Talk of the Devil

Talk of the Devil
Twenty-Four Classic Short Stories of the Fallen Angel

Including Five Bonus Stories

Edited and introduced by
Maximilian J. Rudwin

LEONAUR

Talk of the Devil: Twenty-Four Classic Short Stories of the Fallen Angel
Including Five Bonus Stories
Edited and introduced by Maximilian J. Rudwin

Originally published in 1921 under the title
Devil Stories: an Anthology

The Story by John Masefield has been removed from
this edition for copyright reasons, five additional
stories have been added, these do not have
editor's introductions.

Leonaur is an imprint of Oakpast Ltd

ISBN: 978-0-85706-238-3 (hardcover)
ISBN: 978-0-85706-237-6 (softcover)

http://www.leonaur.com

Publisher's Notes

Contents

To all students of the
supernatural in literature

Introduction

Of all the myths which have come down to us from the East, and of all the creations of Western fancy and belief, the Personality of Evil has had the strongest attraction for the mind of man. The Devil is the greatest enigma that has ever confronted the human intelligence. So large a place has Satan taken in our imagination, and we might also say in our heart, that his expulsion therefrom, no matter what philosophy may teach us, must for ever remain an impossibility. As a character in imaginative literature Lucifer has not his equal in heaven above or on the earth beneath. In contrast to the idea of Good, which is the more exalted in proportion to its freedom from anthropomorphism, the idea of Evil owes to the presence of this element its chief value as a poetic theme. The discrowned archangel may have been inferior to St. Michael in military tactics, but he certainly is his superior in matters literary. The fair angels—all frankness and goodness—are beyond our comprehension, but the fallen angels, with all their faults and sufferings, are kin to us.

There is a legend that the Devil has always had literary aspirations. The German theosophist Jacob Boehme relates that when Satan was asked to explain the cause of God's enmity to him and his consequent downfall, he replied: "I wanted to be an author." Whether or not the Devil has ever written anything over his own signature, he has certainly helped others compose their greatest works. It is a significant fact that the greatest imaginations have discerned an attraction in Diabolus. What would the world's literature be if from it we eliminated Dante's *Divine Comedy*, Calderon's *Marvellous Magician*, Milton's *Paradise Lost*, Goethe's *Faust*, Byron's *Cain*, Vigny's *Eloa*, and Lermontov's *Demon*? Sorry indeed would have been the plight of literature without a judicious admixture of the Diabolical. Without the Devil there would simply be no literature, because without his intervention there would be no plot, and without a plot the story of the world would lose its interest. Even now, when the belief in the Devil has gone out of fashion, and when the very mention of his name, far from causing men to cross themselves, brings a smile to their faces, Satan has continued to be a puissant personage in the realm of letters. As a matter of fact, Beelzebub has perhaps received his greatest elaboration at the hands of writers who believed in him just as little as Shakespeare did in the ghost of Hamlet's father.

Commenting on Anatole France's *The Revolt of the Angels*, an American critic has recently written:

> It is difficult to rehabilitate Beelzebub, not because people are of one mind concerning Beelzebub, but because they are of no mind at all.

How this demon must have laughed when he read these lines! Why, he needs no rehabilitation. The Devil has never been absent from the world of letters, just as he has never been missing from the world of men. Since the days of Job, Satan has taken a deep interest in the affairs of the human race; and while most writers content themselves with recording his activities on this planet, there never have been lacking men of sufficient courage to call upon the prince of darkness in his proper dominions in order to bring back to us, for our instruction and edification, a report of his work there. The most distinguished poet his infernal Highness has ever entertained at his court, it will be recalled, was Dante. The mark which the scorching fires of hell left on Dante's face, was to his contemporaries sufficient proof of the truth of his story.

The subject-matter of literature may always have been in a state of flux, but the Devil has been present in all the stages of literary evolution. All schools of literature in all ages and in all languages set themselves, whether consciously or unconsciously, to represent and interpret the Devil, and each school has treated him in its own characteristic manner.

The Devil is an old character in literature. Perhaps he is as old as literature itself. He is encountered in the story of the paradisiacal sojourn of our first ancestors, and from that day on, Satan has appeared unfailingly, in various forms and with various functions, in all the literatures of the world. His person and his power continued to develop and to multiply with the advance of the centuries, so that in the Middle Ages the world fairly pullulated with demons. From his minor place in the biblical books, the Devil grew to a position of paramount importance in mediaeval literature. The Reformation, which was a movement of progress in so many respects, left his position intact. Indeed, it rather increased his power by withdrawing from the saints the right of intercession in behalf of the sinners. Neither the Renaissance of ancient learning nor the institution of modern science could prevail against Satan. As a matter of fact, the growth of the interest in the Devil has been on a level with the development of the spirit of philosophical inquiry. French classicism, to be sure, occasioned a setback for our hero. As a member of the Christian hierarchy of supernatural personages, the Devil could not help but be affected by the ban under which Boileau placed Christian supernaturalism. But even the eighteenth century, a period so inimical to the Supernatural, produced two master-devils in fiction: Le Sage's Asmodeus and Cazotte's Beelzebub—worthy members of the august company of literary Devils.

But as if to make amends for its long lack of appreciation of the Devil's literary possibilities, France, in the beginning of the nineteenth century, brought about a distinct reaction in his favour. The sympathy extended by that country of revolutionary progress to all victims and to all rebels, whether individuals or classes or nations, could not well be denied to the celestial outlaw. The fighters for political, social, intellectual, and emotional liberty on earth, could not withhold their admiration from the angel who demanded freedom of thought and independence of action in heaven. The rebel of the Empyrean was hailed as the first martyr in the cause of liberty, and his rehabilitation in heaven was demanded by the rebels on earth. Satan became the symbol of the restless, hapless nineteenth century. Through his mouth that age uttered its protest against the monarchs of heaven and earth. The Romantic generation of 1830 thought the world more than ever out of joint, and who was better fitted than the Devil to express their dissatisfaction with the celestial government of terrestrial affairs? Satan is the eternal Malcontent. To Hamlet, Denmark seemed gloomy; to

11

Satan, the whole world appears dark. The admiration of the Romanticists for Satan was mixed with pity and sympathy—so much his melancholy endeared him to their sympathies, so kindred it seemed to their human weakness. The Romanticists felt a deep admiration for solitary grandeur. This "knight of the doleful countenance," laden with a curse and drawing misfortune in his train, was the ideal Romantic hero. Was he not indeed the original *beau tenebreux*? Thus Satan became the typical figure of that period and its poetry. It has been well remarked that if Satan had not existed, the Romanticists would have invented him. The Devil's influence on the Romantic School was so strong and so sustained that soon it was named after him. The terms Romantic and Satanic came to be well-nigh synonymous. The interest which the French Romanticists showed in the Devil, moreover, passed beyond the boundaries of France and the limits of the nineteenth century. The Symbolists, for whom the mysteries of Erebus had a potent attraction, were simply obsessed by Satan. But even the Naturalists, who certainly were not haunted by phantoms, often succumbed to his charms. Foreign writers turning for inspiration to France, where the literature of the last century reached its highest perfection, were also caught in the French enthusiasm for the Devil.

Needless to say that this Devil is not the evil spirit of mediaeval dogma. The Romantic Devil is an altogether new species of the *genus diaboli*. There are fashions in Devils as in dresses, and what is a Devil in one country or one century may not pass muster in another. It is related that after the glory of Greece had departed, a mariner, voyaging along her coast by night, heard from the woods the cry: "Great Pan is dead!" But Pan was not dead; he had fallen asleep to awake again as Satan. In like manner, when the eighteenth century believed Satan to be dead, he was, as a matter of fact, only recuperating his energies for a fresh start in a new form. His new avatar was Prometheus. Satan continued to be the enemy of God, but he was no longer the enemy of man. Instead of a demon of darkness he became a god of grace. This champion of celestial combat was not actuated by hatred and envy of man, as Christianity was thought to teach us, but by love and pity for humankind. The strongest expression of this idea of the Devil in modern literature has been given by August Strindberg, whose Lucifer is a compound of Prometheus, Apollo and Christ. However, this interpretation of the Devil, whatever value it may have from the point of view of originality, is aesthetically as well as theologically not acceptable. Such a revaluation of an old value offends our intellect while it touches our heart. All successful treatment of the Devil in literature and art must be made to correspond with the norm of popular belief. In art we are all orthodox, whatever our views may be in religion. This new conception of Satan will be found chiefly in poetry, while the popular concept has been continued in prose. But even here a gradual evolution of the idea of the Devil will be observed. The nineteenth century Demon is an improvement on his *confrere* of the thirteenth. He differs from his older brother as a cultivated flower from a wild blossom. The Devil as a human projection is bound to partake in the progress of human thought. Says Mephistopheles:

Culture, which the whole world licks,
Also unto the Devil sticks.

The Devil advances with the progress of civilization, because he is what men make him. He has benefited by the modern levelling tendency in characterization. Nowadays supernatural personages, like their human creators, are no longer painted either as wholly white or as wholly black, but in various shades of grey. The Devil, as Renan has aptly remarked, has chiefly benefited by this relativist point of view. The Spirit of Evil is better than he was, because evil is no longer so bad as it was. Satan, even in the popular mind, is no longer a villain of the deepest dye. At his worst he is the general mischief-maker of the universe, who loves to stir up the earth with his pitch-fork. In modern literature the Devil's chief function is that of a satirist. This fine critic directs the shafts of his sarcasm against all the faults and foibles of men. He spares no human institution. In religion, art, society, marriage—everywhere his searching eye can detect the weak spots. The latest demonstration of the Devil's ability as a satirist of men and morals is furnished by Mark Twain in his posthumous romance *The Mysterious Stranger*.

The Devil Lore Series, which opens with this book of Devil Stories, is to serve as documentary evidence of man's abiding interest in the Devil. It will be a sort of portrait-gallery of the literary delineations of Satan. The Anthologies of Diabolical Literature may be considered, I trust, without any risk of offence to any theological or philosophical prepossession. To those alike who accept and who reject the belief in the Devil's spiritual entity apart from man's, there must be profit and pleasure in the contemplation of his literary incarnations. As regards the Devil's fitness as a literary character, all intelligent men and women, believers and unbelievers, may be assumed to have but one opinion.

This Series is wholly devoted to the Christian Devil with the total disregard of his cousins in the other faiths. There will, however, be found a strong Jewish element in Christian demonology. It must be borne in mind that our literature has become saturated through Christian channels with the traditions of the parent creed.

This collection has been limited to twenty tales. Within the bounds thus set, an effort has been made to have this book as representative of national and individual conceptions of the Devil as possible. The tales have been taken from many times and tongues. Selection has been made not only among writers, but also among the stories of each writer. In two instances, however, where the choice was not so easy, an author is represented by two specimens from his pen.

The stories have been arranged in chronological order to show the constant and continuous appeal on the part of the Devil to our story-writers. The mediaeval tale, although published last, was placed first. For obvious reasons, this story has not been given in its original form, but in its modernized version. While this is not meant to be a nursery-book, it has been made *virginibus puerisque*, and for this reason, selections from Boccaccio, Rabelais and Balzac could not find their way into these pages. Moreover, as this volume was limited to narratives in prose, devil's tales in verse by Chaucer, Hans Sachs and La Fontaine could not be considered, either. Nevertheless this collection is sufficiently comprehensive to please all tastes in Devils. The reader will find between the covers of this book Devils fascinating and fearful, Devils powerful and picturesque, Devils serious and humorous, Devils pathetic and comic, Devils fantastic and satiric, Devils gruesome and grotesque. I have tried, though, to keep them all in good humour throughout the book, and can accordingly assure the reader that he need fear no harm from an intimate acquaintance with the diabolical company to which he is herewith introduced.

Maximilian J. Rudwin

The Devil in a Nunnery

Francis Oscar Mann

According to a German legend, the devil is master of all arts, and certainly he has given sufficient proof of his musical talent. Certain Church Fathers ascribed, not without good reason, the origin of music to Satan. "The Devil," says Mr. Huneker in his diabolical story "The Supreme Sin" (1920), "is the greatest of all musicians," and Rowland Hill long ago admitted the fact that the devil has all the good tunes. Perhaps his greatest composition is the *Sonata del Diavolo*, which Tartini wrote down in 1713. This diabolical master-piece is the subject of Gerard de Nerval's story *La Sonate du Diable* (1830). While the devil plays all instruments equally well, he seems to prefer the violin. Satan appears as fiddler in the poem *"Der Teufel mit der Geige,"* which has been ascribed to the Swiss anti-Papist Pamphilus Gengenbach of the sixteenth century. In Leanu's *Faust* (1836) Mephistopheles takes the violin out of the hands of one of the musicians at a peasant-wedding and plays a diabolical *czardas*, which fills the hearts of all who hear it with voluptuousness. An opera *Un Violon du Diable* was played in Paris in 1849. *The Devil's Violin*, an extravaganza in verse by Benjamin Webster, was performed the same year in London. In his story *"Les Tentations ou Eros, Plutus et la Gloire"* Baudelaire presents the Demon of Love as holding in his left hand a violin "which without doubt served to sing his pleasures and pains." The devil also appears as limping fiddler in a California legend, which appeared under the title "The Devil's Fiddle" in a Californian magazine in 1855. Death, the devil's first cousin, if not his alter ego, has the souls, in the Dance of Death, march off to hell to a merry tune on his violin. Death appears as a musician also in the Piper of Hamlin. In this legend, well known to the English world through Browning's poem "Pied Piper of Hamelin" (1843) and Miss Peabody's play *The Piper* (1909), the rats are the human souls, which Death charms with his music into following him. In the Middle Ages the soul was often represented as leaving the body in the form of a mouse. The soul of a good man comes out of his mouth as a white mouse, while at the death of a sinner the soul escapes as a black mouse, which the devil catches and brings to hell. Mephistopheles, it will be recalled, calls himself "the lord of rats and mice" (*Faust*, 1, 1516). Devil-Death has inherited this wind instrument from the goat-footed Pan.

"The Devil is more busy in the convents," we are told by J. K. Huysmans in his novel *En route* (1895), *"than in the cities, as he has a harder job on hand."*

Buckingham is as pleasant a shire as a man shall see on a seven days' journey. Neither was it any less pleasant in the days of our Lord King Edward, the third of that name, he who fought and put the French to shameful discomfiture at Crecy and Poitiers and at many another hard-fought field. May God rest his soul, for he now sleeps in the great Church at Westminster.

Buckinghamshire is full of smooth round hills and woodlands of hawthorn and beech, and it is a famous country for its brooks and shaded waterways running through the low hay meadows. Upon its hills feed a thousand sheep, scattered like the remnants of the spring snow, and it was from these that the merchants made themselves fat purses, sending the wool into Flanders in exchange for silver crowns. There were many strong castles there too, and rich abbeys, and the King's Highway ran through it from North to South, upon which the pilgrims went in crowds to worship at the Shrine of the Blessed Saint Alban. Thereon also rode noble knights and stout men-at-arms, and these you could follow with the eye by their glistening armour, as they wound over hill and dale, mile after mile, with shining spears and shields and fluttering pennons, and anon a trumpet or two sounding the same keen note as that which rang out dreadfully on those bloody fields of France. The girls used to come to the cottage doors or run to hide themselves in the wayside woods to see them go trampling by; for Buckinghamshire girls love a soldier above all men. Nor, I warrant you, were jolly friars lacking in the highways and the by-ways and under the hedges, good men of religion, comfortable of penance and easy of life, who could tip a wink to a housewife, and drink and crack a joke with the good man, going on their several ways with tight paunches, skins full of ale and a merry salutation for every one. A fat pleasant land was this Buckinghamshire; always plenty to eat and drink therein, and pretty girls and lusty fellows; and God knows what more a man can expect in a world where all is vanity, as the Preacher truly says.

There was a nunnery at Maids Moreton, two miles out from Buckingham Borough, on the road to Stony Stratford, and the place was called Maids Moreton because of the nunnery. Very devout creatures were the nuns, being holy ladies out of families of gentle blood. They punctually fulfilled to the letter all the commands of the pious founder, just as they were blazoned on the great parchment Regula, which the Lady Mother kept on her reading-desk in her little cell. If ever any of the nuns, by any chance or subtle machination of the Evil One, was guilty of the smallest backsliding from the conduct that beseemed them, they made full and devout confession thereof to the Holy Father who visited them for this purpose. This good man loved swan's meat and galingale, and the charitable nuns never failed to provide of their best for him on his visiting days; and whatsoever penance he laid upon them they performed to the utmost, and with due contrition of heart.

From Matins to Compline they regularly and decently carried out the services of Holy Mother Church. After dinner, one read aloud to them from the Rule, and again after supper there was reading from the life of some notable Saint or Virgin, that thereby they might find ensample for themselves on their own earthly pilgrimage. For the rest, they tended their herb garden, reared their chickens, which were famous for miles around, and kept strict watch over their hay wards and swineherds. If time was when they had nothing more important on hand, they set to and made the prettiest blood bandages imaginable for the Bishop, the Bishop's Chaplain, the Archdeacon, the neighbouring Abbot and other god-

17

ly men of religion round about, who were forced often to bleed themselves for their health's sake and their eternal salvation, so that these venerable men in process of time came to have by them great chests full of these useful articles. If little tongues wagged now and then as the sisters sat at their sewing in the great hall, who shall blame them, *Eva peccatrice*? Not I; besides, some of them were something stricken in years, and old women are garrulous and hard to be constrained from chattering and gossiping. But being devout women they could have spoken no evil.

One evening after Vespers all these good nuns sat at supper, the Abbess on her high dais and the nuns ranged up and down the hall at the long trestled tables. The Abbess had just said "*Gratias*" and the sisters had sung "*Qui vivit et regnat per omnia saecula saeculorum, Amen*," when in came the Manciple mysteriously, and, with many deprecating bows and outstretchings of the hands, sidled himself up upon the dais, and, permission having been given him, spoke to the Lady Mother thus:

"Madam, there is a certain pilgrim at the gate who asks refreshment and a night's lodging." It is true he spoke softly, but little pink ears are sharp of hearing, and nuns, from their secluded way of life, love to hear news of the great world.

"Send him away," said the Abbess. "It is not fit that a man should lie within this house."

"Madam, he asks food and a bed of straw lest he should starve of hunger and exhaustion on his way to do penance and worship at the Holy Shrine of the Blessed Saint Alban."

"What kind of pilgrim is he?"

"Madam, to speak truly, I know not; but he appears of a reverend and gracious aspect, a young man well spoken and well disposed. Madam knows it waxeth late, and the ways are dark and foul."

"I would not have a young man, who is given to pilgrimages and good works, to faint and starve by the wayside. Let him sleep with the hay wards."

"But, Madam, he is a young man of goodly appearance and conversation; saving your reverence, I would not wish to ask him to eat and sleep with churls."

"He must sleep without. Let him, however, enter and eat of our poor table."

"Madam, I will strictly enjoin him what you command. He hath with him, however, an instrument of music and would fain cheer you with spiritual songs."

A little shiver of anticipation ran down the benches of the great hall, and the nuns fell to whispering.

"Take care, Sir Manciple, that he be not some light juggler, a singer of vain songs, a mocker. I would not have these quiet halls disturbed by wanton music and unholy words. God forbid." And she crossed herself.

"Madam, I will answer for it."

The Manciple bowed himself from the dais and went down the middle of the hall, his keys rattling at his belt. A little buzz of conversation rose from the sisters and went up to the oak roof-trees, like the singing of bees. The Abbess told her beads.

The hall door opened and in came the pilgrim. God knows what manner of man he was; I cannot tell you. He certainly was lean and lithe like a cat, his eyes danced in his head like the very devil, but his cheeks and jaws were as bare of flesh as any hermit's that lives on roots and ditchwater. His yellow-hosed legs went like the tune of a May game, and he screwed and twisted his scarlet-jerkined body in time with them. In his left hand he held a *cithern*, on which he twanged with his right, making a cunning noise that titillated the back-bones of those who heard it, and teased every delicate nerve in the body. Such a tune would have tickled the ribs of Death himself. A queer fellow to go pilgrimaging certainly, but why, when they saw him, all the young nuns tittered and the old nuns grinned, until they showed their red gums, it is hard to tell. Even the Lady Mother on the dais smiled, though she tried to frown a moment later.

The pilgrim stepped lightly up to the dais, the infernal devil in his legs making the nuns think of the games the village folk play all night in the churchyard on Saint John's Eve.

"Gracious Mother," he cried, bowing deeply and in comely wise, "allow a poor pilgrim on his way to confess and do penance at the shrine of Saint Alban to take food in your hall, and to rest with the hay wards this night, and let me thereof make some small recompense with a few sacred numbers, such as your pious founder would not have disdained to hear."

"Young man," returned the Abbess, "right glad am I to hear that God has moved thy heart to godly works and to go on pilgrimages, and verily I wish it may be to thy soul's health and to the respite of thy pains hereafter. I am right willing that thou shouldst refresh thyself with meat and rest at this holy place."

"Madam, I thank thee from my heart, but as some slight token of gratitude for so large a favour, let me, I pray thee, sing one or two of my divine songs, to the uplifting of these holy Sisters' hearts."

Another burst of chatter, louder than before, from the benches in the hall. One or two of the younger Sisters clapped their plump white hands and cried, "Oh!" The Lady Abbess held up her hand for silence.

"Verily, I should be glad to hear some sweet songs of religion, and I think it would be to the uplifting of these Sisters' hearts. But, young man, take warning against singing any wanton lines of vain imagination, such as the ribalds use on the highways, and the idlers and haunters of taverns. I have heard them in my youth, although my ears tingle to think of them now, and I should think it shame that any such light words should echo among these sacred rafters or disturb the slumber of our pious founder, who now sleeps in Christ. Let me remind you of what saith Saint Jeremie, *Onager solitarius, in desiderio animae suae, attraxit ventum amoris*; the wild ass of the wilderness, in the desire of his heart, snuffeth up the wind of love; whereby that holy man signifies that vain earthly love, which is but wind and air, and shall avail nothing at all, when this weak, impure flesh is sloughed away."

"Madam, such songs as I shall sing, I learnt at the mouth of our holy parish priest, Sir Thomas, a man of all good learning and purity of heart."

"In that case," said the Abbess, "sing in God's name, but stand at the end of the hall, for it suits not the dignity of my office a man should stand so near this dais."

Whereon the pilgrim, making obeisance, went to the end of the hall, and the eyes of all the nuns danced after his dancing legs, and their ears hung on the clear, sweet notes he struck out of his *cithern* as he walked. He took his place with his back against the great hall door, in such attitude as men use when they play the *cithern*. A little trembling ran through the nuns, and some rose from their seats and knelt on the benches, leaning over the table, the better to see and hear him. Their eyes sparkled like dew on meadowsweet on a fair morning.

Certainly his fingers were bewitched or else the devil was in his *cithern*, for such sweet sounds had never been heard in the hall since the day when it was built and consecrated to the service of the servants of God. The shrill notes fell like a tinkling rain from the high roof in mad, fantastic trills and dying falls that brought all one's soul to one's lips to suck them in. What he sang about, God only knows; not one of the nuns or even the holy Abbess herself could have told you, although you had offered her a piece of the True Cross or a hair of the Blessed Virgin for a single word. But a divine yearning filled all their hearts; they seemed to hear ten thousand thousand angels singing in choruses, Alleluia, Alleluia, Alleluia; they floated up on impalpable clouds of azure and silver, up through the blissful paradises of the uppermost heaven; their nostrils were filled with the odours of exquisite spices and herbs and smoke of incense; their eyes dazzled at splendours and lights and glories; their ears were full of gorgeous harmonies and all created concords of sweet sounds; the very fibres of being were loosened within them, as though their souls would leap forth from their bodies in exquisite dissolution. The eyes of the younger nuns grew round and large and tender, and their breath almost died upon their velvet lips. As for the old nuns, the great, salt tears coursed down their withered cheeks and fell like rain on their gnarled hands. The Abbess sat on her dais with her lips apart, looking into space, ten thousand thousand miles away. But no one saw her and she saw no one; every one had forgotten every one else in that delicious intoxication.

Then with a shrill cry, full of human yearnings and desire, the minstrel came to a sudden stop—

"Western wind, when wilt thou blow,
"And the small rain will down rain?
"Christ, if my love were in my arms,
"And I in my bed again."

Silence!—not one of the holy Sisters spoke, but some sighed; some put their hands over their hearts, and one put her hand in her hood, but when she felt her hair shorn close to her scalp, drew it out again sharply, as though she had touched red-hot iron, and cried, "O Jesu."

Sister Peronelle, a toothless old woman, began to speak in a cracked, high voice, quickly and monotonously, as though she spoke in a dream. Her eyes were wet and red, and her thin lips trembled. "God knows," she said, "I loved him; God knows it. But I bid all those who be maids here, to be mindful of the woods. For they are green, but they are deep and dark, and it is merry in the springtime with the thick turf below and the good boughs above, all alone with your heart's darling—all alone in the green wood. But God help me, he would not stay any more than snow at Easter. I thought just now that I was back with him in the woods. God keep all those that be maids from the green woods."

The pretty Sister Ursula, who had only just finished her novitiate, was as white as a sheet. Her breath came thickly and quick as though she bore a great burden up hill. A great sigh made her comely shoulders rise and fall. "Blessed Virgin," she cried. "Ah, ye ask too much; I did not know; God help me, I did not know," and her grey eyes filled with sudden tears, and she dropped her head on her arms on the table, and sobbed aloud. Then cried out Sister Katherine, who looked as old and dead as a twig dropped from a tree of last autumn, and at whom the younger Sisters privily mocked, "It is the wars, the wars, the cursed wars. I have held his head in this lap, I tell you; I have kissed his soul into mine. But now he lies dead, and his pretty limbs all dropped away into earth. Holy Mother, have pity on me. I shall never kiss his sweet lips again or look into his jolly eyes. My heart is broken long since. Holy Mother! Holy Mother!"

"He must come oftener," said a plump Sister of thirty, with a little nose turned up at the end, eyes black as sloes and lips round as a plum. "I go to the orchard day after day, and gather my lap full of apples. He is my darling. Why does he not come? I look for him every time that I gather the ripe apples. He used to come; but that was in the spring, and Our Lady knows that is long ago. Will it not be spring again soon? I have gathered many ripe apples."

Sister Margarita rocked herself to and fro in her seat and crossed her arms on her breast. She was singing quietly to herself.

"Lulla, lullay, thou tiny little child,
"Lulla, lullay, lullay;
"Suck at my breast that am thereat beguiled,
"Lulla, lullay, lullay."

She moaned to herself, "I have seen the village women go to the well, carrying their babies with them, and they laugh as they go by on the way. Their babies hold them tight round the neck, and their mothers comfort them, saying, 'Hey, hey, my little son; hey, hey, my sweeting.' Christ and the blessed Saints know that I have never felt a baby's little hand in my bosom—and now I shall die without it, for I am old and past the age of bearing children."

> *"Lulla, lullay, thou tiny little boy,*
> *"Lulla, lullay, lullay;*
> *"To feel thee suck doth soothe my great annoy,*
> *"Lulla, lullay, lullay."*

"I have heard them on a May morning, with their pipes and tabors and jolly, jolly music," cried Sister Helen; "I have seen them too, and my heart has gone with them to bring back the white hawthorn from the woods. 'A man and a maid to a hawthorn bough,' as it says in the song. They sing outside my window all Saint John's Eve so that I cannot say my prayers for the wild thoughts they put into my brain, as they go dancing up and down in the churchyard; I cannot forget the pretty words they say to each other, 'Sweet love, a kiss'; 'kiss me, my love, nor let me go'; 'As I went through the garden gate'; 'A bonny black knight, a bonny black knight, and what will you give to me? A kiss, and a kiss, and no more than a kiss, under the wild rose tree.' Oh, Mary Mother, have pity on a poor girl's heart, I shall die, if no one love me, I shall die."

"In faith, I am truly sorry, William," said Sister Agnes, who was gaunt and hollow-eyed with long vigils and over fasting, for which the good father had rebuked her time after time, saying that she over tasked the poor weak flesh. "I am truly sorry that I could not wait. But the neighbours made such a clamour, and my father and mother buffeted me too sorely. It is under the oak tree, no more than a foot deep, and covered with the red and brown leaves. It was a pretty sight to see the red blood on its neck, as white as whalebone, and it neither cried nor wept, so I put it down among the leaves, the pretty poppet; and it was like thee, William, it was like thee. I am sorry I did not wait, and now I'm worn and wan for thy sake, this many a long year, and all in vain, for thou never comst. I am an old woman now, and I shall soon be quiet and not complain any more."

Some of the Sisters were sobbing as if their hearts would break; some sat quiet and still, and let the tears fall from their eyes unchecked; some smiled and cried together; some sighed a little and trembled like aspen leaves in a southern wind. The great candles in the hall were burning down to their sockets. One by one they spluttered out. A ghostly, flickering light fell upon the legend over the broad dais, "*Connubium mundum sed virginitas paradisum complet*"— "Marriage replenisheth the World, but virginity Paradise."

"Dong, dong, dong." Suddenly the great bell of the Nunnery began to toll. With a cry the Abbess sprang to her feet; there were tear stains on her white cheeks, and her hand shook as she pointed fiercely to the door.

"Away, false pilgrim," she cried. "Silence, foul blasphemer! *Retro me, Satanas*." She crossed herself again and again, saying *Pater Noster*.

The nuns screamed and trembled with terror. A little cloud of blue smoke arose from where the minstrel had stood. There was a little tongue of flame, and he had disappeared. It was almost dark in the hall. A few sobs broke the silence. The dying light of a single candle fell on the form of the Lady Mother.

"Tomorrow," she said, "we shall fast and sing *Placebo* and *Dirige* and the *Seven Penitential Psalms*. May the Holy God have mercy upon us for all we have done and said and thought amiss this night. *Amen*."

Belphagor

Niccolo Machiavelli

This story of the devil Belphagor, who was sent by his infernal chief Pluto up to earth, where he married an earthly wife, but finally left her in disgust to go back to hell, is also of mediaeval origin. It was first printed by Giovanni Brevio in 1545, and appeared for the second time with the name of Machiavelli in 1549, twenty-two years after the death of the diabolical statesman. The two authors did not borrow from each other, but had a common source in a mediaeval Latin manuscript, which seems to have first fallen into the hands of Italians, but was later brought to France where it has been lost. The tale of the marriage of the devil appeared in several other Italian versions during the sixteenth century. Among the Italian novelists, who retold it for the benefit of their married friends, may be mentioned Giovan-Francesco Straparola, Francesco Sansovino, and Gabriel Chappuys. In England this story was no less popular. Barnabe Riche inserted it in his collection of narratives in 1581, and we meet it again later in the following plays: *Grim, the Collier of Croydon*, ascribed to Ulpian Fulwell (1599); *The Devil and his Dame* by P. M. Houghton (1600); *Machiavel and the Devil* by Daborne and Henslowe (1613); *The Devil is an Ass* by Ben Jonson (1616); and Belphagor, or the Marriage of the Devil (1690). In France the story was treated in verse by La Fontaine (1694), and in Germany it served the Nuremberg poet Hans Sachs as the subject for a farce (1557). The *Encyclopaedia Britannica* is authority for the statement that Machiavelli's own married life had nothing to do with the plot of his story.

The notion of this story is ingenious, and might have been made productive of entertaining incident, had Belphagor been led by his connubial connections from one crime to another. But Belphagor is only unfortunate, and in no respect guilty; nor did anything occur during his abode on earth that testified to the power of woman in leading us to final condemnation. The story of the peasant and the possession of the princesses bears no reference to the original idea with which the tale commences, and has no connection with the object of the infernal deputy's terrestrial sojourn.

J. C. Dunlop, *History of Fiction*

To this criticism Mr. Thomas Roscoe replies that:

. . . . part of the humour of the story seems to consist in Belphagor's earthly career being cut short before he had served the full term of his apprenticeship. But from the follies and extravagances into which he had already plunged, we are now authorized to believe that, even if he had been able longer to support the asperities of the lady's temper, he must, from the course he was pursuing, have been led from crime to crime, or at least from folly to folly, to such a degree that he would infallibly have been condemned.

T. Roscoe, *Italian Novelists*

The demon of Machiavelli offers no features of a deep psychology, but he distinguishes himself from the other demons of his period by his elegant manners. Like creator, like creature.

Belphagor, the god of the Moabites, like all other pagan gods, joined the infernal forces of Satan when driven off the earth by the Church Triumphant.

The parliament of devils, which we find in this story, was taken from the mystery-plays where the ruler of hell is represented as holding occasional receptions when he listens to the reports of their recent achievements on his behalf, and consults their opinion on matters of state. Satan, who has always wished to rival God, has instituted the infernal council in imitation of the celestial council described in the Book of

Job. The source for the parliament of devils is the apocryphal book *Evangelium Nicodemi*. An early metrical tract under the title of the *Parlement of Devils* was printed two or three times in London about 1520. A "Pandemonium" is also found in Tasso, Milton, and Chateaubriand. The *Parlement of Foules* (14th century) is but a modification of the *Parlement of Devils*, for the devil and the fool were originally identical in person and may be traced back to the demonic clown of the ancient heathen cult (cf. the present writer's book, *The Origin of the German Carnival Comedy*). A far echo is Thomas Chatterton's poem 'The Parliament of Sprites'.

This story recalls to us the saying that the heart of a beautiful woman is the most beloved hiding-place of at least seven devils.

We read in the ancient archives of Florence the following account, as it was received from the lips of a very holy man, greatly respected by every one for the sanctity of his manners at the period in which he lived. Happening once to be deeply absorbed in his prayers, such was their efficacy, that he saw an infinite number of condemned souls, belonging to those miserable mortals who had died in their sins, undergoing the punishment due to their offences in the regions below. He remarked that the greater part of them lamented nothing so bitterly as their folly in having taken wives, attributing to them the whole of their misfortunes. Much surprised at this, Minos and Rhadamanthus, with the rest of the infernal judges, unwilling to credit all the abuse heaped upon the female sex, and wearied from day to day with its repetition, agreed to bring the matter before Pluto. It was then resolved that the conclave of infernal princes should form a committee of inquiry, and should adopt such measures as might be deemed most advisable by the court in order to discover the truth or falsehood of the calumnies which they heard. All being assembled in council, Pluto addressed them as follows: "Dearly beloved demons! though by celestial dispensation and the irreversible decree of fate this kingdom fell to my share, and I might strictly dispense with any kind of celestial or earthly responsibility, yet, as it is more prudent and respectful to consult the laws and to hear the opinion of others,

I have resolved to be guided by your advice, particularly in a case that may chance to cast some imputation upon our government. For the souls of all men daily arriving in our kingdom still continue to lay the whole blame upon their wives, and as this appears to us impossible, we must be careful how we decide in such a business, lest we also should come in for a share of their abuse, on account of our too great severity; and yet judgment must be pronounced, lest we be taxed with negligence and with indifference to the interests of justice. Now, as the latter is the fault of a careless, and the former of an unjust judge, we, wishing to avoid the trouble and the blame that might attach to both, yet hardly seeing how to get clear of it, naturally enough apply to you for assistance, in order that you may look to it, and contrive in some way that, as we have hitherto reigned without the slightest imputation upon our character, we may continue to do so for the future."

The affair appearing to be of the utmost importance to all the princes present, they first resolved that it was necessary to ascertain the truth, though they differed as to the best means of accomplishing this object. Some were of opinion that they ought to choose one or more from among themselves, who should be commissioned to pay a visit to the world, and in a human shape endeavour personally to ascertain how far such reports were grounded in truth. To many others it appeared that this might be done without so much trouble merely by compelling some of the wretched souls to confess the truth by the application of a variety of tortures. But the majority being in favour of a journey to the world, they abided by the former proposal. No one, however, being ambitious of undertaking such a task, it was resolved to leave the affair to chance. The lot fell upon the arch-devil Belphagor, who, previous to the Fall, had enjoyed the rank of archangel in a higher world. Though he received his commission with a very ill grace, he nevertheless felt himself constrained by Pluto's imperial mandate, and prepared to execute whatever had been determined upon in council. At the same time he took an oath to observe the tenor of his instructions, as they had been drawn up with all due solemnity and ceremony for the purpose of his mission. These were to the following effect:—*Imprimis*, that the better to promote the object in view, he should be furnished with a hundred thousand gold ducats; secondly, that he should make use of the utmost expedition in getting into the world; thirdly, that after assuming the human form he should enter into the marriage state; and lastly, that he should live with his wife for the space of ten years. At the expiration of this period, he was to feign death and return home, in order to acquaint his employers, by the fruits of experience, what really were the respective conveniences and inconveniences of matrimony. The conditions further ran, that during the said ten years he should be subject to all kinds of miseries and disasters, like the rest of mankind, such as poverty, prisons, and diseases into which men are apt to fall, unless, indeed, he could contrive by his own skill and ingenuity to avoid them. Poor Belphagor having signed these conditions and received the money, forthwith came into the world, and having set up his equipage, with a numerous train of servants, he made a very splendid entrance into Florence. He selected this city in preference to all others, as being most favourable for obtaining an usurious interest of his money; and having assumed the name of Roderigo, a native of Castile, he took a house in the suburbs of Ognissanti. And because he was unable to explain the instructions under which he acted, he gave out that he was a merchant, who having had poor prospects in Spain, had gone to Syria, and succeeded in acquiring his fortune at Aleppo, whence he had lastly set out for Italy, with the intention of marrying and settling there, as one of the most polished and agreeable countries he knew.

Roderigo was certainly a very handsome man, apparently about thirty years of age, and he lived in a style of life that showed he was in pretty easy circumstances, if not possessed of immense wealth. Being, moreover, extremely affable and liberal, he soon attracted the notice of many noble citizens blessed with large families of daughters and small incomes. The former of these were soon offered to him, from among whom Roderigo chose a very beautiful girl of the name of Onesta, a daughter of Amerigo Donati, who had also three sons, all grown up, and three more daughters, also nearly marriageable. Though of a noble family and enjoying a good reputation in Florence, his father-in-law was extremely poor, and maintained as poor an establishment. Roderigo, therefore, made very splendid nuptials, and omitted nothing that might tend to confer honour upon such a festival, being liable, under the law which he received on leaving his infernal abode, to feel all kinds of vain and earthly passions. He therefore soon began to enter into all the pomps and vanities of the world, and to aim at reputation and consideration among mankind, which put him to no little expense. But more than this, he had not long enjoyed the society of his beloved Onesta, before he became tenderly attached to her, and was unable to behold her suffer the slightest inquietude or vexation. Now, along with her other gifts of beauty and nobility, the lady had brought into the house of Roderigo such an insufferable portion of pride, that in this respect Lucifer himself could not equal her; for her husband, who had experienced the effects of both, was at no loss to decide which was the most intolerable of the two. Yet it became infinitely worse when she discovered the extent of Roderigo's attachment to her, of which she availed herself to obtain an ascendancy over him and rule him with a rod of iron. Not content with this, when she found he would bear it, she continued to annoy him with all kinds of insults and taunts, in such a way as to give him the most indescribable pain and uneasiness. For what with the influence of her father, her brothers, her friends, and relatives, the duty of the matrimonial yoke, and the love he bore her, he suffered all for some time with the patience of a saint. It would be useless to recount the follies and extravagancies into which he ran in order to gratify her taste for dress, and every article of the newest fashion, in which our city, ever so variable in its nature, according to its usual habits, so much abounds. Yet, to live upon easy terms with her, he was obliged to do more than this; he had to assist his father-in-law in portioning off his other daughters; and she next asked him to furnish one of her brothers with goods to sail for the Levant, another with silks for the West, while a third was to be set up in a goldbeater's establishment at Florence. In such objects the greatest part of his fortune was soon consumed. At length the Carnival season was at hand; the festival of St. John was to be celebrated, and the whole city, as usual, was in a ferment. Numbers of the noblest families were about to vie with each other in the splendour of their parties, and the Lady Onesta, being resolved not to be outshone by her acquaintance, insisted that Roderigo should exceed them all in the richness of their feasts. For the reasons above stated, he submitted to her will; nor, indeed, would he have scrupled at doing much more, however difficult it might have been, could he have flattered himself with a hope of preserving the peace and comfort of his household, and of awaiting quietly the consummation of his ruin. But this was not the case, inasmuch as the arrogant temper of his wife had grown to such a height of asperity by long indulgence, that he was at a loss in what way to act. His domestics, male and female, would no longer remain in the house, being unable to support for any length of time the intolerable life they led. The inconvenience which he suffered in consequence of having no one to whom he could entrust his affairs it is impossible to express. Even his own familiar devils, whom he had brought along with him, had already deserted him, choosing to return below rather than longer submit to the tyranny of his wife. Left, then, to himself, amidst this turbulent and unhappy life, and having dissipated all the ready money he possessed, he was compelled to live upon the hopes of the returns expected from his ventures in the East and the West. Being still in good credit, in order to support his rank he resorted to bills of exchange; nor was it long before, accounts running against him, he found himself in the same situation as many other unhappy speculators in that market. Just as his case became extremely delicate, there arrived sudden tidings both from East and West that one of his wife's brothers had dissipated the whole of Roderigo's profits in play, and that while the other was returning with a rich cargo uninsured, his ship had the misfortune to be wrecked, and he himself was lost. No sooner did this affair transpire than his creditors assembled, and supposing it must be all over with him, though their bills had not yet become due, they resolved to keep a strict watch over him in fear that he might abscond. Roderigo, on his part, thinking that there was no other remedy, and feeling how deeply he was bound by the Stygian law, determined at all hazards to make his escape. So taking horse one morning early, as he luckily lived near the Prato gate, in that direction he went off. His departure was soon known; the creditors were all in a bustle; the magistrates were applied to, and the officers of justice, along with a great part of the populace, were dispatched in pursuit. Roderigo had hardly proceeded a mile before he heard this hue and cry, and the pursuers were soon so close at his heels that the only resource he had left was to abandon the highroad and take to the open country, with the hope of concealing himself in the fields. But finding himself unable to make way over the hedges and ditches, he left his horse and took to his heels, traversing fields of vines and canes, until he reached Peretola, where he entered the house of Matteo del Bricca, a labourer of Giovanna del Bene. Finding him at home, for he was busily providing fodder for his cattle, our hero earnestly entreated him to save him from the hands of his adversaries close behind, who would infallibly starve him to death in a dungeon, engaging that if Matteo would give him refuge, he would make him one of the richest men alive, and afford him such proofs of it before he took his leave as would convince him of the truth of what he said; and if he failed to do this, he was quite content that Matteo himself should deliver him into the hands of his enemies.

Now Matteo, although a rustic, was a man of courage, and concluding that he could not lose anything by the speculation, he gave him his hand and agreed to save him. He then thrust our hero under a heap of rubbish, completely enveloping him in weeds; so that when his pursuers arrived they found themselves quite at a loss, nor could they extract from Matteo the least information as to his appearance. In this dilemma there was nothing left for them but to proceed in the pursuit, which they continued for two days, and then returned, jaded and disappointed, to Florence. In the meanwhile, Matteo drew our hero from his hiding-place, and begged him to fulfil his engagement. To this his friend Roderigo replied: "I confess, brother, that I am under great obligations to you, and I mean to return them. To leave no doubt upon your mind, I will inform you who I am;" and he proceeded to acquaint him with all the particulars of the affair: how he had come into the world, and married, and run away. He next described to his preserver the way in which he might become rich, which was briefly as follows: As soon as Matteo should hear of some lady in the neighbourhood being said to be possessed, he was to conclude that it was Roderigo himself who had taken possession of her; and he gave him his word, at the same time, that he would never leave her until Matteo should come and conjure him to depart. In this way he might obtain what sum he pleased from the lady's friends for the price of exorcizing her; and having mutually agreed upon this plan, Roderigo disappeared.

Not many days elapsed before it was reported in Florence that the daughter of Messer Ambrogio Amedei, a lady married to Buonajuto Tebalducci, was possessed by the devil. Her relations did not fail to apply every means usual on such occasions to expel him, such as making her wear upon her head St. Zanobi's cap, and the cloak of St. John of Gualberto; but these had only the effect of making Roderigo laugh. And to convince them that it was really a spirit that possessed her, and that it was no flight of the imagination, he made the young lady talk Latin, hold a philosophical dispute, and reveal the frailties of many of her acquaintance. He particularly accused a certain friar of having introduced a lady into his monastery in male attire, to the no small scandal of all who heard it, and the astonishment of the brotherhood. Messer Ambrogio found it impossible to silence him, and began to despair of his daughter's cure. But the news reaching Matteo, he lost no time in waiting upon Ambrogio, assuring him of his daughter's recovery on condition of his paying him five hundred florins, with which to purchase a farm at Peretola. To this Messer Ambrogio consented; and Matteo immediately ordered a number of masses to be said, after which he proceeded with some unmeaning ceremonies calculated to give solemnity to his task. Then approaching the young lady, he whispered in her ear: "Roderigo, it is Matteo that is come. So do as we agreed upon, and get out." Roderigo replied: "It is all well; but you have not asked enough to make you a rich man. So when I depart I will take possession of the daughter of Charles, king of Naples, and I will not leave her till you come. You may then demand whatever you please for your reward; and mind that you never trouble me again." And when he had said this, he went out of the lady, to the no small delight and amazement of the whole city of Florence.

It was not long again before the accident that had happened to the daughter of the king of Naples began to be buzzed about the country, and all the monkish remedies having been found to fail, the king, hearing of Matteo, sent for him from Florence. On arriving at Naples, Matteo, after a few ceremonies, performed the cure. Before leaving the princess, however, Roderigo said: "You see,

Matteo, I have kept my promise and made a rich man of you, and I owe you nothing now. So, henceforward you will take care to keep out of my way, lest as I have hitherto done you some good, just the contrary should happen to you in future." Upon this Matteo thought it best to return to Florence, after receiving fifty thousand *ducats* from his majesty, in order to enjoy his riches in peace, and never once imagined that Roderigo would come in his way again. But in this he was deceived; for he soon heard that a daughter of Louis, king of France, was possessed by an evil spirit, which disturbed our friend Matteo not a little, thinking of his majesty's great authority and of what Roderigo had said. Hearing of Matteo's great skill, and finding no other remedy, the king dispatched a messenger for him, whom Matteo contrived to send back with a variety of excuses. But this did not long avail him; the king applied to the Florentine council, and our hero was compelled to attend. Arriving with no very pleasant sensations at Paris, he was introduced into the royal presence, when he assured his majesty that though it was true he had acquired some fame in the course of his demoniac practice, he could by no means always boast of success, and that some devils were of such a desperate character as not to pay the least attention to threats, enchantments, or even the exorcisms of religion itself. He would, nevertheless, do his majesty's pleasure, entreating at the same time to be held excused if it should happen to prove an obstinate case. To this the king made answer, that be the case what it might, he would certainly hang him if he did not succeed. It is impossible to describe poor Matteo's terror and perplexity on hearing these words; but at length mustering courage, he ordered the possessed princess to be brought into his presence. Approaching as usual close to her ear, he conjured Roderigo in the most humble terms, by all he had ever done for him, not to abandon him in such a dilemma, but to show some sense of gratitude for past services and to leave the princess. "Ah! thou traitorous villain!" cried Roderigo, "hast thou, indeed, ventured to meddle in this business? Dost thou boast thyself a rich man at my expense? I will now convince the world and thee of the extent of my power, both to give and to take away. I shall have the pleasure of seeing thee hanged before thou leavest this place." Poor Matteo finding there was no remedy, said nothing more, but, like a wise man, set his head to work in order to discover some other means of expelling the spirit; for which purpose he said to the king, "Sire, it is as I feared: there are certain spirits of so malignant a character that there is no keeping any terms with them, and this is one of them. However, I will make a last attempt, and I trust that it will succeed according to our wishes. If not, I am in your majesty's power, and I hope you will take compassion on my innocence. In the first place, I have to entreat that your majesty will order a large stage to be erected in the centre of the great square, such as will admit the nobility and clergy of the whole city. The stage ought to be adorned with all kinds of silks and with cloth of gold, and with an altar raised in the middle. Tomorrow morning I would have your majesty, with your full train of lords and ecclesiastics in attendance, seated in order and in magnificent array, as spectators of the scene at the said place. There, after having celebrated solemn mass, the possessed princess must appear; but I have in particular to entreat that on one side of the square may be stationed a band of men with drums, trumpets, horns, tambours, bagpipes, cymbals, and kettle-drums, and all other kinds of instruments that make the most infernal noise. Now, when I take my hat off, let the whole band strike up, and approach with the most horrid uproar towards the stage. This, along with a few other secret remedies which I shall apply, will surely compel the spirit to depart."

These preparations were accordingly made by the royal command; and when the day, being Sunday morning, arrived, the stage was seen crowded with people of rank and the square with the people. Mass was celebrated, and the possessed princess conducted between two bishops, with a train of nobles, to the spot. Now, when Roderigo beheld so vast a concourse of people, together with all this awful preparation, he was almost struck dumb with astonishment, and said to himself, "I wonder what that cowardly wretch is thinking of doing now? Does he imagine I have never seen finer things than these in the regions above—ay! and more horrid things below? However, I will soon make him repent it, at all events." Matteo then approaching him, besought him to come out; but Roderigo replied, "Oh, you think you have done a fine thing now! What do you mean to do with all this trumpery? Can you escape my power, think you, in this way, or elude the vengeance of the king? Thou poltroon villain, I will have thee hanged for this!" And as Matteo continued the more to entreat him, his adversary still vilified him in the same strain. So Matteo, believing there was no time to be lost, made the sign with his hat, when all the musicians who had been stationed there for the purpose suddenly struck up a hideous din, and ringing a thousand peals, approached the spot. Roderigo pricked up his ears at the sound, quite at a loss what to think, and rather in a perturbed tone of voice he asked Matteo what it meant. To this the latter returned, apparently much alarmed: "Alas! dear Roderigo, it is your wife; she is coming for you!" It is impossible to give an idea of the anguish of Roderigo's mind and the strange alteration which his feelings underwent at that name. The moment the name of "wife" was pronounced, he had no longer presence of mind to consider whether it were probable, or even possible, that it could be her. Without replying a single word, he leaped out and fled in the utmost terror, leaving the lady to herself, and preferring rather to return to his infernal abode and render an account of his adventures, than run the risk of any further sufferings and vexations under the matrimonial yoke. And thus Belphagor again made his appearance in the infernal domains, bearing ample testimony to the evils introduced into a household by a wife; while Matteo, on his part, who knew more of the matter than the devil, returned triumphantly home, not a little proud of the victory he had achieved.

The Devil and Tom Walker

Washington Irving

By his interest in popular legends the first of the great American writers shows his sympathy with the Romantic movement, which prevailed in his time in all the countries of Europe. His devil, however, has not been imported from the lands across the Atlantic, but is a part of the superstitions of the New World. The author himself did not believe in "Old Scratch." The real devils for him were the slave-traders and the witch-hunters of Salem fame. It is interesting now to read a contemporary critic of Washington Irving's devil-story: "If Mr. Irving believes in the existence of Tom Walker's master, we can scarcely conceive how he can so earnestly jest about him; at all events, we would counsel him to beware lest his own spells should prove fatal to him" (*Eclectic Review*, 1825). Few people in those days had the courage to take Old Nick good-naturedly. "Even the clever Madame de Stael," said Goethe, "was greatly scandalized that I kept the devil in such good-humour."

The devil appears in many colours, principally, however, in black and red. It is a common belief in Scotland that the devil is a black man, as may also be seen in Robert Louis Stevenson's story "Thrawn Janet." There is no warrant in the biblical tradition for a black devil. Satan, however, appeared as an Ethiopian as far back as the days of the Church Fathers. The black colour presumably is intended to suggest his place of abode, whereas red denotes the scorching fires of hell. The devil was considered as a sort of eternal Salamander. In the New Testament he is described as a fiery fiend. Red was considered by Oriental nations as a diabolical colour. In Egypt red hair and red animals of all kinds were considered infernal. The Apis was also red-coloured. Satan's red beard recalls the Scandinavian god Donar or Thor, who is of Phoenician origin. Judas was always represented in mediaeval mystery-plays with a red beard; and down to the present day red hair is the mark of a suspicious character. The devil also appears as yellow, and even blue, but never as white or green. The yellow devil is but a shade less bright than his fiery brother. The blue devil is a sulphur-constitutioned individual. He is the demon of melancholy, and fills us with "the blues." As the spirit of darkness and death, the devil cannot assume the colours of white or green, which are the symbols of light and life. The devil's dragon-tail is, according to Sir Walter Scott, of biblical tradition, coming from a literal interpretation of a figurative expression.

A few interesting remarks on the expression "The Devil and Tom Walker" current in certain parts of this country as a caution to usurers will be found in Dr. Blondheim's article "The Devil and Doctor Foster" in *Modern Language Notes* for 1918.

A few miles from Boston in Massachusetts, there is a deep inlet, winding several miles into the interior of the country from Charles Bay, and terminating in a thickly-wooded swamp or morass. On one side of this inlet is a beautiful dark grove; on the opposite side the land rises abruptly from the water's edge into a high ridge, on which grow a few scattered oaks of great age and immense size. Under one of these gigantic trees, according to old stories, there was a great amount of treasure buried by Kidd the pirate. The inlet allowed a facility to bring the money in a boat secretly and at night to the very foot of the hill; the elevation of the place permitted a good lookout to be kept that no one was at hand; while the remarkable trees formed good landmarks by which the place might easily be found again. The old stories add, moreover, that the devil presided at the hiding of the money, and took it under his guardianship; but this, it is well known, he always does with buried treasure, particularly when it has been ill-gotten. Be that as it may, Kidd never returned to recover his wealth; being shortly after seized at Boston, sent out to England, and there hanged for a pirate.

About the year 1727, just at the time that earthquakes were prevalent in New England, and shook many tall sinners down upon their knees, there lived near this place a meagre, miserly fellow, of the name of Tom Walker. He had a wife as miserly as himself: they were so miserly that they even conspired to cheat each other. Whatever the woman could lay hands on, she hid away; a hen could not cackle but she was on the alert to secure the new-laid egg. Her husband was continually prying about to detect her secret hoards, and many and fierce were the conflicts that took place about what ought to have been common property. They lived in a forlorn-looking house that stood alone, and had an air of starvation. A few straggling *savin*-trees, emblems of sterility, grew near it; no smoke ever curled from its chimney; no traveller stopped at its door. A miserable horse, whose ribs were as articulate as the bars of a gridiron, stalked about a field, where a thin carpet of moss, scarcely covering the ragged beds of pudding-stone, tantalized and balked his hunger; and sometimes he would lean his head over the fence, look piteously at the passer-by, and seem to petition deliverance from this land of famine.

The house and its inmates had altogether a bad name. Tom's wife was a tall termagant, fierce of temper, loud of tongue, and strong of arm. Her voice was often heard in wordy warfare with her husband; and his face sometimes showed signs that their conflicts were not confined to words. No one ventured, however, to interfere between them. The lonely wayfarer shrunk within himself at the horrid clamour and clapper-clawing; eyed the den of discord askance; and hurried on his way, rejoicing, if a bachelor, in his celibacy.

One day that Tom Walker had been to a distant part of the neighbourhood, he took what he considered a short cut homeward, through the swamp. Like most short cuts, it was an ill-chosen route. The swamp was thickly grown with great gloomy pines and hemlocks, some of them ninety feet high, which made it dark at noonday, and a retreat for all the owls of the neighbourhood. It was full of pits and quagmires, partly covered with weeds and mosses, where the green surface often betrayed the traveller into a gulf of black, smothering mud: there were also dark and stagnant pools, the abodes of the tadpole, the bull-frog, and the water-snake; where the trunks of pines and hemlocks lay half-drowned, half-rotting, looking like alligators sleeping in the mire.

Tom had long been picking his way cautiously through this treacherous forest; stepping from tuft to tuft of rushes and roots, which afforded precarious footholds among deep sloughs; or pacing carefully, like a cat, along the prostrate trunks of trees; startled now and then by the sudden screaming of the bittern, or the quacking of a wild duck rising on the wing from some solitary pool. At length he arrived at a firm piece of ground, which ran out like a peninsula into the deep bosom of the swamp. It had been one of the strongholds of the Indians during their wars with the first colonists. Here they had thrown up a kind of fort, which they had looked upon as almost impregnable, and had used as a place of refuge for their squaws and children. Nothing remained of the old Indian fort but a few embankments, gradually sinking to the level of the surrounding earth, and already overgrown in part by oaks and other forest trees, the foliage of which formed a contrast to the dark pines and hemlocks of the swamp.

It was late in the dusk of evening when Tom Walker reached the old fort, and he paused there awhile to rest himself. Any one but he would have felt unwilling to linger in this lonely, melancholy place, for the common people had a bad opinion of it, from the stories handed down from the time of the Indian wars; when it was asserted that the savages held incantations here, and made sacrifices to the evil spirit.

Tom Walker, however, was not a man to be troubled with any fears of the kind. He reposed himself for some time on the trunk of a fallen hemlock, listening to the boding cry of the tree-toad, and delving with his walking-staff into a mound of black mould at his feet. As he turned up the soil unconsciously, his staff struck against something hard. He raked it out of the vegetable mould, and lo! a cloven skull, with an Indian tomahawk buried deep in it, lay before him. The rust on the weapon showed the time that had elapsed since this death-blow had been given. It was a dreary memento of the fierce struggle that had taken place in this last foothold of the Indian warriors.

"Humph!" said Tom Walker, as he gave it a kick to shake the dirt from it.

"Let that skull alone!" said a gruff voice. Tom lifted up his eyes, and beheld a great black man seated directly opposite him, on the stump of a tree. He was exceedingly surprised, having neither heard nor seen any one approach; and he was still more perplexed on observing, as well as the gathering gloom would permit, that the stranger was neither negro nor Indian. It is true he was dressed in a rude half Indian garb, and had a red belt or sash swathed round his body; but his face was neither black nor copper-colour, but swarthy and dingy, and begrimed with soot, as if he had been accustomed to toil among fires and forges. He had a shock of coarse black hair, that stood out from his head in all directions, and bore an axe on his shoulder.

He scowled for a moment at Tom with a pair of great red eyes.

"What are you doing on my grounds?" said the black man, with a hoarse growling voice.

"Your grounds!" said Tom, with a sneer, "no more your grounds than mine; they belong to Deacon Peabody."

"Deacon Peabody be d—d," said the stranger, "as I flatter myself he will be, if he does not look more to his own sins and less to those of his neighbours. Look yonder, and see how Deacon Peabody is faring."

Tom looked in the direction that the stranger pointed, and beheld one of the great trees, fair and flourishing without, but rotten at the core, and saw that it had been nearly hewn through, so that the first high wind was likely to blow it down. On the bark of the tree was scored the name of Deacon Peabody, an eminent man, who had waxed wealthy by driving shrewd bargains with the Indians. He now looked around, and found most of the tall trees marked with the name of some great man of the colony, and all more or less scored by the axe. The one on which he had been seated, and which had evidently just been hewn down, bore the name of Crowninshield; and he recollected a mighty rich man of that name, who made a vulgar display of wealth, which it was whispered he had acquired by buccaneering.

"He's just ready for burning!" said the black man, with a growl of triumph. "You see I am likely to have a good stock of firewood for winter."

41

"But what right have you," said Tom, "to cut down Deacon Peabody's timber?"

"The right of a prior claim," said the other. "This woodland belonged to me long before one of your white-faced race put foot upon the soil."

"And pray, who are you, if I may be so bold?" said Tom.

"Oh, I go by various names. I am the wild huntsman in some countries; the black miner in others. In this neighbourhood I am known by the name of the black woodsman. I am he to whom the red men consecrated this spot, and in honour of whom they now and then roasted a white man, by way of sweet-smelling sacrifice. Since the red men have been exterminated by you white savages, I amuse myself by presiding at the persecutions of Quakers and Anabaptists; I am the great patron and prompter of slave-dealers, and the grand-master of the Salem witches."

"The upshot of all which is, that, if I mistake not," said Tom, sturdily, "you are he commonly called Old Scratch."

"The same, at your service!" replied the black man, with a half civil nod.

Such was the opening of this interview, according to the old story; though it has almost too familiar an air to be credited. One would think that to meet with such a singular personage, in this wild, lonely place, would have shaken any man's nerves; but Tom was a hard-minded fellow, not easily daunted, and he had lived so long with a termagant wife, that he did not even fear the devil.

It is said that after this commencement they had a long and earnest conversation together, as Tom returned homeward. The black man told him of great sums of money buried by Kidd the pirate, under the oak-trees on the high ridge, not far from the morass. All these were under his command, and protected by his power, so that none could find them but such as propitiated his favour. These he offered to place within Tom Walker's reach, having conceived an especial kindness for him; but they were to be had only on certain conditions. What these conditions were may be easily surmised, though Tom never disclosed them publicly. They must have been very hard, for he required time to think of them, and he was not a man to stick at trifles when money was in view. When they had reached the edge of the swamp, the stranger paused. "What proof have I that all you have been telling me is true?" said Tom. "There's my signature," said the black man, pressing his finger on Tom's forehead. So saying, he turned off among the thickets of the swamp, and seemed, as Tom said, to go down, down, down, into the earth, until nothing but his head and shoulders could be seen, and so on, until he totally disappeared.

When Tom reached home, he found the black print of a finger burnt, as it were, into his forehead, which nothing could obliterate.

The first news his wife had to tell him was the sudden death of Absalom Crowninshield, the rich buccaneer. It was announced in the papers with the usual flourish, that "A great man had fallen in Israel."

Tom recollected the tree which his black friend had just hewn down, and which was ready for burning. "Let the freebooter roast," said Tom, "who cares!" He now felt convinced that all he had heard and seen was no illusion.

He was not prone to let his wife into his confidence; but as this was an uneasy secret, he willingly shared it with her. All her avarice was awakened at the mention of hidden gold, and she urged her husband to comply with the black man's terms, and secure what would make them wealthy for life. However Tom might have felt disposed to sell himself to the Devil, he was determined not to do so to oblige his wife; so he flatly refused, out of the mere spirit of contradiction. Many and bitter were the quarrels they had on the subject; but the more she talked, the more resolute was Tom not to be damned to please her.

At length she determined to drive the bargain on her own account, and if she succeeded, to keep all the gain to herself. Being of the same fearless temper as her husband, she set off for the old Indian fort towards the close of a summer's day. She was many hours absent. When she came back, she was reserved and sullen in her replies. She spoke something of a black man, whom she had met about twilight hewing at the root of a tall tree. He was sulky, however, and would not come to terms: she was to go again with a propitiatory offering, but what it was she forbore to say.

The next evening she set off again for the swamp, with her apron heavily laden. Tom waited and waited for her, but in vain; midnight came, but she did not make her appearance: morning, noon, night returned, but still she did not come. Tom now grew uneasy for her safety, especially as he found she had carried off in her apron the silver tea-pot and spoons, and every portable article of value. Another night elapsed, another morning came; but no wife. In a word, she was never heard of more.

What was her real fate nobody knows, in consequence of so many pretending to know. It is one of those facts which have become confounded by a variety of historians. Some asserted that she lost her way among the tangled mazes of the swamp, and sank into some pit or slough; others, more charitable, hinted that she had eloped with the household booty, and made off to some other province; while others surmised that the tempter had decoyed her into a dismal quagmire, on the top of which her hat was found lying. In confirmation of this, it was said a great black man, with an axe on his shoulder, was seen late that very evening coming out of the swamp, carrying a bundle tied in a check apron, with an air of surly triumph.

The most current and probable story, however, observes, that Tom Walker grew so anxious about the fate of his wife and his property, that he set out at length to seek them both at the Indian fort. During a long summer's afternoon he searched about the gloomy place, but no wife was to be seen. He called her name repeatedly, but she was nowhere to be heard. The bittern alone responded to his voice, as he flew screaming by; or the bull-frog croaked dolefully from a neighbouring pool. At length, it is said, just in the brown hour of twilight, when the owls began to hoot, and the bats to flit about, his attention was attracted by the clamour of carrion crows hovering about a cypress-tree. He looked up, and beheld a bundle tied in a check apron, and hanging in the branches of the tree, with a great vulture perched hard by, as if keeping watch upon it. He leaped with joy; for he recognized his wife's apron, and supposed it to contain the household valuables.

"Let us get hold of the property," said he, consolingly to himself, "and we will endeavour to do without the woman."

As he scrambled up the tree, the vulture spread its wide wings, and sailed off, screaming, into the deep shadows of the forest. Tom seized the checked apron, but, woeful sight! found nothing but a heart and liver tied up in it!

Such, according to this most authentic old story, was all that was to be found of Tom's wife. She had probably attempted to deal with the black man as she had been accustomed to deal with her husband; but though a female scold is generally considered a match for the devil, yet in this instance she appears to have had the worst of it. She must have died game, however; for it is said Tom noticed many prints of cloven feet deeply stamped about the tree, and found handfuls of hair, that looked as if they had been plucked from the coarse black shock of the woodman. Tom knew his wife's prowess by experience. He shrugged his shoulders, as he looked at the signs of a fierce clapper-clawing. "Egad," said he to himself, "Old Scratch must have had a tough time of it!"

Tom consoled himself for the loss of his property, with the loss of his wife, for he was a man of fortitude. He even felt something like gratitude towards the black woodman, who, he considered, had done him a kindness. He sought, therefore, to cultivate a further acquaintance with him, but for some time without success; the old black-legs played shy, for whatever people may think, he is not always to be had for calling for: he knows how to play his cards when pretty sure of his game.

At length, it is said, when delay had whetted Tom's eagerness to the quick, and prepared him to agree to anything rather than not gain the promised treasure, he met the black man one evening in his usual woodman's dress, with his axe on his shoulder, sauntering along the swamp, and humming a tune. He affected to receive Tom's advances with great indifference, made brief replies, and went on humming his tune.

By degrees, however, Tom brought him to business, and they began to haggle about the terms on which the former was to have the pirate's treasure. There was one condition which need not be mentioned, being generally understood in all cases where the devil grants favours; but there were others about which, though of less importance, he was inflexibly obstinate. He insisted that the money found through his means should be employed in his service. He proposed, therefore, that Tom should employ it in the black traffic; that is to say, that he should fit out a slave-ship. This, however, Tom resolutely refused: he was bad enough in all conscience; but the devil himself could not tempt him to turn slave-trader.

Finding Tom so squeamish on this point, he did not insist upon it, but proposed, instead, that he should turn usurer; the devil being extremely anxious for the increase of usurers, looking upon them as his peculiar people.

To this no objections were made, for it was just to Tom's taste.

"You shall open a broker's shop in Boston next month," said the black man.

"I'll do it tomorrow, if you wish," said Tom Walker.

"You shall lend money at two per cent. a month."

"Egad, I'll charge four!" replied Tom Walker.

"You shall extort bonds, foreclose mortgages, drive the merchants to bankruptcy"—

"I'll drive them to the d—l," cried Tom Walker.

"You are the usurer for my money!" said black-legs with delight. "When will you want the rhino?"

"This very night."

"Done!" said the devil.

"Done!" said Tom Walker.—So they shook hands and struck a bargain.

A few days' time saw Tom Walker seated behind his desk in a counting-house in Boston.

His reputation for a ready-moneyed man, who would lend money out for a good consideration, soon spread abroad. Everybody remembers the time of Governor Belcher, when money was particularly scarce. It was a time of paper credit. The country had been deluged with government bills, the famous Land Bank had been established; there had been a rage for speculating; the people had run mad with schemes for new settlements; for building cities in the wilderness; land-jobbers went about with maps of grants, and townships, and Eldorados, lying nobody knew where, but which everybody was ready to purchase. In a word, the great speculating fever which breaks out every now and then in the country, had raged to an alarming degree, and everybody was dreaming of making sudden fortunes from nothing. As usual the fever had subsided; the dream had gone off, and the imaginary fortunes with it; the patients were left in doleful plight, and the whole country resounded with the consequent cry of "hard times."

At this propitious time of public distress did Tom Walker set up as usurer in Boston. His door was soon thronged by customers. The needy and adventurous; the gambling speculator; the dreaming land-jobber; the thriftless tradesman; the merchant with cracked credit; in short, every one driven to raise money by desperate means and desperate sacrifices, hurried to Tom Walker.

Thus Tom was the universal friend of the needy, and acted like a "friend in need"; that is to say, he always exacted good pay and good security. In proportion to the distress of the applicant was the hardness of his terms. He accumulated bonds and mortgages; gradually squeezed his customers closer and closer: and sent them at length, dry as a sponge, from his door.

In this way he made money hand over hand; became a rich and mighty man, and exalted his cocked hat upon 'Change. He built himself, as usual, a vast house, out of ostentation; but left the greater part of it unfinished and unfurnished, out of parsimony. He even set up a carriage in the fullness of his vainglory, though he nearly starved the horses which drew it; and as the ungreased wheels groaned and screeched on the axle-trees, you would have thought you heard the souls of the poor debtors he was squeezing.

As Tom waxed old, however, he grew thoughtful. Having secured the good things of this world, he began to feel anxious about those of the next. He thought with regret on the bargain he had made with his black friend, and set his wits to work to cheat him out of the conditions. He became, therefore, all of a sudden, a violent church-goer. He prayed loudly and strenuously, as if heaven were to be taken by force of lungs. Indeed, one might always tell when he had sinned most during the week, by the clamour of his Sunday devotion. The quiet Christians who had been modestly and steadfastly travelling Zionward, were struck with self-reproach at seeing themselves so suddenly outstripped in their career by this new-made convert. Tom was as rigid in religious as in money matters; he was a stern supervisor and censurer of his neighbours, and seemed to think every sin entered up to their account became a credit on his own side of the page. He even talked of the expediency of reviving the persecution of Quakers and Anabaptists. In a word, Tom's zeal became as notorious as his riches.

Still, in spite of all this strenuous attention to forms, Tom had a lurking dread that the devil, after all, would have his due. That he might not be taken unawares, therefore, it is said he always carried a small Bible in his coat-pocket. He had also a great folio Bible on his counting-house desk, and would frequently be found reading it when people called on business; on such occasions he would lay his green spectacles in the book, to mark the place, while he turned round to drive some usurious bargain.

Some say that Tom grew a little crack-brained in his old days, and that, fancying his end approaching, he had his horse new shod, saddled and bridled, and buried with his feet uppermost; because he supposed that at the last day the world would be turned upside down; in which case he should find his horse standing ready for mounting, and he was determined at the worst to give his old friend a run for it. This, however, is probably a mere old wives' fable. If he really did take such a precaution, it was totally superfluous; at least so says the authentic old legend; which closes his story in the following manner.

One hot summer afternoon in the dog-days, just as a terrible black thunder-gust was coming up, Tom sat in his counting-house, in his white linen cap and India silk morning-gown. He was on the point of foreclosing a mortgage, by which he would complete the ruin of an unlucky land-speculator for whom he had professed the greatest friendship. The poor land-jobber begged him to grant a few months' indulgence. Tom had grown testy and irritated, and refused another day.

"My family will be ruined, and brought upon the parish," said the land-jobber. "Charity begins at home," replied Tom; "I must take care of myself in these hard times."

"You have made so much money out of me," said the speculator.

Tom lost his patience and his piety. "The devil take me," said he, "if I have made a farthing!"

Just then there were three loud knocks at the street-door. He stepped out to see who was there. A black man was holding a black horse, which neighed and stamped with impatience.

"Tom, you're come for," said the black fellow, gruffly. Tom shrank back, but too late. He had left his little Bible at the bottom of his coat-pocket, and his big Bible on the desk buried under the mortgage he was about to foreclose: never was sinner taken more unawares. The black man whisked him like a child into the saddle, gave the horse the lash, and away he galloped, with Tom on his back, in the midst of the thunder-storm. The clerks stuck their pens behind their ears, and stared after him from the windows. Away went Tom Walker, dashing down the street; his white cap bobbing up and down; his morning-gown fluttering in the wind, and his steed striking fire out of the pavement at every bound. When the clerks turned to look for the black man, he had disappeared.

Tom Walker never returned to foreclose the mortgage. A countryman, who lived on the border of the swamp, reported that in the height of the thunder-gust he had heard a great clattering of hoofs and a howling along the road, and running to the window caught sight of a figure, such as I have described, on a horse that galloped like mad across the fields, over the hills, and down into the black hemlock swamp towards the old Indian fort; and that shortly after a thunder-bolt falling in that direction seemed to set the whole forest in a blaze.

The good people of Boston shook their heads and shrugged their shoulders, but had been so much accustomed to witches and goblins, and tricks of the devil, in all kinds of shapes, from the first settlement of the colony, that they were not so much horror-struck as might have been expected. Trustees were appointed to take charge of Tom's effects. There was nothing, however, to administer upon. On searching his coffers, all his bonds and mortgages were found reduced to cinders. In place of gold and silver, his iron chest was filled with chips and shavings; two skeletons lay in his stable instead of his half-starved horses, and the very next day his great house took fire and was burnt to the ground.

Such was the end of Tom Walker and his ill-gotten wealth. Let all griping money-brokers lay this story to heart. The truth of it is not to be doubted. The very hole under the oak-trees, whence he dug Kidd's money, is to be seen to this day; and the neighbouring swamp and old Indian fort are often haunted in stormy nights by a figure on horseback, in morning-gown and white cap, which is doubtless the troubled spirit of the usurer. In fact, the story has resolved itself into a proverb, and is the origin of that popular saying, so prevalent throughout New England, of "The Devil and Tom Walker."

From the Memoirs of Satan

Wilhelm Hauff

Wilhelm Hauff, the author of this book, ranks honourably among the members of the Romantic School in Germany. As the work of a man of only twenty-two years, just out of the university, the book is a credit to its author. It must be admitted, however, that it was not altogether original with him. The idea was taken from E. Th. A. Hoffmann,—Devil-Hoffmann, as he was called by his contemporaries,—who in his short-story "Der Teufel in Berlin" also has the devil travel incognito in Germany; and the title was borrowed from Jean Paul Richter, who also claimed to edit Selections from the Devil's Papers (*Auswahl aus des Teufels Papieren*, 1789). There were others, too, who claimed to have been honoured by his Satanic Majesty to edit his "journal." J. R. Beard, a Unitarian minister, published in 1872 an *Autobiography of Satan*. Another autobiography of Satan is said to have been found among the posthumous works of Leonid Andreev, author of that original diabolical work *Anathema, a Tragedy* (Engl. tr. 1910). This book has just appeared in English under the title *Satan's Diary*. Frederic Soulie's *Les Memoires du Diable* (1837/8) consist of memoirs not of the devil himself, but of other people, which the Count de Luizzi, the human partner to the diabolical pact, is very anxious to know. Hauff's book consists of a series of papers, which are but loosely connected. In certain passages we hear nothing of the autobiographer. The Suavian writer apparently could digest the Diabolical only in homeopathic doses. His Satan, moreover, is a very youthful and quite harmless devil. He is nothing but

50

a personified echo of the author's student-days. The book by Hauff is perhaps the most popular personification of the devil in German literature.

The passage presented here shows the fantastic element of the book at its best. The short introductory synopsis will give an idea of its satirical aspect. The humorous aspect has pretty nearly been lost in translation. Professor Brander Matthews has aptly said: "The German humour is like the simple Italian wines—it will not stand export."

Of all the peoples, the Germans seem to have had the most kindly feelings towards the devil. This is because they knew him better. To judge from the many bridges and cathedrals, which the demon, according to legends, has built in Germany, he must have been a frequent visitor to that country. In Frankfort, where with his own hands our author received the memoirs from the autobiographer, there is a gilded cock above the bridge in memory of the bargain the bridge-builder once made with Satan to give him the first living thing that should cross the river. The day the bridge was finished, a cock fluttered from a woman's market-basket and ran over the bridge. A claw-like hand reached down and claimed the prize.

The distinguished personage, whose adventures form the subject of this book, does not figure in it under his own name, nor does he appear here in the gala attire of tail, horns and cloven foot with which he graces the revels on the Blocksberg. He borrows for the nonce a tall, gentlemanly figure, surmounted by delicate features, dresses well, is fastidious about his ring and linen, travels post and stops at the best hotels. He begins his earthly career by studying at the renowned university of—. As he can boast of abundant means, a handsome wardrobe and the name of Herr von Barbe, it is no wonder that on the first evening he should be politely received, the next morning have a confidential friend, and the second evening embrace "brothers till death." He becomes much puzzled at the extraordinary manners of the students, and at their language, so different from that of every rational German. He remarks: "Over a glass of beer they often fell into singularly transcendental investigations, of which I understood little or nothing. However, I observed the principal words, and when drawn into a conversation, replied with a grave air—'Freedom, Fatherland, Nationality.'" He attends the lectures of a celebrated professor, whose profundity of thought and terseness of style are so astounding, that the German world set him down as possessed; the critical student, however, differs somewhat from that conclusion, observing—

"I have borne a great deal in the world. I have even entered into swine," ("The devil," said Luther, "knows Scripture well and he uses it in argument") "but into such a philosopher? No, indeed! I had rather be excused."

The episode here reprinted occurred in a hotel in Frankfort, where our incognito is known as Herr von Natas (which, it will be noticed, is his more familiar name read backwards). His brilliant powers of conversation, his adroit flattery, courteous gallantry, and elegant, though wayward flights of imagination, soon rendered him the delight of the whole *table d'hote*. All guests, including our author, were fascinated by the mysterious stranger. But we will let the author himself tell his story.

In this way the jovial stranger had kept myself, and twelve or fifteen other gentlemen and ladies (our fellow guests), in a perpetual whirl of delight. Scarcely any had any special business to detain them at the hotel, and yet none ventured to entertain the mere idea of departure, even at a distant day. On the other hand, after we had slept for some time late on mornings, sat long at dinner, sung and played long of evenings, and drank, chatted, and laughed long of nights, the magic tie which bound us to this hotel seemed to have woven new chains around us.

This intoxication, however, was soon to be put an end to, perhaps for our good. On the seventh day of our rejoicings, a Sunday, our friend Von Natas was not to be found anywhere. The waiters gave as his apology a short journey; he could not return before sunset, but would certainly be in time for tea and supper.

The enjoyment of his society had already become such a necessity, that this piece of information made us helpless and ill at ease.

The conversation turned naturally on our absent friend and his striking, brilliant apparition among us. It was strange, but I could not get it out of my head that I had already met with him in my walk through life, but in a different shape; and, absurd as the idea was, it still forced itself irresistibly on my mind once and again. I called to mind, from years long gone by, the recollection of a man who in his whole demeanour, but more especially in his glance, had the greatest resemblance to him. The one of whom I now speak was a foreign physician, who occasionally visited my native town, and there lived at first in great retirement, though he soon found a crowd of worshippers collected around him. The thought of this man was always a melancholy one, for it was asserted that some serious misfortune always followed his visits; still I could not shake off the idea that Natas resembled him strikingly, in fact that he was one and the same person.

I mentioned to my next neighbour at table the idea that incessantly haunted me, and how unpleasant it was to identify so horrible a being as the stranger who had so afflicted my native city, with our mutual friend who had so fully gained my esteem and affection; but it will seem still more incredible when I assure my readers that all my neighbours were full of precisely the same idea, and that all fancied they had seen our agreeable companion in some entirely different shape.

"You are enough to make one downright melancholy," said Baroness von Thingen, who sat near me; "you make our friend Natas out to be the Wandering Jew, or God knows what more!"

A little old man, a professor in Tibsingen, who had joined our circle some days before, and passed his time in quiet, silent enjoyment, enlivened by an occasional deep conference with the Rhine wine, had kept smiling to himself during what he called our "comparative anatomy," and twirling his huge snuff-box between his fingers with such skilful rapidity, that it revolved like a coach-wheel.

"I cannot longer refrain from a remark I wished to make," exclaimed he at last. "Under your favour, gracious lady, I do not look upon him as being precisely the Wandering Jew, but still as being a very strange mortal. As long as he was present, the thought would, it is true, now and then flash up in my mind, 'You have seen this man before, but pray where was it?' but these recollections were driven away as if by magic whenever he fastened upon me those dark wandering eyes of his."

"So was it with me—and with me—and with me," exclaimed we all in astonishment.

"Hem! hem!" smiled the Professor. "Even now the scales seem to fall from my eyes, and I see that he is the very same person I saw in Stuttgart twelve years ago."

"What, you have seen him then, and in what circumstances?" asked Lady von Thingen eagerly, and almost blushed at the eagerness she displayed.

The Professor took a pinch of snuff, shook the superfluous grains off his waistcoat, and answered—"It may be now about twelve years since I was forced by a law-suit to spend some months in Stuttgart. I lived at one of the best hotels, and generally dined with a large company at the *table d'hote*. Once upon a time I made my first appearance at table after a lapse of several days, during which I had been forced to keep my room. The company were talking very eagerly about a certain Signor Barighi, who for some time past had been delighting the other visitors with his lively wit, and his fluency in all languages. All were unanimous in his praise, but they could not exactly agree as to his occupation; some making him out a diplomatist, others a teacher of languages, a third party a distinguished political exile, and a fourth a spy of the police. The door opened, all seemed silent, even confused, at having carried on the dispute in so loud a tone; I judged that the person spoken of must be among us, and saw—"

"Who, pray?"

"Under favour, the same person who has amused us so agreeably for some days past. There was nothing supernatural in this, to be sure, but listen a moment; for two days Signor Barighi, as the stranger was called, had given a new relish to our meals by his brilliant conversation, when mine host interrupted us suddenly—'Gentlemen,' said he, 'prepare yourself for an unique entertainment which will be provided for you tomorrow.'

"We asked what this meant, and a grey headed captain, who had presided at the hotel table many years, informed us of the joke as follows—Exactly opposite this dining room, an old bachelor lives, solitary and alone, in a large deserted house; he is a retired Counsellor of State—lives on a handsome premium, and has an enormous fortune besides. He is, however, a downright fool, and has some of the strangest peculiarities; thus, for instance, he often gives himself entertainments on a scale of extravagant luxury. He orders covers for twelve, from the hotel, he has excellent wines in his cellar, and one or the other of our waiters has the honour to attend table. You think, perhaps, that at these feasts he feeds the hungry, and gives drink to the thirsty—no such thing; on the chairs lie old yellow leaves of parchment, from the family record, and the old hunks is as jovial as if he had the merriest set of fellows around him; he talks and laughs with them, and the whole thing is said to be so fearful to look upon, that the youngest waiters are always sent over, for whoever has been to one such supper will enter the deserted house no more.

"The day before yesterday he had a supper, and our new waiter, Frank, there, calls heaven and earth to witness that nobody shall ever induce him to go there a second time. The next day after the entertainment comes the Counsellor's second freak. Early in the morning he leaves the city, and comes back the morning after; not, however, to his own house, which during this time is fast locked and bolted, but into this hotel. Here he treats people he has been in the habit of seeing for a whole year, as strangers; dines, and afterwards places himself at one of the windows, and examines his own house across the way from top to bottom.

"'Who does that house opposite belong to?' he then asks the host.

"The other regularly bows and answers, 'It belongs to the Counsellor of State, Hasentreffer, at your Excellency's service.'"

"But, Professor," here observed I, "what has this silly Hasentreffer of yours to do with our Natas?"

"A moment's patience, Doctor," answered the Professor, "the light will soon break in upon you. Hasentreffer then examines the house, and learns that it belongs to Hasentreffer. 'Oh, what!' he asks, 'the same that was a student with me at Tibsingen'—then throws open the window, stretches his powdered head out, and calls out—'Ha-asentreffer—Ha-asentreffer!'

"Of course no one answers, but he remarks: 'The old fellow would never forgive me if I was not to look in on him for a moment,' then takes up his hat and cane, unlocks his own house, goes in, and all goes on after as before.

"All of us," the Professor proceeded in his story, "were greatly astonished at this singular story, and highly delighted at the idea of the next day's merriment. Signor Barighi, however, obliged us to promise that we would not betray him, as he said he was preparing a capital joke to play off on the Counsellor.

"We all met at the *table d'hote* earlier than usual, and besieged the windows. An old tumble down carriage, drawn by two blind steeds, came crawling down the street; it stopped before the hotel. *There's Hasentreffer, there's Hasentreffer,* was echoed by every mouth; and we were filled with extravagant merriment when we saw the little man get out, neatly powdered, dressed in an iron grey *surtout* with a huge *meerschaum* in hand. An escort of at least ten servants followed him in, and in this guise he entered the dining-room.

"We sat down at once. I have seldom laughed as much as I did then; for the old chap insisted, with the greatest coolness, that he came direct from Carrel, and that he had six days before been extremely well entertained at the Swan Inn at Frankfort. Barighi must have disappeared before the dessert, for when the Counsellor left the table, and the other guests, full of curiosity, imitated his example, Barighi was nowhere to be seen.

"The Counsellor took his seat at the window; we all followed his example and watched his movements. The house opposite seemed desolate and uninhabited. Grass grew on the threshold, the shutters were closed, and on some of them birds seemed to have built their nests.

"'A fine house that, opposite,' said the old man to our host, who kept standing behind him in the third position. 'Who does it belong to?'

"'To the Counsellor of State, Hasentreffer, at your Excellency's service.'

"'Ah, indeed! that must be the same one that was a fellow-student with me,' exclaimed he; 'he would never forgive me if I was not to inform him that I was here.' He opened the window,— 'Ha-asentreffer—Hasentreffer!' cried he, in a hoarse voice. But who can paint our terror, when opposite, in the empty house, which we knew was firmly locked and bolted, a window-shutter was slowly raised, a window opened, and out of it peered the Counsellor of State, Hasentreffer, in his chintz morning-gown and white nightcap, under which a few thin grey locks were visible; this, this exactly, was his usual morning costume. Down to the minutest wrinkle on the pallid visage, the figure across the street was precisely the same as the one that stood by our side. But a panic seized us, when the figure in the morning-gown called out across the street, in just the same hoarse voice, 'What do you want? who are you calling to, hey?'

"'Are you the Counsellor of State, Hasentreffer?' said the one on our side of the way, pale as death, in a trembling voice, and quaking as he leaned against the window for support.

"'I'm the man,' squeaked the other, and nodded his head in a friendly way; 'have you any commands for me?'

"'But I'm the man too,' said our friend mournfully, 'how can it be possible?'

"'You are mistaken, my dear friend,' answered he across the way, 'you are the thirteenth, be good enough just to step across the street to my house, and let me twist your neck for you! it is by no means painful.'

"'Waiter! my hat and stick,' said the Counsellor, pale as death, and his voice escaped in mournful tones from his hollow chest. 'The devil is in my house and seeks my soul; a pleasant evening to you, gentlemen,' added he, turning to us with a polite bow, and thereupon left the room.

"'What does this mean?' we asked each other; 'are we all beside ourselves?'

"The gentleman in the morning-gown kept looking quietly out of the window, while our good silly old friend crossed the street at his usual formal pace. At the front-door, he pulled a huge bunch of keys out of his pocket, unlocked the heavy creaking door—he of the morning-gown looking carelessly on, and walked in.

"The latter now withdrew from the window, and we saw him go forward to meet our acquaintance at the room-door.

"Our host and the ten waiters were all pale with fear, and trembled. 'Gentlemen,' said the former, 'God pity poor Hasentreffer, for one of those two must be the devil in human shape.' We laughed at our host, and tried to persuade ourselves that it was a joke of Barighi's; but our host assured us that no one could have obtained access to the house except he was in possession of the Counsellor's very artificially contrived keys; also, that Barighi was seated at table not ten minutes before the prodigy happened; how then could he have disguised himself so completely in so short a time, even supposing him to have known how to unlock a strange house? He added, that the two were so fearfully like one another, that he who had lived in the neighbourhood for twenty years could not distinguish the true one from the counterfeit. 'But, for God's sake, gentlemen, do you not hear the horrid shrieks opposite?'

"We rushed to the window—terrible and fearful voices rang across from the empty house; we fancied we saw the old Counsellor, pursued by his image in the morning-gown, hurry past the window repeatedly. On a sudden all was quiet.

"We gazed on each other; the boldest among us proposed to cross over to the house—we all agreed to it. We crossed the street—the huge bell at the old man's door was rung thrice, but nothing could be heard in answer; we sent to the police and to a blacksmith's—the door was broken open, the whole tide of anxious visitors poured up the wide silent staircase—all the doors were fastened; at length one was opened. In a splendid apartment, the Counsellor, his iron-grey frock-coat torn to pieces, his neatly dressed hair in horrible disorder, lay dead, strangled, on the sofa.

"Since that time no traces of Barighi have been found, neither in Stuttgart nor elsewhere."

St. John's Eve

Nikolai Gogol

This story, taken from *Evenings on a Farm Near Dikanka*, a series of sketches of the life of the Ukrainian peasants, offers a good illustration of the author's art, which was a combination of the romantic and realistic elements. In these pages Gogol wished to record the myths and legends still current among the plain folk of his beloved Ukrainia. The devil naturally enough peeps out here and there through the pages of this book. Gogol's devil is a product of the Russian soil, "the spirit of mischief and cunning, whom Russian literature is always trying to outplay and overcome" (Mme. Jarintzow, *Russian Poets and Poems*). According to European superstition St. John's Eve is the only evening in the year when his Satanic Majesty reveals himself in his proper shape to the eyes of men. If you wish to behold his Highness face to face, stand on St. John's Eve at midnight near a mustard-plant. It is suggested by Sir James Frazer in his *Golden Bough* that, in the chilly air of the upper world, this prince from a warmer clime may be attracted by the warmth of the mustard. It is believed in many parts of Europe that treasures can be found on St. John's Eve by means of the fern-seed. Even without the use of this plant treasures are sometimes said to bloom or burn in the earth, or to reveal their presence by a bluish flame on Midsummer Eve. As guardian of treasures the devil is the successor of the gnome.

Thoma Grigorovich had a very strange sort of eccentricity: to the day of his death, he never liked to tell the same thing twice. There were times, when, if you asked him to relate a thing afresh, behold, he would interpolate new matter, or alter it so that it was impossible to recognize it. Once on a time, one of those gentlemen (it is hard for us simple people to put a name to them, to say whether they are scribblers, or not scribblers: but it is just the same thing as the usurers at our yearly fairs; they clutch and beg and steal every sort of frippery, and issue mean little volumes, no thicker than an A B C book, every month, or even every week),—one of these gentlemen wormed this same story out of Thoma Grigorovich, and he completely forgot about it. But that same young gentleman in the pea-green *caftan*, whom I have mentioned, and one of whose tales you have already read, I think, came from Poltava, bringing with him a little book, and, opening it in the middle, shows it to us. Thoma Grigorovich was on the point of setting his spectacles astride of his nose, but recollected that he had forgotten to wind thread about them, and stick them together with wax, so he passed it over to me. As I understand something about reading and writing, and do not wear spectacles, I undertook to read it. I had not turned two leaves, when all at once he caught me by the hand, and stopped me.

"Stop! tell me first what you are reading."

I confess that I was a trifle stunned by such a question.

"What! what am I reading, Thoma Grigorovich? These were your very words."

"Who told you that they were my words?"

"Why, what more would you have? Here it is printed: *Related by such and such a sacristan.*"

"Spit on the head of the man who printed that! he lies, the dog of a Moscow pedlar! Did I say that? *'Twas just the same as though one hadn't his wits about him!* Listen, I'll tell it to you on the spot."

We moved up to the table, and he began.

****

My grandfather (the kingdom of heaven be his! may he eat only wheaten rolls and *makovniki*[1] with honey in the other world!) could tell a story wonderfully well. When he used to begin on a tale, you wouldn't stir from the spot all day, but keep on listening. He was no match for the story-teller of the present day, when he

---

1. Poppy-seeds cooked in honey, and dried in square cakes.

begins to lie, with a tongue as though he had had nothing to eat for three days, so that you snatch your cap, and flee from the house. As I now recall it, my old mother was alive then, in the long winter evenings when the frost was crackling out of doors, and had so sealed up hermetically the narrow panes of our cottage, she used to sit before the hackling-comb, drawing out a long thread in her hand, rocking the cradle with her foot, and humming a song, which I seem to hear even now.

The fat-lamp, quivering and flaring up as though in fear of something, lighted us within our cottage; the spindle hummed; and all of us children, collected in a cluster, listened to grandfather, who had not crawled off the oven for more than five years, owing to his great age. But the wondrous tales of the incursions of the Zaporozhian Cossacks, the Poles, the bold deeds of Podkova, of Poltor-Kozhukh, and Sagaidatchnii, did not interest us so much as the stories about some deed of old which always sent a shiver through our frames, and made our hair rise upright on our heads. Sometimes such terror took possession of us in consequence of them, that, from that evening on, Heaven knows what a marvel everything seemed to us. If you chanced to go out of the cottage after nightfall for anything, you imagine that a visitor from the other world has lain down to sleep in your bed; and I should not be able to tell this a second time were it not that I had often taken my own smock, at a distance, as it lay at the head of the bed, for the Evil One rolled up in a ball! But the chief thing about grandfather's stories was, that he never had lied in his life; and whatever he said was so, was so.

I will now relate to you one of his marvellous tales. I know that there are a great many wise people who copy in the courts, and can even read civil documents, who, if you were to put into their hand a simple prayer-book, could not make out the first letter in it, and would show all their teeth in derision—which is wisdom. These people laugh at everything you tell them. Such incredulity has spread abroad in the world! What then? (Why, may God and the Holy Virgin cease to love me if it is not possible that even you will not believe me!) Once he said something about witches;—What then? Along comes one of these head-breakers,—and doesn't believe in witches! Yes, glory to God that I have lived so long in the world! I have seen heretics, to whom it would be easier to lie in confession than it would for our brothers and equals to take snuff, and those people would deny the existence of witches! But let them just dream about something, and they won't even tell what it was! There's no use in talking about them!

****

No one could have recognized this village of ours a little over a hundred years ago: a hamlet it was, the poorest kind of a hamlet. Half a score of miserable *izbas*, unplastered, badly thatched, were scattered here and there about the fields. There was not an enclosure or a decent shed to shelter animals or wagons. That was the way the wealthy lived: and if you had looked for our brothers, the poor,—why, a hole in the ground,—that was a cabin for you! Only by the smoke could you tell that a God-created man lived there. You ask, why they lived so? It was not entirely through poverty: almost every one led a wandering, Cossack life, and gathered not a little plunder in foreign lands; it was rather because there was no reason for setting up a well-ordered *khata*². How many people were wandering all over the country,—Crimeans, Poles, Lithuanians! It was quite possible that their own countrymen might make a descent, and plunder everything. Anything was possible.

In this hamlet a man, or rather a devil in human form, often made his appearance. Why he came, and whence, no one knew. He prowled about, got drunk, and suddenly disappeared as if into the air, and there was not a hint of his existence. Then, again, behold, and he seemed to have dropped from the sky, and went flying about the street of the village, of which no trace now remains, and which was not more than a hundred paces from Dikanka. He would collect together all the Cossacks he met; then there were songs, laughter, money in abundance, and vodka flowed like water—He would address the pretty girls, and give them ribbons, earrings, strings of beads,—more than they knew what to do with. It is true that the pretty girls rather hesitated about accepting his presents: God knows, perhaps they had passed through unclean hands. My grandfather's aunt, who kept a tavern at the time, in which Basavriuk (as they called that devil-man) often

---

2. Wooden house.

62

had his carouses, said that no consideration on the face of the earth would have induced her to accept a gift from him. And then, again, how avoid accepting? Fear seized on every one when he knit his bristly brows, and gave a sidelong glance which might send your feet, God knows whither: but if you accept, then the next night some fiend from the swamp, with horns on his head, comes to call, and begins to squeeze your neck, when there is a string of beads upon it; or bite your finger, if there is a ring upon it; or drag you by the hair, if ribbons are braided in it. God have mercy, then, on those who owned such gifts! But here was the difficulty: it was impossible to get rid of them; if you threw them into the water, the diabolical ring or necklace would skim along the surface, and into your hand.

There was a church in the village,—St. Pantelei, if I remember rightly. There lived there a priest, Father Athanasii of blessed memory. Observing that Basavriuk did not come to Church, even on Easter, he determined to reprove him, and impose penance upon him. Well, he hardly escaped with his life. "Hark ye, *pannotche!*"[3] he thundered in reply, "learn to mind your own business instead of meddling in other people's, if you don't want that goat's throat of yours stuck together with boiling *kutya.*"[4] What was to be done with this unrepentant man? Father Athanasii contented himself with announcing that any one who should make the acquaintance of Basavriuk would be counted a Catholic, an enemy of Christ's church, not a member of the human race.

In this village there was a Cossack named Korzh, who had a labourer whom people called Peter the Orphan—perhaps because no one remembered either his father or mother. The church *starost*,[5] it is true, said that they had died of the pest in his second year; but my grandfather's aunt would not hear to that, and tried with all her might to furnish him with parents, although poor Peter needed them about as much as we need last year's snow. She said that his father had been in Zaporozhe, taken prisoner by the Turks, underwent God only knows what tortures, and having, by some miracle, disguised himself as a eunuch, had made his

---

3. Sir.
4. A dish of rice or wheat flour, with honey and raisins, which is brought to the church on the celebration of memorial masses.
5. Elder.

escape. Little cared the black-browed youths and maidens about his parents. They merely remarked, that if he only had a new coat, a red sash, a black lambskin cap, with dandified blue crown, on his head, a Turkish sabre hanging by his side, a whip in one hand and a pipe with handsome mountings in the other, he would surpass all the young men. But the pity was, that the only thing poor Peter had was a grey *svitka* with more holes in it than there are gold pieces in a Jew's pocket. And that was not the worst of it, but this: that Korzh had a daughter, such a beauty as I think you can hardly have chanced to see. My deceased grandfather's aunt used to say—and you know that it is easier for a woman to kiss the Evil One than to call anybody a beauty, without malice be it said—that this Cossack maiden's cheeks were as plump and fresh as the pinkest poppy when just bathed in God's dew, and, glowing, it unfolds its petals, and coquets with the rising sun; that her brows were like black cords, such as our maidens buy nowadays, for their crosses and ducats, of the Moscow pedlars who visit the villages with their baskets, and evenly arched as though peeping into her clear eyes; that her little mouth, at sight of which the youth smacked their lips, seemed made to emit the songs of nightingales; that her hair, black as the raven's wing, and soft as young flax (our maidens did not then plait their hair in clubs interwoven with pretty, bright-hued ribbons), fell in curls over her *kuntush*.[6] Eh! may I never intone another alleluia in the choir, if I would not have kissed her, in spite of the grey which is making its way all through the old wool which covers my pate, and my old woman beside me, like a thorn in my side! Well, you know what happens when young men and maids live side by side. In the twilight the heels of red boots were always visible in the place where Pidorka chatted with her Petrus. But Korzh would never have suspected anything out of the way, only one day—it is evident that none but the Evil One could have inspired him—Petrus took it into his head to kiss the Cossack maiden's rosy lips with all his heart in the passage, without first looking well about him; and that same Evil One—may the son of a dog dream of the holy cross!—caused the old greybeard, like a fool, to open the cottage-door at that same moment. Korzh was petrified, dropped his jaw,

6. Upper garment in Little Russia.

and clutched at the door for support. Those unlucky kisses had completely stunned him. It surprised him more than the blow of a pestle on the wall, with which, in our days, the *muzhik* generally drives out his intoxication for lack of fusees and powder.

Recovering himself, he took his grandfather's hunting-whip from the wall, and was about to belabour Peter's back with it, when Pidorka's little six-year-old brother Ivas rushed up from somewhere or other, and, grasping his father's legs with his little hands, screamed out, "Daddy, daddy! don't beat Petrus!" What was to be done? A father's heart is not made of stone. Hanging the whip again upon the wall, he led him quietly from the house. "If you ever show yourself in my cottage again, or even under the windows, look out, Petro! by Heaven, your black moustache will disappear; and your black locks, though wound twice about your ears, will take leave of your pate, or my name is not Terentii Korzh." So saying, he gave him a little taste of his fist in the nape of his neck, so that all grew dark before Petrus, and he flew headlong. So there was an end of their kissing. Sorrow seized upon our doves; and a rumour was rife in the village, that a certain Pole, all embroidered with gold, with moustaches, sabre, spurs, and pockets jingling like the bells of the bag with which our sacristan Taras goes through the church every day, had begun to frequent Korzh's house. Now, it is well known why the father is visited when there is a black-browed daughter about. So, one day, Pidorka burst into tears, and clutched the hand of her Ivas. "Ivas, my dear! Ivas, my love! fly to Petrus, my child of gold, like an arrow from a bow. Tell him all: I would have loved his brown eyes, I would have kissed his white face, but my fate decrees not so. More than one towel have I wet with burning tears. I am sad, I am heavy at heart. And my own father is my enemy. I will not marry that Pole, whom I do not love. Tell him they are preparing a wedding, but there will be no music at our wedding: ecclesiastics will sing instead of pipes and *kobzas*.[7] I shall not dance with my bridegroom: they will carry me out. Dark, dark will be my dwelling,—of maple wood; and, instead of chimneys, a cross will stand upon the roof."

Petro stood petrified, without moving from the spot, when the innocent child lisped out Pidorka's words to him. "And I, unhappy

---

7. Eight-stringed musical instrument.

65

man, thought to go to the Crimea and Turkey, win gold and return to thee, my beauty! But it may not be. The evil eye has seen us. I will have a wedding, too, dear little fish, I, too; but no ecclesiastics will be at that wedding. The black crow will caw, instead of the pope, over me; the smooth field will be my dwelling; the dark blue clouds my roof-tree. The eagle will claw out my brown eyes: the rain will wash the Cossack's bones, and the whirlwinds will dry them. But what am I? Of whom, to whom, am I complaining? 'Tis plain, God willed it so. If I am to be lost, then so be it!" and he went straight to the tavern.

My late grandfather's aunt was somewhat surprised on seeing Petrus in the tavern, and at an hour when good men go to morning mass; and she stared at him as though in a dream, when he demanded a jug of brandy, about half a pailful. But the poor fellow tried in vain to drown his woe. The vodka stung his tongue like nettles, and tasted more bitter than wormwood. He flung the jug from him upon the ground. "You have sorrowed enough, Cossack," growled a bass voice behind him. He looked round—Basavriuk! Ugh, what a face! His hair was like a brush, his eyes like those of a bull. "I know what you lack: here it is." Then he jingled a leather purse which hung from his girdle, and smiled diabolically. Petro shuddered. "He, he, he! yes, how it shines!" he roared, shaking out *ducats* into his hand: "he, he, he! and how it jingles! And I only ask one thing for a whole pile of such shiners."—"It is the Evil One!" exclaimed Petro:—"Give them here! I am ready for anything!" They struck hands upon it. "See here, Petro, you are ripe just in time: tomorrow is St. John the Baptist's day. Only on this one night in the year does the fern blossom. Delay not. I will await thee at midnight in the Bear's ravine."

I do not believe that chickens await the hour when the woman brings their corn, with as much anxiety as Petrus awaited the evening. And, in fact, he looked to see whether the shadows of the trees were not lengthening, if the sun were not turning red towards setting; and, the longer he watched, the more impatient he grew. How long it was! Evidently, God's day had lost its end somewhere. And now the sun is gone. The sky is red only on one side, and it is already growing dark. It grows colder in the fields. It gets dusky, and more dusky, and at last quite dark. At last! With heart almost bursting from his bosom, he set out on his way, and cautiously descended through the dense woods into the deep hollow called the Bear's ravine. Basavriuk was already waiting there. It was so dark, that you could not see a yard before you. Hand in hand they penetrated the thin marsh, clinging to the luxuriant thorn-bushes, and stumbling at almost every step. At last they reached an open spot. Petro looked about him: he had never chanced to come there before. Here Basavriuk halted.

"Do you see, before you stand three hillocks? There are a great many sorts of flowers upon them. But may some power keep you from plucking even one of them. But as soon as the fern blossoms, seize it, and look not round, no matter what may seem to be going on behind thee."

Petro wanted to ask—and behold, he was no longer there. He approached the three hillocks—where were the flowers? He saw nothing. The wild *steppe*-grass darkled around, and stifled everything in its luxuriance. But the lightning flashed; and before him stood a whole bed of flowers, all wonderful, all strange: and there were also the simple fronds of fern. Petro doubted his senses, and stood thoughtfully before them, with both hands upon his sides.

"What prodigy is this? one can see these weeds ten times in a day: what marvel is there about them? was not devil's-face laughing at me?"

Behold! the tiny flower-bud crimsons, and moves as though alive. It is a marvel, in truth. It moves, and grows larger and larger, and flashes like a burning coal. The tiny star flashes up, something bursts softly, and the flower opens before his eyes like a flame, lighting the others about it. "Now is the time," thought Petro, and extended his hand. He sees hundreds of shaggy hands reach from behind him, also for the flower; and there is a running about from place to place, in the rear. He half shut his eyes, plucked sharply at the stalk, and the flower remained in his hand. All became still. Upon a stump sat Basavriuk, all blue like a corpse. He moved not so much as a finger. His eyes were immovably fixed on something visible to him alone: his mouth was half open and speechless. All about, nothing stirred. Ugh! it was horrible!—But then a whistle was heard, which made Petro's heart grow cold within him; and it seemed to him that the grass whispered, and the flowers began to talk among themselves in delicate voices, like little silver bells; the trees rustled in waving contention;—Basavriuk's face suddenly became full of life and his eyes sparkled. "The witch has just returned," he muttered between his teeth. "See here, Petro: a beauty will stand before you in a moment; do whatever she commands; if not—you are lost for ever." Then he parted the thorn-bush with a knotty stick, and before him stood a tiny *izba*, on chicken's legs, as they say. Basavriuk smote it with his fist, and the wall trembled. A large black dog ran out to meet them, and with a whine, transforming itself into a cat, flew straight at his eyes. "Don't be angry, don't be angry, you old Satan!" said Basavriuk, employing such words as would have made a good man stop his ears. Behold, instead of a cat, an old woman with a face wrinkled like a baked apple, and all bent into a bow: her nose and chin were like a pair of nut-crackers. "A stunning beauty!" thought Petro; and cold chills ran down his back. The witch tore the flower from his hand, bent over, and muttered over it for a long time, sprinkling it with some kind of water. Sparks flew from her mouth, froth appeared on her lips.

"Throw it away," she said, giving it back to Petro.

Petro threw it, and what wonder was this? the flower did not fall straight to the earth, but for a long while twinkled like a fiery ball through the darkness, and swam through the air like a boat: at last it began to sink lower, and fell so far away, that the little star, hardly larger than a poppy-seed, was barely visible. "Here!" croaked the old woman, in a dull voice: and Basavriuk, giving him a spade, said, "Dig here, Petro: here you will find more gold than you or Korzh ever dreamed of."

Petro spat on his hands, seized the spade, applied his foot, and turned up the earth, a second, a third, a fourth time—There was something hard: the spade clinked, and would go no farther. Then his eyes began to distinguish a small, iron-bound coffer. He tried to seize it; but the chest began to sink into the earth, deeper, farther, and deeper still: and behind him he heard a laugh, more like a serpent's hiss. "No, you shall not see the gold until you procure human blood," said the witch, and led up to him a child of six, covered with a white sheet, indicating by a sign that he was to cut off his head. Petro was stunned. A trifle, indeed, to cut off a man's or even an innocent child's head for no reason whatever! In wrath he tore off the sheet enveloping his head, and behold! before him stood Ivas. And the poor child crossed his little hands, and hung his head—Petro flew upon the witch with the knife like a madman, and was on the point of laying hands on her—

"What did you promise for the girl?"—thundered Basavriuk; and like a shot he was on his back. The witch stamped her foot: a blue flame flashed from the earth; it illumined it all inside, and it was as if moulded of crystal; and all that was within the earth became visible, as if in the palm of the hand. *Ducats*, precious stones in chests and kettles, were piled in heaps beneath the very spot they stood on. His eyes burned,—his mind grew troubled—He grasped the knife like a madman, and the innocent blood spurted into his eyes. Diabolical laughter resounded on all sides. Misshaped monsters flew past him in herds. The witch, fastening her hands in the headless trunk, like a wolf, drank its blood—All went round in his head. Collecting all his strength, he set out to run. Everything turned red before him. The trees seemed steeped in blood, and burned and groaned. The sky glowed and glowered—Burning point, like lightning, flickered before his eyes. Utterly exhausted, he rushed into his miserable hovel, and fell to the ground like a log. A death-like sleep overpowered him.

Two days and two nights did Petro sleep, without once awakening. When he came to himself, on the third day, he looked long at all the corners of his hut; but in vain did he endeavour to recollect; his memory was like a miser's pocket, from which you cannot entice a quarter of a kopek. Stretching himself, he heard something clash at his feet. He looked—two bags of gold. Then only, as if in a dream, he recollected that he had been seeking some treasure, that something had frightened him in the woods—But at what price he had obtained it, and how, he could by no means understand.

Korzh saw the sacks,—and was mollified. "Such a Petrus, quite unheard of! yes, and did I not love him? Was he not to me as my own son?" And the old fellow carried on his fiction until it reduced him to tears. Pidorka began to tell him some passing gipsies had stolen Ivas; but Petro could not even recall him—to such a degree had the Devil's influence darkened his mind! There was no reason for delay. The Pole was dismissed, and the wedding-feast prepared; rolls were baked, towels and handkerchiefs embroidered; the young people were seated at table; the wedding-loaf was cut; *banduras*, cymbals, pipes, *kobzi*, sounded, and pleasure was rife—

A wedding in the olden times was not like one of the present day. My grandfather's aunt used to tell—what doings!—how the maidens—in festive head-dresses of yellow, blue, and pink ribbons, above which they bound gold braid; in thin *chemisettes* embroidered on all the seams with red silk, and strewn with tiny silver flowers; in morocco shoes, with high iron heels—danced the *gorlitza* as swimmingly as peacocks, and as wildly as the whirlwind; how the youths—with their ship-shaped caps upon their heads, the crowns of gold brocade, with a little slit at the nape where the hair-net peeped through, and two horns projecting, one in front and another behind, of the very finest black lambskin; in *kuntushas* of the finest blue silk with red borders—stepped forward one by one, their arms akimbo in stately form, and executed the *gopak*; how the lads—in tall Cossack caps, and light cloth *svitkas*, girt with silver embroidered belts, their short pipes in their teeth—skipped before them, and talked nonsense. Even Korzh could not contain himself, as he gazed at the young people, from getting gay in his old age. *bandura* in hand, alternately puffing at his pipe and singing, a brandy-glass upon his head, the greybeard began the national dance amid loud shouts from the merry-makers. What will not people devise in merry mood! They even began to disguise their faces. They did not look like human beings. They are not to be compared with the disguises which we have at our weddings nowadays. What do they do now? Why, imitate gipsies and Moscow pedlars. No! then one used to dress himself as a Jew, another as the Devil: they would begin by kissing each other, and end by seizing each other by the hair— God be with them! you laughed till you held your sides. They dressed themselves in Turkish and Tartar garments. All upon them glowed like a conflagration—and then they began to joke and play pranks—Well, then away with the saints!

An amusing thing happened to my grandfather's aunt, who was at this wedding. She was dressed in a voluminous Tartar robe, and, wineglass in hand, was entertaining the company. The Evil One instigated one man to pour vodka over her from behind. Another, at the same moment, evidently not by accident, struck a light, and touched it to her;—the flame flashed up; poor aunt, in terror, flung her robe from her, before them all—Screams, laughter, jests, arose, as if at a fair. In a word, the old folks could not recall so merry a wedding.

Pidorka and Petrus began to live like a gentleman and lady. There was plenty of everything, and everything was handsome—But honest people shook their heads when they looked at their way of living. "From the Devil no good can come," they unanimously agreed. "Whence, except from the tempter of orthodox people, came this wealth? Where else could he get such a lot of gold? Why, on the very day that he got rich, did Basavriuk vanish as if into thin air?" Say, if you can, that people imagine things! In fact, a month had not passed, and no one would have recognized Petrus. Why, what had happened to him? God knows. He sits in one spot, and says no word to any one: he thinks continually, and seems to be trying to recall something. When Pidorka succeeds in getting him to speak, he seems to forget himself, carries on a conversation, and even grows cheerful; but if he inadvertently glances at the sacks, "Stop, stop! I have forgotten," he cries, and again plunges into reverie, and again strives to recall something. Sometimes when he has sat long in a place, it seems to him as though it were coming, just coming back to mind,—and again all fades away. It seems as if he is sitting in the tavern: they bring him vodka; vodka stings him; vodka is repulsive to him. Some one comes along, and strikes him on the shoulder;—but beyond that everything is veiled in darkness before him. The perspiration streams down his face, and he sits exhausted in the same place.

What did not Pidorka do? She consulted the sorceress; and they poured out fear, and brewed stomach-ache,[8]—but all to no avail. And so the summer passed. Many a Cossack had mowed and reaped: many a Cossack, more enterprising than the rest, had set off upon an expedition. Flocks of ducks were already crowding our marshes, but there was not even a hint of improvement.

It was red upon the *steppes*. Ricks of grain, like Cossacks' caps, dotted the fields here and there. On the highway were to be encoun-

8. "To pour out fear," is done with us in case of fear; when it is desired to know what caused it, melted lead or wax is poured into water and the object whose form it assumes is the one which frightened the sick person; after this, the fear departs. *Sonvashnitza* is brewed for giddiness, and pain in the bowels. To this end, a bit of stump is burned, thrown into a jug, and turned upside down into a bowl filled with water, which is placed on the patient's stomach: after an incantation, he is given a spoonful of this water to drink.

tered wagons loaded with brushwood and logs. The ground had become more solid, and in places was touched with frost. Already had the snow begun to besprinkle the sky, and the branches of the trees were covered with rime like rabbit-skin. Already on frosty days the red-breasted finch hopped about on the snow-heaps like a foppish Polish nobleman, and picked out grains of corn; and children, with huge sticks, chased wooden tops upon the ice; while their fathers lay quietly on the stove, issuing forth at intervals with lighted pipes in their lips, to growl, in regular fashion, at the orthodox frost, or to take the air, and thresh the grain spread out in the barn. At last the snow began to melt, and the ice rind slipped away: but Petro remained the same; and, the longer it went on, the more morose he grew. He sat in the middle of the cottage as though nailed to the spot, with the sacks of gold at his feet. He grew shy, his hair grew long, he became terrible; and still he thought of but one thing, still he tried to recall something, and got angry and ill-tempered because he could not recall it. Often, rising wildly from his seat, he gesticulates violently, fixes his eyes on something as though desirous of catching it: his lips move as though desirous of uttering some long-forgotten word— and remain speechless. Fury takes possession of him: he gnaws and bites his hands like a man half crazy, and in his vexation tears out his hair by the handful, until, calming down, he falls into forgetfulness, as it were, and again begins to recall, and is again seized with fury and fresh tortures—What visitation of God is this?

Pidorka was neither dead nor alive. At first it was horrible to her to remain alone in the cottage; but, in course of time, the poor woman grew accustomed to her sorrow. But it was impossible to recognize the Pidorka of former days. No blush, no smile: she was thin and worn with grief, and had wept her bright eyes away. Once, some one who evidently took pity on her, advised her to go to the witch who dwelt in the Bear's ravine, and enjoyed the reputation of being able to cure every disease in the world. She determined to try this last remedy: word by word she persuaded the old woman to come to her. This was St. John's Eve, as it chanced. Petro lay insensible on the bench, and did not observe the new-comer. Little by little he rose, and looked about him. Suddenly he trembled in every limb, as though he were on the scaffold: his hair rose upon his head,—and he laughed such a laugh as pierced Pidorka's heart with fear. "I have remembered, remembered!" he cried in terrible joy; and, swinging a hatchet round his head, he flung it at the old woman with all his might. The hatchet penetrated the oaken door two *vershok*.[9] The old woman disappeared; and a child of seven in a white blouse, with covered head, stood in the middle of the cottage—The sheet flew off. "Ivas!" cried Pidorka, and ran to him; but the apparition became covered from head to foot with blood, and illumined the whole room with red light—She ran into the passage in her terror, but, on recovering herself a little, wished to help him; in vain! the door had slammed to behind her so securely that she could not open it. People ran up, and began to knock: they broke in the door, as though there were but one mind among them. The whole cottage was full of smoke; and just in the middle, where Petrus had stood, was a heap of ashes, from which smoke was still rising. They flung themselves upon the sacks: only broken potsherds lay there instead of *ducats*. The Cossacks stood with staring eyes and open mouths, not daring to move a hair, as if rooted to the earth, such terror did this wonder inspire in them.

I do not remember what happened next. Pidorka took a vow to go upon a pilgrimage, collected the property left her by her father, and in a few days it was as if she had never been in the village. Whither she had gone, no one could tell. Officious old women would have dispatched her to the same place whither Petro had gone; but a Cossack from Kiev reported that he had seen, in a cloister, a nun withered to a mere skeleton, who prayed unceasingly; and her fellow-villagers recognized her as Pidorka, by all the signs,— that no one had ever heard her utter a word; that she had come on foot, and had brought a frame for the icon of God's mother, set with such brilliant stones that all were dazzled at the sight.

But this was not the end, if you please. On the same day that the Evil One made way with Petrus, Basavriuk appeared again; but all fled from him. They knew what sort of a bird he was,—none else than Satan, who had assumed human form in order to unearth treasures; and, since treasures do not yield to unclean hands, he seduced the young. That same year, all deserted their earth huts, and collected in a village; but, even there, there was no peace, on account of that accursed Basavriuk. My late grandfather's aunt said that he

---

9. Three inches and a half.

was particularly angry with her, because she had abandoned her former tavern, and tried with all his might to revenge himself upon her. Once the village elders were assembled in the tavern, and, as the saying goes, were arranging the precedence at the table, in the middle of which was placed a small roasted lamb, shame to say. They chattered about this, that, and the other,—among the rest about various marvels and strange things. Well, they saw something; it would have been nothing if only one had seen it, but all saw it; and it was this: the sheep raised his head; his goggling eyes became alive and sparkled; and the black, bristling moustache, which appeared for one instant, made a significant gesture at those present. All, at once, recognized Basavriuk's countenance in the sheep's head: my grand-father's aunt thought it was on the point of asking for vodka—The worthy elders seized their hats, and hastened home.

Another time, the church *starost* himself, who was fond of an occasional private interview with my grandfather's brandy-glass, had not succeeded in getting to the bottom twice, when he beheld the glass bowing very low to him. "Satan take you, let us make the sign of the cross over you!"—And the same marvel happened to his better half. She had just begun to mix the dough in a huge kneading-trough, when suddenly the trough sprang up. "Stop, stop! where are you going?" Putting its arms akimbo, with dignity, it went skipping all about the cottage—You may laugh, but it was no laughing-matter to your grandfathers. And in vain did Father Athanasii go through all the village with holy water, and chase the Devil through the streets with his brush; and my late grandfather's aunt long complained, that, as soon as it was dark, some one came knocking at her door, and scratching at the wall.

Well! All appears to be quiet now, in the place where our village stands; but it was not so very long ago—my father was still alive— that I remember how a good man could not pass the ruined tavern, which a dishonest race had long managed for their own interest. From the smoke-blackened chimneys, smoke poured out in a pillar, and rising high in the air, as if to take an observation, rolled off like a cap, scattering burning coals over the *steppe*; and Satan (the son of a dog should not be mentioned) sobbed so pitifully in his lair, that the startled ravens rose in flocks from the neighbouring oak-wood, and flew through the air with wild cries.

The Devil's Wager

William Makepeace Thackeray

'The Devil's Wager' is Thackeray's earliest attempt at story-writing, was contributed to a weekly literary paper with the imposing title *The National Standard, and Journal of Literature, Science, Music, Theatricals, and the Fine Arts*, of which he was proprietor and editor, and was reprinted in the *Paris Sketch Book* (1840). The story first ended with the very Thackerayesque touch: "The moral of this story will be given in several successive numbers." In the *Paris Sketch Book* the last three words are changed into "the second edition." This comical tale was illustrated by an excellent wood-cut, representing the devil as sailing through the air, dragging after him the fat Sir Roger de Rollo by means of his tail, which is wound round Sir Roger's neck.

In the "Advertisement to the First Edition" of his *Paris Sketch Book*, Thackeray admits the French origin of this as well as of his other devil-story, 'The Painter's Bargain', to be found in the same volume. It was Thackeray's good fortune to live in Paris during the wildest and most brilliant years of Romanticism; and while his attitude towards this movement and its leaders, as presented in the *Paris Sketch Book*, is not wholly sympathetic, he is indebted to it for his interest in supernatural subjects. The Romanticism of Thackeray has been denied with great obstinacy and almost passion, for like Heinrich Heine, the chief of German Romantic ironists, he poked fun at this movement. But "to laugh at what you love," as Mr. George Saintsbury has pointed out in his *History of the French Novel*, "is not only permissible, but a sign of the love itself."

Mercurius makes a pun on the familiar quotation "*rara avis*" from Horace (Sat. 2, 2. 26), where it means a rare bird. This expression is commonly applied to a singular person. It is also found in the *Satires* of Juvenal (VI, 165).

It was the hour of the night when there be none stirring save church-yard ghosts—when all doors are closed except the gates of graves, and all eyes shut but the eyes of wicked men.

When there is no sound on the earth except the ticking of the grasshopper, or the croaking of obscene frogs in the pool.

And no light except that of the blinking stars, and the wicked and devilish wills-o'-the-wisp, as they gambol among the marshes, and lead good men astray.

When there is nothing moving in heaven except the owl, as he flappeth along lazily; or the magician, as he rideth on his infernal broomstick, whistling through the air like the arrows of a Yorkshire archer.

It was at this hour (namely, at twelve o'clock of the night,) that two beings went winging through the black clouds, and holding converse with each other.

Now the first was Mercurius, the messenger, not of gods (as the heathens feigned), but of demons; and the second, with whom he held company, was the soul of Sir Roger de Rollo, the brave knight. Sir Roger was Count of Chauchigny, in Champagne; Seigneur of Santerre, Villacerf and *autre lieux*. But the great die as well as the humble; and nothing remained of brave Roger now, but his coffin and his deathless soul.

And Mercurius, in order to keep fast the soul, his companion, had bound him round the neck with his tail; which, when the soul was stubborn, he would draw so tight as to strangle him well-nigh, sticking into him the barbed point thereof; whereat the poor soul, Sir Rollo, would groan and roar lustily.

Now they two had come together from the gates of purgatory, being bound to those regions of fire and flame where poor sinners fry and roast in saecula saeculorum.

"It is hard," said the poor Sir Rollo, as they went gliding through the clouds, "that I should thus be condemned for ever, and all for want of a single *ave*."

"How, Sir Soul?" said the demon. "You were on earth so wicked, that not one, or a million of *aves*, could suffice to keep from hell-flame a creature like thee; but cheer up and be merry; thou wilt be but a subject of our lord the Devil, as am I; and, perhaps, thou wilt be advanced to posts of honour, as am I also:" and to show his authority, he lashed with his tail the ribs of the wretched Rollo.

"Nevertheless, sinner as I am, one more *ave* would have saved me; for my sister, who was Abbess of St. Mary of Chauchigny, did so prevail, by her prayer and good works, for my lost and wretched soul, that every day I felt the pains of purgatory decrease; the pitch-forks which, on my first entry, had never ceased to vex and torment my poor carcass, were now not applied above once a week; the roasting had ceased, the boiling had discontinued; only a certain warmth was kept up, to remind me of my situation."

"A gentle stew," said the demon.

"Yea, truly, I was but in a stew, and all from the effects of the prayers of my blessed sister. But yesterday, he who watched me in purgatory told me, that yet another prayer from my sister, and my bonds should be unloosed, and I, who am now a devil, should have been a blessed angel."

"And the other *ave*?" said the demon.

"She died, sir—my sister died—death choked her in the middle of the prayer." And hereat the wretched spirit began to weep and whine piteously; his salt tears falling over his beard, and scalding the tail of Mercurius the devil.

"It is, in truth, a hard case," said the demon; "but I know of no remedy save patience, and for that you will have an excellent op-portunity in your lodgings below."

"But I have relations," said the Earl; "my kinsman Randal, who has inherited my lands, will he not say a prayer for his uncle?"

"Thou didst hate and oppress him when living."

"It is true; but an *ave* is not much; his sister, my niece, Matilda—"

"You shut her in a convent, and hanged her lover."

"Had I not reason? besides, has she not others?"

"A dozen, without a doubt."

"And my brother, the prior?"

"A liege subject of my lord the Devil: he never opens his mouth, except to utter an oath, or to swallow a cup of wine."

"And yet, if but one of these would but say an *ave* for me, I should be saved."

"*Aves* with them are *rarae aves*," replied Mercurius, wagging his tail right waggishly; "and, what is more, I will lay thee any wager that no one of these will say a prayer to save thee."

"I would wager willingly," responded he of Chauchigny; "but what has a poor soul like me to stake?"

"Every evening, after the day's roasting, my lord Satan giveth a cup of cold water to his servants; I will bet thee thy water for a year, that none of the three will pray for thee."

"Done!" said Rollo.

"Done!" said the demon; "and here, if I mistake not, is thy castle of Chauchigny."

Indeed, it was true. The soul, on looking down, perceived the tall towers, the courts, the stables, and the fair gardens of the castle. Although it was past midnight, there was a blaze of light in the banqueting-hall, and a lamp burning in the open window of the Lady Matilda.

"With whom shall we begin?" said the demon: "with the baron or the lady?"

"With the lady, if you will."

"Be it so; her window is open, let us enter."

So they descended, and entered silently into Matilda's chamber.

****

The young lady's eyes were fixed so intently on a little clock, that it was no wonder that she did not perceive the entrance of her two visitors. Her fair cheek rested in her white arm, and her white arm on the cushion of a great chair in which she sat, pleasantly supported by sweet thoughts and swan's down; a lute was at her side, and a book of prayers lay under the table (for piety is always modest). Like the amorous Alexander, she sighed and looked (at the clock)—and sighed for ten minutes or more, when she softly breathed the word "Edward!"

At this the soul of the Baron was wroth. "The jade is at her old pranks," said he to the devil; and then addressing Matilda: "I pray thee, sweet niece, turn thy thoughts for a moment from that villainous page, Edward, and give them to thine affectionate uncle."

When she heard the voice, and saw the awful apparition of

her uncle (for a year's sojourn in purgatory had not increased the comeliness of his appearance), she started, screamed, and of course fainted.

But the devil Mercurius soon restored her to herself. "What's o'clock?" said she, as soon as she had recovered from her fit: "is he come?"

"Not thy lover, Maude, but thine uncle—that is, his soul. For the love of heaven, listen to me: I have been frying in purgatory for a year past, and should have been in heaven but for the want of a single *ave*."

"I will say it for thee tomorrow, uncle."

"Tonight, or never."

"Well, tonight be it:" and she requested the devil Mercurius to give her the prayer-book, from under the table; but he had no sooner touched the holy book than he dropped it with a shriek and a yell. "It was hotter," he said, "than his master Sir Lucifer's own particular pitchfork." And the lady was forced to begin her *ave* without the aid of her missal.

At the commencement of her devotions the demon retired, and carried with him the anxious soul of poor Sir Roger de Rollo.

The lady knelt down—she sighed deeply; she looked again at the clock, and began—

"Ave Maria."

When a lute was heard under the window, and a sweet voice singing—

"Hark!" said Matilda.

Now the toils of day are over,
And the sun hath sunk to rest,
Seeking, like a fiery lover,
The bosom of the blushing west—

The faithful night keeps watch and ward,
Raising the moon, her silver shield,
And summoning the stars to guard
The slumbers of my fair Mathilde!

"For mercy's sake!" said Sir Rollo, "the *ave* first, and next the song."

So Matilda again dutifully betook her to her devotions, and began—

"Ave Maria gratia plena!" but the music began again, and the prayer ceased of course.

The faithful night!
Now all things lie
Hid by her mantle dark and dim,
In pious hope I hither hie,
And humbly chant mine ev'ning hymn.

Thou art my prayer,
My saint, my shrine!
(For never holy pilgrim kneel'd,
Or wept at feet more pure than thine),
My virgin love, my sweet Mathilde!

"Virgin love!" said the Baron. "Upon my soul, this is too bad!" and he thought of the lady's lover whom he had caused to be hanged.

But *she* only thought of him who stood singing at her window.

"Niece Matilda!" cried Sir Roger, agonizedly, "wilt thou listen to the lies of an impudent page, whilst thine uncle is waiting but a dozen words to make him happy?"

At this Matilda grew angry: "Edward is neither impudent nor a liar, Sir Uncle, and I will listen to the end of the song."

"Come away," said Mercurius; "he hath yet got wield, field, sealed, congealed, and a dozen other rhymes beside; and after the song will come the supper."

So the poor soul was obliged to go; while the lady listened, and the page sung away till morning.

****

"My virtues have been my ruin," said poor Sir Rollo, as he and Mercurius slunk silently out of the window. "Had I hanged that knave Edward, as I did the page his predecessor, my niece would have sung mine *ave*, and I should have been by this time an angel in heaven."

"He is reserved for wiser purposes," responded the devil: "he will assassinate your successor, the lady Mathilde's brother; and, in consequence, will be hanged. In the love of the lady he will be succeeded by a gardener, who will be replaced by a monk, who will give way to an ostler, who will be deposed by a Jew pedlar, who shall, finally, yield to a noble earl, the future husband of the fair Mathilde. So that, you see, instead of having one poor soul a-frying, we may now look forward to a goodly harvest for our lord the Devil."

The soul of the Baron began to think that his companion knew too much for one who would make fair bets; but there was no help for it; he would not, and he could not cry off: and he prayed inwardly that the brother might be found more pious than the sister.

But there seemed little chance of this. As they crossed the court, lackeys, with smoking dishes and full jugs, passed and repassed continually, although it was long past midnight. On entering the hall, they found Sir Randal at the head of a vast table, surrounded by a fiercer and more motley collection of individuals than had congregated there even in the time of Sir Rollo. The lord of the castle had signified that "it was his royal pleasure to be drunk," and the gentlemen of his train had obsequiously followed their master. Mercurius was delighted with the scene, and relaxed his usually rigid countenance into a bland and benevolent smile, which became him wonderfully.

The entrance of Sir Roger, who had been dead about a year, and a person with hoofs, horns, and a tail, rather disturbed the hilarity of the company. Sir Randal dropped his cup of wine; and Father Peter, the confessor, incontinently paused in the midst of a profane song, with which he was amusing the society.

"Holy Mother!" cried he, "it is Sir Roger."

"Alive!" screamed Sir Randal.

"No, my lord," Mercurius said; "Sir Roger is dead, but cometh on a matter of business; and I have the honour to act as his counsellor and attendant."

"Nephew," said Sir Roger, "the demon saith justly; I am come on a trifling affair, in which thy service is essential."

"I will do anything, uncle, in my power."

"Thou canst give me life, if thou wilt?" But Sir Randal looked very blank at this proposition. "I mean life spiritual, Randal," said Sir Roger; and thereupon he explained to him the nature of the wager.

Whilst he was telling his story, his companion Mercurius was playing all sorts of antics in the hall; and, by his wit and fun, became so popular with this godless crew, that they lost all the fear which his first appearance had given them. The friar was wonderfully taken with him, and used his utmost eloquence and endeavours to convert the devil; the knights stopped drinking to listen to the argument; the men-at-arms forbore brawling; and the wicked little pages crowded round the two strange disputants, to hear their edifying discourse. The ghostly man, however, had little chance in the controversy, and certainly little learning to carry it on. Sir Randal interrupted him. "Father Peter," said he, "our kinsman is condemned for ever, for want of a single *ave*: wilt thou say it for him?"

"Willingly, my lord," said the monk, "with my book;" and accordingly he produced his missal to read, without which aid it appeared that the holy father could not manage the desired prayer. But the crafty Mercurius had, by his devilish art, inserted a song in the place of the *ave*, so that Father Peter, instead of chanting an hymn, sang the following irreverent ditty:

"Some love the matin-chimes, which tell
"The hour of prayer to sinner:
"But better far's the mid-day bell,
"Which speaks the hour of dinner;
"For when I see a smoking fish,
"Or capon drowned in gravy,
"Or noble haunch on silver dish,
"Full glad I sing mine ave.

"My pulpit is an ale-house bench,
"Whereon I sit so jolly;
"A smiling rosy country wench
"My saint and patron holy.
"I kiss her cheek so red and sleek,
"I press her ringlets wavy.
"And in her willing ear I speak
"A most religious ave.

"And if I'm blind, yet heaven is kind,
"And holy saints forgiving;
"For sure he leads a right good life
"Who thus admires good living.
"Above, they say, our flesh is air,
"Our blood celestial ichor:
"Oh, grant! mid all the changes there,
"They may not change our liquor!"

And with this pious wish the holy confessor tumbled under the table in an agony of devout drunkenness; whilst the knights, the men-at-arms, and the wicked little pages, rang out the last verse with a most melodious and emphatic glee.

"I am sorry, fair uncle," hiccupped Sir Randal, "that, in the matter of the *ave*, we could not oblige thee in a more orthodox manner; but the holy father has failed, and there is not another man in the hall who hath an idea of a prayer."

"It is my own fault," said Sir Rollo; "for I hanged the last confessor." And he wished his nephew a surly goodnight, as he prepared to quit the room.

"*Au revoir*, gentlemen," said the devil Mercurius; and once more fixed his tail round the neck of his disappointed companion.

The spirit of poor Rollo was sadly cast down; the devil, on the contrary, was in high good humour. He wagged his tail with the most satisfied air in the world, and cut a hundred jokes at the expense of his poor associate. On they sped, cleaving swiftly through the cold night winds, frightening the birds that were roosting in the woods, and the owls that were watching in the towers.

In the twinkling of an eye, as it is known, devils can fly hundreds of miles: so that almost the same beat of the clock which left these two in Champagne found them hovering over Paris. They dropped into the court of the Lazarist Convent, and winded their way, through passage and cloister, until they reached the door of the prior's cell. Now the prior, Rollo's brother, was a wicked and malignant sorcerer; his time was spent in conjuring devils and doing wicked deeds, instead of fasting, scourging, and singing holy psalms: this Mercurius knew; and he, therefore, was fully at ease as to the final result of his wager with poor Sir Roger.

"You seem to be well acquainted with the road," said the knight.

"I have reason," answered Mercurius, "having, for a long period, had the acquaintance of his reverence, your brother; but you have little chance with him."

"And why?" said Sir Rollo.

"He is under a bond to my master, never to say a prayer, or else his soul and his body are forfeited at once."

"Why, thou false and traitorous devil!" said the enraged knight; "and thou knewest this when we made our wager?"

"Undoubtedly: do you suppose I would have done so had there been any chance of losing?"

And with this they arrived at Father Ignatius's door.

"Thy cursed presence threw a spell on my niece, and stopped the tongue of my nephew's chaplain; I do believe that had I seen either of them alone, my wager had been won."

"Certainly; therefore, I took good care to go with thee; however, thou mayest see the prior alone, if thou wilt; and lo! his door is open. I will stand without for five minutes when it will be time to commence our journey."

It was the poor Baron's last chance: and he entered his brother's room more for the five minutes' respite than from any hope of success.

Father Ignatius, the prior, was absorbed in magic calculations: he stood in the middle of a circle of skulls, with no garment except his long white beard, which reached to his knees; he was waving a silver rod, and muttering imprecations in some horrible tongue.

But Sir Rollo came forward and interrupted his incantation. "I am," said he, "the shade of thy brother Roger de Rollo; and have come, from pure brotherly love, to warn thee of thy fate."

"Whence camest thou?"

"From the abode of the blessed in Paradise," replied Sir Roger, who was inspired with a sudden thought; "it was but five minutes ago that the Patron Saint of thy church told me of thy danger, and of thy wicked compact with the fiend. 'Go,' said he, 'to thy miserable brother, and tell him there is but one way by which he may escape from paying the awful forfeit of his bond.'"

"And how may that be?" said the prior; "the false fiend hath deceived me; I have given him my soul, but have received no worldly benefit in return. Brother! dear brother! how may I escape?"

"I will tell thee. As soon as I heard the voice of blessed St. Mary Lazarus" (the worthy Earl had, at a pinch, coined the name of a saint), "I left the clouds, where, with other angels, I was seated, and sped hither to save thee. 'Thy brother,' said the Saint, 'hath but one day more to live, when he will become for all eternity the subject of Satan; if he would escape, he must boldly break his bond, by saying an *ave*.'"

"It is the express condition of the agreement," said the unhappy monk, "I must say no prayer, or that instant I become Satan's, body and soul."

"It is the express condition of the Saint," answered Roger, fiercely; "pray, brother, pray, or thou art lost for ever."

So the foolish monk knelt down, and devoutly sung out an *ave*. "Amen!" said Sir Roger, devoutly.

"Amen!" said Mercurius, as, suddenly, coming behind, he seized Ignatius by his long beard, and flew up with him to the top of the church-steeple.

The monk roared, and screamed, and swore against his brother; but it was of no avail: Sir Roger smiled kindly on him, and said, "Do not fret, brother; it must have come to this in a year or two."

And he flew alongside of Mercurius to the steeple-top: *but this time the devil had not his tail round his neck.* "I will let thee off thy bet," said he to the demon; for he could afford, now, to be generous.

"I believe, my lord," said the demon, politely, "that our ways separate here." Sir Roger sailed gaily upwards: while Mercurius having bound the miserable monk faster than ever, he sunk downwards to earth, and perhaps lower. Ignatius was heard roaring and screaming as the devil dashed him against the iron spikes and buttresses of the church.

The Painter's Bargain

William Makepeace Thackeray

The belief in compacts with the devil is of great antiquity. Satan, contending with God for the possession of the human race, was supposed to have developed a passion for catching souls. At the death of every man a real fight takes place over his soul between an angel, who wishes to lead it to heaven, and a devil, who attempts to drag it to hell (Jude 9). In order to assure the soul for himself in advance, Satan attempts to purchase it from the owner while he is still living—*vivente corpore*, as he tells the *restaurateur* in Poe's story. As prince of this world he can easily grant even the most extravagant wishes of man in exchange for his soul. Office, wealth and pleasure are mainly the objects for which a man enters into a pact with the Evil One. Count de Luizzi in Frederic Soulie's *Les Memoires du Diable* sells his soul to the devil for an uncommon consideration. It is not wealth or pleasure that tempts him. What he wants in exchange for his soul is to know the past lives of his fellowmen and women, "a thing," as Mr. Saintsbury well remarks, "which a person of sense and taste would do anything, short of selling himself to the devil, *not* to know." The devil fulfils every wish of his contractor for a stipulated period of time, at the expiration of which the soul becomes his. Pope Innocent VIII, in his fatal bull *"Summis desiderantes"* of the year 1484, officially recognized the possibility of a compact with the devil. Increase Mather, the New England preacher, also affirms that many men have made "cursed covenants with the prince of darkness."

St. Theophilus, of Cilicia, in the sixth century, was the first to make the notable discovery that a man could enter into a pact of this nature. The price he set for his soul was a bishopric. This story has been superseded during the Renaissance period by a similar legend concerning the German Dr. Faustus. Other famous personages reputed to have sold their souls to the devil for one consideration or another are Don Juan in Spain, Twardowski in Poland, Merlin in England, and Robert le Diable in France. Socrates, Apuleius, Scaliger and Cagliostro are also said to have entered into compacts with him.

In devil-contracts the Evil One insists that his human negotiator sign the deed with his own blood, while the man never requires the devil to sign it even in ink. The human party to the transaction has always had full confidence in the word of the fiend. There is a universal belief that the devil invariably fulfils his engagement. In no single instance of folk-lore has Satan tried to evade the fulfilment of his share in the agreement. But the man, in violation of the written pact, has often cheated the devil out of his legal due by technical quibbles. "It is peculiar to the German tradition," says Gustav Freytag, "that the devil endeavours to fulfil zealously and honestly his part of the contract; the deceiver is man." In regard to fidelity to his word, the father of lies has always set an example to his victims. "You men," said Satan, "are cheats; you make all sorts of promises so long as you need me, and leave me in the lurch as soon as you have got what you wanted." Mediaeval man had no scruples about his breach of contract with the devil. He always considered the legal document signed with his own blood as "a scrap of paper."

"But still the pact is with the enemy; the man is not bound beyond the letter, and may escape by any trick. It is still the ethics of war. We are very close to the principle that a man by stratagem or narrow observance of the letter may escape the eternal retribution which God decrees conditionally and the devil delights in" (H. D. Taylor, *Mediaeval Mind*). We now can understand why in Eugene Field's story "Daniel and the Devil" it seems to Satan so strange that he should be asked for a written guarantee that he too would fulfil his part of the contract. Apparently this was the first time that the devil had any transactions with an American business man, who has not even faith in Old Nick.

Reference is made in this story by the devil himself to the popular saying that the devil is not so black as he is painted. Even the devout George Herbert wrote—

We paint the devil black, yet he
Hath some good in him all agree.

This story recalls to us the proverb: *"Talk of the devil, and he will either come or send."*

Washington Irving, as we have seen, thinks that he is not always very obliging.

Satan, the father of lies, is said to be the patron of lawyers. The men of the London bar formed a "Temple" corps, which was dubbed "The Devil's Own." The tavern of the lawyers on Fleet Street in London was called "The Devil."

Simon Gambouge was the son of Solomon Gambouge; and as all the world knows, both father and son were astonishingly clever fellows at their profession. Solomon painted landscapes, which nobody bought; and Simon took a higher line, and painted portraits to admiration, only nobody came to sit to him.

As he was not gaining five pounds a year by his profession, and had arrived at the age of twenty, at least, Simon determined to better himself by taking a wife,—a plan which a number of other wise men adopt, in similar years and circumstances. So Simon prevailed upon a butcher's daughter (to whom he owed considerable for cutlets) to quit the meat-shop and follow him. Griskinissa—such was the fair creature's name—"was as lovely a bit of mutton," her father said, "as ever a man would wish to stick a knife into." She had sat to the painter for all sorts of characters; and the curious who possess any of Gambouge's pictures will see her as Venus, Minerva, Madonna, and in numberless other characters: Portrait of a lady—Griskinissa; Sleeping Nymph—Griskinissa, without a rag of clothes, lying in a forest; Maternal Solicitude—Griskinissa again, with young Master Gambouge, who was by this time the offspring of their affections.

The lady brought the painter a handsome little fortune of a couple of hundred pounds; and as long as this sum lasted no woman could be more lovely or loving. But want began speedily to attack their little household; baker's bills were unpaid; rent was due, and the reckless landlord gave no quarter; and, to crown the whole, her father, unnatural butcher! suddenly stopped the supplies of mutton-chops; and swore that his daughter, and the dauber, her husband, should have no more of his wares. At first they embraced tenderly, and, kissing and crying over their little infant, vowed to heaven that they would do without: but in the course of the evening Griskinissa grew peckish, and poor Simon pawned his best coat.

When this habit of pawning is discovered, it appears to the poor a kind of Eldorado. Gambouge and his wife were so delighted, that they, in course of a month, made away with her gold chain, her great warming-pan, his best crimson plush inexpressibles, two wigs, a wash hand basin and ewer, fire-irons, window-curtains, crockery, and arm-chairs. Griskinissa said, smiling, that she had found a second father in *her uncle*,—a base pun, which showed that her mind was corrupted, and that she was no longer the tender, simple Griskinissa of other days.

I am sorry to say that she had taken to drinking; she swallowed the warming-pan in the course of three days, and fuddled herself one whole evening with the crimson plush breeches.

Drinking is the devil—the father, that is to say, of all vices. Griskinissa's face and her mind grew ugly together; her good humour changed to bilious, bitter discontent; her pretty, fond epithets, to foul abuse and swearing; her tender blue eyes grew watery and blear, and the peach-colour on her cheeks fled from its old habitation, and crowded up into her nose, where, with a number of pimples, it stuck fast. Add to this a dirty, draggle-tailed chintz; long, matted hair, wandering into her eyes, and over her lean shoulders, which were once so snowy, and you have the picture of drunkenness and Mrs. Simon Gambouge.

Poor Simon, who had been a gay, lively fellow enough in the days of his better fortune, was completely cast down by his present ill luck, and cowed by the ferocity of his wife. From morning till night the neighbours could hear this woman's tongue, and understand her doings; bellows went skimming across the room, chairs were flumped down on the floor, and poor Gambouge's oil and varnish pots went clattering through the windows, or down the stairs. The baby roared all day; and Simon sat pale and idle in a corner, taking a small sup at the brandy-bottle, when Mrs. Gambouge was out of the way.

One day, as he sat disconsolately at his easel, furbishing up a picture of his wife, in the character of Peace, which he had commenced a year before, he was more than ordinarily desperate, and cursed and swore in the most pathetic manner. "O miserable fate of genius!" cried he, "was I, a man of such commanding talents, born for this? to be bullied by a fiend of a wife; to have my masterpieces neglected by the world, or sold only for a few pieces? Cursed be the love which has misled me; cursed be the art which is unworthy of me! Let me dig or steal, let me sell myself as a soldier, or sell myself to the Devil, I should not be more wretched than I am now!"

"Quite the contrary," cried a small, cheery voice.

"What!" exclaimed Gambouge, trembling and surprised. "Who's there?—where are you?—who are you?"

"You were just speaking of me," said the voice.

Gambouge held, in his left hand, his palette; in his right, a bladder of crimson lake, which he was about to squeeze out upon the mahogany. "Where are you?" cried he again.

"S-q-u-e-e-z-e!" exclaimed the little voice.

Gambouge picked out the nail from the bladder, and gave a squeeze; when, as sure as I'm living, a little imp spurted out from the hole upon the palette, and began laughing in the most singular and oily manner.

When first born he was little bigger than a tadpole; then he grew to be as big as a mouse; then he arrived at the size of a cat; and then he jumped off the palette, and, turning head over heels, asked the poor painter what he wanted with him.

****

The strange little animal twisted head over heels, and fixed himself at last upon the top of Gambouge's easel,—smearing out, with his heels, all the white and vermilion which had just been laid on the allegoric portrait of Mrs. Gambouge.

"What!" exclaimed Simon, "is it the—"

"Exactly so; talk of me, you know, and I am always at hand: besides, I am not half so black as I am painted, as you will see when you know me a little better."

"Upon my word," said the painter, "it is a very singular surprise which you have given me. To tell truth, I did not even believe in your existence."

The little imp put on a theatrical air, and with one of Mr. Macready's best looks, said,—

"There are more things in heaven and earth, Gambogio,
"Than are dreamed of in your philosophy."

Gambouge, being a Frenchman, did not understand the quotation, but felt somehow strangely and singularly interested in the conversation of his new friend.

Diabolus continued: "You are a man of merit, and want money; you will starve on your merit; you can only get money from me. Come, my friend, how much is it? I ask the easiest interest in the world: old Mordecai, the usurer, has made you pay twice as heavily before now: nothing but the signature of a bond, which is a mere ceremony, and the transfer of an article which, in itself, is a supposition—a valueless, windy, uncertain property of yours, called by some poet of your own, I think, an *animula, vagula, blandula*—bah! there is no use beating about the bush—I mean *a soul*. Come, let me have it; you know you will sell it some other way, and not get such good pay for your bargain!"—and, having made this speech, the Devil pulled out from his fob a sheet as big as a double *Times*, only there was a different *stamp* in the corner.

It is useless and tedious to describe law documents: lawyers only love to read them; and they have as good in Chitty as any that are to be found in the Devil's own; so nobly have the apprentices emulated the skill of the master. Suffice it to say, that poor Gambouge read over the paper, and signed it. He was to have all he wished for seven years, and at the end of that time was to become the property of the—; *provided* that during the course of the seven years, every single wish which he might form should be gratified by the other of the contracting parties; otherwise the deed became *null* and *nonavenue*, and Gambouge should be left "to go to the—his own way."

"You will never see me again," said Diabolus, in shaking hands with poor Simon, on whose fingers he left such a mark as is to be seen at this day—"never, at least, unless you want me; for everything you ask will be performed in the most quiet and every-day manner: believe me, it is the best and most gentlemanlike, and avoids anything like scandal. But if you set me about anything which is extraordinary, and out of the course of nature, as it were, come I must, you know; and of this you are the best judge." So saying, Diabolus disappeared; but whether up the chimney, through the keyhole, or by any other aperture or contrivance, nobody knows. Simon Gambouge was left in a fever of delight, as, heaven forgive me! I believe many a worthy man would be, if he were allowed an opportunity to make a similar bargain.

"*Heigho!*" said Simon. "I wonder whether this be a reality or a dream.—I am sober, I know; for who will give me credit for the means to be drunk? and as for sleeping, I'm too hungry for that. I wish I could see a capon and a bottle of white wine."

"*Monsieur Simon!*" cried a voice on the landing-place.

"*C'est ici,*" quoth Gambouge, hastening to open the door. He did so; and lo! there was a *restaurateur's* boy at the door, supporting a tray, a tin-covered dish, and plates on the same; and, by its side, a tall amber-coloured flask of Sauterne.

"I am the new boy, sir," exclaimed this youth, on entering; "but I believe this is the right door, and you asked for these things."

Simon grinned, and said, "Certainly, I did *ask for* these things." But such was the effect which his interview with the demon had had on his innocent mind, that he took them, although he knew they were for old Simon, the Jew dandy, who was mad after an opera girl, and lived on the floor beneath.

"Go, my boy," he said; "it is good: call in a couple of hours, and remove the plates and glasses."

The little waiter trotted down stairs, and Simon sat greedily down to discuss the capon and the white wine. He bolted the legs, he devoured the wings, he cut every morsel of flesh from the breast;—seasoning his repast with pleasant draughts of wine, and caring nothing for the inevitable bill which was to follow all.

"Ye gods!" said he, as he scraped away at the back-bone, "what a dinner! what wine!—and how gaily served up too!" There were silver forks and spoons, and the remnants of the fowl were upon a silver dish. "Why the money for this dish and these spoons," cried Simon, "would keep me and Mrs. G. for a month! *I wish*"—and here Simon whistled, and turned round to see that no one was peeping—"I wish the plate were mine."

Oh, the horrid progress of the Devil! "Here they are," thought Simon to himself; "why should not I *take them?*" and take them he did. "Detection," said he, "is not so bad as starvation; and I would as soon live at the galleys as live with Madame Gambouge."

So Gambouge shovelled dish and spoons into the flap of his *surtout*, and ran down stairs as if the Devil were behind him—as, indeed, he was.

He immediately made for the house of his old friend the pawn-broker—that establishment which is called in France the Mont de Piete. "I am obliged to come to you again, my old friend," said Simon, "with some family plate, of which I beseech you to take care."

The pawnbroker smiled as he examined the goods. "I can give you nothing upon them," said he.

"What!" cried Simon; "not even the worth of the silver?"

"No; I could buy them at that price at the 'Cafe Morisot,' Rue de la Verrerie, where, I suppose, you got them a little cheaper." And, so saying, he showed to the guilt-stricken Gambouge how the name of that coffee-house was inscribed upon every one of the articles which he wished to pawn.

The effects of conscience are dreadful indeed. Oh! how fearful is retribution, how deep is despair, how bitter is remorse for crime—*when crime is found out!*—otherwise, conscience takes matters much more easily. Gambouge cursed his fate, and swore henceforth to be virtuous.

"But, hark ye, my friend," continued the honest broker, "there is no reason why, because I cannot lend upon these things, I should not buy them: they will do to melt, if for no other purpose. Will you have half the money?—speak, or I peach."

Simon's resolves about virtue were dissipated instantaneously. "Give me half," he said, "and let me go.—What scoundrels are these pawnbrokers!" ejaculated he, as he passed out of the accursed shop, "seeking every wicked pretext to rob the poor man of his hard-won gain."

When he had marched forwards for a street or two, Gambouge

counted the money which he had received, and found that he was in possession of no less than a hundred *francs*. It was night, as he reckoned out his equivocal gains, and he counted them at the light of a lamp. He looked up at the lamp, in doubt as to the course he should next pursue: upon it was inscribed the simple number, 152. "A gambling-house," thought Gambouge. "*I wish* I had half the money that is now on the table, up stairs."

He mounted, as many a rogue has done before him, and found half a hundred persons busy at a table of *rouge et noir*. Gambouge's five *napoleons* looked insignificant by the side of the heaps which were around him; but the effects of the wine, of the theft, and of the detection by the pawnbroker, were upon him, and he threw down his capital stoutly upon the 00.

It is a dangerous spot that 00, or double zero; but to Simon it was more lucky than to the rest of the world. The ball went spinning round—in "its predestined circle rolled," as Shelley has it, after Goethe—and plumped down at last in the double zero. One hundred and thirty-five gold *napoleons* (*louis* they were then) were counted out to the delighted painter. "Oh, Diabolus!" cried he, "now it is that I begin to believe in thee! Don't talk about merit," he cried; "talk about fortune. Tell me not about heroes for the future—tell me of *zeroes*." And down went twenty *napoleons* more upon the 0.

The Devil was certainly in the ball: round it twirled, and dropped into zero as naturally as a duck pops its head into a pond. Our friend received five hundred pounds for his stake; and the croupiers and lookers-on began to stare at him.

There were twelve thousand pounds upon the table. Suffice it to say, that Simon won half, and retired from the Palais Royal with a thick bundle of bank-notes crammed into his dirty three-cornered hat. He had been but half an hour in the place, and he had won the revenues of a prince for half a year!

Gambouge, as soon as he felt that he was a capitalist, and that he had a stake in the country, discovered that he was an altered man. He repented of his foul deed, and his base purloining of the *restaurateur's* plate. "O honesty!" he cried, "how unworthy is an action like this of a man who has a property like mine!" So he went back to the pawnbroker with the gloomiest face imaginable.

"My friend," said he, "I have sinned against all that I hold most sacred: I have forgotten my family and my religion. Here is thy money. In the name of heaven, restore me the plate which I have wrongfully sold thee!"

But the pawnbroker grinned, and said, "Nay, Mr. Gambouge, I will sell that plate for a thousand *francs* to you, or I will never sell it at all."

"Well," cried Gambouge, "thou art an inexorable ruffian, Troisboules; but I will give thee all I am worth." And here he produced a billet of five hundred *francs*. "Look," said he, "this money is all I own; it is the payment of two years' lodging. To raise it, I have toiled for many months; and, failing, I have been a criminal. O heaven! I *stole* that plate that I might pay my debt, and keep my dear wife from wandering houseless. But I cannot bear this load of ignominy—I cannot suffer the thought of this crime. I will go to the person to whom I did wrong. I will starve, I will confess; but I will, I *will* do right!"

The broker was alarmed. "Give me thy note," he cried; "here is the plate."

"Give me an acquittal first," cried Simon, almost broken-hearted; "sign me a paper, and the money is yours." So Troisboules wrote according to Gambouge's dictation: "Received, for thirteen ounces of plate, twenty pounds."

"Monster of iniquity!" cried the painter, "fiend of wickedness! thou art caught in thine own snares. Hast thou not sold me five pounds' worth of plate for twenty? Have I it not in my pocket? Art thou not a convicted dealer in stolen goods? Yield, scoundrel, yield thy money, or I will bring thee to justice!"

The frightened pawnbroker bullied and battled for a while; but he gave up his money at last, and the dispute ended. Thus it will be seen that Diabolus had rather a hard bargain in the wily Gambouge. He had taken a victim prisoner, but he had assuredly caught a Tartar. Simon now returned home, and, to do him justice, paid the bill for his dinner, and restored the plate.

****

And now I may add (and the reader should ponder upon this, as a profound picture of human life), that Gambouge, since he had grown rich, grew likewise abundantly moral. He was a most exemplary father. He fed the poor, and was loved by them. He scorned a base action. And I have no doubt that Mr. Thurtell, or the late lamented Mr. Greenacre, in similar circumstances, would have acted like the worthy Simon Gambouge.

There was but one blot upon his character—he hated Mrs. Gam. worse than ever. As he grew more benevolent, she grew more virulent: when he went to plays, she went to Bible societies, and *vice versa*: in fact, she led him such a life as Xantippe led Socrates, or as a dog leads a cat in the same kitchen. With all his fortune—for, as may be supposed, Simon prospered in all worldly things—he was the most miserable dog in the whole city of Paris. Only in the point of drinking did he and Mrs. Simon agree; and for many years, and during a considerable number of hours in each day, he thus dissipated, partially, his domestic chagrin. O philosophy! we may talk of thee: but, except at the bottom of the wine-cup, where thou liest like truth in a well, where shall we find thee?

He lived so long, and in his worldly matters prospered so much, there was so little sign of devilment in the accomplishment of his wishes, and the increase of his prosperity, that Simon, at the end of six years, began to doubt whether he had made any such bargain at all, as that which we have described at the commencement of this history. He had grown, as we said, very pious and moral. He went regularly to mass, and had a confessor into the bargain. He resolved, therefore, to consult that reverend gentleman, and to lay before him the whole matter.

"I am inclined to think, holy sir," said Gambouge, after he had concluded his history, and shown how, in some miraculous way, all his desires were accomplished, "that, after all, this demon was no other than the creation of my own brain, heated by the effects of that bottle of wine, the cause of my crime and my prosperity."

The confessor agreed with him, and they walked out of church comfortably together, and entered afterwards a cafe, where they sat down to refresh themselves after the fatigues of their devotion.

A respectable old gentleman, with a number of orders at his button-hole, presently entered the room, and sauntered up to the marble table, before which reposed Simon and his clerical friend. "Excuse me, gentlemen," he said, as he took a place opposite them, and began reading the papers of the day.

"Bah!" said he, at last,—"*sont-ils grands ces journaux anglais?* Look, sir," he said, handing over an immense sheet of *The Times* to Mr. Gambouge, "was ever anything so monstrous?"

Gambouge smiled, politely, and examined the proffered page. "It is enormous," he said; "but I do not read English."

"Nay," said the man with the orders, "look closer at it, Signor Gambouge; it is astonishing how easy the language is."

Wondering, Simon took the sheet of paper. He turned pale as he looked at it, and began to curse the ices and the waiter. "Come, M. l'Abbe," he said; "the heat and glare of this place are intolerable."

****

The stranger rose with them. *"Au plaisir de vous revoir, mon cher monsieur,"* said he; "I do not mind speaking before the Abbe here, who will be my very good friend one of these days; but I thought it necessary to refresh your memory, concerning our little business transaction six years since; and could not exactly talk of it *at church*, as you may fancy."

Simon Gambouge had seen, in the double-sheeted *Times*, the paper signed by himself, which the little Devil had pulled out of his fob.

****

There was no doubt on the subject; and Simon, who had but a year to live, grew more pious, and more careful than ever. He had consultations with all the doctors of the Sorbonne and all the lawyers of the Palais. But his magnificence grew as wearisome to him as his poverty had been before; and not one of the doctors whom he consulted could give him a pennyworth of consolation.

Then he grew outrageous in his demands upon the Devil, and put him to all sorts of absurd and ridiculous tasks; but they were all punctually performed, until Simon could invent no new ones, and the Devil sat all day with his hands in his pockets doing nothing.

One day, Simon's confessor came bounding into the room, with the greatest glee. "My friend," said he, "I have it! *Eureka!*—I have found it. Send the Pope a hundred thousand crowns, build a new Jesuit college at Rome, give a hundred gold candlesticks to St. Peter's; and tell his Holiness you will double all if he will give you absolution!"

Gambouge caught at the notion, and hurried off a courier to Rome *ventre a terre*. His Holiness agreed to the request of the petition, and sent him an absolution, written out with his own fist, and all in due form.

"Now," said he, "foul fiend, I defy you! arise. Diabolus! your contract is not worth a jot: the Pope has absolved me, and I am safe on the road to salvation." In a fervour of gratitude he clasped the hand of his confessor, and embraced him: tears of joy ran down the cheeks of these good men.

They heard an inordinate roar of laughter, and there was Diabolus sitting opposite to them holding his sides, and lashing his tail about, as if he would have gone mad with glee.

"Why," said he, "what nonsense is this! do you suppose I care about *that*?" and he tossed the Pope's missive into a corner. "M. l'Abbe knows," he said, bowing and grinning, "that though the Pope's paper may pass current *here*, it is not worth twopence in our country. What do I care about the Pope's absolution? You might just as well be absolved by your under butler."

"Egad," said the Abbe, "the rogue is right—I quite forgot the fact, which he points out clearly enough."

"No, no, Gambouge," continued Diabolus, with horrid familiarity, "go thy ways, old fellow, that *cock won't fight*." And he retired up the chimney, chuckling at his wit and his triumph. Gambouge heard his tail scuttling all the way up, as if he had been a sweeper by profession.

Simon was left in that condition of grief in which, according to the newspapers, cities and nations are found when a murder is committed, or a lord ill of the gout—a situation, we say, more easy to imagine than to describe.

To add to his woes, Mrs. Gambouge, who was now first made acquainted with his compact, and its probable consequences, raised such a storm about his ears, as made him wish almost that his seven years were expired. She screamed, she scolded, she swore, she wept, she went into such fits of hysterics, that poor Gambouge, who had completely knocked under to her, was worn out of his life. He was allowed no rest, night or day: he moped about his fine house, solitary and wretched, and cursed his stars that he ever had married the butcher's daughter.

It wanted six months of the time.

A sudden and desperate resolution seemed all at once to have taken possession of Simon Gambouge. He called his family and his friends together—he gave one of the greatest feasts that ever was known in the city of Paris—he gaily presided at one end of his table, while Mrs. Gam., splendidly arrayed, gave herself airs at the other extremity. After dinner, using the customary formula, he called upon Diabolus to appear. The old ladies screamed and hoped he would not appear naked; the young ones tittered, and longed to see the monster: everybody was pale with expectation and affright.

A very quiet, gentlemanly man, neatly dressed in black, made his appearance, to the surprise of all present, and bowed all round to the company. "I will not show my *credentials*," he said, blushing, and pointing to his hoofs, which were cleverly hidden by his pumps and shoe-buckles, "unless the ladies absolutely wish it; but I am the person you want, Mr. Gambouge; pray tell me what is your will."

"You know," said that gentleman, in a stately and determined voice, "that you are bound to me, according to our agreement, for six months to come."

"I am," replied the new comer.

"You are to do all that I ask, whatsoever it may be, or you forfeit the bond which I gave you?"

"It is true."

"You declare this before the present company?"

"Upon my honour, as a gentleman," said Diabolus, bowing, and laying his hand upon his waistcoat.

A whisper of applause ran round the room: all were charmed with the bland manners of the fascinating stranger.

"My love," continued Gambouge, mildly addressing his lady, "will you be so polite as to step this way? You know I must go soon, and I am anxious, before this noble company, to make a provision for one who, in sickness as in health, in poverty as in riches, has been my truest and fondest companion."

Gambouge mopped his eyes with his handkerchief—all the company did likewise. Diabolus sobbed audibly, and Mrs. Gambouge sidled up to her husband's side, and took him tenderly by the hand. "Simon!" said she, "is it true? and do you really love your Griskinissa?"

Simon continued solemnly: "Come hither, Diabolus; you are bound to obey me in all things for the six months during which our contract has to run; take, then, Griskinissa Gambouge, live alone with her for half a year, never leave her from morning till night, obey all her caprices, follow all her whims, and listen to all the abuse which falls from her infernal tongue. Do this, and I ask no more of you; I will deliver myself up at the appointed time."

Not Lord G—, when flogged by Lord B—, in the House,—not Mr. Cartlitch, of Astley's Amphitheatre, in his most pathetic passages, could look more crestfallen, and howl more hideously, than Diabolus did now. "Take another year, Gambouge," screamed he; "two more—ten more—a century; roast me on Lawrence's gridiron, boil me in holy water, but don't ask that: don't, don't bid me live with Mrs. Gambouge!"

Simon smiled sternly. "I have said it," he cried; "do this, or our contract is at an end."

The Devil, at this, grinned so horribly that every drop of beer in the house turned sour: he gnashed his teeth so frightfully that every person in the company well-nigh fainted with the cholic. He slapped down the great parchment upon the floor, trampled upon it madly, and lashed it with his hoofs and his tail: at last, spreading out a mighty pair of wings as wide as from here to Regent Street, he slapped Gambouge with his tail over one eye, and vanished, abruptly, through the keyhole.

****

Gambouge screamed with pain and started up. "You drunken, lazy scoundrel!" cried a shrill and well-known voice, "you have been asleep these two hours:" and here he received another terrific box on the ear.

It was too true, he had fallen asleep at his work; and the beautiful vision had been dispelled by the thumps of the tipsy Griskinissa. Nothing remained to corroborate his story, except the bladder of lake, and this was spurted all over his waistcoat and breeches.

"I wish," said the poor fellow, rubbing his tingling cheeks, "that dreams were true;" and he went to work again at his portrait.

****

My last accounts of Gambouge are, that he has left the arts, and is footman in a small family. Mrs. Gam. takes in washing; and it is said that her continual dealings with soap-suds and hot water have been the only things in life which have kept her from spontaneous combustion.

Bon-Bon

Edgar Allan Poe

This writer, to whom the inner world was more of a reality than the external world, had many visions, especially of the devil. The two seem to have been on a familiar footing. The devil, we must admit, filled Poe's imagination even if we will not go so far as to agree with his critics that he had Satan substituted for soul. His contemporaries, as is well known, would say of him: "He hath a demon, yea, seven devils are entered into him." His detractors actually regarded this unhappy poet as an incarnation of the ruler of Hades (cf. *North American Review*, 1856; *Edinburgh Review*, 1858; *Dublin University Magazine*, 1875). It was but recently that a writer in the *New York Times* declared Poe to have been "grub-staked by demons."

The story "Bon-Bon" offers a specimen of Poe's grimly grotesque humour. It first appeared in the *Broadway Journal* of August, 1835.

The devil of this most un-American of all American authors is not the child of New World fancy, but part of European imagination. The scenery of the story is aptly laid in the land of Robert le Diable.

Poe's description of the devil is, on the whole, fully in accord with the universally accredited conception of his ordinary appearance. His brutal hoofs and savage horns and beastly tail are all there, only discreetly hid under a dress which any gentleman might wear. The devil is very proud of this epithet given him by William Shakespeare; and from that time on, it has been his greatest ambition to be a gentleman, in outer appearance at least; and to his credit it must be said that he has so well succeeded in his efforts to resemble a gentleman that it is now very hard to tell the two apart. The devil is accredited in popular imagination with long ears, a long (sometimes upturned) nose, a wide mouth, and teeth of a lion. It is on account of his fangs that Satan has been called a lion by the biblical writers. But although the prince of darkness can assume any form in the heavens above, in the earth beneath, and in the waters under the earth, he has never appeared as a lion. This, I believe, is out of deference to Judah, whom his father also called a lion. Hairiness is a pretty general characteristic of the devil. His hairy skin he probably inherited from the ancient fauns and satyrs. Esau is believed to have been a hairy demon. "Old Harry" is a corruption of "Old Hairy." As a rule, Old Nick is not pictured as bald, but has a head covered with locks like serpents. These snaky tresses, which already "Monk" Lewis wound around the devil's head, are borrowed, according to Sir Walter Scott, from the shield of Minerva. His face, however, is usually hairless. A beard has rarely been accorded to Satan. His red beard on the mediaeval stage probably came from Donar, whom, as Jacob Grimm says, the modern notions of the devil so often have in the background. Long bearded devils are nowhere normal except in the representations of the Eastern Church of the monarch of hell as counterpart of the monarch of heaven. The eyeless devil is original with our writer. His disciple Baudelaire in his story 'Les Tentations ou Eros, Plutus et la Gloire' presents the second of these three Tempters as an eyeless monster. The mediaeval devil had saucer eyes. According to a Russian legend, the all-seeing spirit of evil is all covered with eyes. The cadaverous aspect of the devil is traditional. With but one remarkable exception (the Egyptian Typhon), demons are always represented lean. "A devil," said Caesarius of Heisterbach of the thirteenth century, "is usually so thin as to cast no shadow" (*Dialogus Miraculorum*, iii). This characteristic is a heritage of the ancient hunger-demon, who, himself a shadow, casts no shadow. In the course of the centuries, however, the devil has gained flesh. His faded suit of black cloth recalls the mediaeval devil who appeared "in his feathers all ragged and rent."

It is not altogether improbable that the ecclesiastical appearance of the devil in this story was not wholly unintentional, as the author believes. While Satan cannot be said to be "one of those who take to the ministry mostly," he often likes to slip into priestly robes. In the "Temptation of Jesus" by Lucas van Leyden the devil is habited as a monk with a pointed cowl.

In the comparison of a soul with a shadow there is a reminiscence of Adalbert von Chamisso, whose *Peter Schlemihl* (1814) sells his shadow to the devil. In his story 'The Fisherman and His Soul' Oscar Wilde considers the shadow of the body as the body of the soul.

That the devils in hell eat the damned consigned there for punishment is also in accord with mediaeval tradition. This idea probably is of Oriental origin. The seven Assyrian evil spirits have a predilection for human flesh and blood. Ghouls and vampires belong to this class of demons.

The devil's pitchfork is not the forked sceptre of Pluto supplemented by another tine, as is commonly assumed. It is the ancient sign of fertility, which is still used as a fertility charm by the Hindus in India and the Zuni and Aztec Indians of North America and Mexico. A related symbol is the trident of Poseidon or Neptune. This symbol was recently carried in a children's May Day parade through Central Park in New York.

> *Quand un bon vin meuble mon estomac,*
> *Je suis plus savant que Balzac—*
> *Plus sage que Pibrac;*
> *Mon bras seul faisant l'attaque*
> *De la nation cossaque,*
> *La mettroit au sac;*
> *De Charon je passerois le lac*
> *En dormant dans son bac;*
> *J'irois au fier Eac,*
> *Sans que mon coeur fit tic ni tac,*
> *Presenter du tabac.*

French Vaudeville

That Pierre Bon-Bon was a *restaurateur* of uncommon quali-
fications, no man who, during the reign of—, frequented
the little cafe in the *cul-de-sac* Le Febvre at Rouen, will, I imagine,
feel himself at liberty to dispute. That Pierre Bon-Bon was, in an
equal degree, skilled in the philosophy of that period is, I presume,
still more especially undeniable. His *pates a la fois* were beyond doubt
immaculate; but what pen can do justice to his essays *sur la Nature*—
his thoughts *sur l'Ame*—his observations *sur l'Esprit?* If his *omelettes*—if his *fricandeaux* were inestimable, what *litterateur* of that day
would not have given twice as much for an *"Idee de Bon-Bon"* as for
all the trash of all the *"Idees"* of all the rest of the *savants?* Bon-Bon
had ransacked libraries which no other man had ransacked—had
read more than any other would have entertained a notion of reading—had understood more than any other would have conceived
the possibility of understanding; and although, while he flourished,
there were not wanting some authors at Rouen to assert "that his
dicta evinced neither the purity of the Academy, nor the depth of
the Lyceum"—although, mark me, his doctrines were by no means
very generally comprehended, still it did not follow that they were
difficult of comprehension. It was, I think, on account of their self-
evidency that many persons were led to consider them abstruse. It
is to Bon-Bon—but let this go no further—it is to Bon-Bon that
Kant himself is mainly indebted for his metaphysics. The former was
indeed not a Platonist, nor strictly speaking an Aristotelian—nor
did he, like the modern Leibnitz, waste those precious hours which
might be employed in the invention of a *fricassee* or, *facili gradu*, the
analysis of a sensation, in frivolous attempts at reconciling the obstinate oils and waters of ethical discussion. Not at all. Bon-Bon was
Ionic—Bon-Bon was equally Italic. He reasoned *a priori*—He reasoned *a posteriori*. His ideas were innate—or otherwise. He believed
in George of Trebizond—he believed in Bossarion. Bon-Bon was
emphatically a—Bon-Bonist.

I have spoken of the philosopher in his capacity of *restaurateur.* I would not, however, have any friend of mine imagine that,
in fulfilling his hereditary duties in that line, our hero wanted a
proper estimation of their dignity and importance. Far from it. It
was impossible to say in which branch of his profession he took
the greater pride. In his opinion the powers of the intellect held

intimate connection with the capabilities of the stomach. I am not sure, indeed, that he greatly disagreed with the Chinese, who hold that the soul lies in the abdomen. The Greeks at all events were right, he thought, who employed the same word for the mind and the diaphragm. By this I do not mean to insinuate a charge of gluttony, or indeed any other serious charge to the prejudice of the metaphysician. If Pierre Bon-Bon had his failings—and what great man has not a thousand?—if Pierre Bon-Bon, I say, had his failings, they were failings of very little importance—faults indeed which, in other tempers, have often been looked upon rather in the light of virtues. As regards one of these foibles, I should not even have mentioned it in this history but for the remarkable prominency— the extreme *alto relievo*—in which it jutted out from the plane of his general disposition. He could never let slip an opportunity of making a bargain.

Not that he was avaricious—no. It was by no means necessary to the satisfaction of the philosopher, that the bargain should be to his own proper advantage. Provided a trade could be effected—a trade of any kind, upon any terms, or under any circumstances—a triumphant smile was seen for many days thereafter to enlighten his countenance, and a knowing wink of the eye to give evidence of his sagacity.

At any epoch it would not be very wonderful if a humour so peculiar as the one I have just mentioned, should elicit attention and remark. At the epoch of our narrative, had this peculiarity *not* attracted observation, there would have been room for wonder indeed. It was soon reported that, upon all occasions of the kind, the smile of Bon-Bon was found to differ widely from the downright grin with which he would laugh at his own jokes, or welcome an acquaintance. Hints were thrown out of an exciting nature; stories were told of perilous bargains made in a hurry and repented of at leisure; and instances were adduced of unaccountable capacities, vague longings, and unnatural inclinations implanted by the author of all evil for wise purposes of his own.

The philosopher had other weaknesses—but they are scarcely worthy our serious examination. For example, there are few men of extraordinary profundity who are found wanting in an inclination for the bottle. Whether this inclination be an exciting cause, or rather a valid proof, of such profundity, it is a nice thing to say. Bon-Bon, as far as I can learn, did not think the subject adapted to minute investigation;—nor do I. Yet in the indulgence of a propensity so truly classical, it is not to be supposed that the *restaurateur* would lose sight of that intuitive discrimination which was wont to characterize, at one and the same time, his *essais* and his *omelettes*. In his seclusions the Vin de Bourgogne had its allotted hour, and there were appropriate moments for the Cotes du Rhone. With him Sauternes was to Medoc what Catullus was to Homer. He would sport with a syllogism in sipping St. Peray, but unravel an argument over Clos-Vougeot, and upset a theory in a torrent of Chambertin. Well had it been if the same quick sense of propriety had attended him in the peddling propensity to which I have formerly alluded—but this was by no means the case. Indeed to say the truth, *that* trait of mind in the philosophic Bon-Bon *did* begin at length to assume a character of strange intensity and mysticism, and appeared deeply tinctured with the *diablerie* of his favourite German studies.

To enter the little cafe in the *cul-de-sac* Le Febvre was, at the period of our tale, to enter the *sanctum* of a man of genius. Bon-Bon was a man of genius. There was not a *sous-cuisinier* in Rouen who could not have told you that Bon-Bon was a man of genius. His very cat knew it, and forbore to whisk her tail in the presence of the man of genius. His large water-dog was acquainted with the fact, and upon the approach of his master, betrayed his sense of inferiority by a sanctity of deportment, a debasement of the ears, and a dropping of the lower jaw not altogether unworthy of a dog. It is, however, true that much of this habitual respect might have been attributed to the personal appearance of the metaphysician. A distinguished exterior will, I am constrained to say, have its way even with a beast; and I am willing to allow much in the outward man of the *restaurateur* calculated to impress the imagination of the quadruped. There is a peculiar majesty about the atmosphere of the little great—if I may be permitted so equivocal an expression—which mere physical bulk alone will be found at all times inefficient in creating. If, however, Bon-Bon was barely three feet in height, and if his head was diminutively small, still it was impossible to behold the rotundity of his stomach without a sense of magnificence nearly bordering upon the sublime. In its size both dogs and men must have seen a type of his acquirements—in its immensity a fitting habitation for his immortal soul.

I might here—if it so pleased me—dilate upon the matter of habiliment, and other mere circumstances of the external metaphysician. I might hint that the hair of our hero was worn short, combed smoothly over his forehead, and surmounted by a conical-shaped white flannel cap and tassels—that his pea-green jerkin was not after the fashion of those worn by the common class of *restaurateurs* at that day—that the sleeves were something fuller than the reigning costume permitted—that the cuffs were turned up, not as usual in that barbarous period, with cloth of the same quality and colour as the garment, but faced in a more fanciful manner with the particoloured velvet of Genoa—that his slippers were of bright purple, curiously filigreed, and might have been manufactured in Japan, but for the exquisite pointing of the toes, and the brilliant tints of the binding and embroidery—that his breeches were of the yellow satin-like material called *aimable*—that his sky-blue cloak, resembling in form a dressing-wrapper, and richly bestudded all over with crimson devices, floated cavalierly upon his shoulders like a mist of the morning—and that his *tout ensemble* gave rise to the remarkable words of Benevenuta, the Improvisatrice of Florence, "that it was difficult to say whether Pierre Bon-Bon was indeed a bird of Paradise, or the rather a very Paradise of perfection." I might, I say, expatiate upon all these points if I pleased,—but I forbear; merely personal details may be left to historical novelists,— they are beneath the moral dignity of matter-of-fact.

I have said that "to enter the cafe in the *cul-de-sac* Le Febvre was to enter the *sanctum* of a man of genius"—but then it was only the man of genius who could duly estimate the merits of the *sanctum*. A sign, consisting of a vast folio, swung before the entrance. On one side of the volume was painted a bottle; on the reverse a *pate*. On the back were visible in large letters *Oeuvres de Bon-Bon*. Thus was delicately shadowed forth the twofold occupation of the proprietor.

Upon stepping over the threshold, the whole interior of the building presented itself to view. A long, low-pitched room, of antique construction, was indeed all the accommodation afforded by the cafe. In a corner of the apartment stood the bed of the metaphysician. An array of curtains, together with a canopy *a la grecque*, gave it an air at once classic and comfortable. In the corner diagonally opposite, appeared, in direct family communion, the properties of the kitchen and the *bibliotheque*. A dish of polemics stood peacefully upon the dresser. Here lay an ovenful of the latest ethics—there a kettle of duodecimo *melanges*. Volumes of German morality were hand and glove with the gridiron—a toasting-fork might be discovered by the side of Eusebius—Plato reclined at his ease in the frying-pan—and contemporary manuscripts were filed away upon the spit.

In other respects the Cafe de Bon-Bon might be said to differ little from the usual restaurants of the period. A large fireplace yawned opposite the door. On the right of the fireplace an open cupboard displayed a formidable array of labelled bottles.

It was here, about twelve o'clock one night, during the severe winter of—, that Pierre Bon-Bon, after having listened for some time to the comments of his neighbours upon his singular propensity—that Pierre Bon-Bon, I say, having turned them all out of his house, locked the door upon them with an oath, and betook himself in no very pacific mood to the comforts of a leather-bottomed arm-chair, and a fire of blazing fagots.

It was one of those terrific nights which are only met with once or twice during a century. It snowed fiercely, and the house tottered to its centre with the floods of wind that, rushing through the crannies of the wall, and pouring impetuously down the chimney, shook awfully the curtains of the philosopher's bed, and disorganized the economy of his *pate*-pans and papers. The huge folio sign that swung without, exposed to the fury of the tempest, creaked ominously, and gave out a moaning sound from its stanchions of solid oak.

It was in no placid temper, I say, that the metaphysician drew up his chair to its customary station by the hearth. Many circumstances of a perplexing nature had occurred during the day, to disturb the serenity of his meditations. In attempting *des oeufs a la Princesse*, he had unfortunately perpetrated an *omelette a la Reine*; the discovery of a principle in ethics had been frustrated by the overturning of a stew; and last, not least, he had been thwarted in one of those admirable bargains which he at all times took such especial delight in bringing to a successful termination. But in the chafing of his mind at these unaccountable vicissitudes, there did not fail to be mingled some degree of that nervous anxiety which the fury of a boisterous night is so well calculated to produce. Whistling to his more immediate vicinity the large black water-dog we have spoken of before, and settling himself uneasily in his chair, he could not help casting a wary and unquiet eye toward those distant recesses of the apartment whose inexorable shadows not even the red fire-light itself could more than partially succeed in overcoming. Having completed a scrutiny whose exact purpose was perhaps unintelligible to himself, he drew close to his seat a small table covered with books and papers, and soon became absorbed in the task of retouching a voluminous manu-script, intended for publication on the morrow.

He had been thus occupied for some minutes, when "I am in no hurry, Monsieur Bon-Bon," suddenly whispered a whining voice in the apartment.

"The devil!" ejaculated our hero, starting to his feet, overturn-ing the table at his side, and staring around him in astonishment.

"Very true," calmly replied the voice.

"Very true!—what is very true?—how came you here?" vocif-erated the metaphysician, as his eye fell upon something which lay stretched at full length upon the bed.

"I was saying," said the intruder, without attending to the interrogatories,—"I was saying that I am not at all pushed for time—that the business, upon which I took the liberty of calling, is of no pressing importance—in short, that I can very well wait until you have finished your Exposition."

"My Exposition!—there now!—how do *you* know?—how came *you* to understand that I was writing an Exposition—good God!"

"Hush!" replied the figure, in a shrill undertone; and, arising quickly from the bed, he made a single step toward our hero, while an iron lamp that depended overhead swung convulsively back from his approach.

The philosopher's amazement did not prevent a narrow scru-tiny of the stranger's dress and appearance. The outlines of his fig-ure, exceedingly lean, but much above the common height, were rendered minutely distinct by means of a faded suit of black cloth which fitted tight to the skin, but was otherwise cut very much in the style of a century ago. These garments had evidently been intended for a much shorter person than their present owner. His ankles and wrists were left naked for several inches. In his shoes, however, a pair of very brilliant buckles gave the lie to the extreme poverty implied by the other portions of his dress. His head was bare, and entirely bald, with the exception of the hinder-part, from which depended a *queue* of considerable length. A pair of green spectacles, with side glasses, protected his eyes from the influence of the light, and at the same time prevented our hero from ascertaining either their colour or their conformation. About the entire person there was no evidence of a shirt; but a white cravat, of filthy appearance, was tied with extreme precision around the throat, and the ends, hanging down formally side by side gave (although I dare say unintentionally) the idea of an ecclesiastic. Indeed, many other points both in his appearance and demeanour might have very well sustained a conception of that nature. Over his left ear, he carried, after the fashion of a modern clerk, an instrument resembling the *stylus* of the ancients. In a breast-pocket of his coat appeared conspicuously a small black volume fastened with clasps of steel. This book, whether accidentally or not, was so turned outwardly from the person as to discover the words *"Rituel Catholique"* in white letters upon the back. His entire physiognomy was interestingly saturnine—even cadaverously pale. The forehead was lofty, and deeply furrowed with the ridges of contemplation. The corners of the mouth were drawn down into an expression of the most submissive humility. There was also a clasping of the hands, as he stepped towards our hero—a deep sigh—and altogether a look of such utter sanctity as could not have failed to be unequivocally prepossessing. Every shadow of anger faded from the countenance of the metaphysician, as, having completed a satisfactory survey of his visitor's person, he shook him cordially by the hand, and conducted him to a seat.

There would however be a radical error in attributing this instantaneous transition of feeling in the philosopher to any one of those causes which might naturally be supposed to have had an influence. Indeed, Pierre Bon-Bon, from what I have been able to understand of his disposition, was of all men the least likely to be imposed upon by any speciousness of exterior deportment. It was impossible that so accurate an observer of men and things should have failed to discover, upon the moment, the real character of the personage who had thus intruded upon his hospitality. To say no more, the conformation of his visitor's feet was sufficiently remarkable—he maintained lightly upon his head an inordinately tall hat—there was a tremulous swelling about the hinder-part of his breeches—and the vibration of his coat tail was a palpable fact. Judge, then, with what feelings of satisfaction our hero found himself thrown thus at once into the society of a person for whom he had at all times entertained the most unqualified respect. He was, however, too much of the diplomatist to let escape him any intimation of his suspicions in regard to the true state of affairs. It was not his cue to appear at all conscious of the high honour he thus unexpectedly enjoyed; but, by leading his guest into conversation, to elicit some important ethical ideas, which might, in obtaining a place in his contemplated publication, enlighten the human race, and at the same time immortalize himself—ideas which, I should have added, his visitor's great age, and well-known proficiency in the science of morals, might very well have enabled him to afford.

Actuated by these enlightened views, our hero bade the gentleman sit down, while he himself took occasion to throw some fagots upon the fire, and place upon the now re-established table some bottles of Mousseaux. Having quickly completed these operations, he drew his chair *vis-a-vis* to his companion's, and waited until the latter should open the conversation. But plans even the most skilfully matured are often thwarted in the outset of their application—and the *restaurateur* found himself *nonplussed* by the very first words of his visitor's speech.

"I see you know me, Bon-Bon," said he; *"ha! ha! ha!—he! he! he!—hi! hi! hi—ho! ho! ho!—hu! hu! hu!"*—and the Devil, dropping at once the sanctity of his demeanour, opened to its fullest extent a mouth from ear to ear, so as to display a set of jagged and fang-like teeth, and, throwing back his head, laughed long, loudly, wickedly, and uproariously, while the black dog, crouching down upon his haunches, joined lustily in the chorus, and the tabby cat, flying off a tangent, stood up on end, and shrieked in the farthest corner of the apartment

Not so the philosopher: he was too much a man of the world either to laugh like the dog, or by shrieks to betray the indecorous trepidation of the cat. It must be confessed, he felt a little astonishment to see the white letters which formed the words "*Rituel Catholique*" on the book in his guest's pocket, momently changing both their colour and their import, and in a few seconds, in place of the original title, the words "*Registre des Condamnes*" blaze forth in characters of red. This startling circumstance, when Bon-Bon replied to his visitor's remark, imparted to his manner an air of embarrassment which probably might not otherwise have been observed.

"Why, sir," said the philosopher, "why, sir, to speak sincerely—I believe you are—upon my word—the d—dest—that is to say, I think—I imagine—I *have* some faint—some *very* faint idea—of the remarkable honour—"

"Oh!—ah!—yes!—very well!" interrupted his Majesty; "say no more—I see how it is." And hereupon, taking off his green spectacles, he wiped the glasses carefully with the sleeve of his coat, and deposited them in his pocket.

If Bon-Bon had been astonished at the incident of the book, his amazement was now much increased by the spectacle which here presented itself to view. In raising his eyes, with a strong feeling of curiosity to ascertain the colour of his guest's, he found them by no means black, as he had anticipated—nor grey, as might have been imagined—nor yet hazel nor blue—nor indeed yellow nor red—nor purple—nor white—nor green—nor any other colour in the heavens above, or in the earth beneath, or in the waters under the earth. In short, Pierre Bon-Bon not only saw plainly that his Majesty had no eyes whatsoever, but could discover no indications of their having existed at any previous period—for the space where eyes should naturally have been was, I am constrained to say, simply a dead level of flesh.

It was not in the nature of the metaphysician to forbear making some inquiry into the sources of so strange a phenomenon; and the reply of his Majesty was at once prompt, dignified, and satisfactory.

"Eyes! my dear Bon-Bon—eyes! did you say?—oh!—ah!—I perceive! The ridiculous prints, eh, which are in circulation, have given you a false idea of my personal appearance. Eyes!—true. Eyes, Pierre Bon-Bon, are very well in their proper place—*that*, you would say, is the head?—right—the head of a worm. To *you*, likewise, these optics are indispensable—yet I will convince you that my vision is more penetrating than your own. There is a cat I see in the corner—a pretty cat—look at her—observe her well. Now, Bon-Bon, do you behold the thoughts—the thoughts, I say—the ideas—the reflections—which are being engendered in her *pericranium*? There it is now—you do not! She is thinking we admire the length of her tail and the profundity of her mind. She has just concluded that I am the most distinguished of ecclesiastics, and that you are the most superficial of metaphysicians. Thus you see I am not altogether blind; but to one of my profession, the eyes you speak of would be merely an encumbrance, liable at any time to be put out by a toasting-iron or a pitchfork. To you, I allow, these optical affairs are indispensable. Endeavour, Bon-Bon, to use them well; *my* vision is the soul."

Hereupon the guest helped himself to the wine upon the table, and pouring out a bumper for Bon-Bon, requested him to drink it without scruple, and make himself perfectly at home.

"A clever book that of yours, Pierre," resumed his Majesty, tapping our friend knowingly upon the shoulder, as the latter put down his glass after a thorough compliance with his visitor's injunction. "A clever book that of yours, upon my honour. It's a work after my own heart. Your arrangement of the matter, I think, however, might be improved, and many of your notions remind me of Aristotle. That philosopher was one of my most intimate acquaintances. I liked him as much for his terrible ill temper, as for his happy knack at making a blunder. There is only one solid truth in all that he has written, and for that I gave him the hint out of pure compassion for his absurdity. I suppose, Pierre Bon-Bon, you very well know to what divine moral truth I am alluding?"

"Cannot say that I—"

"Indeed!—why it was I who told Aristotle that, by sneezing, men expelled superfluous ideas through the proboscis."

"Which is—*hiccup!*—undoubtedly the case," said the metaphysician, while he poured out for himself another bumper of Mousseaux, and offering his snuff-box to the fingers of his visitor.

"There was Plato, too," continued his Majesty, modestly declining the snuff-box and the compliment it implied—"there was

Plato, too, for whom I, at one time, felt all the affection of a friend. You knew Plato, Bon-Bon?—ah, no, I beg a thousand pardons. He met me at Athens, one day, in the Parthenon, and told me he was distressed for an idea. I bade him write down that—*ho nous estin aulos*.[1] He said that he would do so, and went home, while I stepped over to the pyramids. But my conscience smote me for having uttered a truth, even to aid a friend, and hastening back to Athens, I arrived behind the philosopher's chair as he was inditing the *aulos*.[2]

"Giving the *lambda* a fillip with my finger, I turned it upside down. So the sentence now reads *ho nous estin augos*,[3] and is, you perceive, the fundamental doctrine in his metaphysics."

"Were you ever at Rome?" asked the *restaurateur*, as he finished his second bottle of Mousseaux, and drew from the closet a larger supply of Chambertin.

"But once, Monsieur Bon-Bon, but once. There was a time," said the Devil, as if reciting some passage from a book—"there was a time when occurred an anarchy of five years, during which the republic, bereft of all its officers, had no magistracy besides the tribunes of the people, and these were not legally vested with any degree of executive power—at that time, Monsieur Bon-Bon—at that time *only* I was in Rome, and I have no earthly acquaintance, consequently, with any of its philosophy."[4]

"What do you think of—what do you think of—*hiccup!*—Epicurus?"

"What do I think of *whom*?" said the Devil, in astonishment; "you surely do not mean to find any fault with Epicurus! What do I think of Epicurus! Do you mean me, sir?—I am Epicurus! I am the same philosopher who wrote each of the three hundred treatises commemorated by Diogenes Laertes."

"That's a lie!" said the metaphysician, for the wine had gotten a little into his head.

"Very well!—very well, sir!—very well, indeed, sir!" said his Majesty, apparently much flattered.

---

1. 'ὁ νοῦς ἐστιν αὐλός.'

2. 'αὐλός.'

3. 'ὁ νοῦς ἐστιν αὐγος'

4. *Ils ecrivaient sur la philosophie* (Cicero, Lucretius, Seneca)*, mais c'etait la philosophie grecque.*—Condorcet.

"That's a lie!" repeated the *restaurateur*, dogmatically; "that's a-*hiccup!*—a lie!"

"Well, well, have it your own way!" said the Devil, pacifically, and Bon-Bon, having beaten his Majesty at an argument, thought it his duty to conclude a second bottle of Chambertin.

"As I was saying," resumed the visitor—"as I was observing a little while ago, there are some very *outre* notions in that book of yours, Monsieur Bon-Bon. What, for instance, do you mean by all that humbug about the soul? Pray, sir, what is the soul?"

"The—*hiccup!*—soul," replied the metaphysician, referring to his MS., "is undoubtedly—"

"No, sir!"

"Indubitably—"

"No, sir!"

"Indisputably—"

"No, sir!"

"Evidently—"

"No, sir!"

"Incontrovertibly—"

"No, sir!"

"Hiccup!—"

"No, sir!"

"And beyond all question, a—"

"No, sir, the soul is no such thing!" (Here the philosopher, looking daggers, took occasion to make an end, upon the spot, of his third bottle of Chambertin.)

"Then—*hiccup!*—pray, sir—what—what is it?"

"That is neither here nor there, Monsieur Bon-Bon," replied his Majesty, musingly. "I have tasted—that is to say, I have known some very bad souls, and some too—pretty good ones." Here he smacked his lips, and, having unconsciously let fall his hand upon the volume in his pocket, was seized with a violent fit of sneezing.

He continued:

"There was the soul of Cratinus—passable: Aristophanes—racy: Plato—exquisite—not *your* Plato, but Plato the comic poet; your Plato would have turned the stomach of Cerberus—faugh! Then let me see! there were Naevius, and Andronicus, and Plautus, and Terentius. Then there were Lucilius, and Catullus, and Naso, and

Quintus Flaccus,—dear Quinty! as I called him when he sang a *saeculare* for my amusement, while I toasted him, in pure good humour, on a fork. But they want *flavour*, these Romans. One fat Greek is worth a dozen of them, and besides will *keep*, which cannot be said of a Quirite. Let us taste your Sauterne."

Bon-Bon had by this time made up his mind to the *nil admirari*, and endeavoured to hand down the bottles in question. He was, however, conscious of a strange sound in the room like the wagging of a tail. Of this, although extremely indecent in his Majesty, the philosopher took no notice:—simply kicking the dog, and requesting him to be quiet. The visitor continued:

"I found that Horace tasted very much like Aristotle;—you know I am fond of variety. Terentius I could not have told from Menander. Naso, to my astonishment, was Nicander in disguise. Virgilius had a strong twang of Theocritus. Martial put me much in mind of Archilochus—and Titus Livius was positively Polybius and none other."

"Hiccup!" here replied Bon-Bon, and his Majesty proceeded:

"But if I *have* a *penchant*, Monsieur Bon-Bon—if I *have* a *penchant*, it is for a philosopher. Yet, let me tell you, sir, it is not every dev—I mean it is not every gentleman who knows how to *choose* a philosopher. Long ones are *not* good; and the best, if not carefully shelled, are apt to be a little rancid on account of the gall."

"Shelled!!"

"I mean taken out of the carcass."

"What do you think of a—*hiccup!*—physician?"

"*Don't* mention them!—ugh! ugh!" (Here his Majesty retched violently.) "I never tasted but one—that rascal Hippocrates!—smelt of *asafoetida*—ugh! ugh! ugh!—caught a wretched cold washing him in the Styx—and after all he gave me the *cholera-morbus*."

"The—*hiccup!*—wretch!" ejaculated Bon-Bon, "the—*hiccup!*—abortion of a pill-box!"—and the philosopher dropped a tear.

"After all," continued the visitor, "after all, if a dev—if a gentleman wishes to *live*, he must have more talents than one or two; and with us a fat face is an evidence of diplomacy."

"How so?"

"Why we are sometimes exceedingly pushed for provisions. You must know that, in a climate so sultry as mine, it is frequently impossible to keep a spirit alive for more than two or three hours; and after death, unless pickled immediately (and a pickled spirit is *not* good), they will—smell—you understand, eh? Putrefaction is always to be apprehended when the souls are consigned to us in the usual way."

"Hiccup!—*hiccup!*—good God! how *do* you manage?"

Here the iron lamp commenced swinging with redoubled violence, and the Devil half started from his seat;—however, with a slight sigh, he recovered his composure, merely saying to our hero in a low tone: "I tell you what, Pierre Bon-Bon, we *must* have no more swearing."

The host swallowed another bumper, by way of denoting thorough comprehension and acquiescence, and the visitor continued:

"Why, there are *several* ways of managing. The most of us starve: some put up with the pickle: for my part I purchase my spirits *vivente corpore*, in which case I find they keep very well."

"But the body!—*hiccup!*—the body!!"

"The body, the body—well, what of the body?—oh! ah! I perceive. Why, sir, the body is not *at all* affected by the transaction. I have made innumerable purchases of the kind in my day, and the parties never experienced any inconvenience. There were Cain and Nimrod, and Nero, and Caligula, and Dionysius, and Pisistratus, and—and a thousand others, who never knew what it was to have a soul during the latter part of their lives; yet, sir, these men adorned society. Why isn't there A—, now, whom you know as well as I? Is *he* not in possession of all his faculties, mental and corporeal? Who writes a keener epigram? Who reasons more wittily? Who—but, stay! I have his agreement in my pocket-book."

Thus saying, he produced a red leather wallet, and took from it a number of papers. Upon some of these Bon-Bon caught a glimpse of the letters *Machi—Maza—Robesp*—with the words *Caligula, George, Elizabeth*. His Majesty selected a narrow slip of parchment, and from it read aloud the following words:

"In consideration of certain mental endowments which it is unnecessary to specify, and in further consideration of one thousand *louis d'or*, I, being aged one year and one month, do hereby make over to the bearer of this agreement all my right, title, and appurtenance in the shadow called my soul. (Signed) A—"[2] (Here

---

2. Query.—*Arouet?*

His Majesty repeated a name which I do not feel myself justified in indicating more unequivocally.)

"A clever fellow that," resumed he; "but, like you, Monsieur Bon-Bon, he was mistaken about the soul. The soul a shadow, truly! The soul a shadow! *Ha! ha! ha!—he! he! he!—hu! hu! hu!* Only think of a *fricasseed* shadow!"

"*Only* think—*hiccup!*—of a *fricasseed* shadow!" exclaimed our hero, whose faculties were becoming much illuminated by the profundity of His Majesty's discourse. "Only think of a—*hiccup!*—*fricasseed* shadow!! Now, damme!—*hiccup!*—humph! If *I* would have been such a—*hiccup!*—nincompoop! My soul, Mr.—humph!"

"*Your* soul, Monsieur Bon-Bon?"

"Yes, sir—*hiccup!*—my soul is—"

"What, sir?"

"*No* shadow, damme!"

"Did you mean to say—"

"Yes, sir, *my* soul is—*hiccup!*—humph!—yes, sir."

"Did you not intend to assert—"

"*My* soul is—*hiccup!*—peculiarly qualified for—*hiccup!*—a—"

"What, sir?"

"Stew."

"Ha!"

"*Soufflé.*"

"Eh!"

"*Fricassee.*"

"Indeed!"

"*Ragout* and *fricandeau*—and see here, my good fellow! I'll let you have it—*hiccup!*—a bargain." Here the philosopher slapped His Majesty upon the back.

"Couldn't think of such a thing," said the latter calmly, at the same time rising from his seat. The metaphysician stared.

"Am supplied at present," said His Majesty.

"Hic-cup!—e-h?" said the philosopher.

"Have no funds on hand."

"What?"

"Besides, very unhandsome in me—"

"Sir!"

"To take advantage of—"

"Hic-cup!"

"Your present disgusting and ungentlemanly situation."

Here the visitor bowed and withdrew—in what manner could not precisely be ascertained—but in a well-concerted effort to discharge a bottle at "the villain," the slender chain was severed that depended from the ceiling, and the metaphysician prostrated by the downfall of the lamp.

The Printer's Devil

Anonymous

The term "Printer's Devil" is usually accounted for by the fact that Aldus Manutius, the great Venetian printer, employed in his printing shop (about 1485) a black slave, who was popularly thought to be an imp of Satan. This expression may have a deeper significance. It may owe its origin to the fact that Fust, the inventor of the printing press, was believed to have connections with the Evil One. It will be remembered that during the Middle Ages and, in Catholic countries, even for a long time afterwards every discovery of science, every invention of material benefit to man, was believed to have been secured by a compact with the devil. Our ancestors deemed the human mind incapable, without the aid of the Evil One, of producing anything beyond their own comprehension. The red letters which Fust used at the close of his earliest printed volumes to give his name, with the place and date of publication, were interpreted in Paris as indications of the diabolical origin of the works so easily produced by him. (M. D. Conway, *Demonology and Devil-Lore.*) Sacred days, as is well known, are printed in the Catholic calendar with red letters, and the devil has also employed them in books of magic. This is but another instance of the mimicry by "God's Ape" of the sanctities of the Church.

In the infernal economy, where a strict division of labour prevails, the printer's devil is the librarian of hell. The books over which he has charge must be as numerous as the sands on the sea-shore. For nearly every book written without priestly command was associated in the good old days with the devil. The assertion that Satan hates nothing so much as writing or printer's ink apparently is a very great calumny. He has often even been accused of stealing manuscripts in order to prevent their publication. The prince of darkness naturally rather shuns than courts inquiry. On one occasion Joseph Goerres, the defender of Catholicism, complained that the devil, provoked by his interference in Satanic affairs (he is the author of *Die Christliche Mystik*, which is a rich source for diabolism, diabolical possession and exorcism), had stolen one of his manuscripts; it was, however, found some time afterwards in his bookcase, and the devil was completely exonerated.

The concluding paragraph of this story is especially interesting in the light of the present agitation for unbound books and a eulogy of the old Franklin Square Library.

As I was sitting in my armchair and preparing an essay on the Devil in literature, sleep overpowered me; the pen fell from my hands, and my head reclined upon the desk. I had been thinking so much about the Devil in my waking hours, that the same idea pursued me after I had fallen asleep. I heard a gentle rap at the door, and having bawled out as usual, "Come in," a little gentleman entered, wrapped in a large blue cloth cloak, with a slouched hat, and goggles over his eyes. After bowing and scraping with considerable ceremony, he took off his hat, and threw his cloak over the back of a chair, when I immediately perceived that my visitor was no mortal. His face was hideously ugly; the skin appearing very much like wet paper, and the forehead covered with those cabalistic signs whose wondrous significance is best known to those who correct the press. On the end of his long hooked nose there seemed to me to be growing, like a carbuncle, the first letter of the alphabet, glittering with ink and ready to print. I observed, also, that each of his fingers and toes, or rather claws, was in the same manner terminated by one of the letters of the alphabet; and as he slashed round his tail to brush a fly off his nose, I noticed that the letter Z formed the extremity of that useful member. While I was looking with no small astonishment and some trepidation at my extraordinary visitor, he took occasion to inform me that he had taken liberty to call, as he was afraid I might forget him in the treatise which I was writing—an omission which he assured me would cause him no little mortification. "In me," says he, "you behold the prince and patron of printers' devils. My province is to preside over the hell of books; and if you will only take the trouble to accompany me a little way, I will show you some of the wonders of that world." As my imagination had lately been much excited by perusing Dante's *Inferno*, I was delighted with an adventure which promised to turn out something like his wonderful journey, and I readily consented to visit my new friend's dominions, and we sallied forth together. As we pursued our way, my conductor endeavoured to give me some information respecting the world I was about to enter, in order to prepare me for the wonders I should encounter there. "You must know," remarked he, "that books have souls as well as men; and the moment any work is published, whether successful or not, its soul appears in precisely the same form in another world; either in this domain, which is subject to me, or in a better region, over which I have no control. I have power only to exhibit the place of punishment for bad books, periodicals, pamphlets, and, in short, publications of every kind."

We now arrived at the mouth of a cavern, which I did not remember to have ever noticed before, though I had repeatedly passed the spot in my walks. It looked to me more like the entrance to a coalmine than anything else, as the sides were entirely black. Upon examining them more closely, I found that they were covered with a black fluid which greatly resembled printer's ink, and which seemed to corrode and wear away the rocks of the cavern wherever it touched them. "We have lately received a large supply of political publications," said my companion; "and hell is perfectly saturated with their maliciousness. We carry on a profitable trade upon the earth, by retailing this ink to the principal political editors. Unfortunately, it is not found to answer very well for literary publications, though they have tried it with considerable success in printing the London *Quarterly* and several of the other important reviews."

The cavern widened as we advanced, and we came presently into a vast open plain, which was bounded on one side by a wall so high that it seemed to reach the very heavens. As we approached the wall I observed a vast gateway before us, closed up by folding doors. The gates opened at our approach, and we entered. I found myself in a warm sandy valley, bounded on one side by a steep range of mountains. A feeble light shone upon it, much like that of a sick chamber, and the air seemed confined and stifling like that of the abode of illness. My ears were assailed by a confused whining noise, as if all the litters of new-born puppies, kittens with their eyes unopened, and babes just come to light, in the whole world, were brought into one spot, and were whelping, mewing, and squalling at once. I turned in mute wonder to my guide for explanation; and he informed me that I now beheld the destined abode of all still-born and abortive publications; and the infantine noises which I heard were only their feeble wailing for the miseries they had endured in being brought into the world. I now saw what the feebleness of the light had prevented my observing before, that the soil was absolutely covered with books of every size and shape, from the little diamond almanac up to the respectable quarto. I saw folios there. These books were crawling about and tumbling over each other like blind whelps, uttering, at the same time, the most mournful cries. I observed one, however, which remained quite still, occasionally groaning a little, and appeared like an overgrown toad oppressed with its own heaviness. I drew near, and read upon the back, "*Resignation*, a Novel." The cover flew open, and the title-page immediately began to address me. I walked off, however, as fast as possible, only distinguishing a few words about "the injustice and severity of critics;" "bad taste of the public;" "very well considering;" "first effort;" "feminine mind," &c. &c. I presently discovered a very important-looking little book, stalking about among the rest in a great passion, kicking the others out of the way, and swearing like a trooper; till at length, apparently exhausted with its efforts, it sunk down to rise no more. "Ah ha!" exclaimed my little diabolical friend, "here is a new comer; let's see who he is;" and coming up, he turned it over with his foot so that we could see the back of it, upon which was printed "*The Monikins*, by the Author of, &c. &c." I noticed that the book had several marks across it, as if some one had been flogging the unfortunate work. "It is only the marks of the scourge," said my companion, "which the critics have used rather more severely, I think, than was necessary." I expected, after all the passion I had seen, and the great importance of feeling, arrogance, and vanity the little work had manifested, that it would have some pert remarks to make to us; but it was so much exhausted that it could not say a word. At the bottom of the valley was a small pond of a milky hue, from which there issued a perfume very much like the smell of bread and butter. An immense number of thin, prettily bound manuscript books were soaking in this pond of milk, all of which, I was informed, were *Young Ladies' Albums*, which it was necessary to souse in the slough, to prevent them from stealing passages from the various works about them. As soon as I heard what they were, I ran away with all my speed, having a mortal dread of these books.

We had now traversed the valley, and, approaching the barrier of mountains, we found a passage cut through, which greatly resembled the Pausilipo, near Naples; it was closed on the side towards the valley, only with a curtain of white paper, upon which were printed the names of the principal reviews, which my conductor assured me were enough to prevent any of the unhappy works we had seen from coming near the passage.

As we advanced through the mountains, occasional gleams of light appeared before us, and immediately vanished, leaving us in darkness. My guide, however, seemed to be well acquainted with the way, and we went on fearlessly till we emerged into an open field, lighted up by constant flashes of lightning, which glared from every side; the air was hot, and strongly impregnated with sulphur. "Each department of my dominions," said the Devil, "receives its light from the works which are sent there. You are now surrounded by the glittering but evanescent coruscations of the more recent novels. This department of hell was never very well supplied till quite lately, though Fielding, Smollett, Maturin, and Godwin, did what they could for us. Our greatest benefactors have been Disraeli, Bulwer, and Victor Hugo; and this glare of light, so painful to our eyes, proceeds chiefly from their books." There was a tremendous noise like the rioting of an army of drunken men, with horrible cries and imprecations, and fiend-like laughing, which made my blood curdle; and such a scrambling and fighting among the books, as I never saw before. I could not imagine at first what could be the cause of this, till I discovered at last a golden hill rising up like a cone in the midst of the plane, with just room enough for one book on the summit; and I found that the novels were fighting like so many devils for the occupation of this place. One work, however, had gained possession of it, and seemed to maintain its hold with a strength and resolution which bade defiance to the rest. I could not at first make out the name of this book, which seemed to stand upon its golden throne like the Prince of Hell; but presently the whole arch of the heavens glared with new brilliancy, and the magic name of *Vivian Grey* flashed from the book in letters of scorching light. I was much afraid, however, that *Vivian* would not long retain his post; for I saw *Pelham* and *Peregrine Pickle*, and the terrible *Melmoth* with his glaring eyes, coming together to the assault, when a whirlwind seized them all four and carried them away to a vast distance, leaving the elevation vacant for some other competitor. "There is no peace to the wicked, you see," said my Asmodeus. "These books are longing for repose, and they can get none on account of the insatiable vanity of their authors, whose desire for distinction made them careless of the sentiments they expressed and the principles they advocated. The great characteristic of works of this stamp is action, intense, painful action. They have none of that beautiful serenity which shines in Scott and Edgeworth; and they are condemned to illustrate, by an eternity of contest here, the restless spirit with which they are inspired."

While I was looking on with fearful interest in the mad combat before me, the horizon seemed to be darkened, and a vast cloud rose up in the image of a gigantic eagle, whose wings stretched from the east to the west till he covered the firmament. In his talons he carried an open book, at the sight of which the battle around me was calmed; the lightnings ceased to flash, and there was an awful stillness. Then suddenly there glared from the book a sheet of fire, which rose in columns a thousand feet high, and filled the empyrean with intense light; the pillars of flame curling and wreathing themselves into monstrous letters, till they were fixed in one terrific glare, and I read—"*Byron*." Even my companion quailed before the awful light, and I covered my face with my hands. When I withdrew them, the cloud and the book had vanished, and the contest was begun again—"You have seen the Prince of this division of hell," said my guide.

We now began rapidly to descend into the bowels of the earth; and, after sinking some thousand feet, I found myself on *terra firma* again, and walking a little way, we came to a gate of massive ice, over which was written in vast letters—"My heritage is despair." We passed through, and immediately found ourselves in a vast basin of lead, which seemed to meet the horizon on every side. A bright light shone over the whole region; but it was not like the genial light of the sun. It chilled me through; and every ray that fell upon me seemed like the touch of ice. The deepest silence prevailed; and though the valley was covered with books, not one moved or uttered a sound. I drew near to one, and I shivered with intense cold as I read upon it—"*Voltaire.*"

"Behold," said the demon, "the hell of infidel books; the light which emanates from them is the light of reason, and they are doomed to everlasting torpor." I found it too cold to pursue my investigations any farther in this region, and I gladly passed on from the leaden gulf of Infidelity.

I had no sooner passed the barrier which separated this department from the next, than I heard a confused sound like the quacking of myriads of ducks and geese, and a great flapping of wings; of which I soon saw the cause. "You are in the hell of newspapers," said my guide. And sure enough, when I looked up I saw thousands of newspapers flying about with their great wooden back-bones, and the padlock dangling like a bobtail at the end, flapping their wings and hawking at each other like mad. After circling about in the air for a little while, and biting and tearing each other as much as they could, they plumped down, head first, into a deep black-looking pool, and were seen no more. "We place these newspapers deeper in hell than the Infidel publications," said the Devil; "because they are so much more extensively read, and thereby do much greater mischief. It is a kind of pest of which there is no end; and we are obliged to allot the largest portion of our dominions to containing them."

We now came to an immense pile of a leaden hue, which I found at last to consist of old worn-out type, which was heaped up to form the wall of the next division. A monstrous u, turned bottom upwards formed the arch of a gateway through which we passed; and then traversed a draw-bridge, which was thrown across a river of ink, upon whose banks millions of horrible little demons were sporting. I presently saw that they were employed in throwing into the black stream a quantity of books which were heaped up on the shore. As I looked down into the stream, I saw that they were immediately devoured by the most hideous and disgusting monsters which were floundering about there. I looked at one book, which had crawled out after being thrown into the river; it was dripping with filth, but I distinguished on the back the words—*Don Juan*. It had hardly climbed up the bank, however, when one of the demons gave it a kick, and sent it back into the stream, where it was immediately swallowed. On the back of some of the books which the little imps were tossing in, I saw the name of—*Rochester*, which showed me the character of those which were sent into this division of the infernal regions.

Beyond this region rose up a vast chain of mountains, which we were obliged to clamber over. After toiling for a long time, we reached the summit, and I looked down upon an immense labyrinth built upon the plain below, in which I saw a great number of large folios, stalking about in solemn pomp, each followed by a number of small volumes and pamphlets, like so many pages or footmen watching the beck of their master. "You behold here," said the demon, "all the false works upon theology which have been written since the beginning of the Christian era. They are condemned to wander about to all eternity in the hopeless maze of this labyrinth, each folio drawing after it all the minor works to which it gave origin." A faint light shone from these ponderous tomes; but it was like the shining of a lamp in a thick mist, shorn of its rays, and illuminating nothing around it. And if my companion had not held a torch before me, I should not have discerned the outlines of this department of the Infernal world. As my eye became somewhat accustomed to the feeble light, I discovered beyond the labyrinth a thick mist, which appeared to rise from some river or lake. "That," said my companion, "is the distinct abode of German Metaphysical works, and other treatises of a similar unintelligible character. They are all obliged to pass through a press; and if there is any sense in them, it is thus separated from the mass of nonsense in which it is imbedded, and is allowed to escape to a better world. Very few of the works, however, are found to be materially diminished by passing through the press." We had now crossed the plain, and stood near the impenetrable fog, which rose up like a wall before us. In front of it was the press managed by several ugly little demons, and surrounded by an immense number of volumes of every size and shape, waiting for the process which all were obliged to undergo. As I was watching their operations, I saw two very respectable German folios, with enormous clasps, extended like arms, carrying between them a little volume, which they were fondling like a pet child with marks of doting affection. These folios proved to be two of the most abstruse, learned, and incomprehensible of the metaphysical productions of Germany; and the bantling which they seemed to embrace with so much affection, was registered on the back—"*Records of a School.*" I did not find that a single ray of intelligence had been extracted from either of the two after being subjected to the press. As soon as the volumes had passed through the operation of yielding up all the little sense they contained, they plunged into the intense fog, and disappeared for ever.

We next approached the verge of a gulf, which appeared to be bottomless; and there was dreadful noise, like the war of the elements, and forked flames shooting up from the abyss, which reminded me of the crater of Vesuvius. "You have now reached the ancient limits of hell," said the demon, "and you behold beneath your feet the original chaos on which my domains are founded. But within a few years we have been obliged to build a yet deeper division beyond the gulf, to contain a class of books that were unknown in former times."

"Pray, what class can be found," I asked, "worse than those which I have already seen, and for which it appears hell was not bad enough?"

"They are American re-prints of English publications," replied he, "and they are generally works of such a despicable character, that they would have found their way here without being republished; but even where the original work was good, it is so degenerated by the form under which it re-appears in America, that its merit is entirely lost, and it is only fit for the seventh and lowest division of hell."

I now perceived a bridge spanning over the gulf, with an arch that seemed as lofty as the firmament. We hastily passed over, and found that the farthest extremity of the bridge was closed by a gate, over which was written three words. "They are the names of the three furies who reign over this division," said my guide. I of course did not contradict him; but the words looked very much like some I had seen before; and the more I examined them, the more difficult was it to convince myself that the inscription was not the same thing as the sign over a certain publishing house in Philadelphia.

"These," said the Devil, "are called the three furies of the hell of books; not from the mischief they do there to the works about them, but for the unspeakable wrong they did to the same works upon the earth, by re-printing them in their hideous brown paper editions." As soon as they beheld me, they rushed towards me with such piteous accents and heart-moving entreaties, that I would intercede to save them from their torment, that I was moved with the deepest compassion, and began to ask my conductor if there were no relief for them. But he hurried me away, assuring me that they only wanted to sell me some of their infernal editions, and the idea of owning any such property was so dreadful that it woke me up directly.

The Devil's Mother-in-Law

Fernan Caballero

Fernan Caballero is the pseudonym of Mrs. Cecilia Boehl von Faber, Marchioness de Arco-Hermoso, who was a Swiss by birth, daughter of the literary historian Johann Boehl von Faber, the Johannes of Campe's *Robinson* (1779). Her father initiated her early into Spanish literature, which he interpreted for her in the spirit of the Romantic movement of those early days. The interest in mediaeval traditions, which she owes to this early training, increased when, later, she went to Catholic Spain. The charm of her popular Andalusian tales consists in the fact that she fully shares with the Catholic peasants of that province an implicit faith in the truth of these mediaeval legends. In her stories we find perhaps the purest expression of medievalism in modern times. Fernan Caballero gradually drifted to the extreme Right in all questions of religion, art and life. She hated every liberal expression in matters of faith or art with the fanaticism of a Torquemada. This author not only shared the somewhat general Catholic view that all Protestants were eternally damned, but she naively believed that every son of Israel had a tail (Julian Schmidt).

The story of woman's triumph over the Devil is well characteristic of the Land of the Blessed Lady, as Andalusia is commonly called.

The legend of a devil imprisoned in a phial is also found in the work of the Spaniard Luis Velez de Guevara called *El Diablo Cojuelo* (1641), from whom Alain Le Sage borrowed both title and plot for his novel *Le Diable Boiteux*

(1707). Asmodeus, liberated from a bottle, into which he had been confined by a magician, entertains his deliverer with the secret sights of a big city at midnight, by unroofing the houses of the Spanish capital and showing him the life that was going on in them. The legend was introduced into Spain from the East by the Moors and finally acclimated to find a place in local traditions. From that country it spread over the whole of Europe. The Asiatics believed that by abstinence and special prayers evil spirits could be reduced into obedience and confined in black bottles. The tradition forms a part of the Solomonic lore, and is frequently told in esoteric works. In the cabalistic book *Vinculum Spirituum*, which is of Eastern origin, it is said that Solomon discovered, by means of a certain learned book, the valuable secret of inclosing in a bottle of black glass three millions of infernal spirits, with seventy-two of their kings, of whom Beleh was the chief, Beliar (alias Belial) the second, and Asmodeus the third. Solomon afterwards cast this bottle into a deep well near Babylon. Fortunately for the contents, the Babylonians, hoping to find a treasure in the well, descended into it, broke the bottle, and freed the demons (cf. also *The Little Key of Rabbi Solomon, containing the Names, Seals and Characters of the 72 Spirits with whom he held converse, also the Art Almadel of Rabbi Solomon, carefully copied by "Raphael,"* London, 1879). This legend is also found in the tale of the Fisherman and the Djinn in the *Arabian Nights*, which was also treated by the German poet Klopstock in his poem "Wintermaerchen" (1776).

The devil, as it is said in this story, has a mortal hatred of the sound of bells. The origin of ringing the church bells was, according to Sir James Frazer, to drive away devils and witches. The devil in Poe's story "The Devil in the Belfry" (1839) was, indeed, very courageous in invading the belfry.

The concluding part of the story is identical with the Machiavellian tale of Belphagor.

This tale of the Devil's mother-in-law first appeared in the volume *Cuentos y Poesias Populares Andaluces* (Seville, 1859), which was translated the same year into French by

Germond de Lavigne under the title *Nouvelles Andalouses*. An English translation under the title *Spanish Fairy Tales* appeared in 1881. This particular story was rendered again into English two years later and included in *Tales from Twelve Tongues*, London, 1883.

In a town, named Villagananes, there was once an old widow uglier than the sergeant of Utrera, who was considered as ugly as ugly could be; drier than hay; older than foot-walking, and more yellow than the jaundice. Moreover, she had so cross-grained a disposition that Job himself could not have tolerated her. She had been nicknamed "Mother Holofernes," and she had only to put her head out of doors to put all the lads to flight. Mother Holofernes was as clean as a new pin, and as industrious as an ant, and in these respects suffered no little vexation on account of her daughter Panfila, who was, on the contrary, so lazy, and such an admirer of the Quietists, that an earthquake would not move her. So it came to pass that Mother Holofernes began quarrelling with her daughter almost from the day that the girl was born.

"You are," she said, "as flaccid as Dutch tobacco, and it would take a couple of oxen to draw you out of your room. You fly work as you would the pest, and nothing pleases you but the window, you shameless girl. You are more amorous than Cupid himself, but, if I have any power, you shall live as close as a nun."

On hearing all this, Panfila got up, yawned, stretched herself, and turning her back on her mother, went to the street door. Mother Holofernes, without paying attention to this, began to sweep with most tremendous energy, accompanying the noise of the broom with a monologue of this tenor:—

"In my time girls had to work like men."

The broom gave the accompaniment of *shis, shis, shis.*

"And lived as secluded as nuns."

And the broom went *shis, shis, shis.*

"Now they are a pack of fools."—*Shis, shis.*

"Of idlers."—*Shis, shis.*

"And think of nothing but husbands.—*Shis, shis.*

"And are a lot of good-for-nothings."

The broom following with its chorus.

By this time she had nearly reached the street door, when she saw her daughter making signs to a youth; and the handle of the broom, as the handiest implement, descended upon the shoulders of Panfila, and effected the miracle of making her run. Next, Mother Holofernes, grasping the broom, made for the door; but scarcely had the shadow of her head appeared, than it produced the customary effect, and the aspirant disappeared so swiftly that it seemed as if he must have had wings on his feet.

"Drat that fellow!" shouted the mother; "I should like to break all the bones in his body."

"What for? Why should I not think of getting married?"

"What are you saying? You get married, you fool! not while I live!"

"Why were you married, madam? and my grandmother? and my great grandmother?"

"Nicely I have been repaid for it, by you, you sauce-box! And understand me, that if I chose to get married, and your grandmother also, and your great grandmother also, I do not intend that you shall marry; nor my granddaughter, nor my great granddaughter! Do you hear me?"

In these gentle disputes the mother and daughter passed their lives, without any other result than that the mother grumbled more and more every day, and the daughter became daily more and more desirous of getting a husband.

Upon one occasion, when Mother Holofernes was doing the washing, and as the lye was on the point of boiling, she had to call her daughter to help her lift the caldron, in order to pour its contents on to the tub of clothes. The girl heard her with one ear, but with the other was listening to a well-known voice which sang in the street:—

"I would like to love thee,
"Did thy mother let me woo!
"May the demon meddle
"In all she tries to do!"

The sound outside being more attractive for Panfila than the caldron within, she did not hasten to her mother, but went to the window. Mother Holofernes, meanwhile, seeing that her daughter did not come, and that time was passing, attempted to lift the caldron by herself, in order to pour the water upon the linen; and as the good woman was small, and not very strong, it turned over, and burnt her foot. On hearing the horrible groans Mother Holofernes made, her daughter went to her.

"Wretch, wretch!" cried the enraged Mother Holofernes to her daughter, "may you love Barabbas! And as for marrying—may Heaven grant you may marry the Evil One himself!"

Sometime after this accident an aspirant presented himself: he was a little man, young, fair, red-haired, well-mannered, and had well-furnished pockets. He had not a single fault, and Mother Holofernes was not able to find any in all her arsenal of negatives. As for Panfila, it wanted little to send her out of her senses with delight. So the preparations for the wedding were made, with the usual grumbling accompaniment on the part of the bridegroom's future mother-in-law. Everything went on smoothly straightforward, and without a break—like a railroad—when, without knowing why, the popular voice—a voice which is as the personification of conscience,—began to rise in a murmur against the stranger, despite the fact that he was affable, humane, and liberal; that he spoke well and sang better; and freely took the black and horny hands of the labourers between his own white and beringed fingers. They began to feel neither honoured nor overpowered by so much courtesy; his reasoning was always so coarse, although forcible and logical.

"By my faith!" said Uncle Blas; "why does this ill-faced gentleman call me Mr. Blas, as if that would make me any better? What does it look like to you?"

"Well, as for me," said Uncle Gil, "did he not come to shake hands with me as if we had some plot between us? Did he not call me citizen? I, who have never been out of the village, and never want to go."

As for Mother Holofernes, the more she saw of her future son-in-law, the less regard she had for him. It seemed to her that between that innocent red hair and the cranium were located certain protuberances of a very curious kind; and she remembered with emotion that malediction she had uttered against her daughter on that ever memorable day on which her foot was injured and her washing spoilt.

At last, the wedding day arrived. Mother Holofernes had made pastry and reflections—the former sweet, the latter bitter; a great *olla podrida* for the food, and a dangerous project for supper; she had prepared a barrel of wine that was generous, and a line of conduct that was not. When the bridal pair were about to retire to the nuptial chamber, Mother Holofernes called her daughter aside, and said: "When you are in your room, be careful to close the door and windows; shut all the shutters, and do not leave a single crevice open but the keyhole of the door. Take with you this branch of consecrated olive, and beat your husband with it as I advise you; this ceremony is customary at all marriages, and signifies that the woman is going to be master, and is followed in order to sanction and establish the rule."

Panfila, for the first time obedient to her mother, did everything that she had prescribed.

No sooner did the bridegroom espy the branch of consecrated olive in the hands of his wife, than he attempted to make a precipitous retreat. But when he found the doors and windows closed, and every crevice stopped up, seeing no other means of escape than by passing through the keyhole, he crept into that; this spruce, red-and-white, and well-spoken bachelor being, as Mother Holofernes had suspected, neither more nor less than the Evil One himself, who, availing himself of the right given him by the anathema launched against Panfila by her mother, thought to amuse himself with the pleasures of a marriage, and encumber himself with a wife of his own, whilst so many husbands were supplicating him to take theirs off their hands.

But this gentleman, despite his reputation for wisdom, had met with a mother-in-law who knew more than he did; and Mother Holofernes was not the only specimen of that genus. Therefore, scarcely had his lordship entered into the keyhole, congratulating himself upon having, as usual, discovered a method of escape, than he found himself in a phial, which his foreseeing mother-in-law had ready on the other side of the door; and no sooner had he got into it than the provident old dame sealed the vessel hermetically. In a most tender voice, and with most humble supplications, and most pathetic gestures, her son-in-law addressed her, and desired that she would grant him his liberty. But Mother Holofernes was not to be deceived by the demon, nor disconcerted by orations, nor imposed upon by honeyed words; she took charge of the bottle and its contents, and went off to a mountain. The old lady vigorously climbed to the summit of this mountain, and there, on its most elevated crest, in a rocky and secluded spot, deposited the phial, taking leave of her son-in-law with a shake of her closed fist as a farewell greeting.

And there his lordship remained for ten years. What years those ten were! The world was as quiet as a pool of oil. Everybody attended to his own affairs, without meddling in those of other people. Nobody coveted the position, nor the wife, nor the property of other persons; theft became a word without signification; arms rusted; powder was only consumed in fireworks; prisons stood empty; finally, in this decade of the golden age, only one single deplorable event occurred—the lawyers died from hunger and quietude.

Alas! that so happy a time should have an end! But everything has an end in this world, even the discourses of the most eloquent fathers of the country. At last the much-to-be-envied decade came to a termination in the following way.

A soldier named Briones had obtained permission for a few days' leave to enable him to visit his native place, which was Villagananes. He took the road which led to the lofty mountain upon whose summit the son-in-law of Mother Holofernes was cursing all mothers-in-law, past, present, and future, promising as soon as ever he regained his power to put an end to that class of vipers, and by a very simple method—the abolition of matrimony. Much of his time was spent in composing and reciting satires against the invention of washing linen, the primal cause of his present trouble.

Arrived at the foot of the mountain, Briones did not care to go round the mountain like the road, but wished to go straight ahead, assuring the carriers who were with him, that if the mountain would not go to the right-about for him he would pass over its summit, although it were so high that he should knock his head against the sky.

When he reached the summit, Briones was struck with amazement on seeing the phial borne like a pimple on the nose of the mountain. He took it up, looked through it, and on perceiving the demon, who with years of confinement and fasting, the sun's rays, and sadness, had dwindled and become as dried as a prune, exclaimed in surprise:

"Whatever vermin is this? What a phenomenon!"

"I am an honourable and meritorious demon," said the captive, humbly and courteously. "The perversity of a treacherous mother-in-law, into whose clutches I fell, has held me confined here during the last ten years; liberate me, valiant warrior, and I will grant any favour you choose to solicit."

"I should like my demission from the army," said Briones.

"You shall have it; but uncork, uncork quickly, for it is a most monstrous anomaly to have thrust into a corner, in these revolutionary times, the first revolutionist in the world."

Briones drew the cork out slightly, and a noxious vapour issued from the bottle and ascended to his brain. He sneezed, and immediately replaced the stopper with such a violent blow from his hand that the cork was suddenly depressed, and the prisoner, squeezed down, gave a shout of rage and pain.

"What are you doing, vile earthworm, more malicious and perfidious than my mother-in-law?" he exclaimed.

"There is another condition," responded Briones, "that I must add to our treaty; it appears to me that the service I am going to do you is worth it."

"And what is this condition, tardy liberator?" inquired the demon.

"I should like for thy ransom four dollars daily during the rest of my life. Think of it, for upon that depends whether you stay in or come out."

"Miserable avaricious one!" exclaimed the demon, "I have no money."

"Oh!" replied Briones, "what an answer from a great lord like you! Why, friend, that is the Minister of War's answer! If you can't pay me I cannot help you."

"Then you do not believe me," said the demon, "only let me out, and I will aid you to obtain what you want as I have done for many others. Let me out, I say, let me out."

"Gently," responded the soldier, "there is nothing to hurry about. Understand me that I shall have to hold you by the tail until you have performed your promise to me; and if not, I have nothing more to say to you."

"Insolent, do you not trust me then!" shouted the demon.

"No," responded Briones.

"What you desire is contrary to my dignity," said the captive, with all the arrogance that a being of his size could express.

"Now I must go," said Briones.

"Goodbye," said the demon, in order not to say *adieu*.

But seeing that Briones went off, the captive made desperate jumps in the phial, shouting loudly to the soldier.

"Return, return, dear friend," he said; and muttered to himself, "I should like a four-year-old bull to overtake you, you soulless fool!" and then he shouted, "Come, come, beneficent fellow, liberate me, and hold me by the tail, or by the nose, valiant warrior;" and then muttered to himself, "Some one will avenge me, obstinate soldier; and if the son-in-law of Mother Holofernes is not able to do it, there are those who will burn you both, face to face, in the same bonfire, or I have little influence."

On hearing the demon's supplications Briones returned and uncorked the bottle. Mother Holofernes's son-in-law came forth like a chick from its shell, drawing out his head first and then his body, and lastly his tail, which Briones seized; and the more the demon tried to contract it the firmer he held it.

After the ex-captive, who was somewhat cramped, had occasionally stopped to stretch his arms and legs, they took the road to court, the demon grumbling and following the soldier, who carried the tail well secured in his hands.

On their arrival they went to court, and the demon said to his liberator:

"I am going to put myself into the body of the princess, who is extremely beloved by her father, and I shall give her pains that no doctor will be able to cure; then you present yourself and offer to cure her, demanding for your recompense four dollars daily, and your discharge. I will then leave her to you, and our accounts will be settled."

Everything happened as arranged and foreseen by the demon, but Briones did not wish to let go his hold of the tail, and he said:

"Well devised, sir, but four dollars are a ransom unworthy of you, of me, and of the service that we have undertaken. Find some method of showing yourself more generous. To do this will give you honour in the world, where, pardon my frankness, you do not enjoy the best of characters."

"Would that I could get rid of you!" said the demon to himself, "but I am so weak and so numbed that I am not able to go alone. I must have patience! that which men call a virtue. Oh, now I understand why so many fall into my power for not having practised it. Forward then for Naples, for it is necessary to submit in order to liberate my tail. I must go and submit to the arbitration of fate for the satisfaction of this new demand."

Everything succeeded according to his wish. The princess of Naples fell a victim to convulsive pains and took to her bed. The king was greatly afflicted. Briones presented himself with all the arrogance his knowledge that he would receive the demon's aid could give him. The king was willing to make use of his services, but stipulated that if within three days he had not cured the princess, as he confidently promised to, he should be hanged. Briones, certain of a favourable result, did not raise the slightest objection.

Unfortunately, the demon heard this arrangement made, and gave a leap of delight at seeing within his hands the means of avenging himself.

The demon's leap caused the princess such pain that she begged them to take the doctor away.

The following day this scene was repeated. Briones then knew that the demon was at the bottom of it, and intended to let him be hanged. But Briones was not a man to lose his head.

On the third day, when the pretended doctor arrived, they were erecting the gallows in front of the very palace door. As he entered the princess's apartment, the invalid's pains were redoubled and she began to cry out that they should put an end to that impostor.

"I have not exhausted all my resources yet," said Briones gravely, "deign, your Royal Highness, to wait a little while." He then went out of the room and gave orders in the princess's name that all the bells of the city should be rung.

When he returned to the royal apartment, the demon, who has a mortal hatred of the sound of bells, and is, moreover, inquisitive, asked Briones what the bells were ringing for.

"They are ringing," responded the soldier, "because of the arrival of your mother-in-law, whom I have ordered to be summoned."

Scarcely had the demon heard that his mother-in-law had arrived, than he flew away with such rapidity that not even a sun's ray could have caught him. Proud as a peacock, Briones was left in victorious possession of the field.

The Generous Gambler

Charles Baudelaire

This worshipper and singer of Satan shared his American confrere's predilection for the devil. He found his models in the
diabolical scenes of Edgar Allan Poe, whom he interpreted
to the Latin world. "Baudelaire," said Theophile Gautier, his
master and friend, "had a singular prepossession for the devil
as a tempter, in whom he saw a dragon who hurried him into
sin, infamy, crime, and perversity." To Baudelaire, the trier of
men's souls, the Tempter, was as real a person as he was to Job.
He believed that the devil had a great deal to do with the
direction of human destinies. *"C'est le Diable qui tient les fils
qui nous remuent!"* Men are mere puppets in the hands of the
devil. "Baudelaire's motto," as Mr. James Huneker has well remarked, "might be the reverse of Browning's lines: The Devil
is in his heaven. All's wrong with the world."

Baudelaire's devil is a dandy and a boulevardier with
wings. Each author, it has been said, creates the devil in his
own image.

The greatest boon which Satan could offer Baudelaire was
to free him from that great modern monster, *Ennui*, which
selects as its prey the most highly gifted natures. The boredom
of life—this was, indeed, as this unhappy poet admits, the
source of all his maladies and of all his miseries. He called it
the "foulest of vices" and hoped to escape from it "by dreaming of the superlative emotional adventure, by indulging in
infinite, indeterminate desire" (Irving Babbit). His preface
to the *Flowers of Evil*, in which he addresses the reader, ends
with the following statement in regard to the nature of this

modern beast of prey: "Among the jackals, the panthers, the hounds, the apes, the scorpions, the vultures, the serpents—the yelling, howling, growling, grovelling monsters which form the foul menagerie of our vices—there is one which is the most foul, the most wicked, the most unclean of all. This vice, although it uses neither extravagant gestures nor makes a great outcry, would willingly make a ruin of the earth, and swallow up all the world in a yawn. This is *Ennui!* who, with his eye moistened by an involuntary tear, dreams of scaffolds while smoking his hookah. Thou knowest him, this delicate monster, hypocritical reader, my like, my brother!"

In Gorky's story "The Devil" the devil himself suffers from *ennui*.

But Baudelaire believed he had good reason to doubt Satan's word, and, therefore, prayed to the Lord to make the devil keep his promise to him. He had little faith in the father of lies. In his book called *Artificial Paradises* (1860) Baudelaire expressed the thought that the devil would say to the eaters of *hashish*, the smokers of *opium*, as he did in the olden days to our first parents, "If you taste of the fruit, you will be as the gods," and that the devil no more kept his word with them than he did with Adam and Eve, for the next day, the god, tempted, weakened, enervated, descended even lower than the beast.

The representation of the devil in the shape of a he-goat goes back to far antiquity. Goat-formed deities and spirits of the woods existed in the religions of India, Assyria, Greece and Egypt. The Assyrian god was often associated with the goat, which was supposed to possess the qualities for which he was worshipped. The he-goat was also the sacred beast of Donar or Thor, who was brought to Scandinavia by the Phoenicians. (On the relation of satyrs to goats see also James G. Frazer, *The Golden Bough*, vol. VIII.) At the revels on the Blocksberg Satan always appeared as a black buck.

Le bon diable, which is a favourite phrase in France, points to his simplicity of mind rather than generosity of spirit. It generally expresses the half-contemptuous pity with which the giants, these huge beings with weak minds, were regarded.

The idea that Satan would gamble for a human soul is of mediaeval origin and may have been taken by Baudelaire from Gerard de Nerval, who in his mystery play *Le Prince des Sots* (1830) has the devil play at dice with an angel, with human souls as stakes. As a dice-player Satan resembles Wuotan. Mr. H. G. Wells in *The Undying Fire* (1919) has Diabolus play chess with the Deity in Heaven.

The devil in this story falls back into speaking Hebrew when the days of his ancient celestial glory are brought back to his mind. In Louis Menard's *Le Diable au Cafe* the devil calls Hebrew a dead language, and as a modern prefers to be called by the French equivalent of his original Hebrew name. In the Middle Ages the devil's favourite language was Latin. Marlowe's Mephistopheles also speaks this language. Satan is known to be a linguist. "It is the Devil by his several languages," said Ben Jonson.

According to popular belief the devil is a learned scholar and a profound thinker. He has all science, philosophy, and theology at his tongue's end.

The Shavian devil in contradistinction to the Baudelairian fiend does bitterly complain that he is so little appreciated on earth. Walter Scott's devil (in "Wandering Willie's Tale," 1824) also complains that he has been "sair miscaa'd in the world."

The preacher to whom our author refers is the Jesuit Ravignan, who declared that the disbelief in the devil was one of the most cunning devices of the great enemy himself. (*La plus grande force du diable, c'est d'etre parvenu a se faire nier.*) Baudelaire's disciple J. K. Huysmans similarly expresses in his novel *La-Bas* (1891) the view that "the greatest power of Satan lies in the fact that he gets men to deny him." The devil mocks at this theological dictum in Pierre Veber's story "L'Homme qui Vendit son ame au Diable" (1918). In Perkins's story "The Devil-Puzzlers" the devil expresses his satisfaction over his success in this regard.

The story "The Generous Gambler" first appeared in the *Figaro* of February, 1864, was reprinted under the title of "Le Diable" in the *Revue du Dix-Neuvieme Siecle* of June, 1866, and was finally included in *Poemes en Prose*.

Yesterday, across the crowd of the boulevard, I found myself touched by a mysterious Being I had always desired to know, and who I recognized immediately, in spite of the fact that I had never seen him. He had, I imagined, in himself, relatively as to me, a similar desire, for he gave me, in passing, so significant a sign in his eyes that I hastened to obey him. I followed him attentively, and soon I descended behind him into a subterranean dwelling, astonishing to me as a vision, where shone a luxury of which none of the actual houses in Paris could give me an approximate example. It seemed to me singular that I had passed so often that prodigious retreat without having discovered the entrance. There reigned an exquisite, an almost stifling atmosphere, which made one forget almost instantaneously all the fastidious horrors of life; there I breathed a sombre sensuality, like that of opium-smokers when, set on the shore of an enchanted island, over which shone an eternal afternoon, they felt born in them, to the soothing sounds of melodious cascades, the desire of never again seeing their households, their women, their children, and of never again being tossed on the decks of ships by storms.

There were there strange faces of men and women, gifted with so fatal a beauty that I seemed to have seen them years ago and in countries which I failed to remember, and which inspired in me that curious sympathy and that equally curious sense of fear that I usually discover in unknown aspects. If I wanted to define in some fashion or other the singular expression of their eyes, I would say that never had I seen such magic radiance more energetically expressing the horror of *ennui* and of desire—of the immortal desire of feeling themselves alive.

As for mine host and myself, we were already, as we sat down, as perfect friends as if we had always known each other. We drank immeasurably of all sorts of extraordinary wines, and—a thing not less bizarre—it seemed to me, after several hours, that I was no more intoxicated than he was.

However, gambling, this superhuman pleasure, had cut, at various intervals, our copious libations, and I ought to say that I had gained and lost my soul, as we were playing, with an heroical carelessness and light-heartedness. The soul is so invisible a thing, often useless and sometimes so troublesome, that I did not experience, as to this loss, more than that kind of emotion I might have, had I lost my visiting card in the street.

We spent hours in smoking cigars, whose incomparable savour and perfume give to the soul the nostalgia of unknown delights and sights, and, intoxicated by all these spiced sauces, I dared, in an access of familiarity which did not seem to displease him, to cry, as I lifted a glass filled to the brim with wine: "To your immortal health, Old He-Goat!"

We talked of the universe, of its creation and of its future destruction; of the leading ideas of the century—that is to say, of Progress and Perfectibility—and, in general, of all kinds of human infatuations. On this subject his Highness was inexhaustible in his irrefutable jests, and he expressed himself with a splendour of diction and with a magnificence in drollery such as I have never found in any of the most famous conversationalists of our age. He explained to me the absurdity of different philosophies that had so far taken possession of men's brains, and deigned even to take me in confidence in regard to certain fundamental principles, which I am not inclined to share with any one.

He complained in no way of the evil reputation under which he lived, indeed, all over the world, and he assured me that he himself was of all living beings the most interested in the destruction of *Superstition*, and he avowed to me that he had been afraid, relatively as to his proper power, once only, and that was on the day when he had heard a preacher, more subtle than the rest of the human herd, cry in his pulpit: "My dear brethren, do not ever forget, when you hear the progress of lights praised, that the loveliest trick of the Devil is to persuade you that he does not exist!"

The memory of this famous orator brought us naturally on the subject of Academies, and my strange host declared to me that he didn't disdain, in many cases, to inspire the pens, the words, and the consciences of pedagogues, and that he almost always assisted in person, in spite of being invisible, at all the scientific meetings.

Encouraged by so much kindness I asked him if he had any news of God—who has not his hours of impiety?—especially as the old friend of the Devil. He said to me, with a shade of unconcern united with a deeper shade of sadness: "We salute each other when we meet." But, for the rest, he spoke in Hebrew.

It is uncertain if his Highness has ever given so long an audience to a simple mortal, and I feared to abuse it.

Finally, as the dark approached shivering, this famous personage, sung by so many poets, and served by so many philosophers who work for his glory's sake without being aware of it, said to me: "I want you to remember me always, and to prove to you that I—of whom one says so much evil—am often enough *bon diable*, to make use of one of your vulgar locutions. So as to make up for the irremediable loss that you have made of your soul, I shall give you back the stake you ought to have gained, if your fate had been fortunate—that is to say, the possibility of solacing and of conquering, during your whole life, this bizarre affection of *ennui*, which is the source of all your maladies and of all your miseries. Never a desire shall be formed by you that I will not aid you to realize; you will reign over your vulgar equals; money and gold and diamonds, fairy palaces, shall come to seek you and shall ask you to accept them without your having made the least effort to obtain them; you can change your abode as often as you like; you shall have in your power all sensualities without lassitude, in lands where the climate is always hot, and where the women are as scented as the flowers." With this he rose up and said goodbye to me with a charming smile.

If it had not been for the shame of humiliating myself before so immense an assembly, I might have voluntarily fallen at the feet of this generous Gambler, to thank him for his unheard-of munificence. But, little by little, after I had left him, an incurable defiance entered into me; I dared no longer believe in so prodigious a happiness; and as I went to bed, making over again my nightly prayer by means of all that remained in me in the matter of faith, I repeated in my slumber: "My God, my Lord, my God! Do let the Devil keep his word with me!"

The Three Low Masses:
a Christmas Story

Alphonse Daudet

Daudet and Maupassant furnish the best proof of the assertion made in the Introduction to this book that even the Naturalists who, as a rule, disdained the fantastic plots of the Romanticists, whose imagination was rigorously earth-bound, felt themselves nevertheless attracted by devil-lore. Although most of Daudet's subjects are chosen from contemporary French life, this short-story treats a devil-legend of the seventeenth century. This story as "The Pope's Mule" and "The Elixir of the Reverend Pere Gaucher" obviously has no other object but to poke fun at the Catholic Church. It belongs to the literary type known as the Satirical Supernatural.

This story is characteristic of Daudet's art, containing as it does all of his delicacy and daintiness of pathos, of raillery, of humour. It originally appeared in that delightful group of stories *Lettres de Mon Moulin* (1869).

The horns and tail of his Satanic majesty peep out as vividly in this book as the disguised devils in Ingoldsby's *Legend of the North Countrie*.

Although hating all men, the devil has a special hatred for the priests, and he delights in bringing them to fall. Satan loathes the priests, because, as Anatole France says, they teach that "God takes delight in seeing His creatures languish in penitence and abstain from His most precious gifts" (*Les Dieux ont soif*).

It is evident from this story that the popular belief that the devil avoids holy edifices is not based on facts. Here the devil not only enters the church, but even performs the duties of a sacristan at the foot of the altar. According to mediaeval tradition the devil has his agents even in the churches. In the administration of hell where the tasks are carefully parcelled out among the thousands of imps, the church has been assigned to the fiend with the poetic name of Tutevillus. It is his duty to attend all services in order to listen to the gossips and to write down every word they say. After death these women are entertained in hell with their own speeches, which this diabolical church clerk has carefully noted down. Tradition has it that one fine Sunday this demon was sitting in a church on a beam, on which he held himself fast by his feet and his tail, right over two village gossips, who chattered so much during the Blessed Mass that he soon filled every corner of the parchment on both sides. Poor Tutevillus worked so hard that the sweat ran in great drops down his brow, and he was ready to sink with exhaustion. But the gossips ceased not to sin with their tongues, and he had no fair parchment left whereon to record their foul words. So having considered for a little while, he grasped one end of the roll with his teeth and seized the other end with his claws and pulled so hard as to stretch the parchment. He tugged and tugged with all his strength, jerking back his head mightily at each tug, and at last giving such a fierce jerk that he suddenly lost his balance and fell head over heels from the beam to the floor of the church. (From "The Vision of Saint Simon of Blewberry" in F. O. Mann's collection of mediaeval tales.)

1

"Two truffled turkeys, Garrigou?"

"Yes, your reverence, two magnificent turkeys, stuffed with truffles. I should know something about it, for I myself helped to fill them. One would have said their skin would crack as they were roasting, it is that stretched—"

"Jesu-Maria! I who like truffles so much!—Quick, give me my surplice, Garrigou—And have you seen anything else in the kitchen besides the turkeys?"

"Yes, all kinds of good things—Since noon, we have done nothing but pluck pheasants, hoopoes, barn-fowls, and woodcocks. Feathers were flying about all over—Then they have brought eels, gold carp, and trout out of the pond, besides—"

"What size were the trout, Garrigou?"

"As big as that, your reverence—Enormous!"

"Oh heavens! I think I see them—Have you put the wine in the vessels?"

"Yes, your reverence, I have put the wine in the vessels—But la! it is not to be compared to what you will drink presently, when the midnight mass is over. If you only saw that in the dining hall of the chateau! The decanters are all full of wines glowing with every colour!—And the silver plate, the chased *epergnes*, the flowers, the lustres!—Never will such another midnight repast be seen. The noble marquis has invited all the lords of the neighbourhood. At least forty of you will sit down to table, without reckoning the farm bailiff and the notary—Oh, how lucky is your reverence to be one of them!—After a mere sniff of those fine turkeys, the scent of truffles follows me everywhere—Yum!"

"Come now, come now, my child. Let us keep from the sin of gluttony, on the night of the Nativity especially—Be quick and light the wax-tapers and ring the first bell for the mass; for it's nearly midnight and we must not be behind time."

This conversation took place on a Christmas night in the year of grace one thousand six hundred and something, between the Reverend Dom Balaguere (formerly Prior of the Barnabites, now paid chaplain of the Lords of Trinquelague), and his little clerk Garrigou, or at least him whom he took for his little clerk Garrigou, for you must know that the devil had on that night assumed the round face and soft features of the young sacristan, in order the more effectually to lead the reverend father into temptation, and make him commit the dreadful sin of gluttony. Well then, while the supposed Garrigou (hum!) was with all his might making the bells of the baronial chapel chime out, his reverence was putting on his chasuble in the little sacristy of the *chateau*; and with his mind already agitated by all these gastronomic descriptions, he kept saying to himself as he was robing:

"Roasted turkeys,—golden carp,—trout as big as that!—"

Out of doors, the soughing night wind was carrying abroad the music of the bells, and with this, lights began to make their appearance on the dark sides of Mount Ventoux, on the summit of which rose the ancient towers of Trinquelague. The lights were borne by the families of the tenant farmers, who were coming to hear the midnight mass at the *chateau*. They were scaling the hill in groups of five or six together, and singing; the father in front carrying a lantern, and the women wrapped up in large brown cloaks, beneath which their little children snuggled and sheltered. In spite of the cold and the lateness of the hour these good folks were marching blithely along, cheered by the thought that after the mass was over there would be, as always in former years, tables set for them down in the kitchens. Occasionally the glass windows in some lord's carriage, preceded by torch-bearers, would glisten in the moon-light on the rough ascent; or perhaps a mule would jog by with tinkling bells, and by the light of the misty lanterns the tenants would recognize their bailiff and would salute him as he passed with:

"Good evening, Master Arnoton."

"Good evening. Good evening, my friend."

The night was clear, and the stars were twinkling with frost; the north wind was nipping, and at times a fine small hail, that slipped off one's garments without wetting them, faithfully maintained the tradition of Christmas being white with snow. On the summit of the hill, as the goal towards which all were wending, gleamed the chateau, with its enormous mass of towers and gables, and its chapel steeple rising into the blue-black sky. A multitude of little lights were twinkling, coming, going, and moving about at all the windows; they looked like the sparks one sees running about in the ashes of burnt paper.

After you had passed the drawbridge and the postern gate, it was necessary, in order to reach the chapel, to cross the first court, which was full of carriages, footmen and sedan chairs, and was quite illuminated by the blaze of torches and the glare of the kitchen fires. Here were heard the click of turnspits, the rattle of sauce-pans, the clash of glasses and silver plate in the commotion attending the preparation of the feast; while over all rose a warm vapour smelling pleasantly of roast meat, piquant herbs, and complex sauces, and which seemed to say to the farmers, as well as to the chaplain and to the bailiff, and to everybody:

"What a good midnight repast we are going to have after the mass!"

2

Ting-a-ring!—a—ring!

The midnight mass is beginning in the chapel of the *chateau*, which is a cathedral in miniature, with groined and vaulted roofs, oak wood-work as high as the walls, expanded draperies, and tapers all aglow. And what a lot of people! What grand dresses! First of all, seated in the carved stalls that line the choir, is the Lord of Trinquelague in a coat of salmon-coloured silk, and about him are ranged all the noble lords who have been invited.

On the opposite side, on velvet-covered praying-stools, the old dowager marchioness in flame-coloured brocade, and the youthful Lady of Trinquelague wearing a lofty head-dress of plaited lace in the newest fashion of the French court, have taken their places. Lower down, dressed in black, with punctilious wigs, and shaven faces, like two grave notes among the gay silks and the figured damasks, are seen the bailiff, Thomas Arnoton, and the notary Master Ambroy. Then come the stout *major-domos*, the pages, the horsemen, the stewards, Dame Barbara, with all her keys hanging at her side on a real silver ring. At the end, on the forms, are the lower class, the female servants, the cotter farmers and their families; and lastly, down there, near the door, which they open and shut very carefully, are *messieurs* the scullions, who enter in the interval between two sauces, to take a little whiff of mass; and these bring the smell of the repast with them into the church, which now is in high festival and warm from the number of lighted tapers.

Is it the sight of their little white caps that so distracts the celebrant? Is it not rather Garrigou's bell? that mad little bell which is shaken at the altar foot with an infernal impetuosity that seems all the time to be saying: "Come, let us make haste, make haste—The sooner we shall have finished, the sooner shall we be at table." The fact is that every time this devil's bell tinkles the chaplain forgets his mass, and thinks of nothing but the midnight repast. He fancies he sees the cooks bustling about, the stoves glowing with forge-like fires, the two magnificent turkeys, filled, crammed, marbled with truffles—

Then again he sees, passing along, files of little pages carrying dishes enveloped in tempting vapours, and with them he enters the great hall now prepared for the feast. Oh delight! there is the immense table all laden and luminous, peacocks adorned with their feathers, pheasants spreading out their reddish-brown wings, ruby-coloured decanters, pyramids of fruit glowing amid green boughs, and those wonderful fish Garrigou (ah well, yes, Garrigou!) had mentioned, laid on a couch of fennel, with their pearly scales gleaming as if they had just come out of the water, and bunches of sweet-smelling herbs in their monstrous snouts. So clear is the vision of these marvels that it seems to Dom Balaguere that all these wondrous dishes are served before him on the embroidered altar-cloth, and two or three times instead of the *Dominus vobiscum*, he finds himself saying the *Benedicite*. Except these slight mistakes, the worthy man pronounces the service very conscientiously, without skipping a line, without omitting a genuflexion; and all goes tolerably well until the end of the first mass; for you know that on Christmas Day the same officiating priest must celebrate three consecutive masses.

"That's one done!" says the chaplain to himself with a sigh of relief; then, without losing a moment, he motioned to his clerk, or to him whom he supposed to be his clerk, and—

"*Ting-a-ring—Ting-a-ring, a-ring!*"

Now the second mass is beginning, and with it begins also Dom Balaguere's sin. "Quick, quick, let us make haste," Garrigou's bell cries out to him in its shrill little voice, and this time the unhappy celebrant, completely given over to the demon of gluttony, fastens upon the missal and devours its pages with the eagerness of his over-excited appetite. Frantically he bows down, rises up, merely indicates the sign of the cross and the genuflexions, and curtails all his gestures in order to get sooner finished. Scarcely has he stretched out his arms at the gospel, before he is striking his breast at the *Confiteor*. It is a contest between himself and the clerk as to who shall mumble the faster. Versicles and responses are hurried over and run one into another. The words, half pronounced, without opening the mouth, which would take up too much time, terminate in unmeaning murmurs.

"*Oremus ps—ps—ps—*"

"*Mea culpa—pa—pa—*"

Like vintagers in a hurry pressing grapes in the vat, these two paddle in the mass Latin, sending splashes in every direction.

"*Dom—scum!—*" says Balaguere.

"*Stutuo!*" replies Garrigou; and all the time the cursed little bell is tinkling there in their ears, like the jingles they put on post-horses to make them gallop fast. You may imagine at that speed a low mass is quickly disposed of.

"That makes two," says the chaplain quite panting; then without taking time to breathe, red and perspiring, he descends the altar steps and— "*Ting-a-ring!—Ting-a-ring!—*"

Now the third mass is beginning. There are but a few more steps to be taken to reach the dining-hall; but, alas! the nearer the midnight repast approaches the more does the unfortunate Balaguere feel himself possessed by mad impatience and gluttony. The vision becomes more distinct; the golden carps, the roasted turkeys are there, there!—He touches them,—he—oh heavens! The dishes are smoking, the wines perfume the air; and with furiously agitated clapper, the little bell is crying out to him:

"Quick, quick, quicker yet!"

But how could he go quicker? His lips scarcely move. He no longer pronounces the words;—unless he were to impose upon Heaven outright and trick it out of its mass—And that is precisely what he does, the unfortunate man!—From temptation to temptation; he begins by skipping a verse, then two. Then the epistle is too long—he does not finish it, skims over the gospel, passes before the *Credo* without going into it, skips the Pater, salutes the Preface from a distance, and by leaps and bounds thus hurls himself into eternal damnation, constantly followed by the vile Garrigou (*vade retro, Satanas!*), who seconds him with wonderful skill, sustains his chasuble, turns over the leaves two at a time, elbows the reading-desks, upsets the vessels, and is continually sounding the little bell louder and louder, quicker and quicker.

You should have seen the scared faces of all who were present, as they were obliged to follow this mass by mere mimicry of the priest, without hearing a word; some rise when others kneel, and sit down when the others are standing up, and all the phases of this singular service are mixed up together in the multitude of different attitudes presented by the worshippers on the benches—

"The *abbe* goes too fast—One can't follow him," murmured the old dowager, shaking her head-dress in confusion. Master Arnoton with great steel spectacles on his nose is searching in his prayer-book to find where the dickens they are. But at heart all these good folks, who themselves are thinking about feasting, are not sorry that the mass is going on at this post haste; and when Dom Balaguere with radiant face turns towards those present and cries with all his might: "*Ite, missa est,*" they all respond to him a "*Deo gratias*" in but one voice, and that as joyous and enthusiastic, as if they thought themselves already seated at the midnight repast and drinking the first toast.

3

Five minutes afterwards the crowd of nobles were sitting down in the great hall, with the chaplain in the midst of them. The *chateau*, illuminated from top to bottom, was resounding with songs, with shouts, with laughter, with uproar; and the venerable Dom Balaguere was thrusting his fork into the wing of a fowl, and drowning all remorse for his sin in streams of regal wine and the luscious juices of the viands. He ate and drank so much, the dear, holy man, that he died during the night of a terrible attack, without even having had time to repent; and then in the morning when he got to heaven, I leave you to imagine how he was received.

He was told to withdraw on account of his wickedness. His fault was so grievous that it effaced a whole lifetime of virtue— He had robbed them of a midnight mass—He should have to pay for it with three hundred, and he should not enter into Paradise until he had celebrated in his own chapel these three hundred Christmas masses in the presence of all those who had sinned with him and by his fault—

—And now this is the true legend of Dom Balaguere as it is related in the olive country. At the present time the *chateau* of Trinquelague no longer exists, but the chapel still stands on the top of Mount Ventoux, amid a cluster of green oaks. Its decayed door rattles in the wind, and its threshold is choked up with vegetation;

there are birds' nests at the corners of the altar, and in the recesses of the lofty windows, from which the stained glass has long ago disappeared. It seems, however, that every year at Christmas, a supernatural light wanders amid these ruins, and the peasants, in going to the masses and to the midnight repasts, see this phantom of a chapel illuminated by invisible tapers that burn in the open air, even in snow and wind. You may laugh at it if you like, but a vine-dresser of the place, named Garrigue, doubtless a descendant of Garrigou, declared to me that one Christmas night, when he was a little tipsy, he lost his way on the hill of Trinquelague; and this is what he saw—Till eleven o'clock, nothing. All was silent, motionless, inanimate. Suddenly, about midnight, a chime sounded from the top of the steeple, an old, old chime, which seemed as if it were ten leagues off. Very soon Garrigue saw lights flitting about, and uncertain shadows moving in the road that climbs the hill. They passed on beneath the chapel porch, and murmured:

"Good evening, Master Arnoton!"

"Good evening, good evening, my friends!"—

When all had entered, my vine-dresser, who was very courageous, silently approached, and when he looked through the broken door, a singular spectacle met his gaze. All those he had seen pass were seated round the choir, and in the ruined nave, just as if the old seats still existed. Fine ladies in brocade, with lace head-dresses; lords adorned from head to foot; peasants in flowered jackets such as our grandfathers had; all with an old, faded, dusty, tired look. From time to time the night birds, the usual inhabitants of the chapel, who were aroused by all these lights, would come and flit round the tapers, the flames of which rose straight and ill-defined, as if they were burning behind a veil; and what amused Garrigue very much was a certain personage with large steel spectacles, who was ever shaking his tall black wig, in which one of these birds was quite entangled, and kept itself upright by noiselessly flapping its wings—

At the farther end, a little old man of childish figure was on his knees in the middle of the choir, desperately shaking a clapperless and soundless bell, whilst a priest, clad in ancient gold, was coming and going before the altar, reciting prayers of which not a word was heard—Most certainly this was Dom Balaguere in the act of saying his third low mass.

Devil-Puzzlers

Frederick Beecher Perkins

Through Asmodeus the devil became associated with humour and gallantry. Asmodeus sharpened his wits in his conversations with the wisest of kings. It will be recalled that this demon was the familiar spirit of Solomon, whose throne, according to Jewish legend, he occupied for three years. Perhaps it was not Solomon after all but this diabolical usurper who gathered around himself a thousand wives. It is said that Asmodeus is as dangerous to women as Lilith is to men. He loves to decoy young girls in the shape of a handsome young man. His love for the beautiful Sarah is too well known to need any comment. He is a fastidious devil, and will not have the object of his passion subject to the embrace of any other mortal or immortal.

Reference is made by the author to Albert Reville's epitome of Georg Roskoff's *Geschichte des Teufels* (Leipzig, 1869), a standard work on the history of the devil. The review by this French Protestant first appeared in the *Revue des Deux Mondes* for 1870, and was translated into English the following year. A second edition appeared six years later. Roskoff's book, on the other hand, has never appeared in translation.

It is not easy to grasp the scholastic subtleties of mediaeval schoolmen. Dr. Ethel Brewster suggests the following interpretations: *An chimoera bombinans in vacuo devorat secundas intentiones.* Whether a demon buzzing in the air devours our good intentions. This will correspond to our saying that hell is paved with good intentions. *An averia carrucae capta in vetito nomio sint irreplegibilia.* Whether the carriers of a (bishop's) carriage caught in a forbidden district should be punished. We can well understand how even the devil might be puzzled by such questions.

Professor Brander Matthews aptly calls this story "diabolically philosophical."

It will not do at all to disbelieve in the existence of a personal devil. It is not so many years ago that one of our profoundest divines remarked with indignation upon such disbelief. "No such person?" cried the doctor with energy. "Don't tell me! I can hear his tail snap and crack about amongst the churches any day!"

And if the enemy is, in truth, still as vigorously active among the sons of God as he was in the days of Job (that is to say, in the time of Solomon, when, as the critics have found out, the Book of Job was written), then surely still more is he vigilant and sly in his tricks for foreclosing his mortgages upon the souls of the wicked.

And once more: still more than ever is his personal appearance probable in these latter days. The everlasting tooting of the wordy Cumming has proclaimed the end of all things for a quarter of a century; and he will surely see his prophecy fulfilled if he can only keep it up long enough. But, though we discredit the sapient Second-Adventist as to the precise occasion of the diabolic avatar, has there not been a strange coincidence between his noisy declarations, and other evidences of an approximation of the spiritual to the bodily sphere of life? Is not this same quarter of a century that of the Spiritists? Has it not witnessed the development of Od? And of clairvoyance? And have not the doctrines of ghosts, and re-appearances of the dead, and of messages from them, risen into a prominence entirely new, and into a coherence and semblance at least of fact and fixed law such as was never known before? Yea, verily. Of all times in the world's history, to reject out of one's beliefs either good spirits or bad, angelology or diabology, chief good being, or chief bad being, this is the most improper.

Dr. Hicok was trebly liable to the awful temptation, under which he had assuredly fallen, over and above the fact that he was a prig, which makes one feel the more glad that he was so handsomely come up with in the end; such a prig that everybody who knew him, invariably called him (when he wasn't by) Hicok-alorum. This charming surname had been conferred on him by a crazy old fellow with whom he once got into a dispute. Lunatics have the most awfully tricky ways of dodging out of pinches in reasoning; but Hicok knew too much to know *that*; and so he acquired his fine title to teach him one thing more.

Trebly liable, we said. The three reasons are,—

1. He was foreign-born.
2. He was a Scotchman.
3. He was a physician and surgeon.

The way in which these causes operated was as follows (I wish it were allowable to use Artemas Ward's curiously satisfactory vocable "thusly:" like Mrs. Wiggle's soothing syrup, it "supplies a real want"):

Being foreign-born, Dr. Hicok had not the unfailing moral stamina of a native American, and therefore was comparatively easily beset by sin. Being, secondly, a Scotchman, he was not only thoroughly conceited, with a conceit as immovable as the Bass Rock, just as other folks sometimes are, but, in particular, he was perfectly sure of his utter mastery of metaphysics, logic and dialectics, or, as he used to call it, with a snobbish Teutonicalization, *dialectic*. Now, in the latter two, the Scotch can do something, but in metaphysics they are simply imbecile; which quality, in the inscrutable providence of God, has been joined with an equally complete conviction of the exact opposite. Let not man, therefore, put those traits asunder—not so much by reason of any divine ordinance, as because no man in his senses would try to convince a Scotchman—or anybody else, for that matter.

Thirdly, he was a physician and surgeon; and gentlemen of this profession are prone to become either thoroughgoing materialists, or else implicit and extreme Calvinistic Presbyterians, "of the large blue kind." And they are, moreover, positive, hard-headed, bold, and self-confident. So they have good need to be. Did not Majendie say to his students, "Gentlemen, disease is a subject which physicians know nothing about"?

So the doctor both believed in the existence of a personal devil, and believed in his own ability to get the upper hand of that individual in a tournament of the wits. Ah, he learned better by terrible experience! The doctor was a dry-looking little chap, with sandy hair, a freckled face, small grey eyes, and absurd white eyebrows and eyelashes, which made him look as if he had finished off his toilet with just a light flourish from the dredging-box. He was erect of carriage, and of a prompt, ridiculous alertness of step and motion, very much like that of Major Wellington De Boots. And his face commonly wore a kind of complacent serenity such as the Hindus ascribe to Buddha. I know a little snappish dentist's-goods dealer up town, who might be mistaken for Hicok-alorum any day.

Well, well—what had the doctor done? Why—it will sound absurd, probably, to some unbelieving people—but really Dr. Hicok confessed the whole story to me himself: he had made a bargain with the Evil One! And indeed he was such an uncommonly disagreeable-looking fellow, that, unless on some such hypothesis, it is impossible to imagine how he could have prospered as he did. He gained patients, and cured them too; made money; invested successfully; bought a brown-stone front—a house, not a *wiglet*—then bought other real estate; began to put his name on charity subscription lists, and to be made vice-president of various things.

Chiefest of all,—it must have been by some superhuman aid that Dr. Hicok married his wife, the then and present Mrs. Hicok. Dear me! I have described the doctor easily enough. But how infinitely more difficult it is to delineate Beauty than the Beast: did you ever think of it? All I can say is, that she is a very lovely woman now; and she must have been, when the doctor married her, one of the loveliest creatures that ever lived—a lively, graceful, bright-eyed brunette, with thick fine long black hair, pencilled delicate eyebrows, little pink ears, thin high nose, great astonished brown eyes, perfect teeth, a little rosebud of a mouth, and a figure so extremely beautiful that nobody believed she did not pad—hardly even the artists who—those of them at least who work faithfully in the life-school—are the very best judges extant of truth in costume and personal beauty. But, furthermore, she was good, with the innocent unconscious goodness of a sweet little child; and of all feminine charms—even beyond her supreme grace of motion—she possessed the sweetest, the most resistless—a lovely voice; whose tones, whether in speech or song, were perfect in sweetness, and with a strange penetrating sympathetic quality and at the same time with the most wonderful half delaying completeness of articulation and modulation, as if she enjoyed the sound of her own music. No doubt she did; but it was unconsciously, like a bird. The voice was so sweet, the great loveliness and kindness of soul it expressed were so deep, that, like every exquisite beauty, it rayed forth a certain sadness within the pleasure it gave. It awakened infinite, indistinct emotions of beauty and perfection—infinite longings.

It's of no use to tell me that such a spirit—she really ought not to be noted so low down as amongst human beings—that such a spirit could have been made glad by becoming the yoke-fellow of Hicok-alorum, by influences exclusively human. No!—I don't believe it—I won't believe it—it can't be believed. I can't convince you, of course, for you don't know her; but if you did, along with the rest of the evidence, and if your knowledge was like mine, that from the testimony of my own eyes and ears and judgment—you would know, just as I do, that the doctor's possession of his wife was the key-stone of the arch of completed proof on which I found my absolute assertion that he had made that bargain.

He certainly had! A most characteristic transaction too; for while, after the usual fashion, it was agreed by the "party of the first part,"—*viz.*, Old Scratch—that Dr. Hicok should succeed in whatever he undertook during twenty years, and by the party of the second part, that at the end of that time the D—should fetch him in manner and form as is ordinarily provided, yet there was added a peculiar clause. This was, that, when the time came for the doctor to depart, he should be left entirely whole and unharmed, in mind, body, and estate, provided he could put to the Devil three consecutive questions, of which either one should be such that that cunning spirit could not solve it on the spot.

So for twenty years Dr. Hicok lived and prospered, and waxed very great. He did not gain one single pound avoirdupois however, which may perchance seem strange, but is the most natural thing in the world. Who ever saw a little, dry, wiry, sandy, freckled man, with white eyebrows, that did grow fat? And besides, the doctor spent all his leisure time in hunting up his saving trinity of questions; and hard study, above all for such a purpose, is as sure an anti-fattener as Banting.

He knew the Scotch metaphysicians by heart already, *ex-officio* as it were; but he very early gave up the idea of trying to fool the Devil with such mud-pie as that. Yet be it understood, that he found cause to except Sir William Hamilton from the muddle-headed crew. He chewed a good while, and pretty hopefully, upon the Quantification of the Predicate; but he had to give that up too, when he found out how small and how dry a meat rattled within the big, noisy nut-shell. He read Saint Thomas Aquinas, and Peter Dens, and a cartload more of old casuists, Romanist and Protestant.

He exhausted the learning of the Development Theory. He studied and experimented up to the existing limits of knowledge on the question of the Origin of Life, and then poked out alone, as much farther as he could, into the ineffable black darkness that is close at the end of our noses on that, as well as most other questions. He hammered his way through the whole controversy on the Freedom of the Will. He mastered the whole works of Mrs. Henry C. Carey on one side, and of two hundred and fifty English capitalists and American college professors on the other, on the question of Protection or Free Trade. He made, with vast pains, an extensive collection of the questions proposed at debating societies and college-students' societies with long Greek names. The last effort was a failure. Dr. Hicok had got the idea, that, from the spontaneous activity of so many free young geniuses, many wondrous and suggestive thoughts would be born. Having, however, tabulated his collection, he found, that, among all these innumerable gymnasia of intellect, there were only seventeen questions debated! The doctor read me a curious little memorandum of his conclusions on this unexpected fact, which will perhaps be printed some day.

He investigated many other things too; for a sharp-witted little Presbyterian Scotch doctor, working to cheat the Devil out of his soul, can accomplish an amazing deal in twenty years. He even went so far as to take into consideration mere humbugs; for, if he could cheat the enemy with a humbug, why not? The only pain in that case, would be the mortification of having stooped to an inadequate adversary—a foeman unworthy of his steel. So he weighed such queries as the old scholastic *brocard, An chimoera bombinans in vacuo devorat secundas intentiones?* and that beautiful moot point wherewith Sir Thomas More silenced the challenging schoolmen of Bruges, *An averia carrucae capta in vetito nomio sint irreplegibilia?*

He glanced a little at the subject of conundrums; and among the chips from his workshop is a really clever theory of conundrums. He has a classification and discussion of them, all his own, and quite ingenious and satisfactory, which divides them into answerable and unanswerable, and, under each of these, into resemblant and differential.

For instance: let the four classes be distinguished with the initials of those four terms, A. R., A. D., U. R., and U. D.; you will find that the Infinite Possible Conundrum (so to speak) can always be reduced under one of those four heads. Using symbols, as they do in discussing syllogism—indeed, by the way, a conundrum is only a jocular variation in the syllogism, an intentional fallacy for fun (read Whately's *Logic*, Book III., and see if it isn't so)—using symbols, I say, you have these four "figures:"

1. (A. R.) Why is A like B? (answerable): as, Why is a gentleman who gives a young lady a young dog, like a person who rides rapidly up hill? A. Because he gives a gallop up (gal-a-pup).

Sub-variety; depending upon a violation of something like the "principle of excluded middle," a very fallacy of a fallacy; such as the ancient "nigger-minstrel!" case, Why is an elephant like a brick? A. Because neither of them can climb a tree.

2. (A. D.) Why is A *unlike* B? (answerable) usually put thus: What is the difference between A and B? (Figure I., if worded in the same style, would become: What is the similarity between A and B?): as, What is the difference between the old United-States Bank and the Fulton Ferry-boat signals in thick weather? A. One is a fog whistle, and the other is a Whig fossil.

3. (U. R.) Why is A like B? (unanswerable): as Charles Lamb's well-known question, Is that your own hare, or a wig?

4. (U. D.) Why is A *unlike* B? (unanswerable): i.e., What is the difference, &c, as, What is the difference between a facsimile and a sick family; or between hydraulics and raw-hide licks?

But let me not diverge too far into frivolity. All the hopefully difficult questions Dr. Hicok set down and classified. He compiled a set of rules on the subject, and indeed developed a whole philosophy of it, by which he struck off, as soluble, questions or classes of them. Some he thought out himself; others were now and then answered in some learned book, that led the way through the very heart of one or another of his biggest mill-stones.

So it was really none too much time that he had; and, in truth, he did not actually decide upon his three questions, until just a week before the fearful day when he was to put them.

It came at last, as every day of reckoning surely comes; and Dr. Hicok, memorandum in hand, sat in his comfortable library about three o'clock on one beautiful warm summer afternoon, as pale as a sheet, his heart thumping away like Mr. Krupp's biggest steam-hammer at Essen, his mouth and tongue parched and feverish, a pitcher of cold water at hand from which he sipped and sipped, though it seemed as if his throat repelled it into "the globular state," or dispersed it into steam, as red-hot iron does. Around him were the records of the vast army of doubters and quibblers in whose works he had been hunting, as a traveller labours through a jungle, for the deepest doubts, the most remote inquiries.

Sometimes, with that sort of hardihood, rather than reason, which makes a desperate man try to believe by his will what he longs to know to be true, Dr. Hicok would say to himself, "I know I've got him!" And then his heart would seem to fall out of him, it sank so suddenly, and with so deadly a faintness, as the other side of his awful case loomed before him, and he thought, "But if—?" He would not finish *that* question; he could not. The furthest point to which he could bring himself was that of a sort of icy outer stiffening of acquiescence in the inevitable. There was a ring at the street-door. The servant brought in a card, on a silver salver.

Mr. Apollo Lyon

"Show the gentleman in," said the doctor. He spoke with difficulty; for the effort to control his own nervous excitement was so immense an exertion, that he hardly had the self-command and muscular energy even to articulate.

The servant returned, and ushered into the library a handsome, youngish, middle-aged and middle-sized gentleman, pale, with large melancholy black eyes, and dressed in the most perfect and quiet style.

The doctor arose, and greeted his visitor with a degree of steadiness and politeness that did him the greatest credit.

"How do you do, sir?" he said: "I am happy"—but it struck him that he wasn't, and he stopped short.

"Very right, my dear sir," replied the guest, in a voice that was musical but perceptibly sad, or rather patient in tone. "Very right; how hollow those formulas are! I hate all forms and ceremonies! But I am glad to see *you*, doctor. Now, that is really the fact."

No doubt! "Divil doubt him!" as an Irishman would say. So is a cat glad to see a mouse in its paw. Something like these thoughts arose in the doctor's mind; he smiled as affably as he could, and requested the visitor to be seated.

"Thanks!" replied he, and took the chair which the doctor moved up to the table for him. He placed his hat and gloves on the table. There was a brief pause, as might happen if any two friends sat down at their ease for a chat on matters and things in general. The visitor turned over a volume or two that lay on the table.

"*The Devil*," he read from one of them; "*His Origin, Greatness, and Decadence.* By the Rev. A. Reville, D.D."

"Ah!" he commented quietly. "A Frenchman, I observe. If it had been an Englishman, I should fancy he wrote the book for the sake of the rhyme in the title. Do you know, doctor, I fancy that incredulity of his will substitute one dash for the two periods in the reverend gentleman's degree! I know no one greater condition of success in some lines of operation, than to have one's existence thoroughly disbelieved in."

The doctor forced himself to reply: "I hardly know how I came to have the book here. Yet he does make out a pretty strong case. I confess I would like to be certified that he is right. Suppose you allow yourself to be convinced?" And the poor fellow grinned: it couldn't be called a smile.

"Why, really, I'll look into it. I've considered the point though, not that I'm sure I could choose. And you know, as the late J. Milton very neatly observed, one would hardly like to lose one's intellectual being, 'though full of pain;'" and he smiled, not unkindly but sadly, and then resumed: "A Bible too. Very good edition. I remember seeing it stated that a professional person made it his business to find errors of the press in one of the Bible Society's editions—this very one, I think; and the only one he could discover was a single 'wrong font.' Very accurate work—very!"

He had been turning over the leaves indifferently as he spoke, and laid the volume easily back. "Curious old superstition that," he remarked, "that certain personages were made uncomfortable by this work!" And he gave the doctor a glance, as much as to ask, in the most delicate manner in the world, "Did you put that there to scare me with?"

I think the doctor blushed a little. He had not really expected, you know,—still, in case there should be any prophylactic influence—? No harm done, in any event; and that was precisely the observation made by the guest.

"No harm done, my dear fellow!" he said, in his calm, quiet, musical voice. No good, either, I imagine they both of them added to themselves.

There is an often repeated observation, that people under the pressure of an immeasurable misery or agony seem to take on a preternaturally sharp vision for minute details, such as spots in the carpet, and sprigs in the wall-paper, threads on a sleeve, and the like. Probably the doctor felt this influence. He had dallied a little, too, with the crisis; and so did his visitor—from different motives, no doubt; and, as he sat there, his eye fell on the card that had just been brought to him.

"I beg your pardon," he said; "but might I ask a question about your card?"

"Most certainly, doctor: what is it?"

"Why—it's always a liberty to ask questions about a gentleman's name, and we Scotchmen are particularly sensitive on the point; but I have always been interested in the general subject of *patronomatology.*"

The other, by a friendly smile and a deprecating wave of the hand, renewed his welcome to the doctor's question.

"Well, it's this: How did you come to decide upon that form of name—Mr. Apollo Lyon?"

"Oh! just a little fancy of mine. It's a newly-invented variable card, I believe they call it. There's a temporary ink arrangement. It struck me it was liable to abuse in case of an assumption of *aliases*; but perhaps that's none of my business. You can easily take off the upper name, and another one comes out underneath. I'm always interested in inventions. See."

And as the text, "But they have sought out many inventions," passed through Dr. Hicok's mind, the other drew forth a white handkerchief, and, rubbing the card in a careless sort of way, laid it down before the doctor. Perhaps the strain on the poor doctor's nerves was unsteadying him by this time: he may not have seen right; but he seemed to see only one name, as if compounded from the former two.

Apollyon

And it seemed to be in red ink instead of black; and the lines seemed to creep and throb and glow, as if the red were the red of fire, instead of vermilion. But red is an extremely trying colour to the eyes. However, the doctor, startled as he was, thought best not to raise any further queries, and only said, perhaps with some difficulty, "Very curious, I'm sure!"

"Well, doctor," said Mr. Lyon, or whatever his name was, "I don't want to hurry you, but I suppose we might as well have our little business over?"

"Why, yes. I suppose you wouldn't care to consider any question of compromises or substitutes?"

"I fear it's out of the question, really," was the reply, most kindly in tone, but with perfect distinctness.

There was a moment's silence. It seemed to Dr. Hicok as if the beating of his heart must fill the room, it struck so heavily, and the blood seemed to surge with so loud a rush through the carotids up past his ears. "Shall I be found to have gone off with a rush of blood to the head?" he thought to himself. But—it can very often be done by a resolute effort—he gathered himself together as it were, and with one powerful exertion mastered his disordered nerves. Then he lifted his memorandum, gave one glance at the sad, calm face opposite him, and spoke.

"You know they're every once in a while explaining a vote, as they call it, in Congress. It don't make any difference, I know; but it seems to me as if I should put you more fully in possession of my meaning, if I should just say a word or two, about the reasons for my selection."

The visitor bowed with his usual air of pleasant acquiescence.

167

"I am aware," said Dr. Hicok, "that my selection would seem thoroughly commonplace to most people. Yet nobody knows better than you do, my dear sir, that the oldest questions are the newest. The same vitality which is so strong in them, as to raise them as soon as thought begins, is infinite, and maintains them as long as thought endures. Indeed, I may say to you frankly, that it is by no means on novelty, but rather on antiquity, that I rely."

The doctor's hearer bowed with an air of approving interest. "Very justly reasoned," he observed. The doctor went on—

"I have, I may say—and under the circumstances I shall not be suspected of conceit—made pretty much the complete circuit of unsolved problems. They class exactly as those questions do which we habitually reckon as solved: under the three subjects to which they relate—God, the intelligent creation, the unintelligent creation. Now, I have selected my questions accordingly—one for each of those divisions. Whether I have succeeded in satisfying the conditions necessary will appear quickly. But you see that I have not stooped to any quibbling, or begging either. I have sought to protect myself by the honourable use of a masculine reason."

"Your observations interest me greatly," remarked the audience. "Not the less so, that they are so accurately coincident with my own habitual lines of thought—at least, so far as I can judge from what you have said. Indeed, suppose you had called upon me to help you prepare insoluble problems. I was bound, I suppose, to comply to the best of my ability; and, if I had done so, those statements of yours are thus far the very preface I supplied—I beg your pardon—should have supplied—you with. I fancy I could almost state the questions. Well?"

All this was most kind and complimentary; but somehow it did not encourage the doctor in the least. He even fancied that he detected a sneer, as if his interlocutor had been saying, "Flutter away, old bird! That was *my bait* that you have been feeding on: you're safe enough; it is my net that holds you."

"*First Question*," said Dr. Hicok, with steadiness: "Reconcile the foreknowledge and the fore-ordination of God with the free will of man?"

"I thought so, of course," remarked the other. Then he looked straight into the doctor's keen little grey eyes with his deep melancholy black ones, and raised his slender fore-finger. "Most readily. The reconciliation is *your own conscience,* doctor! Do what you know to be right, and you will find that there is nothing to reconcile—that you and your Maker have no debates to settle!"

The words were spoken with a weighty solemnity and conviction that were even awful. The doctor had a conscience, though he had found himself practically forced, for the sake of success, to use a good deal of constraint with it—in fact, to lock it up, as it were, in a private mad-house, on an unfounded charge of lunacy. But the obstinate thing would not die, and would not lose its wits; and now all of a sudden, and from the very last quarter where it was to be expected, came a summons before whose intensity of just requirement no bolts could stand. The doctor's conscience walked out of her prison, and came straight up to the field of battle, and said—

"Give up the first question."

And he obeyed.

"I confess it," he said. "But how could I have expected a great basic truth both religiously and psychologically so, from—from *you?*"

"Ah! my dear sir," was the reply, "you have erred in *that* line of thought, exactly as many others have. The truth is one and the same, to God, man, and devil."

"*Second Question,*" said Dr. Hicok. "Reconcile the development theory, connection of natural selection and sexual relation, with the responsible immortality of the soul."

"Unquestionably," assented the other, as if to say, "Just as I expected."

"No theory of creation has any logical connection with any doctrine of immortality. What was the motive of creation?—*that* would be a question! If you had asked me *that!* But the question, 'Where did men come from?' has no bearing on the question, 'Have they any duties now that they are here?' The two are reconciled, because they do not differ. You can't state any inconsistency between a yard measure and a fifty-six pound weight."

The doctor nodded; he sat down; he took a glass of water, and pressed his hand to his heart. "Now, then," he said to himself, "once more! If I have to stand this fifteen minutes I shall be in *some* other world!"

The door from the inner room opened; and Mrs. Hicok came

singing in, carrying balanced upon her pretty pink fore-finger something or other of an airy bouquet-like fabric. Upon this she was looking with much delight.

"See, dear!" she said: "how perfectly lovely!"

Both gentlemen started, and the lady started too. She had not known of the visit; and she had not, until this instant, seen that her husband was not alone.

Dr. Hicok, of course, had never given her the key to his skeleton-closet; for he was a shrewd man. He loved her too; and he thought he had provided for her absence during the ordeal. She had executed her shopping with unprecedented speed.

Why the visitor started, would be difficult to say. Perhaps her voice startled him. The happy music in it was enough like a beautified duplicate of his own thrilling sweet tones, to have made him acknowledge her for a sister—from heaven. He started, at any rate.

"Mr. Lyon, my wife," said the doctor, somewhat at a loss. Mr. Lyon bowed, and so did the lady.

"I beg your pardon, gentlemen, I am sure," she said. "I did not know you were busy, dear. There is a thunder-shower coming up. I drove home just in season."

"Oh!—only a little wager, about some conundrums," said the doctor. Perhaps he may be excused for his fib. He did not want to annoy her unnecessarily.

"Oh, do let me know!" she said, with much eagerness. "You know how I enjoy them!"

"Well," said the doctor, "not exactly the ordinary kind. I was to puzzle my friend here with one out of three questions; and he has beaten me in two of them already. I've but one more chance."

"Only one?" she asked, with a smile. "What a bright man your friend must be! I thought nobody could puzzle you, dear. Stay; let *me* ask the other question."

Both the gentlemen started again: it was quite a surprise.

"But are you a married man, Mr. Lyon?" she asked, with a blush.

"No, madam," was the reply, with a very graceful bow—"I have a mother, but no wife. Permit me to say, that, if I could believe there was a duplicate of yourself in existence, I would be as soon as possible."

"Oh, what a gallant speech!" said the lady. "Thank you, sir, very much;" and she made him a pretty little curtsy. "Then I am quite sure of my question, sir. Shall I, dear?"

The doctor quickly decided. "I am done for, anyhow," he reflected. "I begin to see that the old villain put those questions into my head himself. He hinted as much. I don't know but I'd rather she would ask it. It's better to have her kill me, I guess, than to hold out the carving-knife to him myself."

"With all my heart, my dear," said the doctor, "if Mr. Lyon consents."

Mr. Lyon looked a little disturbed; but his manner was perfect, as he replied that he regretted to seem to disoblige, but that he feared the conditions of their little bet would not allow it.

"Beg your pardon, I'm sure, for being so uncivil," said the lively little beauty, as she whispered a few words in her husband's ear.

This is what she said—

"What's mine's yours, dear. Take it. Ask him—*buz, buzz, buzz.*"

The doctor nodded. Mrs. Hicok stood by him and smiled, still holding in her pretty pink fore-finger the frail shimmering thing just mentioned; and she gave it a twirl, so that it swung quite round. "Isn't it a love of a bonnet?" she said.

"Yes," the doctor said aloud. "I adopt the question."

"Third Question. Which is the front side of this?"

And he pointed to the bonnet. It must have been a bonnet, because Mrs. Hicok called it so. I shouldn't have known it from the collection of things in a kaleidoscope, bunched up together.

The lady stood before him, and twirled the wondrous fabric round and round, with the prettiest possible unconscious roguish look of defiance. The doctor's very heart stood still.

"Put it on, please," said Mr. Lyon, in the most innocent way in the world.

"Oh, no!" laughed she. "I know I'm only a woman, but I'm not *quite* so silly! But I'll tell you what: you men put it on, if you think that will help you!" And she held out the mystery to him.

Confident in his powers of discrimination, Mr. Lyon took hold of the fairy-like combination of sparkles and threads and feathers and flowers, touching it with that sort of timid apprehension that bachelors use with a baby. He stood before the glass over the mantelpiece. First he put it across his head with one side in front, and then with the other. Then he put it lengthways of his head, and tried the effect of tying one of the two couples of strings under each of his ears. Then he put it on, the other side up; so that it swam on his head like a boat, with a high mounted bow and stern. More than once he did all this, with obvious care and thoughtfulness.

Then he came slowly back, and resumed his seat. It was growing very dark, though they had not noticed it; for the thunder-shower had been hurrying on, and already its advanced guard of wind, heavy laden with the smell of the rain, could be heard, and a few large drops splashed on the window.

The beautiful wife of the doctor laughed merrily to watch the growing discomposure of the visitor, who returned the bonnet, with undiminished courtesy, but with obvious constraint of manner.

He looked down; he drummed on the table; he looked up; and both the doctor and the doctor's wife were startled at the intense sudden anger in the dark, handsome face. Then he sprang up, and went to the window. He looked out a moment, and then said—

"Upon my word, that is going to be a very sharp squall! The clouds are *very* heavy. If I'm any judge, something will be struck. I can feel the electricity in the air."

While he still spoke, the first thunder-bolt crashed overhead. It was one of those close, sudden, overpoweringly awful explosions from clouds very heavy and very near, where the lightning and the thunder leap together out of the very air close about you, even as if you were in them. It was an unendurable burst of sound, and of the intense white sheety light of very near lightning. Dreadfully frightened, the poor little lady clung close to her husband. He, poor man, if possible yet more frightened, exhausted as he was by what he had been enduring, fainted dead away. Don't blame him: a cast-iron bull-dog might have fainted.

Mrs. Hicok, thinking that her husband was struck dead by the lightning, screamed terribly. Then she touched him; and, seeing what was really the matter, administered cold water from the pitcher on the table. Shortly he revived.

"Where is he?" he said.

"I don't know, love. I thought you were dead. He must have gone away. Did it strike the house?"

"Gone away? Thank God! Thank *you*, dear!" cried out the doctor.

Not knowing any adequate cause for so much emotion, she answered him—

"Now, love, don't you ever say women are not practical again. That was a practical question, you see. But didn't it strike the house? What a queer smell. Ozone: isn't that what you were telling me about? How funny, that lightning should have a smell!"

"I believe there's no doubt of it," observed Dr. Hicok.

Mr. Apollo Lyon had really gone, though just how or when, nobody could say.

"My dear," said Dr. Hicok, "I do so like that bonnet of yours! I don't wonder it puzzled him. It would puzzle the Devil himself. I firmly believe I shall call it your Devil-puzzler."

But he never told her what the puzzle had been.

The Devil's Round:
a Tale of Flemish Golf

Charles Deulin

The modern devil is an accomplished gentleman. He is the most all-round being in creation. Mynheer van Belzebuth, as he is called in this story, is indeed the greatest gambler that there is upon or under the earth. On the golf-field as at the roulette-table he is hard to beat. It was the devil who invented cards, and they are, therefore, called the Devil's Bible, and it was also he who taught the Roman soldiers how to cast lots for the raiment of Christ (John xix, 24). Dice are also called the devil's bones.

The devil carries the souls in a sack on his back also in the legend of St. Medard. It is told that this saint, while promenading one day on the shore of the Red Sea in Egypt, saw Satan carrying a bag full of damned souls on his back. The heart of this saint was filled with compassion for the poor souls and he quickly slit the devil's bag open, whereupon the souls scrambled for liberty:

Away went the Quaker—away went the Baker,
Away went the Friar—that fine fat Ghost,
Whose marrow Old Nick Had intended to pick
Dressed like a Woodcock, and served on toast!

Away went the nice little Cardinal's Niece
And the pretty Grisettes, and the Dons from Spain,
And the Corsair's crew, And the coin-cliping Jew,
And they scamper'd, like lamplighters, over the plain!

The Witches' Sabbath is the annual reunion of Satan and his worshippers on earth. The witches, mounted on goats and broomsticks, flock to desolate heaths and hills to hold high revel with their devil.

Beelzebub swears in this story by the horns of his grandfather. While the devil is known to have a grandmother, there has never been found a trace of his grandfather. Satan has probably been adopted by the grandmother of Grendel, the Anglo-Saxon evil demon. The horns have been inherited by Satan from Dionysos. This Greek god had bull-feet and bull's horns.

1

Once upon a time there lived at the hamlet of Coq, near Conde-sur-l'Escaut, a wheelwright called Roger. He was a good fellow, untiring both at his sport and at his toil, and as skilful in lofting a ball with a stroke of his club as in putting together a cartwheel. Every one knows that the game of golf consists in driving towards a given point a ball of cherry wood with a club which has for head a sort of little iron shoe without a heel.

For my part, I do not know a more amusing game; and when the country is almost cleared of the harvest, men, women, children, everybody, drives his ball as you please, and there is nothing cheerier than to see them filing on a Sunday like a flight of starlings across potato fields and ploughed lands.

2

Well, one Tuesday, it was a Shrove Tuesday, the wheelwright of Coq laid aside his plane, and was slipping on his blouse to go and drink his can of beer at Conde, when two strangers came in, club in hand.

"Would you put a new shaft to my club, master?" said one of them.

"What are you asking me, friends? A day like this! I wouldn't give the smallest stroke of the chisel for a brick of gold. Besides, does any one play golf on Shrove Tuesday? You had much better go and see the mummers tumbling in the high street of Conde."

"We take no interest in the tumbling of mummers," replied the stranger. "We have challenged each other at golf and we want to play it out. Come, you won't refuse to help us, you who are said to be one of the finest players of the country?"

"If it is a match, that is different," said Roger.

He turned up his sleeves, hooked on his apron, and in the twinkling of an eye had adjusted the shaft.

"How much do I owe you?" asked the unknown, drawing out his purse.

"Nothing at all, faith; it is not worth while."

The stranger insisted, but in vain.

3

"You are too honest, i'faith," said he to the wheelwright, "for me to be in your debt. I will grant you the fulfilment of three wishes."

"Don't forget to wish what is *best*," added his companion.

At these words the wheelwright smiled incredulously.

"Are you not a couple of the loafers of Capelette?" he asked, with a wink.

The idlers of the crossways of Capelette were considered the wildest wags in Conde.

"Whom do you take us for?" replied the unknown in a tone of severity, and with his club he touched an axle, made of iron, which instantly changed into one of pure silver.

"Who are you, then," cried Roger, "that your word is as good as ready money?"

"I am St. Peter, and my companion is St. Antony, the patron of golfers."

"Take the trouble to walk in, gentlemen," said the wheelwright of Coq; and he ushered the two saints into the back parlour. He offered them chairs, and went to draw a jug of beer in the cellar. They clinked their glasses together, and after each had lit his pipe:

"Since you are so good, sir saints," said Roger, "as to grant me the accomplishment of three wishes, know that for a long while I have desired three things. I wish, first of all, that whoever seats himself upon the elm-trunk at my door may not be able to rise without my permission. I like company and it bores me to be always alone."

St. Peter shook his head and St. Antony nudged his client.

4

"When I play a game of cards, on Sunday evening, at the 'Fighting Cock,'" continued the wheelwright, "it is no sooner nine o'clock than the *garde-champetre* comes to chuck us out. I desire that whoever shall have his feet on my leathern apron cannot be driven from the place where I shall have spread it."

St. Peter shook his head, and St. Antony, with a solemn air, repeated: "Don't forget what is *best*."

"What is best," replied the wheelwright of Coq, nobly, "is to be the first golfer in the world. Every time I find my master at golf it turns my blood as black as the inside of the chimney. So I want a club that will carry the ball as high as the belfry of Conde, and will infallibly win me my match."

"So be it," said St. Peter.

"You would have done better," said St. Antony, "to have asked for your eternal salvation."

"Bah!" replied the other. "I have plenty of time to think of that; I am not yet greasing my boots for the long journey."

The two saints went out and Roger followed them, curious to be present at such a rare game; but suddenly, near the Chapel of St. Antony, they disappeared.

The wheelwright then went to see the mummers tumbling in the high street of Conde.

When he returned, towards midnight, he found at the corner of his door the desired club. To his great surprise it was only a bad little iron head attached to a wretched worn-out shaft. Nevertheless he took the gift of St. Peter and put it carefully away.

5

Next morning the Condeens scattered in crowds over the country, to play golf, eat red herrings, and drink beer, so as to scatter the fumes of wine from their heads and to revive after the fatigues of the Carnival. The wheelwright of Coq came too, with his miserable club, and made such fine strokes that all the players left their games to see him play. The following Sunday he proved still more expert; little by little his fame spread through the land. From ten leagues round the most skilful players hastened to come and be beaten, and it was then that he was named the Great Golfer.

He passed the whole Sunday in golfing, and in the evening he rested himself by playing a game of matrimony at the "Fighting Cock." He spread his apron under the feet of the players, and the devil himself could not have put them out of the tavern, much less the rural policeman. On Monday morning he stopped the pilgrims who were going to worship at Notre Dame de Bon Secours; he induced them to rest themselves upon his *causeuse*, and did not let them go before he had confessed them well.

In short, he led the most agreeable life that a good Fleming can imagine, and only regretted one thing—namely, that he had not wished it might last for ever.

6

Well, it happened one day that the strongest player of Mons, who was called Paternostre, was found dead on the edge of a bunker. His head was broken, and near him was his niblick, red with blood.

They could not tell who had done this business, and as Paternostre often said that at golf he feared neither man nor devil, it occurred to them that he had challenged Mynheer van Belzebuth, and that as a punishment for this he had knocked him on the head. Mynheer van Belzebuth is, as every one knows, the greatest gamester that there is upon or under the earth, but the game he particularly affects is golf. When he goes his round in Flanders one always meets him, club in hand, like a true Fleming.

The wheelwright of Coq was very fond of Paternostre, who, next to himself, was the best golfer in the country. He went to his funeral with some golfers from the hamlets of Coq, La Cigogne, and La Queue de l'Ayache.

On returning from the cemetery they went to the tavern to drink, as they say, to the memory of the dead,[1] and there they lost themselves in talk about the noble game of golf. When they separated, in the dusk of evening:

"A good journey to you," said the Belgian players, "and may St. Antony, the patron of golfers, preserve you from meeting the devil on the way!"

"What do I care for the devil?" replied Roger. "If he challenged me I should soon beat him!"

---

1. *Boire la cervelle du mort.*

The companions trotted from tavern to tavern without misadventure; but the wolf-bell had long tolled for retiring in the belfry of Conde when they returned each one to his own den.

7

As he was putting the key into the lock the wheelwright thought he heard a shout of mocking laughter. He turned, and saw in the darkness a man six feet high, who again burst out laughing.

"What are you laughing at?" said he, crossly.

"At what? Why, at the *aplomb* with which you boasted a little while ago that you would dare measure yourself against the devil."

"Why not, if he challenged me?"

"Very well, my master, bring your clubs. I challenge you!" said Mynheer van Belzebuth, for it was himself. Roger recognized him by a certain odour of sulphur that always hangs about his majesty.

"What shall the stake be?" he asked resolutely.

"Your soul?"

"Against what?"

"Whatever you please."

The wheelwright reflected.

"What have you there in your sack?"

"My spoils of the week."

"Is the soul of Paternostre among them?"

"To be sure! and those of five other golfers; dead, like him, without confession."

"I play you my soul against that of Paternostre."

"Done!"

8

The two adversaries repaired to the adjoining field and chose for their goal the door of the cemetery of Conde.[2] Belzebuth teed a ball on a frozen heap, after which he said, according to custom:

"From here, as you lie, in how many turns of three strokes will you run in?"

"In two," replied the great golfer.

And his adversary was not a little surprised, for from there to the cemetery was nearly a quarter of a league.

2. They play to points, not holes.

"But how shall we see the ball?" continued the wheelwright.

"True!" said Belzebuth.

He touched the ball with his club, and it shone suddenly in the dark like an immense glow-worm.

"Fore!" cried Roger.

He hit the ball with the head of his club, and it rose to the sky like a star going to rejoin its sisters. In three strokes it crossed three-quarters of the distance.

"That is good!" said Belzebuth, whose astonishment redoubled. "My turn to play now!"[3]

With one stroke of the club he drove the ball over the roofs of Coq nearly to Maison Blanche, half a league away. The blow was so violent that the iron struck fire against a pebble.

"Good St. Antony! I am lost, unless you come to my aid," murmured the wheelwright of Coq.

He struck tremblingly; but, though his arm was uncertain, the club seemed to have acquired a new vigour. At the second stroke the ball went as if of itself and hit the door of the cemetery.

"By the horns of my grandfather!" cried Belzebuth, "it shall not be said that I have been beaten by a son of that fool Adam. Give me my revenge."

"What shall we play for?"

"Your soul and that of Paternostre against the souls of two golfers."

9

The devil played up, "pressing" furiously; his club blazed at each stroke with showers of sparks. The ball flew from Conde to Bon-Secours, to Pernwelz, to Leuze. Once it spun away to Tournai, six leagues from there.

It left behind a luminous tail like a comet, and the two golfers followed, so to speak, on its track. Roger was never able to understand how he ran, or rather flew so fast, and without fatigue.

In short, he did not lose a single game, and won the souls of the six defunct golfers. Belzebuth rolled his eyes like an angry tom-cat.

"Shall we go on?" said the wheelwright of Coq.

---

3. After each three strokes the opponent has one hit back—or into a hazard.

"No," replied the other; "they expect me at the Witches' Sabbath on the hill of Copiemont.

"That brigand," said he aside, "is capable of filching all my game."

And he vanished.

Returned home, the great golfer shut up his souls in a sack and went to bed, enchanted to have beaten Mynheer van Belzebuth.

10

Two years after the wheelwright of Coq received a visit which he little expected. An old man, tall, thin and yellow, came into the workshop carrying a scythe on his shoulder.

"Are you bringing me your scythe to haft anew, master?"

"No, faith, *my* scythe is never unhafted."

"Then how can I serve you?"

"By following me: your hour is come."

"The devil," said the great golfer, "could you not wait a little till I have finished this wheel?"

"Be it so! I have done hard work today and I have well earned a smoke."

"In that case, master, sit down there on the *causeuse*. I have at your service some famous tobacco at seven petards the pound."

"That's good, faith; make haste."

And Death lit his pipe and seated himself at the door on the elm trunk.

Laughing in his sleeve, the wheelwright of Coq returned to his work. At the end of a quarter of an hour Death called to him:

"Ho! faith, will you soon have finished?"

The wheelwright turned a deaf ear and went on planing, singing:

"Attendez-moi sur l'orme;
Vous m'attendrez longtemps."

"I don't think he hears me," said Death. "Ho! friend, are you ready?"

"Va-t-en voir s'ils viennent, Jean,
Va-t-en voir s'ils viennent,"

replied the singer.

"Would the brute laugh at me?" said Death to himself.

And he tried to rise.

181

To his great surprise he could not detach himself from the *causeuse*. He then understood that he was the sport of a superior power.

"Let us see," he said to Roger. "What will you take to let me go? Do you wish me to prolong your life ten years?"

"J'ai de bon tabac dans ma tabatiere,"

sang the great golfer.

"Will you take twenty years?"

"Il pleut, il pleut, bergere; Rentre tes blancs moutons."

"Will you take a fifty, wheelwright?—may the devil admire you!"

The wheelwright of Coq intoned:

"Bon voyage, cher Dumollet,

"A Saint-Malo debarquez sans naufrage."

In the meanwhile the clock of Conde had just struck four, and the boys were coming out of school. The sight of this great dry heron of a creature who struggled on the *causeuse*, like a devil in a holy-water pot, surprised and soon delighted them.

Never suspecting that when seated at the door of the old, Death watches the young, they thought it funny to put out their tongues at him, singing in chorus:

"Bon voyage, cher Dumollet,

"A Saint-Malo debarquez sans naufrage."

"Will you take a hundred years?" yelled Death.

"Hein? How? What? Were you not speaking of an extension of a hundred years? I accept with all my heart, master; but let us understand: I am not such a fool as to ask for the lengthening of my old age."

"Then what do you want?"

"From old age I only ask the experience which it gives by degrees. *'Si jeunesse savait, si vieillesse pouvait!'* says the proverb. I wish to preserve for a hundred years the strength of a young man, and to acquire the knowledge of an old one."

"So be it," said Death; "I shall return this day a hundred years."

"Bon voyage, cher Dumollet,

"A Saint-Malo debarquez sans naufrage."

11

The great golfer began a new life. At first he enjoyed perfect happiness, which was increased by the certainty of its not end-ing for a hundred years. Thanks to his experience, he so well understood the management of his affairs that he could leave his mallet and shut up shop.[4]

He experienced, nevertheless, an annoyance he had not foreseen. His wonderful skill at golf ended by frightening the players whom he had at first delighted, and was the cause of his never finding any one who would play against him.

He therefore quitted the canton and set out on his travels over French Flanders, Belgium, and all the greens where the noble game of golf is held in honour. At the end of twenty years he returned to Coq to be admired by a new generation of golfers, after which he departed to return twenty years later.

Alas! in spite of its apparent charm, this existence before long became a burden to him. Besides that, it bored him to win on every occasion; he was tired of passing like the Wandering Jew through generations, and of seeing the sons, grandsons, and great-grandsons of his friends grow old, and die out. He was constantly reduced to making new friendships which were undone by the age or death of his fellows; all changed around him, he only did not change.

He grew impatient of this eternal youthfulness which condemned him to taste the same pleasures for ever, and he sometimes longed to know the calmer joys of old age. One day he caught himself at his looking-glass, examining whether his hair had not begun to grow white; nothing seemed so beautiful to him now as the snow on the forehead of the old.

12

In addition to this, experience soon made him so wise that he was no longer amused at anything. If sometimes in the tavern he had a fancy for making use of his apron to pass the night at cards: "What is the good of this excess?" whispered experience; "it is not sufficient to be unable to shorten one's days, one must also avoid making oneself ill."

He reached the point of refusing himself the pleasure of drinking his pint and smoking his pipe. Why, indeed, plunge into dissipations which enervate the body and dull the brain?

The wretch went further and gave up golf! Experience convinced

---

4. *Vivre a porte close.*

him that the game is a dangerous one, which overheats one, and is eminently adapted to produce colds, catarrhs, rheumatism, and inflammation of the lungs.

Besides, what is the use, and what great glory is it to be reputed the first golfer in the world?

Of what use is glory itself? A vain hope, vain as the smoke of a pipe.

When experience had thus bereft him one by one of his delusions, the unhappy golfer became mortally weary. He saw that he had deceived himself, that delusion has its price, and that the greatest charm of youth is perhaps its inexperience.

He thus arrived at the term agreed on in the contract, and as he had not had a paradise here below, he sought through his hardly-acquired wisdom a clever way of conquering one above.

13

Death found him at Coq at work in his shop. Experience had at least taught him that work is the most lasting of pleasures.

"Are you ready?" said Death.

"I am."

He took his club, put a score of balls in his pocket, threw his sack over his shoulder, and buckled his gaiters without taking off his apron.

"What do you want your club for?"

"Why, to golf in paradise with my patron St. Antony."

"Do you fancy, then, that I am going to conduct you to paradise?"

"You must, as I have half-a-dozen souls to carry there, that I once saved from the clutches of Belzebuth."

"Better have saved your own. *En route, cher Dumollet!*"

The great golfer saw that the old reaper bore him a grudge, and that he was going to conduct him to the paradise of the lost.[5]

Indeed a quarter of an hour later the two travellers knocked at the gate of hell.

"*Toc, toc!*"

"Who is there?"

"The wheelwright of Coq," said the great golfer.

---

5. *Noires glaives.*

"Don't open the door," cried Belzebuth; "that rascal wins at every turn; he is capable of depopulating my empire."

Roger laughed in his sleeve.

"Oh! you are not saved," said Death. "I am going to take you where you won't be cold either."

Quicker than a beggar would have emptied a poor's box they were in purgatory.

"*Toc—toc!*"

"Who is there?"

"The wheelwright of Coq," said the great golfer.

"But he is in a state of mortal sin," cried the angel on duty. "Take him away from here—he can't come in."

"I cannot, all the same, let him linger between heaven and earth," said Death; "I shall shunt him back to Coq."

"Where they will take me for a ghost. Thank you! is there not still paradise?"

14

They were there at the end of a short hour.

"*Toc, toc!*"

"Who is there?"

"The wheelwright of Coq," said the great golfer.

"Ah! my lad," said St. Peter, half opening the door, "I am really grieved. St. Antony told you long ago you had better ask for the salvation of your soul."

"That is true, St. Peter," replied Roger with a sheepish air. "And how is he, that blessed St. Antony? Could I not come in for one moment to return the visit he once paid me?"

"Why, here he comes," said St. Peter, throwing the door wide open.

In the twinkling of an eye the sly golfer had flung himself into paradise, unhooked his apron, let it fall to the ground, and seated himself down on it.

"Good morning, St. Antony," said he with a fine salute. "You see I had plenty of time to think of paradise, for here we are!"

"What! *You* here!" cried St. Antony.

"Yes, I and my company," replied Roger, opening his sack and scattering on the carpet the souls of the six golfers.

"Will you have the goodness to pack right off, all of you?"

"Impossible," said the great golfer, showing his apron.

"The rogue has made game of us," said St. Antony. "Come, St. Peter, in memory of our game of golf, let him in with his souls. Besides, he has had his purgatory on earth."

"It is not a very good precedent," murmured St. Peter.

"Bah!" replied Roger, "if we have a few good golfers in paradise, where is the harm?"

15

Thus, after having lived long, golfed much and drunk many cans of beer, the wheelwright of Coq called the Great Golfer was admitted to paradise; but I advise no one to copy him, for it is not quite the right way to go, and St. Peter might not always be so compliant, though great allowances must be made for golfers.

The Legend of Mont St.-Michel

Guy de Maupassant

No greater proof of the permanence and persistence of the devil as a character in literature can be adduced than the fact that this writer, in whom we find the purest expression of Naturalism, for whom the visible world was absolutely all that there is, was attracted by a devil-legend. But on this point he had a good example in his god-father and master Gustave Flaubert, who, though a realist of realists, showed deep interest in the Tempter of St. Anthony.

This legend of the fraudulent bargain between a sprite and a farmer as to alternate upper- and under-ground crops, with which "the great vision of the guarded mount" is here connected, is of Northern origin, but has travelled South as far as Arabia. It will be found in Grimm's *Fairy Tales* (No. 189); Thiele's *Danish Legends* (No. 122), and T. Sternberg's *The Dialect and Folk-Lore of Northampshire*. Rabelais used it as a French legend, and in its Oriental form it served as a subject for a poem by the German Friedrich Rueckert ("Der betrogene Teufel"). In all these versions the agreement is entered into between the devil (in the Northampshire form it is a bogie or some other field spirit) and a peasant. It was reserved for Maupassant to make St. Michael get the better of Satan on earth as in heaven.

According to this legend the devil broke his leg when, in his flight from St. Michael, he jumped off the roof of the castle into which he had been lured by the saint. The traditional explanation for the devil's broken leg is his fall from heaven. *"I beheld Satan as lightning fall from heaven"* (Luke

187

x, 18). All rebellious deities, who were universally supposed to have fallen from heaven, have crooked or crippled legs. Hephaestos, Vulcan, Loki and Wieland, each has a broken leg. This idea has probably been derived from the crooked lightning flashes. The devil's mother in the mediaeval German mystery-plays walks on crutches. Asmodeus, the Persian demon Aeshma-daeva, also had a lame foot. In Le Sage's book *Le Diable Boiteux* Asmodeus appears as a limping gentleman, who uses two sticks as crutches. According to rabbinical tradition this demon broke his leg when he hurried to meet King Solomon. In addition to his broken leg the devil inherited the goat-foot from Pan, the bull-foot from Dionysius and the horse-foot from Loki. The Ethiopic devil's right foot is a claw, and his left a hoof.

The devil is erroneously represented in this story as very lazy. Industry, it has been said, is the great Satanic virtue. "If we were all as diligent and as conscientious as the devil," observed an old Scotch woman to her minister, "it wad be muckle better for us."

The highest peak of a mountain is always consecrated to St. Michael. The Mont St.-Michel on the Norman Coast played a conspicuous part in the wars of the sons of William the Conqueror. Maupassant uses it as the background for several of the chapters of his novel *Notre Coeur* (1890). The mountain also figures in his story "Le Horla" (1886).

I had first seen it from Cancale, this fairy castle in the sea. I got an indistinct impression of it as of a grey shadow outlined against the misty sky. I saw it again from Avranches at sunset. The immense stretch of sand was red, the horizon was red, the whole boundless bay was red. The rocky castle rising out there in the distance like a weird, *seignorial* residence, like a dream palace, strange and beautiful—this alone remained black in the crimson light of the dying day.

The following morning at dawn I went toward it across the sands, my eyes fastened on this gigantic jewel, as big as a mountain, cut like a cameo, and as dainty as lace. The nearer I approached the greater my admiration grew, for nothing in the world could be more wonderful or more perfect.

As surprised as if I had discovered the habitation of a god, I wandered through those halls supported by frail or massive columns, raising my eyes in wonder to those spires which looked like rockets starting for the sky, and to that marvellous assemblage of towers, of gargoyles, of slender and charming ornaments, a regular fireworks of stone, granite lace, a masterpiece of colossal and delicate architecture.

As I was looking up in ecstasy a Lower Normandy peasant came up to me and told me the story of the great quarrel between Saint Michael and the devil.

A sceptical genius has said: "God made man in his image and man has returned the compliment."

This saying is an eternal truth, and it would be very curious to write the history of the local divinity of every continent, as well as the history of the patron saints in each one of our provinces. The negro has his ferocious man-eating idols; the polygamous Mahomedan fills his paradise with women; the Greeks, like a practical people, deified all the passions.

Every village in France is under the influence of some protecting saint, modelled according to the characteristics of the inhabitants.

Saint Michael watches over Lower Normandy, Saint Michael, the radiant and victorious angel, the sword-carrier, the hero of Heaven, the victorious, the conqueror of Satan.

But this is how the Lower Normandy peasant, cunning, deceitful and tricky, understands and tells of the struggle between the great saint and the devil.

To escape from the malice of his neighbour, the devil, Saint Michael built himself, in the open ocean, this habitation worthy of an archangel; and only such a saint could build a residence of such magnificence.

But, as he still feared the approaches of the wicked one, he surrounded his domains by quicksands, more treacherous even than the sea.

The devil lived in a humble cottage on the hill, but he owned all the salt marshes, the rich lands where grow the finest crops, the wooded valleys and all the fertile hills of the country, while the saint ruled only over the sands. Therefore Satan was rich, whereas Saint Michael was as poor as a church mouse.

After a few years of fasting the saint grew tired of this state of affairs and began to think of some compromise with the devil, but the matter was by no means easy, as Satan kept a good hold on his crops.

He thought the thing over for about six months; then one morning he walked across to the shore. The demon was eating his soup in front of his door when he saw the saint. He immediately rushed toward him, kissed the hem of his sleeve, invited him in and offered him refreshments.

Saint Michael drank a bowl of milk and then began: "I have come here to propose to you a good bargain."

The devil, candid and trustful, answered: "That will suit me."

"Here it is. Give me all your lands."

Satan, growing alarmed, wished to speak: "But—"

The saint continued: "Listen first. Give me all your lands. I will take care of all the work, the ploughing, the sowing, the fertilizing, everything, and we will share the crops equally. How does that suit you?"

The devil, who was naturally lazy, accepted. He only demanded in addition a few of those delicious grey mullet which are caught around the solitary mount. Saint Michael promised the fish.

They grasped hands and spat on the ground to show that it was a bargain, and the saint continued: "See here, so that you will have nothing to complain of, choose that part of the crops which you prefer: the part that grows above ground or the part that stays in the ground." Satan cried out: "I will take all that will be above ground."

"It's a bargain!" said the saint. And he went away.

Six months later, all over the immense domain of the devil, one could see nothing but carrots, turnips, onions, salsify, all the plants whose juicy roots are good and savoury and whose useless leaves are good for nothing but for feeding animals.

Satan wished to break the contract, calling Saint Michael a swindler.

But the saint, who had developed quite a taste for agriculture, went back to see the devil and said: "Really, I hadn't thought of that at all; it was just an accident, no fault of mine. And to make things fair with you, this year I'll let you take everything that is under the ground."

"Very well," answered Satan.

The following spring all the evil spirit's lands were covered with golden wheat, oats as big as beans, flax, magnificent colza, red clover, peas, cabbage, artichokes, everything that develops into grains or fruit in the sunlight.

Once more Satan received nothing, and this time he completely lost his temper. He took back his fields and remained deaf to all the fresh propositions of his neighbour.

A whole year rolled by. From the top of his lonely manor Saint Michael looked at the distant and fertile lands and watched the devil direct the work, take in his crops and thresh the wheat. And he grew angry, exasperated at his powerlessness. As he was no longer able to deceive Satan, he decided to wreak vengeance on him, and he went out to invite him to dinner for the following Monday.

"You have been very unfortunate in your dealings with me," he said; "I know it, but I don't want any ill feeling between us, and I expect you to dine with me. I'll give you some good things to eat."

Satan, who was as greedy as he was lazy, accepted eagerly. On the day appointed he donned his finest clothes and set out for the castle.

Saint Michael sat him down to a magnificent meal. First there was a *vol-au-vent*, full of cocks' crests and kidneys, with meat-balls, then two big grey mullet with cream sauce, a turkey stuffed with chestnuts soaked in wine, some salt-marsh lamb as tender as cake, vegetables which melted in the mouth and nice hot pancake which was brought on smoking and spreading a delicious odour of butter.

They drank new, sweet, sparkling cider and heady red wine, and after each course they whetted their appetites with some old apple brandy.

The devil drank and ate to his heart's content; in fact he took so much that he was very uncomfortable, and began to retch.

Then Saint Michael arose in anger and cried in a voice like thunder: "What! before me, rascal! You dare—before me—"

Satan, terrified, ran away, and the saint, seizing a stick, pursued him. They ran through the halls, turning round the pillars, running up the staircases, galloping along the cornices, jumping from gargoyle to gargoyle. The poor devil, who was woefully ill, was running about madly and trying hard to escape. At last he found himself at the top of the last terrace, right at the top, from which could be seen the immense bay, with its distant towns, sands and pastures. He could no longer escape, and the saint came up behind him and gave him a furious kick, which shot him through space like a cannon-ball.

He shot through the air like a javelin and fell heavily before the town of Mortain. His horns and claws stuck deep into the rock, which keeps through eternity the traces of this fall of Satan.

He stood up again, limping, crippled until the end of time, and as he looked at this fatal castle in the distance, standing out against the setting sun, he understood well that he would always be vanquished in this unequal struggle, and he went away limping, heading for distant countries, leaving to his enemy his fields, his hills, his valleys and his marshes.

And this is how Saint Michael, the patron saint of Normandy, vanquished the devil.

Another people would have dreamed of this battle in an entirely different manner.

The Demon Pope

Richard Garnett

The following two stories by Richard Garnett have been taken from his book *The Twilight of the Gods*, which was first published anonymously in 1888, and in a "new and augmented edition," with the author's name, in 1902. The title recalls Richard Wagner's opera *Goetterdaemmerung*, but may have been directly suggested by Elemir Bourges, whose novel *Le Crepuscule des Dieux* appeared four years earlier than Garnett's collection of stories. In his book Richard Garnett plays havoc with all religions. The demons, naturally enough, fare worse at his hands than the gods. *The Twilight of the Gods* is a panorama of human folly and farce. Franz Cumont has said that human folly is a more interesting study than ancient wisdom. The author finds a great joy in pointing out all the mysterious cobwebs which have collected on the ceiling of man's brain in the course of the ages. Mr. Arthur Symons rightly calls this book "a Punch and Judy show of the comedy of civilization."

The story of "The Demon Pope" is based upon a legend of a compact between a Pope and the devil. It is believed that Gerbert, who later became Pope Silvester II, sold his soul to Satan in order to acquire a knowledge of physics, arithmetic and music. The fullest account of this legend will be found in J. J. Dollinger's Fables Respecting the Popes of the Middle Ages (Engl. Translation, 1871). The History of the Devil and the Idea of Evil by Paul Carus (1900) contains the following passages on this legend:

An English Benedictine monk, William of Malmesbury, says of Pope Sylvester II., who was born in France, his secular name being Gerbert, that he entered the cloister when still a boy. Full of ambition, he flew to Spain where he studied astrology and magic among the Saracens. There he stole a magic-book from a Saracen philosopher, and returned flying through the air to France. Now he opened a school and acquired great fame, so that the king himself became one of his disciples. Then he became Bishop of Rheims, where he had a magnificent clock and an organ constructed. Having raised the treasure of Emperor Octavian which lay hidden in a subterranean vault at Rome, he became Pope. As Pope he manufactured a magic head which replied to all his questions. This head told him that he would not die until he had read Mass in Jerusalem. So the Pope decided never to visit the Holy Land. But once he fell sick, and, asking his magic head, was informed that the church's name in which he had read Mass the other day was 'The Holy Cross of Jerusalem.' The Pope knew at once that he had to die. He gathered all the cardinals around his bed, confessed his crime, and, as a penance, ordered his body to be cut up alive, and the pieces to be thrown out of the church as unclean.

Sigabert tells the story of the Pope's death in a different way. There is no penance on the part of the Pope, and the Devil takes his soul to hell. Others tell us that the Devil constantly accompanied the Pope in the shape of a black dog, and this dog gave him the equivocal prophecy.

The historical truth of the story is that Gerbert was unusually gifted and well educated. He was familiar with the wisdom of the Saracens, for Borell, Duke of Hither Spain, carried him as a youth to his country where he studied mathematics and astronomy. He came early in contact with the most influential men of his time, and became Pope in 999. He was liberal enough to denounce some of his unworthy predecessors as 'monsters of more than human iniquity,' and as 'Antichrist, sitting in the temple of God and playing the part of the Devil' (the text inadvertently reads: and playing the part of God); but at the same time he pursued an independent and vigorous papal policy, foreshadowing in his aims both the pretensions of Gregory the Great and the Crusades.

"So you won't sell me your soul?" said the devil.
"Thank you," replied the student, "I had rather keep it myself, if it's all the same to you."

"But it's not all the same to me. I want it very particularly. Come, I'll be liberal. I said twenty years. You can have thirty."

The student shook his head.

"Forty!"

Another shake.

"Fifty!"

As before.

"Now," said the devil. "I know I'm going to do a foolish thing, but I cannot bear to see a clever, spirited young man throw himself away. I'll make you another kind of offer. We don't have any bargain at present, but I will push you on in the world for the next forty years. This day forty years I come back and ask you for a boon; not your soul, mind, or anything not perfectly in your power to grant. If you give it, we are quits; if not, I fly away with you. What say you to this?"

The student reflected for some minutes. "Agreed," he said at last.

Scarcely had the devil disappeared, which he did instantaneously, ere a messenger reined in his smoking steed at the gate of the University of Cordova (the judicious reader will already have remarked that Lucifer could never have been allowed inside a Christian seat of learning), and, inquiring for the student Gerbert, presented him with the Emperor Otho's nomination to the Abbacy of Bobbio, in consideration, said the document, of his virtue and learning, well-nigh miraculous in one so young. Such messengers were frequent visitors during Gerbert's prosperous career. Abbot, bishop, archbishop, cardinal, he was ultimately enthroned Pope on April 2, 999, and assumed the appellation of Silvester the Second. It was then a general belief that the world would come to an end in the following year, a catastrophe which to many seemed the more imminent from the election of a chief pastor whose celebrity as a theologian, though not inconsiderable, by no means equalled his reputation as a necromancer.

The world, notwithstanding, revolved scatheless through the dreaded twelvemonth, and early in the first year of the eleventh century Gerbert was sitting peacefully in his study, perusing a book of magic. Volumes of algebra, astrology, alchemy, Aristotelian philosophy, and other such light reading filled his bookcase; and on a table stood an improved clock of his invention, next to his introduction of the Arabic numerals his chief legacy to posterity. Suddenly a sound of wings was heard, and Lucifer stood by his side.

"It is a long time," said the fiend, "since I have had the pleasure of seeing you. I have now called to remind you of our little contract, concluded this day forty years."

"You remember," said Silvester, "that you are not to ask anything exceeding my power to perform."

"I have no such intention," said Lucifer. "On the contrary, I am about to solicit a favour which can be bestowed by you alone. You are Pope, I desire that you would make me a Cardinal."

"In the expectation, I presume," returned Gerbert, "of becoming Pope on the next vacancy."

"An expectation," replied Lucifer, "which I may most reasonably entertain, considering my enormous wealth, my proficiency in intrigue, and the present condition of the Sacred College."

"You would doubtless," said Gerbert, "endeavour to subvert the foundations of the Faith, and, by a course of profligacy and licentiousness, render the Holy See odious and contemptible."

"On the contrary," said the fiend, "I would extirpate heresy, and all learning and knowledge as inevitably tending thereunto. I would suffer no man to read but the priest, and confine his reading to his breviary. I would burn your books together with your bones on the first convenient opportunity. I would observe an austere propriety of conduct, and be especially careful not to loosen one rivet in the tremendous yoke I was forging for the minds and consciences of mankind."

"If it be so," said Gerbert, "let's be off!"

"What!" exclaimed Lucifer, "you are willing to accompany me to the infernal regions!"

"Assuredly, rather than be accessory to the burning of Plato and Aristotle, and give place to the darkness against which I have been contending all my life."

"Gerbert," replied the demon, "this is arrant trifling. Know you not that no good man can enter my dominions? that, were such a thing possible, my empire would become intolerable to me, and I should be compelled to abdicate?"

"I do know it," said Gerbert, "and hence I have been able to receive your visit with composure."

"Gerbert," said the devil, with tears in his eyes, "I put it to you— is this fair, is this honest? I undertake to promote your interests in the world; I fulfil my promise abundantly. You obtain through my instrumentality a position to which you could never otherwise have aspired. Often have I had a hand in the election of a Pope, but never before have I contributed to confer the tiara on one eminent for virtue and learning. You profit by my assistance to the full, and now take advantage of an adventitious circumstance to deprive me of my reasonable guerdon. It is my constant experience that the good people are much more slippery than the sinners, and drive much harder bargains."

"Lucifer," answered Gerbert, "I have always sought to treat you as a gentleman, hoping that you would approve yourself such in return. I will not inquire whether it was entirely in harmony with this character to seek to intimidate me into compliance with your demand by threatening me with a penalty which you well knew could not be enforced. I will overlook this little irregularity, and concede even more than you have requested. You have asked to be a Cardinal. I will make you Pope—"

"Ha!" exclaimed Lucifer, and an internal glow suffused his sooty hide, as the light of a fading ember is revived by breathing upon it.

"For twelve hours," continued Gerbert. "At the expiration of that time we will consider the matter further; and if, as I anticipate, you are more anxious to divest yourself of the Papal dignity than you were to assume it, I promise to bestow upon you any boon you may ask within my power to grant, and not plainly inconsistent with religion or morals."

"Done!" cried the demon. Gerbert uttered some cabalistic words, and in a moment the apartment held two Pope Silvesters, entirely indistinguishable save by their attire, and the fact that one limped slightly with the left foot.

"You will find the Pontifical apparel in this cupboard," said Gerbert, and, taking his book of magic with him, he retreated through a masked door to a secret chamber. As the door closed behind him he chuckled, and muttered to himself, "Poor old Lucifer! Sold again!"

If Lucifer was sold he did not seem to know it. He approached a large slab of silver which did duty as a mirror, and contemplated his personal appearance with some dissatisfaction.

"I certainly don't look half so well without my horns," he soliloquized, "and I am sure I shall miss my tail most grievously."

A tiara and a train, however, made fair amends for the deficient appendages, and Lucifer now looked every inch a Pope. He was about to call the master of the ceremonies, and summon a consistory, when the door was burst open, and seven cardinals, brandishing poniards, rushed into the room.

"Down with the sorcerer!" they cried, as they seized and gagged him.

"Death to the Saracen!"

"Practises algebra, and other devilish arts!"

"Knows Greek!"

"Talks Arabic!"

"Reads Hebrew!"

"Burn him!"

"Smother him!"

"Let him be deposed by a general council," said a young and inexperienced Cardinal.

"Heaven forbid!" said an old and wary one, *sotto voce*.

Lucifer struggled frantically, but the feeble frame he was doomed to inhabit for the next eleven hours was speedily exhausted. Bound and helpless, he swooned away.

"Brethren," said one of the senior cardinals, "it hath been delivered by the exorcists that a sorcerer or other individual in league with the demon doth usually bear upon his person some visible token of his infernal compact. I propose that we forthwith institute a search for this stigma, the discovery of which may contribute to justify our proceedings in the eyes of the world."

"I heartily approve of our brother Anno's proposition," said another, "the rather as we cannot possibly fail to discover such a mark, if, indeed, we desire to find it."

The search was accordingly instituted, and had not proceeded far ere a simultaneous yell from all the seven cardinals indicated that their investigation had brought more light than they had ventured to expect.

The Holy Father had a cloven foot!

For the next five minutes the Cardinals remained utterly stunned, silent, and stupefied with amazement. As they gradually recovered their faculties it would have become manifest to a nice observer that the Pope had risen very considerably in their good opinion.

"This is an affair requiring very mature deliberation," said one.

"I always feared that we might be proceeding too precipitately," said another.

"It is written, 'the devils believe,'" said a third: "the Holy Father, therefore, is not a heretic at any rate."

"Brethren," said Anno, "this affair, as our brother Benno well remarks, doth indeed call for mature deliberation. I therefore propose that, instead of smothering his Holiness with cushions, as originally contemplated, we immure him for the present in the dungeon adjoining hereunto, and, after spending the night in meditation and prayer, resume the consideration of the business tomorrow morning."

"Informing the officials of the palace," said Benno, "that his Holiness has retired for his devotions, and desires on no account to be disturbed."

"A pious fraud," said Anno, "which not one of the Fathers would for a moment have scrupled to commit."

The Cardinals accordingly lifted the still insensible Lucifer, and bore him carefully, almost tenderly, to the apartment appointed for his detention. Each would fain have lingered in hopes of his recovery, but each felt that the eyes of his six brethren were upon him: and all, therefore, retired simultaneously, each taking a key of the cell.

Lucifer regained consciousness almost immediately afterwards. He had the most confused idea of the circumstances which had involved him in his present scrape, and could only say to himself that if they were the usual concomitants of the Papal dignity, these were by no means to his taste, and he wished he had been made acquainted with them sooner. The dungeon was not only perfectly dark, but horribly cold, and the poor devil in his present form had no latent store of infernal heat to draw upon. His teeth chattered, he shivered in every limb, and felt devoured with hunger and thirst. There is much probability in the assertion of some of his biographers that it was on this occasion that he invented ardent spirits; but, even if he did, the mere conception of a glass of brandy could only increase his sufferings. So the long January night wore wearily on, and Lucifer seemed likely to expire from inanition, when a key turned in the lock, and Cardinal Anno cautiously glided in, bearing a lamp, a loaf, half a cold roast kid, and a bottle of wine.

"I trust," he said, bowing courteously, "that I may be excused any slight breach of etiquette of which I may render myself culpable from the difficulty under which I labour of determining whether, under present circumstances, 'Your Holiness,' or 'Your infernal Majesty' be the form of address most befitting me to employ."

"*Bub-ub-bub-boo,*" went Lucifer, who still had the gag in his mouth.

"Heavens!" exclaimed the Cardinal, "I crave your Infernal Holiness's forgiveness. What a lamentable oversight!"

And, relieving Lucifer from his gag and bonds, he set out the refection, upon which the demon fell voraciously.

"Why the devil, if I may so express myself," pursued Anno, "did not your Holiness inform us that you *were* the devil? Not a hand would then have been raised against you. I have myself been seeking all my life for the audience now happily vouchsafed me. Whence this mistrust of your faithful Anno, who has served you so loyally and zealously these many years?"

Lucifer pointed significantly to the gag and fetters.

"I shall never forgive myself," protested the Cardinal, "for the part I have borne in this unfortunate transaction. Next to ministering to your Majesty's bodily necessities, there is nothing I have so much at heart as to express my penitence. But I entreat your Majesty to remember that I believed myself to be acting in your Majesty's interest by overthrowing a magician who was accustomed to send your Majesty upon errands, and who might at any time enclose you in a box, and cast you into the sea. It is deplorable that your Majesty's most devoted servants should have been thus misled."

"Reasons of State," suggested Lucifer.

"I trust that they no longer operate," said the Cardinal. "However, the Sacred College is now fully possessed of the whole matter: it is therefore unnecessary to pursue this department of the subject further. I would now humbly crave leave to confer with your Majesty, or rather, perhaps, your Holiness, since I am about to speak of spiritual things, on the important and delicate point of your Holiness's successor. I am ignorant how long your Holiness proposes to occupy the Apostolic chair; but of course you are aware that public opinion will not suffer you to hold it for a term exceeding that of the pontificate of Peter. A vacancy, therefore, must one day occur; and I am humbly to represent that the office could not be filled by one more congenial than myself to the present incumbent, or on whom he could more fully rely to carry out in every respect his views and intentions."

And the Cardinal proceeded to detail various circumstances of his past life, which certainly seemed to corroborate his assertion. He had not, however, proceeded far ere he was disturbed by the grating of another key in the lock, and had just time to whisper impressively, "Beware of Benno," ere he dived under a table.

Benno was also provided with a lamp, wine, and cold viands. Warned by the other lamp and the remains of Lucifer's repast that some colleague had been beforehand with him, and not knowing how many more might be in the field, he came briefly to the point as regarded the Papacy, and preferred his claim in much the same manner as Anno. While he was earnestly cautioning Lucifer against this Cardinal as one who could and would cheat the very Devil himself, another key turned in the lock, and Benno escaped under the table, where Anno immediately inserted his fingers into his right eye. The little squeal consequent upon this occurrence Lucifer successfully smothered by a fit of coughing.

Cardinal No. 3, a Frenchman, bore a Bayonne ham, and exhibited the same disgust as Benno on seeing himself forestalled. So far as his requests transpired they were moderate, but no one knows where he would have stopped if he had not been scared by the advent of Cardinal No. 4. Up to this time he had only asked for an inexhaustible purse, power to call up the Devil *ad libitum*, and a ring of invisibility to allow him free access to his mistress, who was unfortunately a married woman.

Cardinal No. 4 chiefly wanted to be put into the way of poisoning Cardinal No. 5; and Cardinal No. 5 preferred the same petition as respected Cardinal No. 4.

Cardinal No. 6, an Englishman, demanded the reversion of the Archbishoprics of Canterbury and York, with the faculty of holding them together, and of unlimited non-residence. In the course of his harangue he made use of the phrase *non obstantibus*, of which Lucifer immediately took a note.

What the seventh Cardinal would have solicited is not known, for he had hardly opened his mouth when the twelfth hour expired, and Lucifer, regaining his vigour with his shape, sent the Prince of the Church spinning to the other end of the room, and split the marble table with a single stroke of his tail. The six crouched and huddling Cardinals cowered revealed to one another, and at the same time enjoyed the spectacle of his Holiness darting through the stone ceiling, which yielded like a film to his passage, and closed up afterwards as if nothing had happened. After the first shock of dismay they unanimously rushed to the door, but found it bolted on the outside. There was no other exit, and no means of giving an alarm. In this emergency the demeanour of the Italian Cardinals set a bright example to their *ultramontane* colleagues. "*Bisogna pazienzia*," they said, as they shrugged their shoulders. Nothing could exceed the mutual politeness of Cardinals Anno and Benno, unless that of the two who had sought to poison each other. The Frenchman was held to have gravely derogated from good manners by alluding to this circumstance, which had reached his ears while he was under the table: and the Englishman swore so outrageously at the plight in which he found himself that the Italians then and there silently registered a vow that none of his nation should ever be Pope, a maxim which, with one exception, has been observed to this day.

Lucifer, meanwhile, had repaired to Silvester, whom he found arrayed in all the insignia of his dignity; of which, as he remarked, he thought his visitor had probably had enough.

"I should think so indeed," replied Lucifer. "But at the same time I feel myself fully repaid for all I have undergone by the assurance of the loyalty of my friends and admirers, and the conviction that it is needless for me to devote any considerable amount of personal attention to ecclesiastical affairs. I now claim the promised boon, which it will be in no way inconsistent with thy functions to grant, seeing that it is a work of mercy. I demand that the Cardinals be released, and that their conspiracy against thee, by which I alone suffered, be buried in oblivion."

"I hoped you would carry them all off," said Gerbert, with an expression of disappointment.

"Thank you," said the Devil. "It is more to my interest to leave them where they are."

So the dungeon-door was unbolted, and the Cardinals came forth, sheepish and crestfallen. If, after all, they did less mischief than Lucifer had expected from them, the cause was their entire bewilderment by what had passed, and their utter inability to penetrate the policy of Gerbert, who henceforth devoted himself even with ostentation to good works. They could never quite satisfy themselves whether they were speaking to the Pope or to the Devil, and when under the latter impression habitually emitted propositions which Gerbert justly stigmatized as rash, temerarious, and scandalous. They plagued him with allusions to certain matters mentioned in their interviews with Lucifer, with which they naturally but erroneously supposed him to be conversant, and worried him by continual nods and titterings as they glanced at his nether extremities. To abolish this nuisance, and at the same time silence sundry unpleasant rumours which had somehow got abroad, Gerbert devised the ceremony of kissing the Pope's feet, which, in a grievously mutilated form, endures to this day. The stupefaction of the Cardinals on discovering that the Holy Father had lost his hoof surpasses all description, and they went to their graves without having obtained the least insight into the mystery.

Madam Lucifer

Richard Garnett

Perhaps the most fascinating—and the most dangerous—character in the infernal world is this *Mater tenebrarum*—Our Lady of Darkness. "A lady devil," says Daniel Defoe, "is about as dangerous a creature as one could meet." When Lucifer fails to bring a man to his fall, he hands the case over to his better half, and it is said that no man has ever escaped the siren seductions of this Diabo-Lady. A poem, 'The Diabo-Lady, or a Match in Hell,' appeared in London in 1777.

According to Teutonic mythology, this diabolical Madonna is the mother or the grandmother of Satan. The mother or grandmother of Grendel, the Anglo-Saxon evil demon, became Satan's mother or grandmother by adoption. A mother was a necessary part of the devil's equipment. Having set his mind to equal Christ in every detail of his life, Satan had to get a mother somehow. In his story "The Vision Malefic" (1920) Mr. Huneker tells of the appearance of this counterfeit Madonna on a Christmas Eve to the organist of a Roman Catholic church in New York. Partly out of devotion to her and partly also because he could not obtain the sacramental blessing of the Church, Satan was forced to remain single. In the story "Devil-Puzzlers" by Fred B. Perkins the demon Apollyon appears as an old bachelor. "I have a mother, but no wife," he tells the charming Mrs. Hicok. The synagogue was more lenient towards the devil. The rabbis did not hesitate to perform the marriage ceremony for the diabolical pair. According to Jewish tradition the chief of the fallen angels married Lilith, Adam's first wife. She is said to have been in her younger days a woman of great beauty, but with a heart of ice. Now, of course, she is a regular hell-hag. If we can trust Rossetti, who painted her Majesty's portrait, she still is a type of beauty whose fascination is fatal. This woman was created by the Lord to be the help-meet of Adam, but mere man had no attraction for this superwoman. She is said to have started the fight for woman's emancipation from man, and contested Adam's right to be the head of the family. Their married life was very brief. Their incompatibility of character was too great. One fine morning Adam found that his erstwhile angelical wife had deserted him and run away with Lucifer, whom she had formerly known in heaven.

The King-Devil apparently always succeeded somehow or other in breaking the chains with which, according to legend, he had repeatedly been bound and sealed in the lowest depths of hell. From antediluvian times the demons appear to have been attracted by the daughters of men and to have come frequently up to earth to pay court to them. The only devil who must always remain in hell is the stoker, Brendli by name. The fires of hell must not be allowed to go out.

The anatomically melancholic Burton also tells of a devil who was in love with a mortal maiden. Jacques Cazotte tells the story of Beelzebub as a woman in love with an earth-born man.

L ucifer sat playing chess with Man for his soul.
The game was evidently going ill for Man. He had but pawns left, few and struggling. Lucifer had rooks, knights, and, of course, bishops.

It was but natural under such circumstances that Man should be in no great hurry to move. Lucifer grew impatient.

"It is a pity," said he at last, "that we did not fix some period within which the player must move, or resign."

"Oh, Lucifer," returned the young man, in heart-rending accents, "it is not the impending loss of my soul that thus unmans me, but the loss of my betrothed. When I think of the grief of the Lady Adeliza, the paragon of terrestrial loveliness!" Tears choked his utterance; Lucifer was touched.

"Is the Lady Adeliza's loveliness in sooth so transcendent?" he inquired.

"She is a rose, a lily, a diamond, a morning star!"

"If that is the case," rejoined Lucifer, "thou mayest reassure thyself. The Lady Adeliza shall not want for consolation. I will assume thy shape and woo her in thy stead."

The young man hardly seemed to receive all the comfort from this promise which Lucifer no doubt designed. He made a desperate move. In an instant the Devil checkmated him, and he disappeared.

****

"Upon my word, if I had known what a business this was going to be, I don't think I should have gone in for it," soliloquized the Devil as, wearing his captive's semblance and installed in his apartments, he surveyed the effects to which he now had to administer. They included coats, shirts, collars, neckties, foils, cigars, and the like *ad libitum*; and very little else except three challenges, ten writs, and seventy-four unpaid bills, elegantly disposed around the looking-glass. To the poor youth's praise be it said, there were no *billets-doux*, except from the Lady Adeliza herself.

Noting the address of these carefully, the Devil sallied forth, and nothing but his ignorance of the topography of the hotel, which made him take the back stairs, saved him from the clutches of two bailiffs lurking on the principal staircase. Leaping into a cab, he thus escaped a perfumer and a boot maker, and shortly found himself at the Lady Adeliza's feet.

The truth had not been half told him. Such beauty, such wit, such correctness of principle! Lucifer went forth from her presence a love-sick fiend. Not Merlin's mother had produced half the impression upon him; and Adeliza on her part had never found her lover one-hundredth part so interesting as he seemed that morning.

Lucifer proceeded at once to the City, where, assuming his proper shape for the occasion, he negotiated a loan without the smallest difficulty. All debts were promptly discharged, and Adeliza was astonished at the splendour and variety of the presents she was constantly receiving.

Lucifer had all but brought her to name the day, when he was informed that a gentleman of clerical appearance desired to wait upon him.

"Wants money for a new church or mission, I suppose," said he. "Show him up."

But when the visitor was ushered in, Lucifer found with discomposure that he was no earthly clergyman, but a celestial saint; a saint, too, with whom Lucifer had never been able to get on. He had served in the army while on earth, and his address was curt, precise, and peremptory.

"I have called," he said, "to notify to you my appointment as Inspector of Devils."

"What!" exclaimed Lucifer, in consternation. "To the post of my old friend Michael!"

"Too old," said the Saint laconically. "Millions of years older than the world. About your age, I think."

Lucifer winced, remembering the particular business he was then about. The Saint continued:

"I am a new broom, and am expected to sweep clean. I warn you that I mean to be strict, and there is one little matter which I must set right immediately. You are going to marry that poor young fellow's betrothed, are you? Now you know you can not take his wife, unless you give him yours."

"Oh, my dear friend," exclaimed Lucifer, "what an inexpressibly blissful prospect you do open unto me!"

"I don't know that," said the Saint. "I must remind you that the dominion of the infernal regions is unalterably attached to the person of the present Queen thereof. If you part with her you immediately lose all your authority and possessions. I don't care a brass button which you do, but you must understand that you cannot eat your cake and have it too. Good morning!"

Who shall describe the conflict in Lucifer's bosom? If any stronger passion existed therein at that moment than attachment to Adeliza, it was aversion to his consort, and the two combined were well-nigh irresistible. But to disenthrone himself, to descend to the condition of a poor devil!

Feeling himself incapable of coming to a decision, he sent for Belial, unfolded the matter, and requested his advice.

"What a shame that our new inspector will not let you marry Adeliza!" lamented his counsellor. "If you did, my private opinion is that forty-eight hours afterwards you would care just as much for her as you do now for Madam Lucifer, neither more nor less. Are your intentions really honourable?"

"Yes," replied Lucifer, "it is to be a Lucifer match."

"The more fool you," rejoined Belial. "If you tempted her to commit a sin, she would be yours without any conditions at all."

"Oh, Belial," said Lucifer, "I cannot bring myself to be a tempter of so much innocence and loveliness."

And he meant what he said.

"Well then, let me try," proposed Belial.

"You?" replied Lucifer contemptuously; "do you imagine that Adeliza would look at you?"

"Why not?" asked Belial, surveying himself complacently in the glass.

He was humpbacked, squinting, and lame, and his horns stood up under his wig.

The discussion ended in a wager: after which there was no retreat for Lucifer.

The infernal Iachimo was introduced to Adeliza as a distinguished foreigner, and was soon prosecuting his suit with all the success which Lucifer had predicted. One thing protected while it baffled him—the entire inability of Adeliza to understand what he meant. At length he was constrained to make the matter clear by producing an enormous treasure, which he offered Adeliza in exchange for the abandonment of her lover.

The tempest of indignation which ensued would have swept away any ordinary demon, but Belial listened unmoved. When Adeliza had exhausted herself he smilingly rallied her upon her affection for an unworthy lover, of whose infidelity he undertook to give her proof. Frantic with jealousy, Adeliza consented, and in a trice found herself in the infernal regions.

****

Adeliza's arrival in Pandemonium, as Belial had planned, occurred immediately after the receipt of a message from Lucifer, in whose bosom love had finally gained the victory, and who had telegraphed his abdication and resignation of Madam Lucifer to Adeliza's betrothed. The poor young man had just been hauled up from the lower depths, and was beset by legions of demons obsequiously pressing all manner of treasures upon his acceptance.

He stared, helpless and bewildered, unable to realize his position in the smallest degree. In the background grave and serious demons, the princes of the infernal realm, discussed the new departure, and consulted especially how to break it to Madam Lucifer—a commission of which no one seemed ambitious.

"Stay where you are," whispered Belial to Adeliza; "stir not: you shall put his constancy to the proof within five minutes."

Not all the hustling, mowing, and gibbering of the fiends would under ordinary circumstances have kept Adeliza from her lover's side: but what is all hell to jealousy?

In even less time than he had promised, Belial returned, accompanied by Madam Lucifer. This lady's black robe, dripping with blood, contrasted agreeably with her complexion of sulphurous yellow; the absence of hair was compensated by the exceptional length of her nails; she was a thousand million years old, and, but for her remarkable muscular vigour, looked every one of them. The rage into which Belial's communication had thrown her was something indescribable; but, as her eye fell on the handsome youth, a different order of thoughts seemed to take possession of her mind.

"Let the monster go!" she exclaimed; "who cares? Come, my love, ascend the throne with me, and share the empire and the treasures of thy fond Luciferetta."

"If you don't, back you go," interjected Belial.

What might have been the young man's decision if Madam Lucifer had borne more resemblance to Madam Vulcan, it would be wholly impertinent to inquire, for the question never arose.

"Take me away!" he screamed, "take me away, anywhere! anywhere out of her reach! Oh, Adeliza!"

With a bound Adeliza stood by his side. She was darting a triumphant glance at the discomfited Queen of Hell, when suddenly her expression changed, and she screamed loudly. Two adorers stood before her, alike in every lineament and every detail of costume, utterly indistinguishable, even by the eye of Love.

Lucifer, in fact, hastening to throw himself at Adeliza's feet and pray her to defer his bliss no longer, had been thunderstruck by the tidings of her elopement with Belial. Fearing to lose his wife and his dominions along with his sweetheart, he had sped to the nether regions with such expedition that he had had no time to change his costume. Hence the equivocation which confounded Adeliza, but at the same time preserved her from being torn to pieces by the no less mystified Madam Lucifer.

Perceiving the state of the case, Lucifer with true gentlemanly feeling resumed his proper semblance, and Madam Lucifer's talons were immediately inserted into his whiskers.

"My dear! my love!" he gasped, as audibly as she would let him, "is this the way it welcomes its own Lucy-pucy?"

"Who is that person?" demanded Madam Lucifer.

"I don't know her," screamed the wretched Lucifer. "I never saw her before. Take her away; shut her up in the deepest dungeon!"

"Not if I know it," sharply replied Madam Lucifer. "You can't bear to part with her, can't you? You would intrigue with her under my nose, would you? Take that! and that! Turn them both out, I say! turn them both out!"

"Certainly, my dearest love, most certainly," responded Lucifer.

"Oh, Sire," cried Moloch and Beelzebub together, "for Heaven's sake let your Majesty consider what he is doing. The Inspector—"

"Bother the Inspector!" screeched Lucifer. "D'ye think I'm not a thousand times more afraid of your mistress than of all the saints in the calendar? There," addressing Adeliza and her betrothed, "be off! You'll find all debts paid, and a nice balance at the bank. Out! Run!"

They did not wait to be told twice. Earth yawned. The gates of Tartarus stood wide. They found themselves on the side of a steep mountain, down which they scoured madly, hand linked in hand. But fast as they ran, it was long ere they ceased to hear the tongue of Madam Lucifer.

Lucifer

Anatole France

This writer has a great sympathy for devil-lore, and many of his characters show the cloven hoof. An analyst of illusions, he has a profound interest in the greatest of illusions. An assailant of every form of superstition, he has a tender affection for the greatest of superstitions. An exponent of the radical and ironical spirit in French literature, he feels irresistibly drawn to the eternal Denier and Mocker.

The story of the Florentine painter Spinello Spinelli, to whom Lucifer appeared in a dream to ask him in what place he had beheld him under so brutish a form as he had painted him, is told in Giorgio Vasari's *Vite de' piu eccellenti Pittori, Scultori, ed Architteti* (1550), which is the basis of the history of Italian art. It was treated by Barrili in his novel *The Devil's Portrait* (1882; Engl. tr. 1885), from whom Anatole France may have got the idea for his story. But there is also a mediaeval French legend about a monk (*Du moine qui contrefyt l'ymage du Diable, qui s'en corouca*), who was forced by the indignant devil to paint him in a less ugly manner.

The devil is very sensitive in regard to his appearance. On a number of occasions he expressed his bitter resentment at the efforts of a certain class of artists to represent him in a hideous form (cf. M. D. Conway, *Demonology and Devil-Lore*).

Daniel Defoe has well remarked that the devil does not think that the people would be terrified half so much if they were to converse face to face with him. "Really," this biographer of Satan goes on to say, "it were enough to fright the devil himself to meet himself in the dark, dressed up in the several figures which imagination has formed for him in the minds of men." It makes us, indeed, wonder why the devil was always represented in a hideous and horrid form.

Rationally conceived, the devil should by right be the most fascinating object in creation. One of his essential functions, temptation, is destroyed by his hideousness. To do the work of temptation a demon might be expected to approach his intended victim in the most fascinating form he could command. This fact is an additional proof that the devil was for the early Christians but the discarded pagan god, whom they wished to represent as ugly and as repulsive as they could.

The earliest known representation of the devil in human form is found on an ivory diptych of the time of Charles the Bald (9th century). Many artists have since then painted his Majesty's portrait. Schongauer, Duerer, Michelangelo, Titian, Raphael, Rubens, Poussin, Van Dyck, Breughel and other masters on canvas vied with each other to present us with a real likeness of Satan. None has, however, equalled the power of Gustave Dore in the portrayal of the Diabolical. This Frenchman was at his best as an artist of the infernal (Dante's "Great Dis" and Milton's "Satan at the Gates of Hell").

Modern artists frequently represent the devil as a woman. Felicien Rops, Max Klinger, and Franz Stuck may be cited as illustrations. Apparently the devil has in modern times changed sex as well as custom and costume. Victor Hugo has said:

Dieu s'est fait homme; soit.
Le diable s'est fait femme.

"Lucifer," as well as the other stories which form the volume *The Well of St. Claire*, is told by the abbe Jerome Coignard on the edge of Santa Clara's well at Siena. The book was first published serially in the *Echo de Paris* (1895). It has just been rendered into Spanish (*El Pozo de Santa Clara*).

E si compiacque tanto Spinello di farlo orribile e contrafatto, che si dice
(tanto puo alcuna fiata l'immaginazione) che la detta figura da lui
dipinta gli apparve in sogno, domandandolo dove egli l' avesse veduta
si brutta.[1]

(Vite de' piu eccellenti pittori, da Messer
Giorgio Vasari.—*Vita di Spinello.*)

A ndrea Tafi, painter and worker-in-mosaic of Florence, had a
wholesome terror of the Devils of Hell, particularly in the
watches of the night, when it is given to the powers of Darkness to
prevail. And the worthy man's fears were not unreasonable, for in
those days the Demons had good cause to hate the Painters, who
robbed them of more souls with a single picture than a good little
Preaching Friar could do in thirty sermons. No doubt the Monk,
to instil a soul-saving horror in the hearts of the faithful, would
describe to the utmost of his powers "that day of wrath, that day
of mourning," which is to reduce the universe to ashes, *teste David
et Sibylla*, borrowing his deepest voice and bellowing through his
hands to imitate the Archangel's last trump. But there! it was "all
sound and fury, signifying nothing," whereas a painting displayed
on a Chapel wall or in the Cloister, showing Jesus Christ sitting on
the Great White Throne to judge the living and the dead, spoke
unceasingly to the eyes of sinners, and through the eyes chastened
such as had sinned by the eyes or otherwise.

It was in the days when cunning masters were depicting at San-
ta-Croce in Florence and the Campo Santo of Pisa the mysteries of
Divine Justice. These works were drawn according to the account
in verse which Dante Alighieri, a man very learned in Theology
and in Canon Law, wrote in days gone by of his journey to Hell,
and Purgatory and Paradise, whither by the singular great merits
of his lady, he was able to make his way alive. So everything in
these paintings was instructive and true, and we may say surely less
profit is to be had of reading the most full and ample Chronicle

---

1. "And so successful was Spinello with his horrible and portentous Production that
it was commonly reported—so great is always the force of fancy—that the said figure (of Lucifer trodden underfoot by St. Michael in the Altar-Piece of the Church
of St. Agnolo at Arezzo) painted by him had appeared to the artist in a dream, and
asked him in what place he had beheld him under so brutish a form." *Lives of the
most Excellent Painters*, by Giorgio Vasari.—"Life of Spinello."

than from contemplating such representative works of art. Moreover, the Florentine masters took heed to paint, under the shade of orange groves, on the flower-starred turf, fair ladies and gallant knights, with Death lying in wait for them with his scythe, while they were discoursing of love to the sound of lutes and viols. Nothing was better fitted to convert carnal-minded sinners who quaff forgetfulness of God on the lips of women. To rebuke the covetous, the painter would show to the life the Devils pouring molten gold down the throat of Bishop or Abbess, who had commissioned some work from him and then scamped his pay.

This is why the Demons in those days were bitter enemies of the painters, and above all of the Florentine painters, who surpassed all the rest in subtlety of wit. Chiefly they reproached them with representing them under a hideous guise, with the heads of bird and fish, serpents' bodies and bats' wings. This sore resentment which they felt will come out plainly in the history of Spinello of Arezzo.

Spinello Spinelli was sprung of a noble family of Florentine exiles, and his graciousness of mind matched his gentle birth; for he was the most skilful painter of his time. He wrought many and great works at Florence; and the Pisans begged him to complete Giotto's wall-paintings in their Campo Santo, where the dead rest beneath roses in holy earth shipped from Jerusalem. At last, after working long years in divers cities and getting much gold, he longed to see once more the good city of Arezzo, his mother. The men of Arezzo had not forgotten how Spinello, in his younger days, being enrolled in the Confraternity of Santa Maria della Misericordia, had visited the sick and buried the dead in the plague of 1383. They were grateful to him besides for having by his works spread the fame of their city over all Tuscany. For all these reasons they welcomed him with high honours on his return.

Still full of vigour in his old age, he undertook important tasks in his native town. His wife would tell him:

"You are rich, Spinello. Do you rest, and leave younger men to paint instead of you. It is meet a man should end his days in a gentle, religious quiet. It is tempting God to be for ever raising new and worldly monuments, mere heathen towers of Babel. Quit your colours and your varnishes, Spinello, or they will destroy your peace of mind."

So the good dame would preach, but he refused to listen, for his one thought was to increase his fortune and renown. Far from resting on his laurels, he arranged a price with the Wardens of Sant' Agnolo for a history of St. Michael, that was to cover all the Choir of the Church and contain an infinity of figures. Into this enterprise he threw himself with extraordinary ardour. Re-reading the parts of Scripture that were to be his inspiration, he set himself to study deeply every line and every word of these passages. Not content with drawing all day long in his workshop, he persisted in working both at bed and board; while at dusk, walking below the hill on whose brow Arezzo proudly lifts her walls and towers, he was still lost in thought. And we may say the story of the Archangel was already limned in his brain when he started to sketch out the incidents in red chalk on the plaster of the wall. He was soon done tracing these outlines; then he fell to painting above the high altar the scene that was to outshine all the others in brilliancy. For it was his intent therein to glorify the leader of the hosts of Heaven for the victory he won before the beginning of time. Accordingly Spinello represented St. Michael fighting in the air against the serpent with seven heads and ten horns, and he figured with delight, in the bottom part of the picture, the Prince of the Devils, Lucifer, under the semblance of an appalling monster. The figures seemed to grow to life of themselves under his hand. His success was beyond his fondest hopes; so hideous was the countenance of Lucifer, none could escape the nightmare of its foulness. The face haunted the painter in the streets and even went home with him to his lodging.

Presently when night was come, Spinello lay down in his bed beside his wife and fell asleep. In his slumbers he saw an Angel as comely as St. Michael, but black; and the Angel said to him:

"Spinello, I am Lucifer. Tell me, where had you seen me, that you should paint me as you have, under so ignominious a likeness?"

The old painter answered, trembling, that he had never seen him with his eyes, never having gone down alive into Hell, like Messer Dante Alighieri; but that, in depicting him as he had done, he was for expressing in visible lines and colours the hideousness of sin.

Lucifer shrugged his shoulders, and the hill of San Gemignano seemed of a sudden to heave and stagger.

"Spinello," he went on, "will you do me the pleasure to reason awhile with me? I am no mean Logician; He you pray to knows that."

Receiving no reply, Lucifer proceeded in these terms:

"Spinello, you have read the books that tell of me. You know of my enterprise, and how I forsook Heaven to become the Prince of this World. A tremendous adventure,—and a unique one, had not the Giants in like fashion assailed the god Jupiter, as yourself have seen, Spinello, recorded on an ancient tomb where this Titanic war is carved in marble."

"It is true," said Spinello, "I have seen the tomb, shaped like a great tun, in the Church of Santa Reparata at Florence. 'Tis a fine work of the Romans."

"Still," returned Lucifer, smiling, "the Giants are not pictured on it in the shape of frogs or chameleons or the like hideous and horrid creatures."

"True," replied the painter, "but then they had not attacked the true God, but only a false idol of the Pagans. 'Tis a mighty difference. The fact is clear, Lucifer, you raised the standard of revolt against the true and veritable King of Earth and Heaven."

"I will not deny it," said Lucifer. "And how many sorts of sins do you charge me with for that?"

"Seven, it is like enough," the painter answered, "and deadly sins one and all."

"Seven!" exclaimed the Angel of Darkness; "well! the number is canonical. Everything goes by sevens in my history, which is close bound up with God's. Spinello, you deem me proud, angry and envious. I enter no protest, provided you allow that glory was my only aim. Do you deem me covetous? Granted again; Covetousness is a virtue for Princes. For Gluttony and Lust, if you hold me guilty, I will not complain. Remains *Indolence*."

As he pronounced the word, Lucifer crossed his arms across his breast, and shaking his gloomy head, tossed his flaming locks:

"Tell me, Spinello, do you really think I am indolent? Do you take me for a coward? Do you hold that in my revolt I showed a lack of courage? Nay! you cannot. Then it was but just to paint me in the guise of a hero, with a proud countenance. You should wrong no one, not even the Devil. Cannot you see that you insult Him you make prayer to, when you give Him for adversary a vile, monstrous toad? Spinello, you are very ignorant for a man of your age. I have a great mind to pull your ears, as they do to an ill-conditioned schoolboy."

At this threat, and seeing the arm of Lucifer already stretched out towards him, Spinello clapped his hand to his head and began to howl with terror.

His good wife, waking up with a start, asked him what ailed him. He told her with chattering teeth, how he had just seen Lucifer and had been in terror for his ears.

"I told you so," retorted the worthy dame; "I knew all those figures you will go on painting on the walls would end by driving you mad."

"I am not mad," protested the painter. "I saw him with my own eyes; and he is beautiful to look on, albeit proud and sad. First thing tomorrow I will blot out the horrid figure I have drawn and set in its place the shape I beheld in my dream. For we must not wrong even the Devil himself."

"You had best go to sleep again," scolded his wife. "You are talking stark nonsense, and unchristian to boot."

Spinello tried to rise, but his strength failed him and he fell back unconscious on his pillow. He lingered on a few days in a high fever, and then died.

The Devil

Maxim Gorky

This story shows reminiscences of Le Sage's *Le Diable Boiteux*. It will be recalled that Asmodeus also lifts the roofs of the houses of Madrid and exhibits their interior to his benefactor. The fate of a Russian author was, indeed, a very sad affair.

> In all lands have the writers drunk of life's cup of bitterness, have they been bruised by life's sharp corners and torn by life's pointed thorns. Chill penury, public neglect, and ill health have been the lot of many an author in countries other than Russia. But in the land of the Tsar's men of letters had to face problems and perils which were peculiarly their own, and which have not been duplicated in any other country on the globe—Every man of letters was under suspicion. The government of Russia treated every author as its natural enemy, and made him feel frequently the weight of its heavy hand. The wreath of laurels on the brow of almost every poet was turned by the tyrants of his country into a crown of thorns.
>
> (From the present writer's essay "The Gloom and Glory of Russian Literature" in *The Open Court* for July, 1918.)

Life is a burden in the Fall,—the sad season of decay and death!

The grey days, the weeping, sunless sky, the dark nights, the growling, whining wind, the heavy, black autumn shadows—all that drives clouds of gloomy thoughts over the human soul, and fills it with a mysterious fear of life where nothing is permanent, all is in an eternal flux; things are born, decay, die—why?—for what purpose?—

Sometimes the strength fails us to battle against the tenebrous thoughts that enfold the soul late in the autumn, therefore those who want to assuage their bitterness ought to meet them half way. This is the only way by which they will escape from the chaos of despair and doubt, and will enter on the terra firma of self-confidence.

But it is a laborious path, it leads through thorny brambles that lacerate the living heart, and on that path the devil always lies in ambush. It is that best of all the devils, with whom the great Goethe has made us acquainted—

My story is about that devil.

****

The devil suffered from ennui.

He is too wise to ridicule everything.

He knows that there are phenomena of life which the devil himself is not able to rail at; for example, he has never applied the sharp scalpel of his irony to the majestic fact of his existence. To tell the truth, our favourite devil is more bold than clever, and if we were to look more closely at him, we might discover that, like ourselves, he wastes most of his time on trifles. But we had better leave that alone; we are not children that break their best toys in order to discover what is in them.

The devil once wandered over the cemetery in the darkness of an autumn night: he felt lonely and whistled softly as he looked around himself in search of a distraction. He whistled an old song— my father's favourite song,—

When, in autumnal days,
A leaf from its branch is torn
And on high by the wind is borne.

And the wind sang with him, soughing over the graves and among the black crosses, and heavy autumnal clouds slowly crawled over the heaven and with their cold tears watered the narrow dwellings of the dead. The mournful trees in the cemetery timidly creaked under the strokes of the wind and stretched their bare branches to the speechless clouds. The branches were now and then caught by the crosses, and then a dull, shuffling, awful sound passed over the churchyard—

The devil was whistling, and he thought:

"I wonder how the dead feel in such weather! No doubt, the dampness goes down to them, and although they are secure against rheumatism ever since the day of their death, yet, I suppose, they do not feel comfortable. How, if I called one of them up and had a talk with him? It would be a little distraction for me, and, very likely, for him also. I will call him! Somewhere around here they have buried an old friend of mine, an author—I used to visit him when he was alive—why not renew our acquaintance? People of his kind are dreadfully exacting. I shall find out whether the grave satisfies him completely. But where is his grave?"

And the devil who, as is well known, knows everything, wandered for a long time about the cemetery, before he found the author's grave—

"Oh there!" he called out as he knocked with his claws at the heavy stone under which his acquaintance was put away.

"Get up!"

"What for?" came the dull answer from below.

"I need you."

"I won't get up."

"Why?"

"Who are you, anyway?"

"You know me."

"The censor?"

"Ha, ha, ha! No!"

"Maybe a secret policeman?"

"No, no!"

"Not a critic, either?"

"I am the devil."

"Well, I'll be out in a minute."

The stone lifted itself from the grave, the earth burst open, and a skeleton came out of it. It was a very common skeleton, just the kind that students study anatomy by: only it was dirty, had no wire connections, and in the empty sockets there shone a blue phosphoric light instead of eyes. It crawled out of the ground, shook its bones in order to throw off the earth that stuck to them, making a dry, rattling noise with them, and raising up its skull, looked with its cold, blue eyes at the murky, cloud-covered sky. "I hope you are well!" said the devil.

"How can I be?" curtly answered the author. He spoke in a strange, low voice, as if two bones were grating against each other.

"Oh, excuse my greeting!" the devil said pleasantly.

"Never mind!—But why have you raised me?"

"I just wanted to take a walk with you, though the weather is very bad.

"I suppose you are not afraid of catching a cold?" asked the devil.

"Not at all, I got used to catching colds during my lifetime."

"Yes, I remember, you died pretty cold."

"I should say I did! They had poured enough cold water over me all my life."

They walked beside each other over the narrow path, between graves and crosses. Two blue beams fell from the author's eyes upon the ground and lit the way for the devil. A drizzling rain sprinkled over them, and the wind freely passed between the author's bare ribs and through his breast where there was no longer a heart.

"We are going to town?" he asked the devil.

"What interests you there?"

"Life, my dear sir," the author said impassionately.

"What! It still has a meaning for you?"

"Indeed it has!"

"But why?"

"How am I to say it? A man measures all by the quantity of his effort, and if he carries a common stone down from the summit of Ararat, that stone becomes a gem to him."

"Poor fellow!" smiled the devil.

"But also happy man!" the author retorted coldly.

The devil shrugged his shoulders.

They left the churchyard, and before them lay a street,—two rows of houses, and between them was darkness in which the miserable lamps clearly proved the want of light upon earth.

"Tell me," the devil spoke after a pause, "how do you like your grave?"

"Now I am used to it, and it is all right: it is very quiet there."

"Is it not damp down there in the Fall?" asked the devil.

"A little. But you get used to that. The greatest annoyance comes from those various idiots who ramble over the cemetery and accidentally stumble on my grave. I don't know how long I have been lying in my grave, for I and everything around me is unchangeable, and the concept of time does not exist for me."

"You have been in the ground four years,—it will soon be five," said the devil.

"Indeed? Well then, there have been three people at my grave during that time. Those accursed people make me nervous. One, you see, straight away denied the fact of my existence: he read my name on the tombstone and said confidently: 'There never was such a man! I have never read him, though I remember such a name: when I was a boy, there lived a man of that name who had a broker's shop in our street.' How do you like that? And my articles appeared for sixteen years in the most popular periodicals, and three times during my lifetime my books came out in separate editions."

"There were two more editions since your death," the devil informed him.

"Well, you see? Then came two, and one of them said: 'Oh, that's that fellow!' 'Yes, that is he!' answered the other. 'Yes, they used to read him in the auld lang syne.' 'They read a lot of them.' 'What was it he preached?' 'Oh, generally, ideas of beauty, goodness, and so forth.' 'Oh, yes, I remember.' 'He had a heavy tongue.' 'There is a lot of them in the ground:—yes, Russia is rich in talents'—And those asses went away. It is true, warm words do not raise the temperature of the grave, and I do not care for that, yet it hurts me. And oh, how I wanted to give them a piece of my mind!"

"You ought to have given them a fine tongue-lashing!" smiled the devil.

"No, that would not have done. On the verge of the twentieth century it would be absurd for dead people to scold, and, besides, it would be hard on the materialists."

The devil again felt the ennui coming over him.

This author had always wished in his lifetime to be a bridegroom at all weddings and a corpse at all burials, and now that all is dead in him, his egotism is still alive. Is man of any importance to life?

Of importance is only the human spirit, and only the spirit deserves applause and recognition—How annoying people are! The devil was on the point of proposing to the author to return to his grave, when an idea flashed through his evil head. They had just reached a square, and heavy masses of buildings surrounded them on all sides. The dark, wet sky hung low over the square; it seemed as though it rested on the roofs and murkily looked at the dirty earth.

"Say," said the devil as he inclined pleasantly towards the author, "don't you want to know how your wife is getting on?"

"I don't know whether I want to," the author spoke slowly.

"I see, you are a thorough corpse!" called out the devil to annoy him.

"Oh, I don't know?" said the author and jauntily shook his bones. "I don't mind seeing her; besides, she will not see me, or if she will, she cannot recognize me!"

"Of course!" the devil assured him.

"You know, I only said so because she did not like for me to go away long from home," explained the author.

And suddenly the wall of a house disappeared or became as transparent as glass. The author saw the inside of large apartments, and it was so light and cosy in them.

"Elegant appointments!" he grated his bones approvingly: "Very fine appointments! If I had lived in such rooms, I would be alive now."

"I like it, too," said the devil and smiled. "And it is not expensive—it only costs some three thousands."

"Hem, that not expensive? I remember my largest work brought me 815 *roubles*, and I worked over it a whole year. But who lives here?"

"Your wife," said the devil.

"I declare! That is good—for her."

"Yes, and here comes her husband."

"She is so pretty now, and how well she is dressed! Her husband, you say? What a fine looking fellow! Rather a *bourgeois phiz*,—kind, but somewhat stupid! He looks as if he might be cunning,—well, just the face to please a woman."

"Do you want me to heave a sigh for you?" the devil proposed and looked maliciously at the author. But he was taken up with the scene before him.

"What happy, jolly faces both have! They are evidently satisfied with life. Tell me, does she love him?"

"Oh, yes, very much!"

"And who is he?"

"A clerk in a millinery shop."

"A clerk in a millinery shop," the author repeated slowly and did not utter a word for some time. The devil looked at him and smiled a merry smile.

"Do you like that?" he asked.

The author spoke with an effort:

"I had some children—I know they are alive—I had some children—a son and a daughter—I used to think then that my son would turn out in time a good man—"

"There are plenty of good men, but what the world needs is perfect men," said the devil coolly and whistled a jolly march.

"I think the clerk is probably a poor pedagogue—and my son—"

The author's empty skull shook sadly.

"Just look how he is embracing her! They are living an easy life!" exclaimed the devil.

"Yes. Is that clerk a rich man?"

"No, he was poorer than I, but your wife is rich."

"My wife? Where did she get the money from?"

"From the sale of your books!"

"Oh!" said the author and shook his bare and empty skull. "Oh! Then it simply means that I have worked for a certain clerk?"

"I confess it looks that way," the devil chimed in merrily.

The author looked at the ground and said to the devil: "Take me back to my grave!"

—It was late. A rain fell, heavy clouds hung in the sky, and the author rattled his bones as he marched rapidly to his grave—The devil walked behind him and whistled merrily.

****

My reader is, of course, dissatisfied. My reader is surfeited with literature, and even the people that write only to please him, are rarely to his taste. In the present case my reader is also dissatisfied because I have said nothing about hell. As my reader is justly convinced that after death he will find his way there, he would like to know something about hell during his lifetime. Really, I can't tell anything pleasant to my reader on that score, because there is no hell, no fiery hell which it is so easy to imagine. Yet, there is something else and infinitely more terrible.

The moment the doctor will have said about you to your friends: "He is dead!" you will enter an immeasurable, illuminated space, and that is the space of the consciousness of your mistakes.

You lie in the grave, in a narrow coffin, and your miserable life rotates about you like a wheel.

It moves painfully slow, and passes before you from your first conscious step to the last moment of your life.

You will see all that you have hidden from yourself during your lifetime, all the lies and meanness of your existence: you will think over anew all your past thoughts, and you will see every wrong step of yours,—all your life will be gone over, to its minutest details!

And to increase your torments, you will know that on that narrow and stupid road which you have traversed, others are marching, and pushing each other, and hurrying, and lying—And you understand that they are doing it all only to find out in time how shameful it is to live such a wretched, soulless life.

And though you see them hastening on towards their destruction, you are in no way able to warn them: you will not move nor cry, and your helpless desire to aid them will tear your soul to pieces.

Your life passes before you, and you see it from the start, and there is no end to the work of your conscience, and there will be no end—and to the horror of your torments there will never be an end—never!

Bonus Stories

Young Goodman Brown

Nathaniel Hawthorne

Young Goodman Brown came forth at sunset into the street at Salem village; but put his head back, after crossing the threshold, to exchange a parting kiss with his young wife. And Faith, as the wife was aptly named, thrust her own pretty head into the street, letting the wind play with the pink ribbons of her cap while she called to Goodman Brown.

"Dearest heart," whispered she, softly and rather sadly, when her lips were close to his ear, "prithee put off your journey until sunrise and sleep in your own bed tonight. A lone woman is troubled with such dreams and such thoughts that she's afeard of herself sometimes. Pray tarry with me this night, dear husband, of all nights in the year."

"My love and my Faith," replied young Goodman Brown, "of all nights in the year, this one night must I tarry away from thee. My journey, as thou callest it, forth and back again, must needs be done 'twixt now and sunrise. What, my sweet, pretty wife, dost thou doubt me already, and we but three months married?"

"Then God bless you!" said Faith, with the pink ribbons; "and may you find all well when you come back."

"*Amen!*" cried Goodman Brown. "Say thy prayers, dear Faith, and go to bed at dusk, and no harm will come to thee."

So they parted; and the young man pursued his way until, being about to turn the corner by the meeting-house, he looked back and saw the head of Faith still peeping after him with a melancholy air, in spite of her pink ribbons.

"Poor little Faith!" thought he, for his heart smote him. "What a wretch am I to leave her on such an errand! She talks of dreams, too.

Methought as she spoke there was trouble in her face, as if a dream had warned her what work is to be done tonight. But no, no; 't would kill her to think it. Well, she's a blessed angel on earth; and after this one night I'll cling to her skirts and follow her to heaven."

With this excellent resolve for the future, Goodman Brown felt himself justified in making more haste on his present evil purpose. He had taken a dreary road, darkened by all the gloomiest trees of the forest, which barely stood aside to let the narrow path creep through, and closed immediately behind. It was all as lonely as could be; and there is this peculiarity in such a solitude, that the traveller knows not who may be concealed by the innumerable trunks and the thick boughs overhead; so that with lonely footsteps he may yet be passing through an unseen multitude.

"There may be a devilish Indian behind every tree," said Goodman Brown to himself; and he glanced fearfully behind him as he added, "What if the devil himself should be at my very elbow!"

His head being turned back, he passed a crook of the road, and, looking forward again, beheld the figure of a man, in grave and decent attire, seated at the foot of an old tree. He arose at Goodman Brown's approach and walked onward side by side with him.

"You are late, Goodman Brown," said he. "The clock of the Old South was striking as I came through Boston, and that is full fifteen minutes agone."

"Faith kept me back a while," replied the young man, with a tremor in his voice, caused by the sudden appearance of his companion, though not wholly unexpected.

It was now deep dusk in the forest, and deepest in that part of it where these two were journeying. As nearly as could be discerned, the second traveller was about fifty years old, apparently in the same rank of life as Goodman Brown, and bearing a considerable resemblance to him, though perhaps more in expression than features. Still they might have been taken for father and son. And yet, though the elder person was as simply clad as the younger, and as simple in manner too, he had an indescribable air of one who knew the world, and who would not have felt abashed at the governor's dinner table or in King William's court, were it possible that his affairs should call him thither. But the only thing about him that could be fixed upon as remarkable was his staff, which bore the likeness of a great black snake, so curiously wrought that it might almost be seen to twist and wriggle itself like a living serpent. This, of course, must have been an ocular deception, assisted by the uncertain light.

"Come, Goodman Brown," cried his fellow-traveller, "this is a dull pace for the beginning of a journey. Take my staff, if you are so soon weary."

"Friend," said the other, exchanging his slow pace for a full stop, "having kept covenant by meeting thee here, it is my purpose now to return whence I came. I have scruples touching the matter thou wot'st of."

"Sayest thou so?" replied he of the serpent, smiling apart. "Let us walk on, nevertheless, reasoning as we go; and if I convince thee not thou shalt turn back. We are but a little way in the forest yet."

"Too far! too far!" exclaimed the goodman, unconsciously resuming his walk. "My father never went into the woods on such an errand, nor his father before him. We have been a race of honest men and good Christians since the days of the martyrs; and shall I be the first of the name of Brown that ever took this path and kept—"

"Such company, thou wouldst say," observed the elder person, interpreting his pause. "Well said, Goodman Brown! I have been as well acquainted with your family as with ever a one among the Puritans; and that's no trifle to say. I helped your grandfather, the constable, when he lashed the Quaker woman so smartly through the streets of Salem; and it was I that brought your father a pitch-pine knot, kindled at my own hearth, to set fire to an Indian village, in King Philip's war. They were my good friends, both; and many a pleasant walk have we had along this path, and returned merrily after midnight. I would fain be friends with you for their sake."

"If it be as thou sayest," replied Goodman Brown, "I marvel they never spoke of these matters; or, verily, I marvel not, seeing that the least rumour of the sort would have driven them from New England. We are a people of prayer, and good works to boot, and abide no such wickedness."

"Wickedness or not," said the traveller with the twisted staff, "I have a very general acquaintance here in New England. The deacons of many a church have drunk the communion wine with me; the selectmen of divers towns make me their chairman; and a majority of the Great and General Court are firm supporters of my interest. The governor and I, too—But these are state secrets."

"Can this be so?" cried Goodman Brown, with a stare of amazement at his undisturbed companion. "Howbeit, I have nothing to do with the governor and council; they have their own ways, and are no rule for a simple husbandman like me. But, were I to go on with thee, how should I meet the eye of that good old man, our minister, at Salem village? Oh, his voice would make me tremble both Sabbath day and lecture day."

Thus far the elder traveller had listened with due gravity; but now burst into a fit of irrepressible mirth, shaking himself so violently that his snake-like staff actually seemed to wriggle in sympathy.

"Ha! ha! ha!" shouted he again and again; then composing himself, "Well, go on, Goodman Brown, go on; but, prithee, don't kill me with laughing."

"Well, then, to end the matter at once," said Goodman Brown, considerably nettled, "there is my wife, Faith. It would break her dear little heart; and I'd rather break my own."

"Nay, if that be the case," answered the other, "e'en go thy ways, Goodman Brown. I would not for twenty old women like the one hobbling before us that Faith should come to any harm."

As he spoke he pointed his staff at a female figure on the path, in whom Goodman Brown recognized a very pious and exemplary dame, who had taught him his catechism in youth, and was still his moral and spiritual adviser, jointly with the minister and Deacon Gookin.

"A marvel, truly, that Goody Cloyse should be so far in the wilderness at nightfall," said he. "But with your leave, friend, I shall take a cut through the woods until we have left this Christian woman behind. Being a stranger to you, she might ask whom I was consorting with and whither I was going."

"Be it so," said his fellow-traveller. "Betake you to the woods, and let me keep the path."

Accordingly the young man turned aside, but took care to watch his companion, who advanced softly along the road until he had come within a staff's length of the old dame. She, meanwhile, was making the best of her way, with singular speed for so aged a woman, and mumbling some indistinct words—a prayer, doubtless—as she went. The traveller put forth his staff and touched her withered neck with what seemed the serpent's tail.

"The devil!" screamed the pious old lady.

"Then Goody Cloyse knows her old friend?" observed the traveller, confronting her and leaning on his writhing stick.

"Ah, forsooth, and is it your worship indeed?" cried the good dame. "Yea, truly is it, and in the very image of my old gossip, Goodman Brown, the grandfather of the silly fellow that now is. But—would your worship believe it?—my broomstick hath strangely disappeared, stolen, as I suspect, by that unhanged witch, Goody Cory, and that, too, when I was all anointed with the juice of smallage, and cinquefoil, and wolf's bane."

"Mingled with fine wheat and the fat of a new-born babe," said the shape of old Goodman Brown.

"Ah, your worship knows the recipe," cried the old lady, cackling aloud. "So, as I was saying, being all ready for the meeting, and no horse to ride on, I made up my mind to foot it; for they tell me there is a nice young man to be taken into communion tonight. But now your good worship will lend me your arm, and we shall be there in a twinkling."

"That can hardly be," answered her friend. "I may not spare you my arm, Goody Cloyse; but here is my staff, if you will."

So saying, he threw it down at her feet, where, perhaps, it assumed life, being one of the rods which its owner had formerly lent to the Egyptian *magi*. Of this fact, however, Goodman Brown could not take cognizance. He had cast up his eyes in astonishment, and, looking down again, beheld neither Goody Cloyse nor the serpentine staff, but his fellow-traveller alone, who waited for him as calmly as if nothing had happened.

"That old woman taught me my catechism," said the young man; and there was a world of meaning in this simple comment.

They continued to walk onward, while the elder traveller exhorted his companion to make good speed and persevere in the path, discoursing so aptly that his arguments seemed rather to spring up in the bosom of his auditor than to be suggested by himself. As they went, he plucked a branch of maple to serve for a walking stick, and began to strip it of the twigs and little boughs, which were wet with evening dew. The moment his fingers touched them they became strangely withered and dried up as with a week's sunshine. Thus the pair proceeded, at a good free pace, until suddenly, in a gloomy hollow of the road, Goodman Brown sat himself down on the stump of a tree and refused to go any farther.

"Friend," said he, stubbornly, "my mind is made up. Not another step will I budge on this errand. What if a wretched old woman do choose to go to the devil when I thought she was going to heaven: is that any reason why I should quit my dear Faith and go after her?"

"You will think better of this by and by," said his acquaintance, composedly. "Sit here and rest yourself a while; and when you feel like moving again, there is my staff to help you along."

Without more words, he threw his companion the maple stick, and was as speedily out of sight as if he had vanished into the deepening gloom. The young man sat a few moments by the roadside, applauding himself greatly, and thinking with how clear a conscience he should meet the minister in his morning walk, nor shrink from the eye of good old Deacon Gookin. And what calm sleep would be his that very night, which was to have been spent so wickedly, but so purely and sweetly now, in the arms of Faith! Amidst these pleasant and praiseworthy meditations, Goodman Brown heard the tramp of horses along the road, and deemed it advisable to conceal himself within the verge of the forest, conscious of the guilty purpose that had brought him thither, though now so happily turned from it.

On came the hoof tramps and the voices of the riders, two grave old voices, conversing soberly as they drew near. These mingled sounds appeared to pass along the road, within a few yards of the young man's hiding-place; but, owing doubtless to the depth of the gloom at that particular spot, neither the travellers nor their steeds were visible. Though their figures brushed the small boughs by the wayside, it could not be seen that they intercepted, even for a moment, the faint gleam from the strip of bright sky athwart which they must have passed. Goodman Brown alternately crouched and stood on tiptoe, pulling aside the branches and thrusting forth his head as far as he durst without discerning so much as a shadow. It vexed him the more, because he could have sworn, were such a thing possible, that he recognized the voices of the minister and Deacon Gookin, jogging along quietly, as they were wont to do, when bound to some ordination or ecclesiastical council. While yet within hearing, one of the riders stopped to pluck a switch.

"Of the two, reverend sir," said the voice like the deacon's, "I had rather miss an ordination dinner than tonight's meeting. They tell me that some of our community are to be here from Falmouth and beyond, and others from Connecticut and Rhode Island, besides several of the Indian *powwows*, who, after their fashion, know almost as much deviltry as the best of us. Moreover, there is a goodly young woman to be taken into communion."

"Mighty well, Deacon Gookin!" replied the solemn old tones of the minister. "Spur up, or we shall be late. Nothing can be done, you know, until I get on the ground."

The hoofs clattered again; and the voices, talking so strangely in the empty air, passed on through the forest, where no church had ever been gathered or solitary Christian prayed. Whither, then, could these holy men be journeying so deep into the heathen wilderness? Young Goodman Brown caught hold of a tree for support, being ready to sink down on the ground, faint and overburdened with the heavy sickness of his heart. He looked up to the sky, doubting whether there really was a heaven above him. Yet there was the blue arch, and the stars brightening in it.

"With heaven above and Faith below, I will yet stand firm against the devil!" cried Goodman Brown.

While he still gazed upward into the deep arch of the firmament and had lifted his hands to pray, a cloud, though no wind was stirring, hurried across the zenith and hid the brightening stars. The blue sky was still visible, except directly overhead, where this black mass of cloud was sweeping swiftly northward. Aloft in the air, as if from the depths of the cloud, came a confused and doubtful sound of voices. Once the listener fancied that he could distinguish the accents of towns-people of his own, men and women, both pious and ungodly, many of whom he had met at the communion table, and had seen others rioting at the tavern. The next moment, so indistinct were the sounds, he doubted whether he had heard aught but the murmur of the old forest, whispering without a wind. Then came a stronger swell of those familiar tones, heard daily in the sunshine at Salem village, but never until now from a cloud of night There was one voice of a young woman, uttering lamentations, yet with an uncertain sorrow, and entreating for some favour, which, perhaps, it would grieve her to obtain; and all the unseen multitude, both saints and sinners, seemed to encourage her onward.

"Faith!" shouted Goodman Brown, in a voice of agony and desperation; and the echoes of the forest mocked him, crying, "Faith! Faith!" as if bewildered wretches were seeking her all through the wilderness.

The cry of grief, rage, and terror was yet piercing the night, when the unhappy husband held his breath for a response. There was a scream, drowned immediately in a louder murmur of voices, fading into far-off laughter, as the dark cloud swept away, leaving the clear and silent sky above Goodman Brown. But something fluttered lightly down through the air and caught on the branch of a tree. The young man seized it, and beheld a pink ribbon.

"My Faith is gone!" cried he, after one stupefied moment. "There is no good on earth; and sin is but a name. Come, devil; for to thee is this world given."

And, maddened with despair, so that he laughed loud and long, did Goodman Brown grasp his staff and set forth again, at such a rate that he seemed to fly along the forest path rather than to walk or run. The road grew wilder and drearier and more faintly traced, and vanished at length, leaving him in the heart of the dark wilderness, still rushing onward with the instinct that guides mortal man to evil. The whole forest was peopled with frightful sounds— the creaking of the trees, the howling of wild beasts, and the yell of Indians; while sometimes the wind tolled like a distant church bell, and sometimes gave a broad roar around the traveller, as if all Nature were laughing him to scorn. But he was himself the chief horror of the scene, and shrank not from its other horrors.

"Ha! ha! ha!" roared Goodman Brown when the wind laughed at him.

"Let us hear which will laugh loudest. Think not to frighten me with your deviltry. Come witch, come wizard, come Indian *pow-wow*, come devil himself, and here comes Goodman Brown. You may as well fear him as he fear you."

In truth, all through the haunted forest there could be nothing more frightful than the figure of Goodman Brown. On he flew among the black pines, brandishing his staff with frenzied gestures, now giving vent to an inspiration of horrid blasphemy, and now shouting forth such laughter as set all the echoes of the forest laughing like demons around him. The fiend in his own shape is less hideous than when he rages in the breast of man. Thus sped the demoniac on his course, until, quivering among the trees, he saw a red light before him, as when the felled trunks and branches of a clearing have been set on fire, and throw up their lurid blaze against the sky, at the hour of midnight. He paused, in a lull of the tempest that had driven him onward, and heard the swell of what seemed a hymn, rolling solemnly from a distance with the weight of many voices. He knew the tune; it was a familiar one in the choir of the village meeting-house. The verse died heavily away, and was lengthened by a chorus, not of human voices, but of all the sounds of the benighted wilderness pealing in awful harmony together. Goodman Brown cried out, and his cry was lost to his own ear by its unison with the cry of the desert.

In the interval of silence he stole forward until the light glared full upon his eyes. At one extremity of an open space, hemmed in by the dark wall of the forest, arose a rock, bearing some rude, natural resemblance either to an altar or a pulpit, and surrounded by four blazing pines, their tops aflame, their stems untouched, like candles at an evening meeting. The mass of foliage that had overgrown the summit of the rock was all on fire, blazing high into the night and fitfully illuminating the whole field. Each pendent twig and leafy festoon was in a blaze. As the red light arose and fell, a numerous congregation alternately shone forth, then disappeared in shadow, and again grew, as it were, out of the darkness, peopling the heart of the solitary woods at once.

"A grave and dark-clad company," quoth Goodman Brown.

In truth they were such. Among them, quivering to and fro between gloom and splendour, appeared faces that would be seen next day at the council board of the province, and others which, Sabbath after Sabbath, looked devoutly heavenward, and benignantly over the crowded pews, from the holiest pulpits in the land. Some affirm that the lady of the governor was there. At least there were high dames well known to her, and wives of honoured husbands, and widows, a great multitude, and ancient maidens, all of excellent repute, and fair young girls, who trembled lest their mothers should espy them. Either the sudden gleams of light flashing over the obscure field bedazzled Goodman Brown, or he recognized a score of the church members of Salem village famous for their especial sanctity. Good old Deacon Gookin had arrived, and waited at the skirts of that venerable saint, his revered pastor. But, irreverently consorting with these grave, reputable, and pious people, these elders of the church, these chaste dames and dewy virgins, there were men of dissolute lives and women of spotted fame, wretches given over to all mean and filthy vice, and suspected even of horrid crimes. It was strange to see that the good shrank not from the wicked, nor were the sinners abashed by the saints. Scattered also among their pale-faced enemies were the Indian priests, or powwows, who had often scared their native forest with more hideous incantations than any known to English witchcraft.

"But where is Faith?" thought Goodman Brown; and, as hope came into his heart, he trembled.

Another verse of the hymn arose, a slow and mournful strain, such as the pious love, but joined to words which expressed all that our nature can conceive of sin, and darkly hinted at far more. Unfathomable to mere mortals is the lore of fiends. Verse after verse was sung; and still the chorus of the desert swelled between like the deepest tone of a mighty organ; and with the final peal of that dreadful anthem there came a sound, as if the roaring wind, the rushing streams, the howling beasts, and every other voice of the unconcerted wilderness were mingling and according with the voice of guilty man in homage to the prince of all. The four blazing pines threw up a loftier flame, and obscurely discovered shapes and visages of horror on the smoke wreaths above the impious assembly. At the same moment the fire on the rock shot redly forth and formed a glowing arch above its base, where now appeared a figure. With reverence be it spoken, the figure bore no slight similitude, both in garb and manner, to some grave divine of the New England churches.

"Bring forth the converts!" cried a voice that echoed through the field and rolled into the forest.

At the word, Goodman Brown stepped forth from the shadow of the trees and approached the congregation, with whom he felt a loathful brotherhood by the sympathy of all that was wicked in his heart. He could have well-nigh sworn that the shape of his own dead father beckoned him to advance, looking downward from a smoke wreath, while a woman, with dim features of despair, threw out her hand to warn him back. Was it his mother? But he had no power to retreat one step, nor to resist, even in thought, when the minister and good old Deacon Gookin seized his arms and led him to the blazing rock. Thither came also the slender form of a veiled female, led between Goody Cloyse, that pious teacher of the catechism, and Martha Carrier, who had received the devil's promise to be queen of hell. A rampant hag was she. And there stood the proselytes beneath the canopy of fire.

"Welcome, my children," said the dark figure, "to the communion of your race. Ye have found thus young your nature and your destiny. My children, look behind you!"

They turned; and flashing forth, as it were, in a sheet of flame, the fiend worshippers were seen; the smile of welcome gleamed darkly on every visage.

"There," resumed the sable form, "are all whom ye have reverenced from youth. Ye deemed them holier than yourselves, and shrank from your own sin, contrasting it with their lives of righteousness and prayerful aspirations heavenward. Yet here are they all in my worshipping assembly. This night it shall be granted you to know their secret deeds: how hoary-bearded elders of the church have whispered wanton words to the young maids of their households; how many a woman, eager for widows' weeds, has given her husband a drink at bedtime and let him sleep his last sleep in her bosom; how beardless youths have made haste to inherit their fathers' wealth; and how fair damsels—blush not, sweet ones—have dug little graves in the garden, and bidden me, the sole guest to an infant's funeral. By the sympathy of your human hearts for sin ye shall scent out all the places—whether in church, bedchamber, street, field, or forest—where crime has been committed, and shall exult to behold the whole earth one stain of guilt, one mighty blood spot. Far more than this. It shall be yours to penetrate, in every bosom, the deep mystery of sin, the fountain of all wicked arts, and which inexhaustibly supplies more evil impulses than human power—than my power at its utmost—can make manifest in deeds. And now, my children, look upon each other."

They did so; and, by the blaze of the hell-kindled torches, the wretched man beheld his Faith, and the wife her husband, trembling before that unhallowed altar.

"Lo, there ye stand, my children," said the figure, in a deep and solemn tone, almost sad with its despairing awfulness, as if his once angelic nature could yet mourn for our miserable race. "Depending upon one another's hearts, ye had still hoped that virtue were not all a dream. Now are ye undeceived. Evil is the nature of mankind. Evil must be your only happiness. Welcome again, my children, to the communion of your race."

"Welcome," repeated the fiend worshippers, in one cry of despair and triumph.

And there they stood, the only pair, as it seemed, who were yet hesitating on the verge of wickedness in this dark world. A basin was hollowed, naturally, in the rock. Did it contain water, reddened by the lurid light? or was it blood? or, perchance, a liquid flame? Herein did the shape of evil dip his hand and prepare to lay the mark of baptism upon their foreheads, that they might be partakers of the mystery of sin, more conscious of the secret guilt of others, both in deed and thought, than they could now be of their own. The husband cast one look at his pale wife, and Faith at him. What polluted wretches would the next glance show them to each other, shuddering alike at what they disclosed and what they saw!

"Faith! Faith!" cried the husband, "look up to heaven, and resist the wicked one."

Whether Faith obeyed he knew not. Hardly had he spoken when he found himself amid calm night and solitude, listening to a roar of the wind which died heavily away through the forest. He staggered against the rock, and felt it chill and damp; while a hanging twig, that had been all on fire, besprinkled his cheek with the coldest dew.

The next morning young Goodman Brown came slowly into the street of Salem village, staring around him like a bewildered man. The good old minister was taking a walk along the graveyard to get an appetite for breakfast and meditate his sermon, and bestowed a blessing, as he passed, on Goodman Brown. He shrank from the venerable saint as if to avoid an anathema. Old Deacon Gookin was at domestic worship, and the holy words of his prayer were heard through the open window. "What God doth the wizard pray to?" quoth Goodman Brown. Goody Cloyse, that excellent old Christian, stood in the early sunshine at her own lattice, catechizing a little girl who had brought her a pint of morning's milk. Goodman Brown snatched away the child as from the grasp of the fiend himself. Turning the corner by the meeting-house, he spied the head of Faith, with the pink ribbons, gazing anxiously forth, and bursting into such joy at sight of him that she skipped along the street and almost kissed her husband before the whole village. But Goodman Brown looked sternly and sadly into her face, and passed on without a greeting.

Had Goodman Brown fallen asleep in the forest and only dreamed a wild dream of a witch-meeting?

Be it so if you will; but, alas! it was a dream of evil omen for young Goodman Brown. A stern, a sad, a darkly meditative, a distrustful, if not a desperate man did he become from the night of that fearful dream. On the Sabbath day, when the congregation were singing a holy psalm, he could not listen because an anthem of sin rushed loudly upon his ear and drowned all the blessed strain. When the minister spoke from the pulpit with power and fervid eloquence, and, with his hand on the open Bible, of the sacred truths of our religion, and of saint-like lives and triumphant deaths, and of future bliss or misery unutterable, then did Goodman Brown turn pale, dreading lest the roof should thunder down upon the gray blasphemer and his hearers. Often, waking suddenly at midnight, he shrank from the bosom of Faith; and at morning or eventide, when the family knelt down at prayer, he scowled and muttered to himself, and gazed sternly at his wife, and turned away. And when he had lived long, and was borne to his grave a hoary corpse, followed by Faith, an aged woman, and children and grandchildren, a goodly procession, besides neighbours not a few, they carved no hopeful verse upon his tombstone, for his dying hour was gloom.

The Shoemaker and the Devil

Anton Chekhov

It was Christmas Eve. Marya had long been snoring on the stove; all the paraffin in the little lamp had burnt out, but Fyodor Nilov still sat at work. He would long ago have flung aside his work and gone out into the street, but a customer from Kolokolny Lane, who had a fortnight before ordered some boots, had been in the previous day, had abused him roundly, and had ordered him to finish the boots at once before the morning service.

"It's a convict's life!" Fyodor grumbled as he worked. "Some people have been asleep long ago, others are enjoying themselves, while you sit here like some Cain and sew for the devil knows whom...."

To save himself from accidentally falling asleep, he kept taking a bottle from under the table and drinking out of it, and after every pull at it he twisted his head and said aloud:

"What is the reason, kindly tell me, that customers enjoy themselves while I am forced to sit and work for them? Because they have money and I am a beggar?"

He hated all his customers, especially the one who lived in Kolokolny Lane. He was a gentleman of gloomy appearance, with long hair, a yellow face, blue spectacles, and a husky voice. He had a German name which one could not pronounce. It was impossible to tell what was his calling and what he did. When, a fortnight before, Fyodor had gone to take his measure, he, the customer, was sitting on the floor pounding something in a mortar. Before Fyodor had time to say good-morning the contents of the mortar suddenly flared up and burned with a bright red flame; there was a stink of sulphur and burnt feathers, and the room was filled with a thick pink smoke, so that Fyodor sneezed five times; and as he returned home afterwards, he thought: "Anyone who feared God would not have anything to do with things like that."

When there was nothing left in the bottle Fyodor put the boots on the table and sank into thought. He leaned his heavy head on his fist and began thinking of his poverty, of his hard life with no glimmer of light in it. Then he thought of the rich, of their big houses and their carriages, of their hundred-rouble notes.... How nice it would be if the houses of these rich men—the devil flay them!—were smashed, if their horses died, if their fur coats and sable caps got shabby! How splendid it would be if the rich, little by little, changed into beggars having nothing, and he, a poor shoe-maker, were to become rich, and were to lord it over some other poor shoemaker on Christmas Eve.

Dreaming like this, Fyodor suddenly thought of his work, and opened his eyes.

"Here's a go," he thought, looking at the boots. "The job has been finished ever so long ago, and I go on sitting here. I must take the boots to the gentleman."

He wrapped up the work in a red handkerchief, put on his things, and went out into the street. A fine hard snow was falling, pricking the face as though with needles. It was cold, slippery, dark, the gas-lamps burned dimly, and for some reason there was a smell of paraffin in the street, so that Fyodor coughed and cleared his throat. Rich men were driving to and fro on the road, and every rich man had a ham and a bottle of vodka in his hands. Rich young ladies peeped at Fyodor out of the carriages and sledges, put out their tongues and shouted, laughing:

"Beggar! Beggar!"

Students, officers, and merchants walked behind Fyodor, jeering at him and crying:

"Drunkard! Drunkard! Infidel cobbler! Soul of a boot-leg! Beggar!"

All this was insulting, but Fyodor held his tongue and only spat in disgust. But when Kuzma Lebyodkin from Warsaw, a mas-ter-bootmaker, met him and said: "I've married a rich woman and I have men working under me, while you are a beggar and have nothing to eat," Fyodor could not refrain from running after him. He pursued him till he found himself in Kolokolny Lane. His customer lived in the fourth house from the corner on the very top floor. To reach him one had to go through a long, dark courtyard, and then to climb up a very high slippery stair-case which tottered under one's feet. When Fyodor went in to him he was sitting on the floor pounding something in a mortar, just as he had been the fortnight before.

"Your honour, I have brought your boots," said Fyodor sullenly.

The customer got up and began trying on the boots in silence. Desiring to help him, Fyodor went down on one knee and pulled off his old boot, but at once jumped up and staggered towards the door in horror. The customer had not a foot, but a hoof like a horse's.

"Aha!" thought Fyodor; "here's a go!"

The first thing should have been to cross himself, then to leave everything and run downstairs; but he immediately reflected that he was meeting a devil for the first and probably the last time, and not to take advantage of his services would be foolish. He controlled himself and determined to try his luck. Clasping his hands behind him to avoid making the sign of the cross, he coughed respectfully and began:

"They say that there is nothing on earth more evil and impure than the devil, but I am of the opinion, your honour, that the devil is highly educated. He has—excuse my saying it—hoofs and a tail behind, but he has more brains than many a student."

"I like you for what you say," said the devil, flattered. "Thank you, shoemaker! What do you want?"

And without loss of time the shoemaker began complaining of his lot. He began by saying that from his childhood up he had envied the rich. He had always resented it that all people did not live alike in big houses and drive with good horses. Why, he asked, was he poor? How was he worse than Kuzma Lebyodkin from Warsaw, who had his own house, and whose wife wore a hat? He had the same sort of nose, the same hands, feet, head, and back, as the rich, and so why was he forced to work when others were enjoying themselves? Why was he married to Marya and not to a lady smelling of scent? He had often seen beautiful young ladies in the houses of rich customers, but they either took no notice of him whatever, or else sometimes laughed and whispered to each other:

"What a red nose that shoemaker has!" It was true that Marya was a good, kind, hard-working woman, but she was not educated; her hand was heavy and hit hard, and if one had occasion to speak of politics or anything intellectual before her, she would put her spoke in and talk the most awful nonsense.

"What do you want, then?" his customer interrupted him.

"I beg you, your honour Satan Ivanitch, to be graciously pleased to make me a rich man."

"Certainly. Only for that you must give me up your soul! Before the cocks crow, go and sign on this paper here that you give me up your soul."

"Your honour," said Fyodor politely, "when you ordered a pair of boots from me I did not ask for the money in advance. One has first to carry out the order and then ask for payment."

"Oh, very well!" the customer assented.

A bright flame suddenly flared up in the mortar, a pink thick smoke came puffing out, and there was a smell of burnt feathers and sulphur. When the smoke had subsided, Fyodor rubbed his eyes and saw that he was no longer Fyodor, no longer a shoemaker, but quite a different man, wearing a waistcoat and a watch-chain, in a new pair of trousers, and that he was sitting in an armchair at a big table. Two foot men were handing him dishes, bowing low and saying:

"Kindly eat, your honour, and may it do you good!"

What wealth! The footmen handed him a big piece of roast mutton and a dish of cucumbers, and then brought in a frying-pan a roast goose, and a little afterwards boiled pork with horse-radish cream. And how dignified, how genteel it all was! Fyodor ate, and before each dish drank a big glass of excellent vodka, like some general or some count. After the pork he was handed some boiled grain moistened with goose fat, then an omelette with bacon fat, then fried liver, and he went on eating and was delighted. What more? They served, too, a pie with onion and steamed turnip with *kvass*.

"How is it the gentry don't burst with such meals?" he thought.

In conclusion they handed him a big pot of honey. After dinner the devil appeared in blue spectacles and asked with a low bow:

"Are you satisfied with your dinner, Fyodor Pantelyeitch?"

But Fyodor could not answer one word, he was so stuffed after his dinner. The feeling of repletion was unpleasant, oppressive, and to distract his thoughts he looked at the boot on his left foot.

"For a boot like that I used not to take less than seven and a half *roubles*. What shoemaker made it?" he asked.

"Kuzma Lebyodkin," answered the footman.

"Send for him, the fool!"

Kuzma Lebyodkin from Warsaw soon made his appearance. He stopped in a respectful attitude at the door and asked:

"What are your orders, your honour?"

"Hold your tongue!" cried Fyodor, and stamped his foot. "Don't dare to argue; remember your place as a cobbler! Blockhead! You don't know how to make boots! I'll beat your ugly phiz to a jelly! Why have you come?"

"For money."

"What money? Be off! Come on Saturday! Boy, give him a cuff!"

But he at once recalled what a life the customers used to lead him, too, and he felt heavy at heart, and to distract his attention he took a fat pocketbook out of his pocket and began counting his money. There was a great deal of money, but Fyodor wanted more still. The devil in the blue spectacles brought him another notebook fatter still, but he wanted even more; and the more he counted it, the more discontented he became.

In the evening the evil one brought him a full-bosomed lady in a red dress, and said that this was his new wife. He spent the whole evening kissing her and eating gingerbreads, and at night he went to bed on a soft, downy feather-bed, turned from side to side, and could not go to sleep. He felt uncanny.

"We have a great deal of money," he said to his wife; "we must look out or thieves will be breaking in. You had better go and look with a candle."

He did not sleep all night, and kept getting up to see if his box was all right. In the morning he had to go to church to matins. In church the same honour is done to rich and poor alike. When Fyodor was poor he used to pray in church like this: "God, forgive me, a sinner!" He said the same thing now though he had become rich. What difference was there? And after death Fyodor rich would not be buried in gold, not in diamonds, but in the same black earth as the poorest beggar. Fyodor would burn in the same fire as cobblers. Fyodor resented all this, and, too, he felt weighed down all over by his dinner, and instead of prayer he had all sorts of thoughts in his head about his box of money, about thieves, about his bartered, ruined soul.

He came out of church in a bad temper. To drive away his unpleasant thoughts as he had often done before, he struck up a song at the top of his voice. But as soon as he began a policeman ran up and said, with his fingers to the peak of his cap:

"Your honour, gentlefolk must not sing in the street! You are not a shoemaker!"

Fyodor leaned his back against a fence and fell to thinking: what could he do to amuse himself?

"Your honour," a porter shouted to him, "don't lean against the fence, you will spoil your fur coat!"

Fyodor went into a shop and bought himself the very best concertina, then went out into the street playing it. Everybody pointed at him and laughed.

"And a gentleman, too," the cabmen jeered at him; "like some cobbler...."

"Is it the proper thing for gentlefolk to be disorderly in the street?" a policeman said to him. "You had better go into a tavern!"

"Your honour, give us a trifle, for Christ's sake," the beggars wailed, surrounding Fyodor on all sides.

In earlier days when he was a shoemaker the beggars took no notice of him, now they wouldn't let him pass.

And at home his new wife, the lady, was waiting for him, dressed in a green blouse and a red skirt. He meant to be attentive to her, and had just lifted his arm to give her a good clout on the back, but she said angrily:

"Peasant! Ignorant lout! You don't know how to behave with ladies! If you love me you will kiss my hand; I don't allow you to beat me."

"This is a blasted existence!" thought Fyodor. "People do lead a life! You mustn't sing, you mustn't play the concertina, you mustn't have a lark with a lady.... *Pfoo!*"

He had no sooner sat down to tea with the lady when the evil spirit in the blue spectacles appeared and said:

"Come, Fyodor Pantelyeitch, I have performed my part of the bargain. Now sign your paper and come along with me!"

And he dragged Fyodor to hell, straight to the furnace, and devils flew up from all directions and shouted:

"Fool! Blockhead! Ass!"

There was a fearful smell of paraffin in hell, enough to suffocate one. And suddenly it all vanished. Fyodor opened his eyes and saw his table, the boots, and the tin lamp. The lamp-glass was black, and from the faint light on the wick came clouds of stinking smoke as from a chimney. Near the table stood the customer in the blue spectacles, shouting angrily:

"Fool! Blockhead! Ass! I'll give you a lesson, you scoundrel! You took the order a fortnight ago and the boots aren't ready yet! Do you suppose I want to come traipsing round here half a dozen times a day for my boots? You wretch! you brute!"

Fyodor shook his head and set to work on the boots. The customer went on swearing and threatening him for a long time. At last when he subsided, Fyodor asked sullenly:

"And what is your occupation, sir?"

"I make Bengal lights and fireworks. I am a pyrotechnician."

They began ringing for matins. Fyodor gave the customer the boots, took the money for them, and went to church.

Carriages and sledges with bearskin rugs were dashing to and fro in the street; merchants, ladies, officers were walking along the pavement together with the humbler folk.... But Fyodor did not envy them nor repine at his lot. It seemed to him now that rich and poor were equally badly off. Some were able to drive in a carriage, and others to sing songs at the top of their voice and to play the concertina, but one and the same thing, the same grave, was awaiting all alike, and there was nothing in life for which one would give the devil even a tiny scrap of one's soul.

Billy Duffy and the Devil

Anonymous

Billy Duffy was an Irishman, a blacksmith, and a drunkard. He had the Keltic aversion from steady work, and stuck to his forge only long enough to get money for drink; when that was spent, he returned to work.

Billy was coming home one day after one of these drinking-bouts, soberer than usual, when he exclaimed to himself, for the thirst was upon him, "By God! I would sell myself to the devil if I could get some more drink."

At that moment a tall gentleman in black stepped up to him, and said, "What did you say?"

"I said I would sell myself to the devil if I could get a drink."

"Well, how much do you want for seven years, and the devil to get you then?"

"Well, I can't tell exactly, when it comes to the push."

"Will £700 do you?"

"Yes; I'd take £700."

"And the devil to get you then?"

"Oh, yes; I don't care about that."

When Billy got home he found the money in his smithy. He at once shut the smithy, and began squandering the money, keeping open house.

Amongst the people who flocked to get what they could out of Billy came an old hermit, who said, "I am very hungry, and nearly starved. Will you give me something to eat and drink?"

"Oh, yes; come in and get what you like."

The hermit disappeared, after eating and drinking, and did not reappear for several months, when he received the same kindly welcome, again disappearing. A few months afterwards he again appeared.

"Come in, come in!" said Billy.

After he had eaten and drunk his full, the hermit said to Billy: "Well, three times have you been good and kind to me. I'll give you three wishes, and whatever you wish will be sure to come true."

"I must have time to consider," said Billy.

"Oh, you shall have plenty of time to consider, and mind they are good wishes."

Next morning Billy told the hermit he was ready. "Well, go on; be sure they're good wishes," said the hermit.

"Well, I've got a big sledge-hammer in the smithy, and I wish whoever gets hold of that hammer shall go on striking the anvil, and never break it, till I tell him to stop."

"Oh, that's a bad wish, Billy."

"Oh, no; you'll see it's good. Next thing I wish for is a purse so that no one can take out whatever I put into it."

"Oh, Billy, Billy! that's a bad wish. Be careful now about the third wish," said the hermit.

"Well, I have got an armchair upstairs, and I wish that whoever may sit in that armchair will never be able to get up till I let them."

"Well, well, indeed; they are not very good wishes."

"Oh, yes; I've got my senses about me. I think I'll make them good wishes, after all."

The seven years, all but three days, had passed, and Billy was back working at his forge, for all his money was gone, when the dark gentleman stepped in and said:

"Now, Billy, during these last three days you may have as much money as you like," and he disappeared.

On the last day of his seven years Billy was penniless, and he went to the taproom of his favourite inn, which was full.

"Well, boys," said Billy, "we must have some money tonight. I'll treat you, and give you a pound each," and rising, he placed his tumbler in the middle of the table, and wished for twenty pounds. No sooner had he wished than a ball of fire came through the ceiling, and the twenty sovereigns fell into the tumbler. Everyone was taken aback, and there was a noise as if a bomb had burst, and the fireball disappeared, and rolled down the garden path, the landlord following it. After this they each drank what they liked, and Billy gave them a sovereign apiece before he went home.

The next morning he was in his smithy making a pair of horse-shoes, when the devil came in and said:

"Well, Billy, I'll want you this morning."

"Yes; all right. Take hold of this sledge-hammer, and give me a few hammers till I finish this job before I go."

So the devil seized the hammer and began striking the anvil, but he couldn't stop.

So Billy laughed, and locked him in, and was away three days. During this time the people collected round the smithy, and peeped through the cracks in the shutter, for they could hear the hammer going night and day.

At the end of three days Billy returned and opened the door, and the devil said, "Oh, Billy, you've played a fine trick to me; let me go."

"What are you going to give me if I let you go?"

"Seven years more, twice the money, and two days' grace for wishing for what you like."

The devil paid his money and disappeared, and Billy shut the smithy and took to gambling and drinking, so that at the end of seven years he was without a penny, and working again in his smithy.

On the last night of the seven years he went to his favourite public-house again, and wished for five pounds.

After he wished, a little man entered and spat the sovereigns into the tumbler, and they all drank all night.

Next morning Billy went back to his smithy. The devil, who had grown suspicious, turned himself into a sovereign and appeared on the floor. Billy seized the sovereign and clapped it into his purse. Then he took his purse and lay it upon the anvil, and began to beat it with his sledge-hammer, when the devil began to call out, "Spare my poor limbs, spare my poor limbs!"

"How much now if I let you go?" asked Billy

"Seven more years, three times the money, and one day in which to wish for what you like."

Billy took the sovereign out of his purse and threw it away, when he found his money in the smithy.

Billy carried on worse than ever; gambled and drank and raced, squandering it all before his seven years was gone. On the last day of his term he went to his favourite inn as usual and wished for a tumbler full of sovereigns. A little man with a big head, a big nose, and big mouth, a little body, and little legs, with clubbed feet and a forked tail, brought them in and put them in the tumbler. The drunkards in the room got scared when they saw the little man, for he looked all glowing with fire as he danced on the table. When he finished, he said, "Billy, tomorrow morning our compact is up."

"I know it, old boy, I know it, old boy!" said Billy. Then the devil ran out and disappeared, and the people began to question Billy:

"What is that? I think it is you, Mister Duffy, he is after."

"Oh, it is nothing at all," said Billy.

"I should think there was something," said the man.

"I am afraid my house will get a bad name," croaked the landlord.

"Not in the least! You are only a coward," said Billy.

"But in the name of God, what is it all about?" asked an old man.

"Oh, you'll see by-and-bye," said Billy; "it is nothing at all."

Next morning Billy went to his smithy, but the devil would not come near it.

So he went to his house, and began to quarrel with his wife, and whilst he was quarrelling the devil walked in and said:

"Well, Mr. Duffy, I am ready for you."

"Ah, yes; just sit down and wait a minute or two. I have some papers I want to put to rights before I go."

So the devil sat down in the arm-chair, and Billy went to the smithy and heated a pair of tongs red-hot, and coming back, he got the devil by the nose, and pulled it out as though it had been soft iron. And the devil began yelling, but he could not move, and Billy kept drawing the nose out till it was long enough to reach over the window, when he put an old bell-topper on the end of it. And the devil yelled, and snorted fire from his nose.

The whole of the village crowded round Billy's, house—at a safe distance—calling out, "Billy and the devil! The devil and Billy Duffy!"

The devil got awful savage, and blackguarded Billy Duffy terribly; but it was useless. Billy kept him there for days, till he got civil and said:

"Mr. Duffy, what will you let me go for?"

"Only one thing: I am to live the rest of my life without you, and have as much gold as I like."

The devil agreed, so Billy let him go; and immediately he grew rich. He lived to a good old age squandering money all the time, but at last he died and when he got to the gates of hell the clerk said "Who are you?"

"Billy Duffy," said he. And when the devil, who was standing near, heard, he said:

"Good God! bar the gates and double-lock them for if this Billy Duffy the blacksmith gets in he will ruin us all."

Old Billy saw a pair of red-hot tongs, which he picked up, and seized the devil by the nose. When the devil pulled back his head he left a red-hot bit of his nose in the tongs.

Then Billy Duffy went up to the gates of heaven and St. Peter asked him who he was.

"Billy Duffy the blacksmith," he answered.

"No admittance! You are a bold, bad man," said St. Peter.

"Good God! what will I do?" said Billy, and he went back to the earth, where he and the piece of the devil's nose melted into a ball of fire, and he roves the earth till this day as a will-o'-the-wisp.

The Devil and the Broker

Bret Harte

The church clocks in San Francisco were striking ten. The Devil, who had been flying over the city that evening, just then alighted on the roof of a church near the corner of Bush and Montgomery Streets. It will be perceived that the popular belief that the Devil avoids holy edifices, and vanishes at the sound of a *Credo* or *Paternoster*, is long since exploded. Indeed, modern scepticism asserts that he is not averse to these orthodox discourses, which particularly bear reference to himself, and in a measure recognize his power and importance.

I am inclined to think, however, that his choice of a resting-place was a good deal influenced by its contiguity to a populous thoroughfare. When he was comfortably seated, he began pulling out the joints of a small rod which he held in his hand, and which presently proved to be an extraordinary fishing-pole, with a telescopic adjustment that permitted its protraction to a marvellous extent. Affixing a line thereto, he selected a fly of a particular pattern from a small box which he carried with him, and, making a skilful cast, threw his line into the very centre of that living stream which ebbed and flowed through Montgomery Street.

Either the people were very virtuous that evening or the bait was not a taking one. In vain the Devil whipped the stream at an eddy in front of the Occidental, or trolled his line into the shadows of the Cosmopolitan; five minutes passed without even a nibble. "Dear me!" quoth the Devil, "that's very singular; one of my most popular flies, too! Why, they'd have risen by shoals in Broadway or Beacon Street for that. Well, here goes another." And, fitting a new fly from his well-filled box, he gracefully recast his line.

For a few moments there was every prospect of sport. The line was continually bobbing and the nibbles were distinct and gratifying. Once or twice the bait was apparently gorged and carried off in the upper stories of the hotels to be digested at leisure. At such times the professional manner in which the Devil played out his line would have thrilled the heart of Izaak Walton. But his efforts were unsuccessful; the bait was invariably carried off without hooking the victim, and the Devil finally lost his temper.

"I've heard of these San Franciscans before," he muttered; "wait till I get hold of one,—that's all!" he added malevolently, as he rebaited his hook. A sharp tug and a wriggle foiled his next trial, and finally, with considerable effort, he landed a portly two-hundred-pound broker upon the church roof.

As the victim lay there gasping, it was evident that the Devil was in no hurry to remove the hook from his gills; nor did he exhibit in this delicate operation that courtesy of manner and graceful manipulation which usually distinguished him.

"Come," he said, gruffly, as he grasped the broker by the waistband, "quit that whining and grunting. Don't flatter yourself that you're a prize either. I was certain to have had you. It was only a question of time."

"It is not that, my lord, which troubles me," whined the unfortunate wretch, as he painfully wriggled his head, "but that I should have been fooled by such a paltry bait. What will they say of me down there? To have let 'bigger things' go by, and to be taken in by this cheap trick," he added, as he groaned and glanced at the fly which the Devil was carefully rearranging, "is what,—pardon me, my lord,—is what gets me!"

"Yes," said the Devil, philosophically, "I never caught anybody yet who didn't say that; but tell me, ain't you getting somewhat fastidious down there? Here is one of my most popular flies, the greenback," he continued, exhibiting an emerald-looking insect, which he drew from his box. "This, so generally considered excellent in election season, has not even been nibbled at. Perhaps your sagacity, which, in spite of this unfortunate contretemps, no one can doubt," added the Devil, with a graceful return to his usual courtesy, "may explain the reason or suggest a substitute."

The broker glanced at the contents of the box with a supercilious smile. "Too old-fashioned, my lord,—long ago played out. Yet," he added, with a gleam of interest, "for a consideration I might offer something—*ahem!*—that would make a taking substitute for these trifles. Give me," he continued, in a brisk, business-like way, "a slight percentage and a bonus down, and I'm your man."

"Name your terms," said the Devil, earnestly.

"My liberty and a percentage on all you take, and the thing's done."

The Devil caressed his tail thoughtfully, for a few moments. He was certain of the broker any way, and the risk was slight. "Done!" he said.

"Stay a moment," said the artful broker. "There are certain contingencies. Give me your fishing-rod and let me apply the bait myself. It requires a skilful hand, my lord; even your well-known experience might fail. Leave me alone for half an hour, and if you have reason to complain of my success I will forfeit my deposit,—I mean my liberty."

The Devil in Manuscript

Nathaniel Hawthorne

On a bitter evening of December, I arrived by mail in a large town, which was then the residence of an intimate friend, one of those gifted youths who cultivate poetry and the belles-lettres, and call themselves students at law. My first business, after supper, was to visit him at the office of his distinguished instructor. As I have said, it was a bitter night, clear starlight, but cold as Nova Zembla,—the shop-windows along the street being frosted, so as almost to hide the lights, while the wheels of coaches thundered equally loud over frozen earth and pavements of stone. There was no snow, either on the ground or the roofs of the houses. The wind blew so violently, that I had but to spread my cloak like a main-sail, and scud along the street at the rate of ten knots, greatly envied by other navigators, who were beating slowly up, with the gale right in their teeth. One of these I capsized, but was gone on the wings of the wind before he could even vociferate an oath.

After this picture of an inclement night, behold us seated by a great blazing fire, which looked so comfortable and delicious that I felt inclined to lie down and roll among the hot coals. The usual furniture of a lawyer's office was around us,—rows of volumes in sheepskin, and a multitude of writs, summonses, and other legal papers, scattered over the desks and tables. But there were certain objects which seemed to intimate that we had little dread of the intrusion of clients, or of the learned counsellor himself, who, indeed, was attending court in a distant town. A tall, decanter-shaped bottle stood on the table, between two tumblers, and beside a pile of blotted manuscripts, altogether dissimilar to any law documents recognized in our courts. My friend, whom

I shall call Oberon,—it was a name of fancy and friendship between him and me,—my friend Oberon looked at these papers with a peculiar expression of disquietude.

"I do believe," said he, soberly, "or, at least, I could believe, if I chose, that there is a devil in this pile of blotted papers. You have read them, and know what I mean,—that conception in which I endeavoured to embody the character of a fiend, as represented in our traditions and the written records of witchcraft. Oh, I have a horror of what was created in my own brain, and shudder at the manuscripts in which I gave that dark idea a sort of material existence! Would they were out of my sight!"

"And of mine, too," thought I.

"You remember," continued Oberon, "how the hellish thing used to suck away the happiness of those who, by a simple concession that seemed almost innocent, subjected themselves to his power. Just so my peace is gone, and all by these accursed manuscripts. Have you felt nothing of the same influence?"

"Nothing," replied I, "unless the spell be hid in a desire to turn novelist, after reading your delightful tales."

"Novelist!" exclaimed Oberon, half seriously. "Then, indeed, my devil has his claw on you! You are gone! You cannot even pray for deliverance! But we will be the last and only victims; for this night I mean to burn the manuscripts, and commit the fiend to his retribution in the flames."

"Burn your tales!" repeated I, startled at the desperation of the idea.

"Even so," said the author, despondingly. "You cannot conceive what an effect the composition of these tales has had on me. I have become ambitious of a bubble, and careless of solid reputation. I am surrounding myself with shadows, which bewilder me, by aping the realities of life. They have drawn me aside from the beaten path of the world, and led me into a strange sort of solitude,—a solitude in the midst of men,—where nobody wishes for what I do, nor thinks nor feels as I do. The tales have done all this. When they are ashes, perhaps I shall be as I was before they had existence. Moreover, the sacrifice is less than you may suppose, since nobody will publish them."

"That does make a difference, indeed," said I.

"They have been offered, by letter," continued Oberon, reddening with vexation, "to some seventeen booksellers. It would make you stare to read their answers; and read them you should, only that I burnt them as fast as they arrived. One man publishes nothing but school-books; another has five novels already under examination."

"What a voluminous mass the unpublished literature of America must be!" cried I.

"Oh, the Alexandrian manuscripts were nothing to it!" said my friend. "Well, another gentleman is just giving up business, on purpose, I verily believe, to escape publishing my book. Several, however, would not absolutely decline the agency, on my advancing half the cost of an edition, and giving bonds for the remainder, besides a high percentage to themselves, whether the book sells or not. Another advises a subscription."

"The villain!" exclaimed I.

"A fact!" said Oberon. "In short, of all the seventeen booksellers, only one has vouchsafed even to read my tales; and he—a literary dabbler himself, I should judge—has the impertinence to criticise them, proposing what he calls vast improvements, and concluding, after a general sentence of condemnation, with the definitive assurance that he will not be concerned on any terms."

"It might not be amiss to pull that fellow's nose," remarked I.

"If the whole 'trade' had one common nose, there would be some satisfaction in pulling it," answered the author. "But, there does seem to be one honest man among these seventeen unrighteous ones; and he tells me fairly, that no American publisher will meddle with an American work,—seldom if by a known writer, and never if by a new one,—unless at the writer's risk."

"The paltry rogues!" cried I. "Will they live by literature, and yet risk nothing for its sake? But, after all, you might publish on your own account."

"And so I might," replied Oberon. "But the devil of the business is this. These people have put me so out of conceit with the tales, that I loathe the very thought of them, and actually experience a physical sickness of the stomach, whenever I glance at them on the table. I tell you there is a demon in them! I anticipate a wild enjoyment in seeing them in the blaze; such as I should feel in taking vengeance on an enemy, or destroying something noxious."

I did not very strenuously oppose this determination, being privately of opinion, in spite of my partiality for the author, that his tales would make a more brilliant appearance in the fire than anywhere else. Before proceeding to execution, we broached the bottle of champagne, which Oberon had provided for keeping up his spirits in this doleful business. We swallowed each a tumblerful, in sparkling commotion; it went bubbling down our throats, and brightened my eyes at once, but left my friend sad and heavy as before. He drew the tales towards him, with a mixture of natural affection and natural disgust, like a father taking a deformed infant into his arms.

"Pooh! Pish! Pshaw!" exclaimed he, holding them at arm's-length. "It was Gray's idea of heaven, to lounge on a sofa and read new novels. Now, what more appropriate torture would Dante himself have contrived, for the sinner who perpetrates a bad book, than to be continually turning over the manuscript?"

"It would fail of effect," said I, "because a bad author is always his own great admirer."

"I lack that one characteristic of my tribe,—the only desirable one," observed Oberon. "But how many recollections throng upon me, as I turn over these leaves! This scene came into my fancy as I walked along a hilly road, on a starlight October evening; in the pure and bracing air, I became all soul, and felt as if I could climb the sky, and run a race along the Milky Way. Here is another tale, in which I wrapt myself during a dark and dreary night-ride in the month of March, till the rattling of the wheels and the voices of my companions seemed like faint sounds of a dream, and my visions a bright reality. That scribbled page describes shadows which I summoned to my bedside at midnight: they would not depart when I bade them; the gray dawn came, and found me wide awake and feverish, the victim of my own enchantments!"

"There must have been a sort of happiness in all this," said I, smitten with a strange longing to make proof of it.

"There may be happiness in a fever fit," replied the author. "And then the various moods in which I wrote! Sometimes my ideas were like precious stones under the earth, requiring toil to dig them up, and care to polish and brighten them; but often a delicious stream of thought would gush out upon the page at once, like water sparkling up suddenly in the desert; and when it had passed, I gnawed my pen hopelessly, or blundered on with cold and miserable toil, as if there were a wall of ice between me and my subject."

"Do you now perceive a corresponding difference," inquired I, "between the passages which you wrote so coldly, and those fervid flashes of the mind?"

"No," said Oberon, tossing the manuscripts on the table. "I find no traces of the golden pen with which I wrote in characters of fire. My treasure of fairy coin is changed to worthless dross. My picture, painted in what seemed the loveliest hues, presents nothing but a faded and indistinguishable surface. I have been eloquent and poetical and humorous in a dream,—and behold! it is all nonsense, now that I am awake."

My friend now threw sticks of wood and dry chips upon the fire, and seeing it blaze like Nebuchadnezzar's furnace, seized the champagne bottle, and drank two or three brimming bumpers, successively. The heady liquor combined with his agitation to throw him into a species of rage. He laid violent hands on the tales. In one instant more, their faults and beauties would alike have vanished in a glowing purgatory. But, all at once, I remembered passages of high imagination, deep pathos, original thoughts, and points of such varied excellence, that the vastness of the sacrifice struck me most forcibly. I caught his arm.

"Surely, you do not mean to burn them!" I exclaimed.

"Let me alone!" cried Oberon, his eyes flashing fire. "I will burn them! Not a scorched syllable shall escape! Would you have me a damned author?—To undergo sneers, taunts, abuse, and cold neglect, and faint praise, bestowed, for pity's sake, against the giver's conscience! A hissing and a laughing-stock to my own traitorous thoughts! An outlaw from the protection of the grave,—one whose ashes every careless foot might spurn, un-honoured in life, and remembered scornfully in death! Am I to bear all this, when yonder fire will insure me from the whole? No! There go the tales! May my hand wither when it would write another!"

The deed was done. He had thrown the manuscripts into the hottest of the fire, which at first seemed to shrink away, but soon curled around them, and made them a part of its own fervent brightness. Oberon stood gazing at the conflagration, and shortly began to soliloquize, in the wildest strain, as if Fancy resisted and became riotous, at the moment when he would have compelled her to ascend that funeral pile. His words described objects which he appeared to discern in the fire, fed by his own precious thoughts; perhaps the thousand visions which the writer's magic had incorporated with these pages became visible to him in the dissolving heat, brightening forth ere they vanished forever; while the smoke, the vivid sheets of flame, the ruddy and whitening coals, caught the aspect of a varied scenery.

"They blaze," said he, "as if I had steeped them in the intensest spirit of genius. There I see my lovers clasped in each other's arms. How pure the flame that bursts from their glowing hearts! And yonder the features of a villain writhing in the fire that shall torment him to eternity. My holy men, my pious and angelic women, stand like martyrs amid the flames, their mild eyes lifted heavenward. Ring out the bells! A city is on fire. See!—destruction roars through my dark forests, while the lakes boil up in steaming billows, and the mountains are volcanoes, and the sky kindles with a lurid brightness! All elements are but one pervading flame! *Ha!* The fiend!"

I was somewhat startled by this latter exclamation. The tales were almost consumed, but just then threw forth a broad sheet of fire, which flickered as with laughter, making the whole room dance in its brightness, and then roared portentously up the chimney.

"You saw him? You must have seen him!" cried Oberon. "How he glared at me and laughed, in that last sheet of flame, with just the features that I imagined for him! Well! The tales are gone."

The papers were indeed reduced to a heap of black cinders, with a multitude of sparks hurrying confusedly among them, the traces of the pen being now represented by white lines, and the whole mass fluttering to and fro in the draughts of air. The destroyer knelt down to look at them.

"What is more potent than fire!" said he, in his gloomiest tone. "Even thought, invisible and incorporeal as it is, cannot escape it. In this little time, it has annihilated the creations of long nights and days, which I could no more reproduce, in their first glow and freshness, than cause ashes and whitened bones to rise up and live.

There, too, I sacrificed the unborn children of my mind. All that I had accomplished—all that I planned for future years—has perished by one common ruin, and left only this heap of embers! The deed has been my fate. And what remains? A weary and aimless life,—a long repentance of this hour,—and at last an obscure grave, where they will bury and forget me!"

As the author concluded his dolorous moan, the extinguished embers arose and settled down and arose again, and finally flew up the chimney, like a demon with sable wings. Just as they disappeared, there was a loud and solitary cry in the street below us. "Fire!" Fire! Other voices caught up that terrible word, and it speedily became the shout of a multitude. Oberon started to his feet, in fresh excitement.

"A fire on such a night!" cried he. "The wind blows a gale, and wherever it whirls the flames, the roofs will flash up like gunpowder. Every pump is frozen up, and boiling water would turn to ice the moment it was flung from the engine. In an hour, this wooden town will be one great bonfire! What a glorious scene for my next—*Pshaw!*"

The street was now all alive with footsteps, and the air full of voices. We heard one engine thundering round a corner, and another rattling from a distance over the pavements. The bells of three steeples clanged out at once, spreading the alarm to many a neighbouring town, and expressing hurry, confusion, and terror, so inimitably that I could almost distinguish in their peal the burden of the universal cry,—*"Fire! Fire! Fire!"*

"What is so eloquent as their iron tongues!" exclaimed Oberon. "My heart leaps and trembles, but not with fear. And that other sound, too,—deep and awful as a mighty organ,—the roar and thunder of the multitude on the pavement below! Come! We are losing time. I will cry out in the loudest of the uproar, and mingle my spirit with the wildest of the confusion, and be a bubble on the top of the ferment!"

From the first outcry, my forebodings had warned me of the true object and centre of alarm. There was nothing now but uproar, above, beneath, and around us; footsteps stumbling pell-mell up the public staircase, eager shouts and heavy thumps at the door, the whiz and dash of water from the engines, and the crash of furniture thrown upon the pavement. At once, the truth flashed upon my friend. His frenzy took the hue of joy, and, with a wild gesture of exultation, he leaped almost to the ceiling of the chamber.

"My tales!" cried Oberon. "The chimney! The roof! The Fiend has gone forth by night, and startled thousands in fear and wonder from their beds! Here I stand,—a triumphant author! Huzza! Huzza! My brain has set the town on fire! Huzza!"

The Devil acceded to his request, bowed, and withdrew. Alighting gracefully in Montgomery Street, he dropped into Meade & Co.'s clothing store, where, having completely equipped himself *a la mode*, he sallied forth intent on his personal enjoyment. Determining to sink his professional character, he mingled with the current of human life, and enjoyed, with that immense capacity for excitement peculiar to his nature, the whirl, bustle, and feverishness of the people, as a purely aesthetic gratification unalloyed by the cares of business. What he did that evening does not belong to our story. We return to the broker, whom we left on the roof.

When he made sure that the Devil had retired, he carefully drew from his pocket-book a slip of paper and affixed it on the hook. The line had scarcely reached the current before he felt a bite. The hook was swallowed. To bring up his victim rapidly, disengage him from the hook, and reset his line, was the work of a moment. Another bite and the same result. Another, and another. In a very few minutes the roof was covered with his panting spoil. The broker could himself distinguish that many of them were personal friends; nay, some of them were familiar frequenters of the building on which they were now miserably stranded. That the broker felt a certain satisfaction in being instrumental in thus misleading his fellow-brokers no one acquainted with human nature will for a moment doubt. But a stronger pull on his line caused him to put forth all his strength and skill. The magic pole bent like a coach-whip. The broker held firm, assisted by the battlements of the church. Again and again it was almost wrested from his hand, and again and again he slowly reeled in a portion of the tightening line. At last, with one mighty effort, he lifted to the level of the roof a struggling object. A howl like Pandemonium rang through the air as the broker successfully landed at his feet—the Devil himself!

The two glared fiercely at each other. The broker, perhaps mindful of his former treatment, evinced no haste to remove the hook from his antagonist's jaw. When it was finally accomplished, he asked quietly if the Devil was satisfied. That gentleman seemed absorbed in the contemplation of the bait which he had just taken from his mouth. "I am," he said, finally, "and forgive you; but what do you call this?"

"Bend low," replied the broker, as he buttoned up his coat ready to depart. The Devil inclined his ear.

"I call it *wild cat!*"

LEONAUR

ALSO FROM LEONAUR
AVAILABLE IN SOFTCOVER OR HARDCOVER WITH DUST JACKET

THE FIRST BOOK OF AYESHA *by H. Rider Haggard*—Contains *She & Ayesha: the Return of She.*

THE SECOND BOOK OF AYESHA *by H. Rider Haggard*—Contains *She and Allan & Wisdom's Daughter.*

QUATERMAIN: THE COMPLETE ADVENTURES—1 *by H. Rider Haggard*—Contains *King Solomon's Mines & Allan Quatermain.*

QUATERMAIN: THE COMPLETE ADVENTURES—2 *by H. Rider Haggard*—Contains *Allan's Wife, Maiwa's Revenge & Marie.*

QUATERMAIN: THE COMPLETE ADVENTURES—3 *by H. Rider Haggard*—Contains *Child of Storm & Allan and the Holy Flower.*

QUATERMAIN: THE COMPLETE ADVENTURES—4 *by H. Rider Haggard*—Contains *Finished & The Ivory Child.*

QUATERMAIN: THE COMPLETE ADVENTURES—5 *by H. Rider Haggard*—Contains *The Ancient Allan & She and Allan.*

QUATERMAIN: THE COMPLETE ADVENTURES—6 *by H. Rider Haggard*—Contains *Heu-Heu or, the Monster & The Treasure of the Lake.*

QUATERMAIN: THE COMPLETE ADVENTURES—7 *by H. Rider Haggard*—Contains *Allan and the Ice Gods, Four Short Adventures & Nada the Lily.*

TROS OF SAMOTHRACE 1: WOLVES OF THE TIBER *by Talbot Mundy*—55 B.C.--an adventurer set during the Roman invasion of Britain.

TROS OF SAMOTHRACE 2: DRAGONS OF THE NORTH *by Talbot Mundy*—55 B.C. —Caesar plots, Britons war among themselves and the Vikings are coming.

TROS OF SAMOTHRACE 3: SERPENT OF THE WAVES *by Talbot Mundy*—55 B.C.--Caesar is poised to invade Britain—only a grand strategy can foil him!.

TROS OF SAMOTHRACE 4: CITY OF THE EAGLES *by Talbot Mundy*—54 B.C.—Rome—Tros treads in the streets of his sworn enemies!.

TROS OF SAMOTHRACE 5: CLEOPATRA *by Talbot Mundy*—Tros and the Roman Empire turn to the Egypt of the Pharaohs.

TROS OF SAMOTHRACE 6: THE PURPLE PIRATE *by Talbot Mundy*—The epic saga of the ancient world—Tros of Samothrace—draws to a conclusion in this sixth—and final—volume.

LEONAUR

ALSO FROM LEONAUR
AVAILABLE IN SOFTCOVER OR HARDCOVER WITH DUST JACKET

THE COMPLETE FOUR JUST MEN: VOLUME 2 *by Edgar Wallace*—*The Law of the Four Just Men* & *The Three Just Men*—disillusioned with a world where the wicked and the abusers of power perpetually go unpunished, the Just Men set about to rectify matters according to their own standards, and retribution is dispensed on swift and deadly wings.

THE COMPLETE RAFFLES: 1 *by E. W. Hornung*—*The Amateur Cracksman* & *The Black Mask*—By turns urbane gentleman about town and accomplished cricketer, life is just too ordinary for Raffles and that sets him on a series of adventures that have long been treasured as a real antidote to the 'white knights' who are the usual heroes of the crime fiction of this period.

THE COMPLETE RAFFLES: 2 *by E. W. Hornung*—*A Thief in the Night* & *Mr Justice Raffles*—By turns urbane gentleman about town and accomplished cricketer, life is just too ordinary for Raffles and that sets him on a series of adventures that have long been treasured as a real antidote to the 'white knights' who are the usual heroes of the crime fiction of this period.

THE COLLECTED SUPERNATURAL AND WEIRD FICTION OF WILKIE COLLINS: VOLUME 1 *by Wilkie Collins*—Contains one novel 'The Haunted Hotel', one novella 'Mad Monkton', three novelettes 'Mr Percy and the Prophet', 'The Biter Bit' and 'The Dead Alive' and eight short stories to chill the blood.

THE COLLECTED SUPERNATURAL AND WEIRD FICTION OF WILKIE COLLINS: VOLUME 2 *by Wilkie Collins*—Contains one novel 'The Two Destinies', three novellas 'The Frozen deep', 'Sister Rose' and 'The Yellow Mask' and two short stories to chill the blood.

THE COLLECTED SUPERNATURAL AND WEIRD FICTION OF WILKIE COLLINS: VOLUME 3 *by Wilkie Collins*—Contains one novel 'Dead Secret,' two novelettes 'Mrs Zant and the Ghost' and 'The Nun's Story of Gabriel's Marriage' and five short stories to chill the blood.

FUNNY BONES *selected by Dorothy Scarborough*—An Anthology of Humorous Ghost Stories.

MONTEZUMA'S CASTLE AND OTHER WEIRD TALES *by Charles B. Cory*—Cory has written a superb collection of eighteen ghostly and weird stories to chill and thrill the avid enthusiast of supernatural fiction.

SUPERNATURAL BUCHAN *by John Buchan*—Stories of Ancient Spirits, Uncanny Places & Strange Creatures.